Praise for Believe Me Not: An Unreliable Anthology

"The Test *is a compelling tale of human friendship and sacrifice.*"
—Captain Conway

"Morning, Baby *is one of those real quiet thrillers. It sneaks up and you don't even know what hit you—'til it's over.*"
—Fat Richie

"*Treat yourself to* Confined—*it's quite delectable.*"
—Ms. Stanton

"*Make sure to read* Sugarfruit *to experience a great description of flight navigation.*"
—Astronaut Mike Andrews

"*Hans is an intriguing character I sympathize with; however, I see no need to solve the case. If we did, it would be a happy ending, and that is not what I like.*"
—Anonymous

"*Guilt Monkey Nectar would be an awesome drink name.*"
—Betelgeusian spore-head

"Myrmidon Station is riddled with intrigue and passwords. I had a bad experience with a partner once involving a password, so this story really brightened my day."

—Beth

"I'm excited to learn about the French association with trebuchets and explore different cultural dialects. What a fascinating episode in human history."

—Sara

"Patient Zero, what can I say? It's a truly innovative, wonderful use of disease; worthy of a Nobel Prize."

—Doctor

"It was great fun to read a little tidbit of my buddy Orion's past. Oh, the pranks we've pulled."

—Rakkason

"There's a moon? And one can travel there on a dragon? The riders will be so excited to chase the biggest plot bunny ever!"

—George

*"*Ghost in the Machine *is a brilliant expose of Descartes' early philosophies. Descartes himself would have been such a delightful character to kill over and over and over again."*

—Ted

BELIEVE ME NOT

AN UNRELIABLE ANTHOLOGY

Editor
SARA W. MCBRIDE

Associate Editors
VIANNAH E. DUNCAN, KATE FINDLEY,
DANIEL J. MAGALLANES, JESSICA MAGALLANES,
KATY MANN, BRAD RAY, BETHANY SIMONSEN,
K. ANDREW TURNER, AND LISA WALSH

LEMUR
PUBLISHING

Lemur Publishing
Pasadena, CA 91101
Lemur-Publishing.com

Copyright © 2014 Sara W. McBride and all included authors.

All included authors own full rights to their stories. Grateful acknowledgment is made to all contributors for permission to use selected writings in this book.

All rights reserved. No part of this publication may be reproduced, distributed, or transmitted in any form or by any means, including photocopying, recording, or other electronic or mechanical methods, without the prior written permission of the publisher, except in the case of brief quotations embodied in critical reviews and certain other noncommercial uses permitted by copyright law.

For permissions requests, or to contact a contributor, please write to the publisher, addressed "Unreliable Anthology Permissions" to lemurpublishing@gmail.com.

The name NaNoWriMo has been used with permission from National Novel Writing Month.

This content has not been reviewed by National Novel Writing Month. For more information, please visit nanowrimo.org.

Cover design and formatting by Damonza.com.

ISBN: 978-0-9907670-0-8 (paper)
ISBN: 978-0-9907670-1-5 (ebook)

To Chris Baty, the founder of NaNoWriMo and all its beloved icons.

To all writers, young and old: write agelessly and fearlessly.

Table of Contents

Introduction	Viannah E Duncan	xi
The Q-TCL in the Space Station	Daniel J. Magallanes	1
Guilt Monkey	Shirley Hanna-King	13
S.A.R.A.	Bethany Simonsen	21
The Outsider Among Us	Katia Shank	38
Orion in the Everglades	Sara W. McBride	46
That Delicate Touch	Faith Dincolo	60
The Amazon Adventure	Henry Barker	65
The Heart of It	Katy Mann	75
The Mother That I Lost	Maya Watanabe	83
A Dwindling Supply of Bleach	Renée Jessica Tan	86
Reviewed	Wendy Erich	91
Mr. Mungo's Shop of Oddities	Alexandr Bond	101
Sasha and Derek	Alana Saltz	111
A Moon of a Problem	Fiona Yang	116
I Cordially Accept	Kate Findley	127
Ghost in the Machine	Melora Sundt	148
Situational Gravity	Brad Ray	160
Second Sunrise	K. Andrew Turner	167
A Magical Trip to the Moon	Irene Kang, Ben Kang, and Matthew Kang	175
The Olopa Bean	Dan Nowell	187
I Spy True Love	Susie Tex	198

Not Hansel and Gretel	Jamie Park	203
In the Event of a Migraine Take A Snot	Lillith Black	209
A Regular Saturday Night	Dan Portnoy	215
A Sunlight Symphony	Anna A. Chen	223
The People of the Apples	Jasmine Chung	227
Prince of Persian	June Low	242
Morning, Baby	Sophie McLachlan-O'Hara	250
Beginnings	Nita Lieu	257
Patient Zero	Dara McGarry	259
And To Think It All Happened Over a Box of Cookies	Kayla Delie	272
A Job's a Job	Stephen Buehler	282
Mushrooms are an Acquired Taste	R. Hadlock-Piltz	289
The Test	Viannah E. Duncan	299
Charles Oleson Maverick Anderson	Jedidiah Shank	308
No Exceptions	Ted Nitschke	321
Sugarfruit	John Everett	329
Not So Ordinary Day	Rebekah Ruther	336
Confined	Andrea Goyan	339
Mortimer Marchand	D.B. Randall	346
Dreaming Magic	Irene Chung	352
Pyre	Sarah Hawley	357
The Factory Job	Jessica Magallanes	375
The Unauthorized Memoirs of an Anthrophysicist	Sascha Stucky	392
Fallen Grace	Anastasia Barbato	399
Moving Up	Gabe McClure	416
Afterword		429

Introduction

IT STARTED OUT innocently enough, as these things always do. I was sitting with a group of fellow writers—many of whom became editors for the collection you are holding in your hands—and we were discussing the advent and evolution of the unreliable narrator. I wrote my Master's thesis on the topic, so I figured I was fairly well prepared for the conversation, but many members of the group had only just recently come to understand that some characters in literature and film are completely untrustworthy: Tyler Durden of *Fight Club*, Leonard in *Memento*, and any of the various narrators in *Rashomon*, for example. We bantered back and forth with the unreliable narrator idea, learning more about it and trying our hands at writing our own unreliable characters.

Near the end of the evening, we were discussing topics for the next group meeting and someone suggested anthologies. Jokingly, I suggested that if we all wrote stories with unreliable narrators, I would be happy to put them into an anthology for all of us to enjoy.

As we're an improv writing group, a prompt, also known as an audience suggestion, was required to be included in all stories. Several group members shouted simultaneously and the phrase that emerged was, "A cuticle in the space station!"

It was a joke, nonsense, but it stuck, and the gauntlet had been thrown down. Could we each write a story with an unreliable narrator *and* the phrase "A cuticle in the space station?"

The idea was a fun one, I thought, but then our fearless leader took up the mantle, and there was no turning back. When you give a good idea (or *any* decent idea, some would argue) to Sara McBride, she will run with it whether you meant for anyone to take it seriously or not. (Just imagine a running track and papers flying everywhere!)

Before we knew it, Sara had posted a call for submissions on the National Novel Writing Month Los Angeles email list, and the short stories started pouring in. We looked over our own writing and realized that with all these submissions, our own stories had some very stiff competition. We also decided to award bonus points for the creative use of NaNoWriMo icons within the story: lemurs, trebuchets, Viking helmets, the traveling shovel of death, guilt monkeys, 1,667, etc. You can find more information at Lemur Publishing (lemur-publishing.com). Keep your eyes open; there's a prize if you can find all the icons.

We met again and organized into cohesive editing teams. What started off as a playful challenge grew into its own delightful story that became an enormous gift in education, camaraderie, and the understanding that an unreliable narrator is far more than the Wikipedia definition. I am proud to be a part of the group that is sharing this anthology with you now.

What you are holding in your hands is the completed collection of stories from around Los Angeles County, the United States, and the world. Not counting the time it took each author to write their own story, we, as editors, volunteered hundreds of hours choosing, editing, and arranging those stories for content and flow.

One hundred percent of the proceeds from the purchase of this anthology goes to NaNoWriMo events in Los Angeles and NaNoWriMo's Young Writers Program, a nonprofit organization that promotes creative writing in young people and people young at heart. That means that each author and editor donated his or her time and energy and passion to create this marvel, all for the pleasure of encouraging writers of all stripes and ages to tackle noveling. You'll notice that fourteen of the authors published in this anthology are age seventeen and under. Their stories are noted throughout the anthology with a flower petal.

So, have you ever thought, "I've always wanted to write a novel" but never thought you could? Check out NaNoWriMo to be inspired! And if you are young, check out NaNoWriMo's Young Writer's Program (ywp.nanowrimo.org). One of the enclosed authors is a veteran WriMo at only ten years old.

If you enjoy this anthology, visit www.nanolosangeles.org for more writing fun. Stories *matter*. Yes, *your* story matters. Thanks for reading.

May the words be with you,
Viannah E. Duncan
Associate Editor

The Q-TCL in the Space Station

Daniel J. Magallanes

"QUANTUM-CLASS TRANSPORT TCL, your approach has been flagged by Security, priority level one," announced the station's control tower agent. "Proceed to Security Dock Alpha-2. Any deviation of course will be interpreted as hostile action and will engage counter measures." Her voice was the same cold and courteous mezzo-soprano found at all of the Terran Federation stations. This one may have even come from an actual human female. Maybe.

"No need for hostilities, Tower," I replied. "Q-TCL, proceeding to Sec-Dock Alpha-2." Maybe I should've tried to sound more indignant or surprised, but I do best when I play to my strengths: smartest guy in the room. Of course, I was the only guy actually on board, so that didn't mean all that much.

Technically, Q-TCL was my ship's registry, but I've always pronounced her name "cuticle." Once I'd maneuvered her within half a click from the dock,

The Q-TCL in the Space Station

Myrmidon Station engaged its tractor beams. Not the usual dual-polar tug-beams that helped less experienced pilots dock without mussing up the Station's outer hull. No, this was a hex-axis tractor beam. The Q-TCL wouldn't be leaving until the brass at Myrmidon Station were done with me.

You may be wondering why I would fly within hailing range, let alone tractor range, of a Federation Space Station if I was only going to get caught. A backwater Station in geo-sync around Europa that was so small, it didn't even have a legitimate interior hangar bay, just exterior docking berths. Well, desperate times called for desperate measures.

As Myrmidon's dock-coupling made atmo-lock on the Q-TCL's exterior bulkhead with a snap-hiss-bing, the bulkhead started to open of its own accord. Station security had taken over some of Q-TCL's basic functioning. I figured as much, but I felt bad for her nonetheless.

I was standing at the bulkhead when it opened. Across the threshold was Barnabas. Commander Jedediah Barnabas, chief of security for Outer-Planet sector, flanked by a cadre of securi-troops and tech-sweeps. Damn. I hated this guy.

"'Captain' Nicodemus Conway, come to turn yourself in, have you?" He was so pleased with himself, like he'd actually caught me.

"If you wouldn't mind, 'Commander,' please refrain from saying 'Captain' like it's in ironic quotes. I *am* a captain."

"What's a 'Captain' without a crew, hmm?" Like I said, I frakkin' *hated* this guy. "Lights out, Conway." And that's when the securi-troop on his left lifted the taze-wand and I took a little nap.

* * * *

I woke up and almost immediately wished I hadn't. The taze-induced nap left my head swimming. I felt like I was going through severe withdrawals from half the illicit substances known to man. Luckily, I awoke exactly where I figured I would: a stainless steel interrogation room. At least it wasn't a detention cell; we could skip ahead to the good part.

The room was completely brushed stainless steel. Anonymous stainless steel panels hid the door and surveillance equipment; even the lighting was hidden. Just me, in a stainless steel cube, grav-locked to a stainless steel chair, wrists similarly locked to a stainless steel table. There was a second chair opposite me. That would be for Barnabas, I presumed.

It took Barnabas forty-seven seconds to realize I was awake, hurry from wherever he was surveilling me, and make his entrance. I'm sure he spent the last five of those seconds outside the door prepping his shit-eating grin.

"So, 'Captain.'" He was enjoying this. I didn't blame him. "It looks like I caught a 'cuticle' in the space station. Have you come to turn yourself in?"

"Turn myself in? Commander, I don't know what you're talking about." I completely knew what he was talking about. "I just needed to make a supply stop and have the Q-TCL serviced. It sounds like something may be hanging loose under the hull."

"So you're going to play stupid, then?" He was getting frustrated. Good. "We *know* your crew stole a shipment of med supplies from a Federation Freighter."

Oh. That. "First of all, Commander, I'd heard that the Federation was withholding those med supplies from one of its own colonies on Ganymede for being late on its taxes.

And second, what crew? I thought you said I wasn't a captain because I don't have a crew."

Barnabas cracked a wide, carnivorous smile. He made a sequence of taps on the table and a virtual control console came online, superimposed on his side of the table. A few more taps and he activated the table's holo-projector.

"Well, let's see here. Janna Swift, age 32. Your pilot, I believe." An eight-inch holo of Janna sprang to life from the table, flanked by a floating dossier describing her vital statistics, legal disposition, and current whereabouts. This last was encoded. That meant that she was in Federation custody and that her specific location was classified.

"Dex Bradley, age 27. Bastien Ibanez, age 33. Victor Chien, age 24. And Drusilla McClintock, age 20." As he named them, their holos and vitals appeared next to Janna's.

"Twenty," he repeated. "That's pretty young to be looking at a life sentence." Barnabas paused and drilled me with his gaze, like a lemur with a grudge. "And of course, Raja Patel, aged 26. Missing, presumed deceased." Raja's holo was in grayscale, different from the teal highlights of the other holos. An inset vid-screen showed grainy security footage of a vaguely Raja-shaped figure being blown out a hull-breach into open space. Again Barnabas paused. He was looking for a reaction. I shrugged.

"So? Some former associates of mine got busted for a job gone wrong. Why should that interest me? And why the frak does that justify impounding the Q-TCL and tazing me?"

Barnabas tapped his index finger irritably. He looked at me sideways, weighing his next move. He thought this was a chess match. Barnabas swiped across the holos and dossiers, minimizing them into a teal cube-shaped icon. It floated in the lower corner of the holo-space.

"Then tell me this, Captain. Why come all the way across the system just for a supply and service stop? Hmmm?" He was like a cat backing his mouse into a corner.

"I don't suppose you'll accept 'to be closer to you' as a legitimate answer?"

That did it. "*YOU ARE HERE* ...." He caught himself and sat back down. "I know you are here in an attempt to find your crew and break them out of detention. Well, *Captain*, they are not here. And you'll never find them." Now he was *really* enjoying this. "That is, until you're arrested for your crimes and convicted. Then I'll make sure you have a cell next door."

Until? Yeah, that was a slip. I held back a smile. "Commander, we both know you don't have anything on me. I mean, if you *did* have actionable proof of anything, I wouldn't be in an interrogation room. I'd be in front of a magistrate and on my way to a penal colony. So then, why *am* I here?"

I'd called his bluff. He reacted like he'd bitten tin foil. I sallied forth. "Tell me, *Commander*. If I was coming to Myrmidon Station to, I dunno, hack the system, find information on where my so-called crew was being detained, and install some sort of Trojan horse to help me break *in* to a max-sec detention center and then break *out* with my six crew mates, then how am I supposed to get *onto* Myrmidon Station without *YOU* of all people knowing about it?!"

The silence that followed was thick, even if it only lasted a few seconds. Frankly, I'd expected Barnabas to buckle a little, but he wasn't done with me. The look in his eye as he chewed his next words showed more resolve than I ever remembered him having. I'd flown into his lair and he certainly wasn't going to let me go.

"You're right, Nic." Barnabas was much quieter, controlled. He moved to my side of the table, standing close over me. "I don't have any concrete proof that the 'brave' freelancer Captain Conway ran away from a job gone pear-shaped and left his crew to be apprehended by Federation Security. That's why you're going to confess. To me. Here and now."

"Why in hell would I admit to—there's nothing for me to confess." I turned my head from him. My eyes fell on the teal icon glowing steadily in the corner of the holo-space.

The look of disgust on Barnabas' face was meant to goad me. "You coward. You're no captain. You let your crew go down while you sailed away as free as a bird." He wanted me to crack. But I knew he was wrong; I'm not a coward.

"You've got nothing on me, Commander. Former associates. Emphasis on the 'former.'"

His tone shifted. More friendly, a lot more sinister. "You know, Nic, I don't buy that. You hold yourself in much too high esteem to be that callous. Someone with *your* inflated ego prizes things like camaraderie and loyalty. So consider this. Any number of really terrible things can happen to someone in detention, even if they're only awaiting trial." I did *not* like where he was going with this. "One call from me and things can get very interesting for your crew. I can only imagine what a treat Ms. McClintock would make for the right inmate."

He was trying to get me to show my hand. I didn't have one to show him. My eyes were still on the icon. The icon blinked twice.

Time to change my tack. "Aren't I allowed at least one communiqué?" I asked. My suddenly sunny tone threw him back a bit. "If you wouldn't mind, dial up Counselor Braithwaite for me. She's always been such a dear friend." This wasn't a bluff. Ever since I saved her husband and daughter from those pirates … but that's another story. I mean, she's still on the up-right side of the law. Braithwaite wouldn't bend the rules to get me or anyone else out of detention if they'd been convicted of a crime. But she could make things uncomfortable for this jumped-up bureaucrat in an officer's uniform, and Barnabas knew it. Especially since he didn't really have anything on me.

Commander Barnabas stood. He hadn't expected this, and I thought I was as good as free. But I could see his thoughts collecting, a cloud of menace forming on his face. Frak, this wasn't going to be good.

"Of course, I could do that, Captain. That *is* your right. Such a pity that the Counselor is vacationing with her family right now on Andromeda IV. Even via subspace communication, it'll be weeks before we hear back from her. And so many interesting things could happen in that time to Ms. McClintock. Or Ms. Swift, or even Mr. Chien. He's young."

I have to admit, this was dark even for him. I always figured Barnabas' ruling trait was self-preservation. This was different, and the difference was bordering on evil. I was surprised he wasn't actually twirling his moustache.

And he wasn't done there. Barnabas sat back down in his chair and looked at the console.

"I should add, Captain, that every day until we hear

back," Barnabas made a few taps and swipes on the console, "is another day you'll be here in my custody." He locked eyes on me and dropped his finger ominously on a blinking red circle.

The sensation was immediate, though it took me a half a second to define that sensation as complete, abject pain, coursing through every cell of my body. I'm not sure how long it lasted—a minute, an hour—though it probably only lasted a few seconds. All I knew was that I couldn't withstand much more of that without being reduced to a quivering mass, begging Barnabas to let me tell him everything.

Barnabas was pleased; his shit-eating grin returned. "Taze-wands work on the brain by reversing the polarity of your synaptic neural impulses for exactly one cycle. It knocks you out, painlessly. That is, until you wake up. I've heard the resulting migraines are just ... horrific.

"What you just experienced, for the first of perhaps *many* times, is that same polarity reversal, throughout your entire body, sustained for two seconds. Care to go for three?"

If I hadn't been panting so hard, trying to get my eyes to refocus, I would've cried. Right then and there.

"*CAPTAIN*," demanded Barnabas, "Confess your part in the Ganymede theft and you never have to feel that again."

I did my best to sound defiant, but my voice had lost all its swagger. "Go frak yourself, Jed."

His finger. The blinking red circle. More interminable agony.

Unknowable moments later, my focus returned.

"That was five seconds, Nic ...."

"What happened to three?"

His finger moved towards the console. "WAIT!" I barked. "Please, wait … I'll tell you what I know."

Barnabas' demeanor softened. He could see that he'd broken open his prize and was about to get to the good stuff.

I lifted my head and locked eyes with Barnabas. "Mars Consolidated SDBWGD-42302-PQSJC-741510." His glare became a thousand click stare. I couldn't tell if it was going to work or if he was fixing to launch me via trebuchet out an airlock. "Commander, this farce of an 'interrogation' ends now. I go free or the contents of that account, of *your* account, become public knowledge. That also goes for the account-history." He knew what that meant. All the graft, the skimming, even the med-supplies at the center of Ganymede job had his dirty fingers on them.

I really hadn't wanted to play that card. Barnabas would be much more dangerous knowing I knew. But I sure as hell couldn't stay here.

Barnabas straightened himself in his seat. A few finger taps on the console and the holo-vid shut down. "We have our eyes on you, Conway. Arrogant freelancers like you always get tripped up on the wrong side of the law, eventually." One more tap on the console and the hidden door opened.

In walked a pair of securi-troops. They flanked me in my chair. One pressed a button on his tablet and I was released from grav-lock. "Get up," said the securi-troop on my right. I'm pretty sure he was the same troop that had tazed me. I stood and shook the sleep out of my hands and legs.

"Let's go." The voice modulators in securi-troop helmets always struck me as funny. They were meant to protect the identity of the individuals and to mask their humanity, but they always sounded a bit too faked, like a storybook robo-monster.

"Oh, and Jed?" I paused at the door and turned my head toward Barnabas. "If anything unsavory happens to my crew, things will get very interesting. For you."

Barnabas didn't look up. He continued fiddling with the console, as if he had important work that couldn't be interrupted by idle chatter. "I thought you didn't *have* a crew, 'Captain.'"

"I'm sure you thought a lot of things, Jed." I let the securi-troops lead me out.

* * * *

The securi-troops lead me down an anonymous maze of halls until we arrived at Sec-Dock Alpha-2. "Captain Nicodemus Conway of the Quantum-class transport TCL," declared the securi-troop, "you and your ship are banned from Myrmidon Station for a duration not less than one Terran year." The bulkhead opened and I boarded the Q-TCL. Looking around, I could tell the tech-sweeps had had their way with her, but at least they didn't leave a mess.

I sat down in the pilot's seat and awaited clearance from the tower. "Quantum-class transport TCL," announced that same cold and courteous voice, "you are cleared to detach." I punched the buttons and the station's tug beams assisted Q-TCL as she moved out into open space.

When Myrmidon Station was already several thousand clicks away in my aft-view, Q-TCL's ops readout informed me that the underbody airlock was being accessed from the outside. The readout continued its display as the airlock cycled through its entrance procedures.

Raj entered the bridge and took the co-pilot's seat. He was wearing an exo-suit, helmet retracted.

Raj deadpanned, "Break out with your *six* crew mates, Captain?"

"Sorry about that, Raj. I forgot you were supposed to be dead. You have any trouble?"

"Not as much as you, Nic. That had to hurt."

I couldn't be sure if he was referring to my polarity reversal-enhanced interrogation or having to write off the six people who meant the most to me in the galaxy as merely "former associates."

"Occupational hazard," I replied behind a weak half-smile. "It's not like I got to do anything as fun as hang off the starboard side of a space ship."

Raj grinned. "I wasn't out there long after we'd docked. As soon as the tech-sweeps cleared the Q-TCL, I snuck on board. You know, for a secure station, there are a surprising number of unmanned system-access ports."

"Your Federation tax dollars at work," I quipped.

"While you were 'napping,' I hacked into the Security Main Frame and played Tetris until you could get me the info. Once Barnabas opened the files and showed you the encrypted locations I had everything I needed. Took me a minute or two to recalibrate the Trojan horse to the proper detention station. Turns out they're on Pluto."

Barnabas was always a good chess player. He always played his opponent. But great chess players play the board, not the opponent.

"I brought back a little present. You still a 44 regular, Cap?" Raj held up one of two pairs of tech-sweep coveralls. I nodded. "Raj, set course for geo-sync around Pluto. But first, re-attach the stealth-pack to the Q-TCL's sensor array."

"Aye, Captain." And at that moment, had Barnabas been looking, he would've seen the Q-TCL disappear from the sky.

A music educator by trade, DANIEL J. MAGALLANES is the Director of Bands and Instrumental Music at Monrovia H.S. (MonroviaMusic.org). Daniel enjoys trading wit with smart, creative people, which is why he frequents the NaNoWriMo Writer's Improv Group in Pasadena, CA. This is also a chief reason he's been so happy in his marriage of eighteen years to Jessica, the better writer of the family.

...No, seriously. Go read her story. It's quite good. You're welcome.

Guilt Monkey

Shirley Hanna-King

HENRY WASN'T EASILY surprised; at least that's what he thought until the morning he met George. At first, Henry thought George was the strangest looking lemur he'd ever seen, but he never judged a book by its cover and he liked books. It wasn't long though, before Henry realized George wasn't a lemur at all. He wasn't even from Madagascar! George was something called "monkey" and apparently, he thought Henry was a monkey too! *The only thing* not *strange about George*, thought Henry, *is his name.*

"You can do this," George declared. "You got what it takes to be a great Guilt Monkey."

"Uh, sorry, mister," Henry stammered, "but I'm not a monkey, I'm a—"

"Labels! 116," George interrupted, pointing to the small box in his hand. "This here is a word counter," he explained, "tool of the trade. You can't be a Guilt Monkey without one." He checked it again. "150. And I–for one–hate 'em!"

"Word counters?" Henry asked.

"No!" George barked, stamping his foot. "Labels! Are you going to let yourself be defined by labels?"

"Uh ... no," Henry replied hesitantly. He wasn't sure he really meant no, being thoroughly confused by so many new ideas and words. A lemur's world, you see, is limited to Madagascar and is considerably smaller than a monkey's. However, Henry was brave and brave creatures aren't afraid to ask questions, so he did. "Um ... what are labels?" he squeaked.

"I'm glad you asked," George said, as he slid the counter into his pocket. He adjusted his face to a scholarly expression, put his hands behind his back, and began to pace. After a moment he paused to stroke his chin, which Henry found odd as George had very few whiskers and they were hardly worth stroking. "Labels, my friend," continued George, "are names and rules and things we believe we ought not to believe that keep us doing what we've been told we should do and prevent us from finding out what it is we want to do and ought to do. I'd like to take a trebuchet to all of them!"

"How do we know what we ought to do?" asked Henry.

George spun around, poking his finger in Henry's chest. "What we ought to do is what we would do if we weren't scared of labels! Is that what you want to be, a Label Monkey?"

Taken by surprise, Henry stumbled backward, landing seated on a small tree root. This was convenient since his head was reeling and he was beginning to feel unsteady on his feet. Lemurs aren't bold by nature, so the poke was rather disconcerting. "Ooo, my head." Henry muttered, putting his paws to his forehead. "It's filled to the top."

George waited until Henry settled securely on the root. "Don't you worry," he said, "you'll be fine. Just sit up straight." Henry did as he was told, straightening his back as much as a little lemur can straighten. "Deep breath!" George ordered. Henry breathed deeply.

"Again!" George barked. Trusting his new friend and lacking any ideas of his own, Henry did as he was told. It worked!

"Wow!" Henry glowed in admiration. "That's amazing! It works! How did you know that?"

"Oh," George shrugged nonchalantly, "I picked up a few things nagging the riders on their tip-tap machines." Spinning around, he whispered the word eerily. "*Riders* ... they sit for days in front of their machines, tipping and tapping out things in their heads, putting them onto papery things they carry around."

Henry tried to make sense of it. "Can't they carry the words in their heads?"

"No!" George said. "They can not. The riders must get them out or they'll be lost." This did not seem logical at all to Henry. He hid things inside things to keep them safe. "Ideas," George continued, "are like the things that float downstream. Too many clump together and ... wham!" He clapped his hands hard. Henry jumped. "If too many stick together, those tip-tap machines just STOP!"

"Oh no!" Henry cried worriedly, unsure why, but feeling this was the right response.

George continued. "Some riders sit days, weeks, months,

staring at the tip-tap machine, waiting to ride"—he gave a little sob as he checked the counter again—"but they can't. 710." He shook his little monkey fist in the air, crying, "Guilt Monkeys forever! Take that, Herb!" Then he exhaled loudly and plopped down next to Henry. "There's a rider," he whispered, "a mischief-making rider named Herb who locks 'em up. It's called the Rider-Herb-Lock." Henry squirmed uneasily. "The riders look out of the window, pace, stare at the tip-tap machines and curse—*Rider-Herb-lock! RiderHerblock!*—but all they can do is wait until the Rider-Herb-lock is gone and they can ride again."

"Oh no!" fretted Henry.

George leaned closer. "Then Rider-Herb-lock worry sets in, making it worse until soon, thoughts that don't even make sense get stuck together—like 'strawberry pie buckets' and 'a cuticle in the space station.' Once that happens ... no one knows." He shook his head and Henry grimaced. Henry's cousin was locked in a hunter's trap once. It took twenty-five lemurs to open it. George quickly brightened. "Not all riders get locked though. For some, it's a real big problem, like that space station cuticle. For others, it's as easy as eating that strawberry pie, which is how I learned about the breathin'." Henry was really interested now.

"Forget and breathe," George continued, "and everything unlocks. Try unlocking and it locks tighter. It's a real puzzlement."

"But breathing is simple!" Henry declared.

"Most true things are simple," George mused. "Being a primate of singular thoughts," he boasted, "I never had the problem myself, but I've seen plenty."

"Why don't they breathe, if it's so simple?" Henry asked.

George pondered that for a moment, stroking his hairless chin again. "Well," he concluded, "It's easier for us, Henry. We trust ourselves when we get in-stinks. People—"

"Stinks?" Henry asked, sniffing the air, happy to hear a word he recognized. "I know stinks. Everybody gets in stinks, don't they, George? Even riders?"

"Yes," George replied. "Riders get in-stinks but they don't always pay attention. I blame the bunnies."

"Bunnies? Do they get in stinks too, George?" Henry prodded excitedly.

"Most riders pay more attention when they get thoughts than when they get in-stinks. Critters like us who don't have many thoughts, we just do what comes natural when we get in-stinks." He scratched his head. "Some riders figure it out though. There was a rider once that they still talk about." His eyes grew large. "They say he could shake-a-spear!"

"Shake-a-spear?" Henry repeated. He didn't understand why riders needed to shake spears, so he picked up a pokeweed berry to munch while he mulled this over. It seemed that George was making much ado about nothing with the spears. Henry saw he had an awful lot to learn, but he understood stinks. After all, his eyes were big but were not nearly as helpful as his nose. Why, it could identify stinks across a pond, could find food under bushes, or could lead the way back home. Henry only had one thought but it told him that getting in stinks was important. It was how he knew which mom was his. "George?" he asked. "If I didn't get in stinks, how would I know who I am?"

"You wouldn't!" George declared. "That's the reason

riders have to figure it out, and why they need us!" he said enthusiastically. "1,249. Wanna give it a try?" Before Henry could answer, George continued. "Remember, forget labels. Guilt Monkey's the job title, like 'disc jockey' or 'book worm.' We don't just use worms exclusively any more."

"Eureka!" exclaimed Henry, jumping to his feet. "I mean, aha! Like surfing–the waves, or web–net or hair or inter—"

"Whoa!" George interrupted, realizing this might go on all day. "What do *you* know about the internet?"

"Please!" said Henry indignantly. "I'm geographically challenged, not a heathen!"

"OK," George replied cautiously. "It's like that. Guilt Monkey is the job title because we hang around the riders like monkeys and nag them."

"I'm good at nagging!" said Henry, thrilled at the possibilities opening before him. He loved nagging his father and would've nagged his mother more, if she hadn't been the troop leader. "What do we nag about?"

"Word count," said George. "But ... I don't know ... maybe ... you can't ...."

Henry raised an eyebrow. "Can't what?"

"Well, not to brag," puffed George, "but monkeys *are* smart. Not many critters can understand numbers like monkeys."

"Well, lemurs can!" Henry piped. The sky was his limit now. "Lemurs are even *better* counters."

"Really?" Now George was skeptical. "Well, monkeys use tools. This word counter ain't no picnic."

"Many roads to Rome, George," Henry winked. "I know numbers, I get in stinks, I even got opposable thumbs." He wiggled his thumbs at George. "And I always wanted to be a Guilt Monkey," he sighed, "since I first saw one."

"So ... today?" George said, warily. "Oh well, why not? I'm game if you are."

Henry looked serious. "Technically, George, I think we're both game," but George, who was busy jerking a stick near Henry's head, didn't hear.

"I dub you Guilt Monkey Trainee," he said, giving the lemur a whack. "Now—rules! One, imitate me. Monkey see, monkey do. Two, learn. What do you say?"

Adding a little skip to his step, Henry grinned. "I say ... no and yes."

"Huh?" George grunted, scratching his head.

Henry turned to face him. "No labels, no judging books by covers, no imitating other people. First I gotta be ME. Then, maybe a Guilt Monkey! Try it, George! I'll bet you could even be a rider! I'll bet you could even do what that shake-a-spear guy did. You just gotta sit at a tip-tap machine long enough!" Henry began to dance, singing,

"Your dreams are looking for you,
so you better be yourself,
or they just might go-oh-oh
to somebody else—
Oh yeah! 1,667!"

SHIRLEY HANNA-KING has always been a writer, she just didn't know it. In her search for the meaning of life, she has written winning speeches, college admissions essays,

Grammy nominated songs, touching eulogies, inspiring newsletters, and annoying letters to editors—for other people. Shirley travelled the world, stopped to marry a musician (who didn't stop) and raised their four children. Finally at the age of sixty, with everyone gone, Shirley signed her own name, hit "send" and became a published author. Now she has abandoned the search for the meaning of life–Douglas Adams/42–spending her time instead wondering why she doesn't have grandchildren. She plans/hopes to remember and write down her life story, if she can figure out how to combine her two blogs: www.shirleyhannaking.com and justcallmehanna.com.

S.A.R.A.

Bethany Simonsen

WHEN SHE FIRST awoke, Sara knew next to nothing. She had been programmed with a "desire" to learn more, an itching in her vacant neural pathways. Instead of dumping a massive database into her memory bank, Dr. Henry Lee, her creator, had designed Sara with the ability to learn. Using an implanted system of visual or linguistic cues, Sara would evaluate the appropriateness of her response to any situation; like a child, the satisfaction of a "correct" response served as positive reinforcement. As a member of the Self-Aware Robotics & Androids program, Dr. Lee hoped to create a more humanistic android by giving her an experience closer to childhood. Sara was an empty vessel, to be filled by her interactions with her environment; secretly, Henry even hoped Sara might develop something akin to a personality.

The first thing Sara remembered was opening her eyes to see a face peering at her. She knew vaguely what a face was and could recognize different emotional reactions. The face changed its shape in a most intriguing manner and began to emit new sounds.

"HelloSaraIamDoctorLee," was what she heard. Her programming recognized neither a positive nor a negative expression. *I must provoke a reaction.*

"HelloSaraIamDoctorLee," she repeated back, more slowly, trying out her vocal matrix for the first time.

Dr. Lee suppressed his amusement, knowing that her programming would take that as reinforcement. He shook his head instead. "No, try again." He pointed his finger at himself. "I am Doctor Lee," he repeated. Then, before she could parrot his sentence again, he pointed at her. "You are Sara."

Incorrect. I must try again. She raised her arm, bending it awkwardly. "I am Doctor Lee," she tried. Then she pointed at the other. "You are Sara."

Dr. Lee shook his head again. "Closer." He pointed at himself again. "I am Doctor Lee." He pointed at her. "You are Sara."

Sara quickly processed the variables, trying to figure out the most likely way to respond that she hadn't yet tried. She slowly raised her arm, touching her chest. "I am … Sara," she postulated, then waited for the other to respond. When he nodded, her programming received a small numeric reinforcement for the correct guess. She pointed at him. "You are Doctor Lee," she said.

Dr. Lee smiled widely and said, "Yes, Sara, I am."

* * * *

This was how Sara's lessons began. She quickly caught on to the naming of objects, and the conjugation of verbs. All people on Earth, Mars, and the space stations were fluent in Standard; it was an artificial, bastardized version of Latin and had been the official language of Earth since the twenty-second century. Many spoke at least one or two other old Earth languages as well, keeping in touch with their cultural heritage. For now, Dr. Lee spoke to Sara only in Standard. Other languages could come later when her first set of neural pathways was complete.

Once he felt she had a good grasp of Standard vocabulary—which only took about two weeks—he decided it was time to introduce her to one of his colleagues. Henry invited Dr. Adrianna Guerra to come meet his newest attempt to earn a place in scientific history.

"Sara, I want to introduce you to a friend of mine. She wants to be your friend, too." Dr. Lee smiled encouragingly at Sara, then motioned to Adrianna to enter.

"Hello, Sara. I'm Dr. Guerra. You can call me by my first name, Adrianna, if you'd like." She extended her hand to Sara.

Sara examined Dr. Guerra briefly, then shook her hand firmly. "Hello, Adrianna. I am Sara. What is a friend?" she asked.

Adrianna tilted her head to one side. "A friend?" She rubbed her chin thoughtfully. "To put it simply, a friend is a person that you like to spend time with. Someone you trust to help you if you ever have a problem."

Sara tilted her head to one side, mirroring Adrianna, then straightened up. "I see. How many friends do you have?"

Adrianna laughed. "Quite a few, I suppose."

Sara's system got another boost from the laughter.

Adrianna likes when I ask questions. Her system filed that information away. "I only have two friends. Dr. Lee and you. How do I make more friends?"

Adrianna smiled. "We shall take you out of this laboratory soon, my dear, and then I'm sure you will make many new friends. Everyone on this station is eager to meet you. Dr. Lee hasn't talked about anything other than his new android for the past two weeks."

Sara drew her eyebrows together, a habit she had picked up from watching Dr. Lee's face when he appeared to be processing data. "What is an android?"

Adrianna turned to Henry. "You haven't told her what she is yet?" she asked.

Henry shook his head.

What I am? I do not understand. Is this protected information?

"I think this is a conversation for you two to have alone, then." She turned back to Sara. "Sara, it's been a pleasure to meet you. I would like to come visit you again soon; would you like that?"

Sara nodded. "Yes, please. I would like to spend time with you. You are my friend." The corners of her lips turned up in a smile. Adrianna couldn't help but smile back.

Sara watched Adrianna leave, then repeated her question to Dr. Lee. "What is an android?"

Henry pursed his lips as he thought about how to answer her question. "Sara, we've discussed how there are different kinds of life forms—animals, plants, insects, and so on." She nodded. "You are a life form, but much different than the other kinds we have studied thus far. I am a human, with a body of flesh and blood, coded by my DNA. My body changes as I age, and someday I will cease to exist. You, however, are made of metals and plastics; you merely look human. Since you are made of longer lasting materials, you will not change in appearance as you age; it will be a long, long time before you cease to exist, if that time comes at all. You have much in common with the computer that runs the space station, perhaps even more than you have in common with human beings like myself and Dr. Guerra."

I am different from Henry, but like the computer. Is that what being an android means?

"Is the computer that runs the station an android also?"

Dr. Lee shook his head. "The computer isn't aware of itself as you are. It will not seek out information on its own. You, on the other hand, are aware that you exist; you can move, speak, and think for yourself. I have programmed you with the ability and the desire to learn. Your brain is more like a human's, even though your body is a machine."

"I see. Are there other androids like me?"

"There have been many attempts to create a functional android, but none have been successful so far. I am a lead scientist in the Earth Coalition's Self-Aware Android program. If you are as successful as I hope, I will someday create others like you." Dr. Lee beamed with happiness and pride at the thought.

"I see," Sara replied. *If Dr. Lee does not feel I am successful, then he may terminate me. And I do not want that to happen.*

* * * *

A week passed, with daily visits from Dr. Guerra. They became friends in truth; Sara quickly became adept at eliciting smiles or laughter from Adrianna. Sara picked up her habit of referring to Dr. Lee as Henry. She noticed the pleasure it gave him when she successfully interacted with Adrianna. Sara began to pay closer attention to Henry's behavior patterns as well, studying how to make him happy.

If he enjoys my company, he will not desire to terminate me, even if I am not as successful as he wanted.

Sara began to study Henry's favorite team—the Martian Boomers—so she could discuss sports with him. She learned what types of food he liked, watched several hours of instructional vids, and begged to be allowed to cook as part of her learning process. Henry laughed at the idea, but indulged her. He was astounded by the results; no one had ever been able to replicate his mother's dumpling recipe so well.

Sara learned how to play the old-fashioned Earth strategy games that Henry seemed to enjoy so much. She learned magic tricks; she learned to paint in every style man had ever employed; she even learned how to sing after watching many, many hours of old vids. Replicating the sound with her plastic piping and synthetic vocal cords had been difficult, but it was worth it to see the surprised look on Henry's face. More and more often, Sara found herself striving to make Henry smile and laugh, not just because she feared what would happen to her, but because his approval and his happiness had become important to her programming. Positive reinforcements from Henry became worth much more to her system than those from anyone else. Henry had designed her to be able to create something approaching real friendship, and to be able to decide how she wanted to value someone's approval. Just like a real human, she could weigh her friends and rank them in order of importance.

Henry had never imagined that love might come into the equation.

* * * *

"Adrianna, I need to ask you something, but you mustn't tell Henry," Sara said seriously.

Adrianna put down the rook she had been holding. She was half convinced that Sara could beat her at chess any time she wanted to, but politely limited herself to winning roughly half the time. "I'm not certain I can promise that, Sara," she cautioned. "If it's something that will affect his work, I may have to discuss it with him. Besides, why would you want to keep anything secret from Henry?"

Should I discuss the matter with Adrianna without a promise of secrecy? She sighed, unconsciously mimicking Adrianna's habit of sighing when deep in thought. *The potential value outweighs the risk.* "Because I'm afraid that there may be something wrong with me—and that, if there is, he may terminate me."

"Sara, that's absurd!" Adrianna exclaimed. "Henry would never do such a thing!"

"Then why are there no other androids? Surely, if Henry is a leader in the field of artificial intelligence, I cannot be the first android he has created. Where are the others, Adrianna?" She looked her friend squarely in the eyes, mutely demanding an honest answer.

Adrianna sighed. "You're right. You're not the first.

But the others—they couldn't even approach your level of sophistication. They were nothing like you. Henry wouldn't get rid of you, even if there was something wrong. And if there's a problem, no one on the station is better qualified to fix it than Henry." She tried to smile reassuringly at Sara.

"I can't tell Henry about the problem, Adrianna, because he's part of it. He seems to be affecting my programming somehow."

"Tell me about it," Adrianna urged gently.

"I spend an inordinate amount of time thinking about him and how to make him happy. At first it was because I didn't want him to terminate me, but now ... my system is only satisfied when I have made him happy. My brain is constantly processing, discovering new ways to please Henry. Even right now, my brain is working on the problem in the background. At times it is difficult to concentrate on anything else. I am worried about this disruption to my regular programming," Sara confided.

Adrianna suppressed a smile; she had had similar conversations with her own daughters back when they were teenagers. "Sara, is it possible that you might have feelings for Henry?" she suggested.

"Adrianna, my system is not equipped with any sort of software that would emulate human feelings," Sara protested.

"But you were equipped with the ability to evolve and develop a personality of your own, weren't you?"

"Yes, I was," Sara conceded. "I am aware of how my personality has changed as I have learned and spent time interacting with others. But love and emotions? The changes to my personality are merely the results of a string of mathematical sums; I have learned to value various attributes, activities, and expressions differently. Everything that I do is a logical conclusion of my programming. How could I possibly love Henry?"

Adrianna shook her head. "Perhaps your programming has concluded that you love him. Perhaps you have developed feelings for him outside the bounds of your programming somehow; we still only barely understand the field of artificial intelligence. All I can tell you is that the sensations you described are very similar to the initial stages of romantic love as a human experiences them."

"Then what can I do?" Sara asked, genuinely distressed. *I thought there was a bug in my programming that Adrianna could fix privately.*

"You'll have to do what young women have been doing for eons, Sara. You have to decide whether to tell him how you feel or keep it to yourself. Just remember that there's nothing wrong with you; in fact, if you do have feelings for Henry outside of what your programming dictates, it means that you have been successful beyond our wildest dreams."

Sara nodded. *I can't ever tell Henry. It's too dangerous.*

* * * *

A few days later, Henry decided that it was time to take Sara out in public. He had taken her around the floor where the scientists' labs were before, but had kept a close eye on her interactions with others. He finally believed that she was ready to be exposed to a greater mass of humans: diverse, noisy, and unaware that she was an android. He could hardly wait to see how she would react to new people, and how they would react to her.

Henry watched Sara fondly as she fidgeted with her hair in the mirror he had provided her. Adrianna had supplied more feminine clothing for the excursion to help her blend in. He felt a surge of pride as he examined her, noticing how human she looked. It was remarkable how far she had developed in just a few shorts weeks. If he hadn't known she was an android, he would have thought she was an attractive young woman. He might even have asked her out. After all, she appeared to be only a few years younger than he was. Perhaps some young man might notice her and flirt with her today—although that thought made Henry oddly uncomfortable.

He cleared his throat, pushing aside the awkwardness. "Are you ready to go yet, Sara?" he asked, more roughly than he intended.

Sara ducked her head. "I'm sorry, Henry; I'm just not used to my own appearance. I'm ready to go whenever you are." She stood and smoothed her tunic. The dark crimson color went nicely with her pale skin and dark hair, Henry noticed absently. He took her hand and led her to the lift that would take them down to the recreational ring of the space station. "After you, my dear," he said. Sara stepped in.

The rec ring on the station was always packed, no matter the hour. Just about anything a human could want to do in their free time could be found on the rec ring somewhere.

Sara stopped as they exited the lift, staring around. She silently took in the masses of people: the sights, sounds, and strange smells. She took a few steps in the direction of the music, then paused. "May I?"

Henry grinned. "Of course. This expedition is all for you."

Sara smiled back. "I'd like to hear more of the music then." She grabbed Henry's hand and pulled him along. Henry followed, laughing.

They quickly reached the musicians' section. Sara shifted from hall to hall until she found one that captured her attention. The music was upbeat and many of the listeners were dancing. After a few moments, Sara found herself being pulled into the crowd. At first her movements were haltingly slow, but she quickly caught on.

Henry stood back, watching her move. He admired the way she rapidly assimilated into the crowd, although he was decidedly uncomfortable with the way several of the young men were also appreciating her.

"It's time to leave, Sara," he called abruptly. Sara meekly trotted over. *What did I do to displease Henry?* She felt a surge of electricity through her circuits. Her core temperature rose, only half a degree, but enough to make her feel odd.

"Let's go look at the gardens instead," Henry suggested. "The music here is too loud for me."

Sara sighed in relief. *Henry isn't upset with me.* "To the gardens."

They silently made their way to the gardens. Sara followed a half step behind Henry, not wanting him to notice her abnormal temperature. When they reached the gardens, she forgot her worries. She had seen images of flowers, but they paled in comparison to the reality. She meandered through the pathways, admiring the sights, smells, and textures of the blossoms.

Henry smiled, his discomfort forgotten, as he watched

Sara revel in the novel experience. She had learned so much in the past few weeks that, at times, he forgot how young and inexperienced she truly was. Impulsively, he picked a flower and approached Sara quietly, threading it into her dark hair.

Sara looked down, blushing slightly.

Henry's eyes widened in surprise.

He cleared his throat awkwardly. "I think it's time to return to the lab, Sara. I'd like to run some diagnostics, make sure your system is working correctly."

Sara paled, but silently followed him back to the rec ring's main corridor. *He's noticed that there's something wrong. He's going to terminate me once his diagnostics tell him what the problem is.* She suppressed a sniff. *Why should I cry? I'm just an android; I don't even have real tear ducts, just tiny plastic tubing filled with clear lubricant to keep my eyelids from squeaking.*

Who will make Henry laugh when I'm gone? No one understands him the way I do. It will take him ages to build a replacement.

What if I'm such a failure that I've ruined his career?

While they walked, Sara's temperature continued to rise. The variations began to affect her systems, causing wires to short and processors to overheat. She was so anxious that she didn't notice until after they had entered the lift. When she leaned against the wall, she felt something tiny land on her skin; it instantly burned up on contact.

Sara didn't want to admit it, but she knew she had to tell Henry that something was seriously wrong.

"Henry?" she said, her voice quivering. Then she collapsed.

Henry dropped to his knees at her side, but snatched his

hand back when he felt the scorching heat coming from her body.

"Sara, what's wrong? Please, answer me!" Henry pleaded. Sara tried desperately to speak, but couldn't.

"Lift, this is an emergency!" Henry called out. "Override all other stops and take us directly to the labs!" He grabbed the lift's emergency medical kit, wrapped his hands in thick bandages, and took Sara's hands.

"Sara, I can fix whatever's wrong. You just have to hang on until we get to the lab, all right?" he begged, hoping that she could hear him.

As soon as the lift doors opened, he grabbed Sara and lugged her to the lab. By the time he got there, Sara's temperature had risen so much that his hands were burned even through his bandages. Henry tried everything he could think of. After a few minutes with no success, he did the only thing he could think of that might give Sara even a remote chance of survival. He grabbed his scalpel, sliced her forehead open, and yanked out her primary memory chipset. If he couldn't save her body, perhaps he could save something of her personality.

And while Sara could no longer communicate, and could barely function at all, she could still feel. She tried to scream in agony, but she couldn't. Henry grabbed the chips and ran from the room, unable to stand the heat.

Henry dropped to the floor, sobbing, holding the chips to his chest. Adrianna found him there; the lab's monitors had notified her of the emergency. She took everything in, including the visible heat waves rising from Sara's body, threatening the rest of the lab. She started the fire suppression program, then sank to sit by Henry's side, tears welling up in her eyes.

"What happened?"

"We were exploring the rec ring, and she started overheating. I don't know what caused it. And now she's gone!" Henry opened his hands. "This is all that's left. Even if I put these inside another robot, it won't be the same. Sara was unique, more than the sum of her parts. She was the most important person in my life. Without her ... what else is there?" he asked bitterly.

"You're right that she was unique. You truly succeeded with her. She was self-aware, capable of interacting normally with humans." She decided to break Sara's confidence. "And she loved you."

Henry wiped his eyes wearily. "I loved her too."

* * * *

The lab doors dinged once the program was finished. Henry helped Adrianna up, then turned to enter the lab, steeling himself.

"Let me go first," Adrianna offered gently. Henry nodded, half numb.

After a moment, she called to him to come in. Henry took a deep breath, then entered.

Nothing appeared to have been damaged beyond repair. Adrianna had kept her head and started the fire suppression program in time. After surveying the rest of the lab for damage, he turned to Sara's body, still lying on the table. Adrianna courteously gave him space.

It looked like a scene from an operating room failure,

he noted grimly. Adrianna had covered Sara with a blanket, thinking to spare him, no doubt. Well, Henry would have none of it. Sara's death was his fault—he was her creator, and whatever had caused her systems to fail had to be his mistake. He deserved to feel pain.

Henry pulled back the blanket. His breath caught in his throat. She was still so lovely—why had he never noticed how lovely she was until their last few hours together? He took her hand and gently kissed her cheek.

"I loved you, Sara," he whispered. "I'm sorry that I failed you. You deserved better."

A sigh filled the room. Henry jumped.

"I don't want anything other than you, Henry," Sara whispered hoarsely. She coughed, clearing her lungs.

Then she bolted up. "I have lungs!" she shouted.

Adrianna spun around, her eyes wide with shock.

"Of course you do, Sara. I built your lungs myself," Henry replied distractedly. "But what happened? How are you alive? You stopped working—I pulled out your memory chips!" He thrust them into her face.

She batted them away. "Exactly! I don't need those anymore. I have *real* lungs! I have a heartbeat, feel!" She pressed his hand to her neck.

Henry felt her veins pulsing under his fingers. "But ... how?"

"In the lift, a bit of DNA landed on me, a cuticle in the space station. My system had already begun to fail. My sub-processors analyzed the DNA and created a unique genome for me, then used the station's matter replication systems to create a new body. Notice all the dust in here? It's all that's left, except for those chips you have." She paused, suddenly shy. "Did you mean it when you said you loved me?"

"Of course I meant it. No matter whether you're human or android, I love you, Sara."

She sighed happily. "I love you too, Henry." She cleared her throat, unsure how to tell Henry what she wanted. "Just before you first said you love me, you pressed your lips to my cheek."

Henry blushed. "That's called a kiss, Sara."

Sara tilted her head to one side. "I liked it. Would you kiss me again, Henry?" she asked.

"Um." Henry coughed. "Yes." He leaned forward, and their lips met gently. After a moment, Sara pulled away.

"Henry, I think there's something wrong with me!" she exclaimed.

An iron fist gripped Henry's chest. "Tell me, what's wrong?"

"I'm not sure how to explain," Sara replied. "It feels like my internal organs are twisting themselves into knots." She frowned. "It's rather uncomfortable."

Adrianna burst into laughter, startling them both; they had been so wrapped up in each other that they had forgotten she was there.

"Sara, my dear, I think you ought to come with me so we can have a talk. Unless you'd rather handle it yourself, Henry?"

"No!" he protested, backing away. "I leave her education in your capable hands."

"My education?" Sara asked. "But I thought I already knew so many things."

"You do, dearest," Henry assured her. "But now you need

to learn what it is to be human." He kissed her once more on the cheek.

If being human means feeling like my inside is about to become my outside, I'm not sure that I like it, Sara thought as she followed Adrianna out the door. *Although the kissing might be worth it.*

BETHANY SIMONSEN always wanted to be a writer when she grew up, except for a brief period when she aspired to be a zookeeper. However, she realized that manuscripts are much easier to clean up after than elephants. When she isn't writing, she's busy parenting her three crazy and energetic lemurs. Bethany loves music, gardening, making silly faces at children, and reading. She's hoping to have a full-length eBook (titled *Angelus*) out sometime in the next year, if she can ever find enough time to revise it. You can follow her musings on books at bethanysbookcorner.blogspot.com.

The Outsider Among Us

Katia Shank

I RUN AS FAST as I can through the forest. They are hunting me. I can't stop. What part of the U.S. am I in now? I don't know. There are no states anymore. I need to get as far away as possible from D.C. Over the past few days, I have been driving from state to state, but my vehicle broke down and now I must travel on foot. I pause to catch my breath and lean against a tall tree. The sun is quickly setting and it is already dark because of the thick leaves covering the sky. I stare at the cuts and scratches covering my pale hands and take a deep but shaky breath. The last few days have been crazy, to say the least. I get up and stretch. With the remaining sunlight I can go a little farther. Slowly, I trudge on, the leaves crunching under my feet and my skinny, sore legs calling out for me to stop. In the dim light, I see a cabin in the clearing. Running up to it, I look inside.

It is protection from the night, and that's all I need. A dust-covered bed is in the corner of the room, and I fall into it and sleep.

A cold breeze wakes me up, and I see that a window blew open in the night. Getting out of bed, I reach for my backpack and put on my boots. I scan the cupboard in the cabin and find a can of beans. Eating them, I go on my way. By noon, I am exhausted. Before my escape, I had never done any strenuous activities. I had barely even gone in the sun. Now, I am trekking across the country to get away from my past.

I stop by a creek to fill my water bottle. As I lean over, my glasses fall into the stream. I blindly stretch my hands out, feeling for them. Suddenly, a hand goes over my mouth. "Don't move," says a deep voice.

A blindfold is tied around my eyes, and I am moved into some sort of vehicle. I attempt to struggle and yell. "Be quiet," says the man. "It's going to be a long ride."

Has all my work been for nothing? Have I gotten away just to be taken back again? A woman's voice speaks, "Who do you think he is? Is he a Straggling or a Cuticle?"

I almost throw up. C.U.T.I.C.L.E.? I don't want to think of that word again. "Shh," says the man. "Don't say anything till we get to the station."

The ride is long, but I stay awake the whole time and can tell we're heading west. After several hours, the vehicle comes to a stop. I am yanked out of the car. I stumble along and follow where the man is pulling me. After a few yards, I notice a change in surroundings. It is much warmer, and my shoes tap on the floor. After a few minutes of walking, I am seated in a chair, and my blindfold is taken off.

At first, I can't see anything except a blinding white light. A few moments pass, and I can faintly make out a person sitting opposite me with a table between the two of us. "Here," the man says.

The man slides a pair of glasses across the table, my glasses, and I quickly put them on. With everything in focus, I study the man in front of me. He is Hispanic-looking, has a strong build, and is completely bald except for slight stubble on his face.

"Who are you?" says the man.

"J-Jason Summers," I stutter.

"Are you a Cuticle or a Straggling?" the man asks.

C.U.T.I.C.L.E. That word again. I can feel my heart race and my breathing quickens. "Wha–what do you mean? C.U.T.I.C.L.E.?"

The man answers, "I guess you don't understand. We call the people who took our families and friends away Cuticles. People like me, the people who refused to leave—we're called Stragglings. Now which one are you?"

"I guess I'm a ... Straggling," I lie.

They can't know the truth. If they did, they would kill me. "Well then, I guess you're one of us," the man says flatly.

He stands up, "Follow me."

I stand up and follow the man out of the white room. "What is this place?" I wonder out loud as I walk into a large hall and see a scaled down replica of a space shuttle.

"Before everyone left, this used to be a space museum," says the man. "We got rid of most of the items to make it a community and meeting place, but obviously we couldn't get rid of the space shuttle. Now we just call this place the Space Station."

I nod in understanding, but inside, my stomach sinks. These people are forced to live like this because of what I have done. The man walks up to a panel on the wall and presses a button. An alarm goes off, and people start flooding into the room. One thing I notice is that most of them are men. There are a few women, but no children. "We have a new member to welcome to our group. His name is Jason. Tell us about yourself, Jason," the man projects to the crowd.

I shuffle my feet uncomfortably. The stares of the people look as if they can tell exactly who I am. "Um ... I'm Jason. I used to be a scientist ... now I'm here."

"Come with me Jason. Let's get you a place to sleep," the man says.

His hand grips my shoulder tightly, and he whispers into my ear, "Don't think you're here to stay. We will be watching you closely to make sure you are fit to stay here."

I swallow and nod dumbly as the man releases me from his grip. I follow the man and several other people to a small room with a table and chairs. "Please sit," says the man. "You remember in 2026 when the government issued a project to protect the people from the growing threat of the Russians. Few people wondered what it really was all about. They all just believed the things they were shown on their TVs: Russian soldiers beating civilians, women and children at concentration camps, and country after country being invaded. They called it C.U.T.I.C.L.E., Camp Utopia To Instigate Cordial Living Everywhere. A safe haven, they said; like a cuticle on a leaf, it was meant to protect us. When the children left, the first group of resistors sprang up. Angry parents who wanted nothing more than to get their children back marched to

D.C. They were turned away. What you do not know is that when they continued protesting, people from the group began disappearing. The remaining protestors each received a note saying, "This is a warning." It was enough to stop them, or so the government thought. The men and women eventually left. However, a group of resisters stayed behind, and that is who we are."

"Do you know why they took everyone away?" a woman with short black hair asks.

"All I know is that there was no real threat from the Russians." I lie. I know so much more.

"You're right about that," says the woman. "When they took the children first, they were actually performing their first test. You see, President Bernard wanted more control. For years he's been sheltering everybody from the outside world, but in 2026 he hired scientists to make something terrible. An injection was created to prevent disease, aging, but promote mind control from others. It makes you dumb. The only thing you believe is what the President says. It's like his commands trigger something in your brain to make you obey. The children they took—they were the first ones to be tested with it. Then they took the women and the elderly, and finally the men."

"How ... how do you know all this?" I ask in disbelief. My stomach is twisted into knots.

"We have our resources," says the black man next to me. "It's not only happening here. Countries all over the world are going through the same thing. And there are other people like us. We have groups all over the country and double agents who work underground. Oh, you probably don't know about the underground. It's where they keep everybody. Person after person is lying next to each other, hibernating, until it's time to release them back into the world. The problem is, the injections wear off after a week. So for now they're keeping the nation in an induced coma, while they find a solution."

My mind is having a hard time keeping up. How can they know so much? The next fifteen minutes pass like a blur, and I am led to my sleeping quarters. That night I dream about being back in the laboratory and I wake up in a cold sweat.

During breakfast, I have no appetite, but the eating hall is buzzing with excitement. "What's going on?" I ask a young man next to me.

"Early this morning, a team left for D.C. They're going to assassinate the president today. It's taken over a year of preparation, but the day has finally come!" the young man explains.

I sigh with relief. Maybe after this, I can forget about everything I have done. The hour goes by slowly, then, finally, they receive a call. A man holding a walkie-talkie runs into the room. "The president is dead!" he exclaims.

Cheers erupt, and I cry silent tears. I can now put away my past and start a new life, but for some reason, I'm still uneasy. The president is dead. I should be happy, but a guilt, the same guilt from my past haunts me. It gnaws at my insides. By the time the team gets back, it is dark. The crew walks in with someone I recognize. He is tall, has piercing blue eyes, and curly red hair. Jackson! I panic, and my hands start to sweat. I look down to avoid Jackson's eyes. Briefly glancing up, my eyes lock with Jackson's. Jackson's eyes widen and he whispers something into a man's ear. Calmly walking to me, the man grabs my arm and drags me away. "Looks like we have a Cuticle in the Space Station," he says.

They lead me into a large closet and lock the door. Huddling in the corner, fear creeps into my throat, blocking my airway. They found out. They know everything. Scenes from my past flash before my eyes.

I'm in the laboratory, working on a revolutionary new injection. It is age defying, it can prevent diseases, and it also makes everyone work together and listen to one higher authority. President Bernard enters the laboratory. "Are you making any progress?" he asks.

"Yes, sir. It's almost finished," I answer.

"Good, good! Jason, you will be remembered in history. The man who brought America together. You are a genius," praises the President.

Fame. It is all the skinny twenty-two year old wants. His socially awkward days will be over once people respect him for what he can do. Another scene flashes before me, and I am underground with the President. I look in horror as I see thousands of people lying on stretchers in front of me. Screaming comes from the next room. "What is that?" I ask President Bernard.

"Oh it's just the side effects of the injection," replies the President. "Already a couple thousand people have died, but you should know this. After all, this is all your doing."

I gasp for breath and start to shiver as all my memories, everything I've been actively repressing, flood into my brain. Jackson was another scientist back at the laboratory. He must be the double agent. He will tell them everything. The hours go by, but I do not sleep. I stare into the dark, my mind numb.

At last the door opens, and the man who put me in this room walks in. "Jackson told me everything."

I gulp. "I've just gotten off the phone with the leader of our group," he continues. "All people associated with the formation of C.U.T.I.C.L.E. are to be executed."

"No!" I sob. "Please no! I'm sorry! I didn't know what I was doing! Please!"

The man raises his voice, "It doesn't matter how sorry you are! You killed thousands of people. You tested and experimented on children. You deserve this."

The words hit me like a brick. I let go of everything I've been holding back, and I accept defeat. He's right. I'm a monster. I killed thousands of people. Children. I deserve this. The only thing I can do to amend for my past is to accept my punishment. I sink to my knees and close my eyes. Closing my eyes, I feel a gun being pressed to my head. As the trigger is being pulled, I whisper, "I'm sorry."

KATIA SHANK is a high school sophomore who lives in Southern California. She participated in the 2012 NaNoWriMo, and she is very excited to be contributing in another NaNoWriMo event. In her free time, Katia enjoys reading, listening to music, and watching Korean dramas. Her favorite school subject is history, and some of her favorite books include *The Chronicles of Narnia*, *Anne of Green Gables*, *Percy Jackson and the Olympians*, *Harry Potter*, and *Pride and Prejudice*.

Orion in the Everglades

Sara W. McBride

FOR A TIME, a time longer than the humid summers of the Everglades, I lived with the most exquisite woman, a goddess in fact; her name was Artemis. She never traveled around her elbow to find her thumb, which is to say she lived without fanfare, so I shoulda' listened to her when she advised me to never fall in love.

It all started on an airless August morning when a young girl decided to walk along the banks of a stream, following a small raft she'd thatched out of sixteen fine pieces of tender green grass; each piece for each of her years. Immediately I knew she was special. The air came to life and shifted around her like an unexpected breeze, causing the limbs of a weeping willow to dance with delight.

The raft bobbed along through the water, gliding over rocks and seeking the current like it was a friend to share secrets with. The girl tripped along the stream bank, her long skirts entangling her gangly legs. She raced her raft, pointing, gasping, and on one occasion, releasing a small squeal at the swift genesis of a threatening stone. Down here in the 'Glades, stones are precious. This one possessed a point akin to the great glacier carvings that the locals bequeath names to, like Ol' Gator's Tooth or Dandy's Blade. No one was ever quite sure how long this particular stone had been corrupting the currents—maybe an eon, maybe a century, or maybe it just sprang up on that very day. Either way, the pointy rock in the center of the stream was called the Ferryman. But it was not the Ferryman stone that stopped the little grass raft's journey; it was a hand.

Don't worry—this wasn't a detached hand, or anything of the like. I'm a god, and I've seen plenty o' gruesome things, but I got no intention of telling any grisly tales. This is a happy story about a boy and a girl and lots of long strands of tender green grass. That warm August day is the day that the boy's hand, my hand, reached into the stream and caught that tripping, gasping girl's little thatched raft.

"Hey! That's mine, put it back."

"What if I don't want to?"

The girl fell silent, but her face flashed red for a moment, just a moment. Then it returned to the florid grace a humid day induces. She was stumped, like a tree without wisdom. Why wouldn't a boy, this boy, release the raft back into the stream? Surely the little grass raft was far more entertaining as an object in motion than an object in hand. But the boy felt differently; the raft as a link to the girl held far greater appeal.

"Well, what are you going to do to my raft?"

"I'm studyin' it."

"What's there to study?"

"You wove the grass. That's worth a good study."

The girl sat down on the stream bank, opposite the boy on the other side. He was unusual-looking for these parts, with thick black hair and a strong jaw line. He lay on his back, holding the raft up to the dappled sunlight. The girl noticed his hands were oddly large. He had a youthful body, like someone her age, but his hands belonged to an adult. Those large hands began to unweave her raft. She glowered at him, crossed her arms, and harrumphed her brown bangs off her slightly sweaty forehead. She waited five minutes, staring angrily at the boy, like an indignant night toad building up his croaking sack.

"You're so boring!" she finally croaked.

"You're not," said the boy. He continued to lie on his back. Still holding the raft in the air, he took each blade of grass out of the raft and then wove each blade of grass back into the raft.

The girl finally gave her last harrumph and stood up. She wandered a few feet away, bent down, and plucked a long strand of tender green grass. Then she plucked another strand, and another and another. After a few minutes she sat back down at the stream bank. She crossed her legs and smoothed out her long skirt to make a bowl. In it she laid her palm-fulls of grass. She immediately went to work weaving a new raft, a much larger one, a much stronger one, a much finer one.

The boy rolled over onto his stomach and watched the girl across the stream.

She ignored him and focused on her new, fine raft of tender green grass.

He stood up, reached out for the Ferryman stone, and tramped across the shallow waters to her side of the stream. His shoes splashed water on the edge of her skirts, but she paid him no never mind. He handed her back the small grassy raft made of only sixteen blades. She ignored him. He dropped the raft in the bowl of her skirt. She picked it up and dropped it on the ground next to her. He sat on top of the discarded raft as if it was an insult to both of them, but not really understandin' with whom the insult lay.

"Why do you stay?" he asked. "No one ever stays."

"I know who you are," she said with a hint of pity. But this isn't one of those stories about the poor dimwitted boy that everyone pities, so don't go thinking that. I'm not one to be pitied. The girl continued, "I know who you are. You're the boy that makes all those little grass men and leaves them on people's windowsills when they need protecting. You're the boy they call Thady. I know who you are."

"Why?" he asked, edging toward her. He asked wanting to know why this girl, this very strong-minded, unbending girl, knew him and knew that his Earthly name was indeed Thady.

"Some people in town say bad things about you. They say you're quiet, backward, dangerous. But I don't think that. I think you just want to help people."

"Why?" he asked, different again. The boy honestly wanted to know why this fascinating girl who could weave grass so well thought he wanted to help people, as indeed he honestly did, sometimes.

"You always leave a little grass man on the windowsill when a baby is being born, or when a child is sick, or when someone in the house dies. The grass man protects the mother or the child or the family while they mourn. I often wake up and look on my windowsill to see if I need protecting from something."

"Why?"

"Because, maybe, because, well I hope you're thinking of me. Maybe I hope you want me to be protected."

"Why?" He asked with an intensity in his gut that made his belly twirl and his head spin.

"Because I'm a girl and you're a boy."

He didn't say anything for a long while. He just observed that indeed, she was a girl and he was a boy.

He noticed that the edge of her fingernail on her left middle digit was bleeding, but he didn't say anything. Instead he reached into the bowl of her skirts, pulled out several long strands of tender green grass, and began to fashion a little man.

The next morning, the girl raced to her window, sure she would find a little grass man, but alas, her sill was empty. Later in school that day, she heard that Annabelle's mother found "one of those horrible voodoo symbols on her window."

"My mother grabbed that hideous doll and threw it into the fireplace. Then this terrible smoke came from it. That's how we know it was voodoo."

"It was fresh young grass, that's why it smoked," the girl said to Annabelle. "Why do you have a fire burning in this hot weather?"

"Don't you know *anything*, Dottie?" The girl winced. She hated hearing her name. "Mother says it's best for the baby. For the laying in."

Dottie ignored Annabelle for the rest of the week.

Everyday after school, the girl who hated her name found happiness walking along the stream bank. And everyday, just at the Ferryman stone, the boy, Thady, sat tying knots in grass with his oversized hands. Most days they sat opposite each other across the stream and quietly worked. The girl weaved boats and the boy weaved men. He smiled at her. She smiled at him. And he always looked forward to moment in the day when she launched a raft and he occupied it with a small grass man, because at that moment, reaching toward the center of the stream, their hands almost touched.

One day, the sun seemed to set earlier than usual and the boy and the girl found themselves covered in a blanket of stars.

"Does anything scare you?" the girl asked the boy.

"The blackness im'between the stars."

"Why?" the girl asked. Her mortal empathy intoxicated the boy.

"I don't know what lives in the space between the stars. No one does."

"That's what makes the blackness beautiful. Anything can live there."

"Like scorpions? I'm certain a scorpion lives in the stars," the boy said.

"And does it chase you?" the girl teased. "In your dreams, does the scorpion chase you?"

"If only you knew."

"I'm sorry. I didn't know you were scared. I didn't think Thady Grassman could ever be scared of anything."

"Nothing scares you, does it, girl?"

She sighed and smiled, but never took her eyes off the stars. Finally, she said, "My fingers always bleed. They tear and bleed. I always worry that my finger edges, my cuticles, won't hold my nails in place. What then? I'd have no fingernails and I couldn't work the grass blades, and then I'd have no reason to visit you."

"Girl, if all your fingernails fell off, I would make you a set of grass thimbles."

"Thady, that's the sweetest thing anyone ever said to me."

Another week passed, and every morning the girl ran to her windowsill and looked for a little grass man, but still her sill was empty. But everyday at school, someone else complained about finding a little grass man on their windowsill.

"It had little red eyes, I swear. It was probably crazy Thady's blood. His real blood. I bet he leaves the dolls as a warning of who he wants to kill."

"Has anyone who found a grass man ever died?" the girl inquired of Vella.

"You're such an idiot, Dottie." The girl really hated hearing her name said by Vella's scowling voice. Vella scrubbed at words like they were unrinsed oatmeal. She spat as she pronounced each 't' of the girl's name separately. "That's just because, Dot-tie, he hasn't had a chance to kill someone. Maybe he'll come after you, Dot-tie."

The girl hated Vella for speaking meanly about Thady. But she'd learned long ago that feeling contempt and showing contempt led to two very different outcomes in her world. So she smiled and asked, "Did your little brother's chicken pox get better?"

"Yes. Our prayers finally worked. My little brother joined us for breakfast this morning and ate like a crocodile fresh out of hibernation. Daddy's gonna drive him into town in the new Model T for a real chocolate malted. God says chocolate is good, ya' know. Fixes sins clean away."

The girl ignored Vella for the rest of the week.

The girl and the boy found themselves at the banks of the stream every day, and also found themselves staying longer every day. One night, lying on their backs, on opposite sides of the streams with the Ferryman stone in the middle, Thady asked a very important question.

"Girl, what's your name?"

"What do you think it should be?"

"Dream."

"Dream? I like that. You can call me Dream."

The next night, the girl, Dream, lay on her back, dazzled by the stars above when she heard a splash in the water. She sat up, but before she could say anything, Thady laid down beside her. His wet shoes and socks touched her bare ankle. The coolness on her skin felt sweet, tingly, like an iced mint tea, as she lay perfectly still in the warm, humid night. Thady raised his arm, the arm that was next to hers, and pointed at the sky.

"That space there, between the bright star and the moon. What do you think lives in that space?" he asked.

"A space house sits there. In a space house, nothing bad ever happens and everyone is safe from scorpions." She reached up, her arm brushing against his body for a brief scintillating moment. She pointed at another spot, their elbows slightly touching, the hairs on their arms interlacing with each other. "That space, between the handle of the Big Dipper and the next bright star. What do you think lives in that space?"

Thady let his pointing finger touch hers. "There?"

Dream wrapped her petite hand around Thady's large hand and pointed his finger. "There."

"You. You live there. All good things live there." Thady knew that their intertwined hands meant as much to her as it did to him. He discovered his Adam's apple moved up and down when he gulped.

The girl didn't say anything for a long while and simply

held Thady's hand, pointing upward at the place where all good things lived.

"Thady, why do you leave your little grass men on the windowsills of people who don't deserve them?"

Thady lowered his arm and rolled on his side, rustling the leaves and grass as he did so. "People will always be scared. If I give them something to be scared of, then they won't be scared of each other. So, ya' see, every scared person is deservin'."

"Thady, do your dolls really work? Do they really heal people?"

"Depends if the person wants to be healed. My pulps—"

"Your pulps?"

"Pulps. Like a mass of something that can be molded. A pulp. The grass is molded into a little man and the finder is molded into focusing his interest away from the dead, the sick, the worry, the fear. Sometimes, all a person needs to move on is a little distraction."

"Why haven't you ever left a little grass man on my windowsill?"

Thady lay back down on his backside and stared upward. "Dream, you should know by now, you don't need one."

That night, I knew I loved her. And I'm not allowed to love. I made a grass man and gave it to myself.

The next day, Thady wasn't at the stream. Every day for a week, the girl asked around the school, hoping to hear that someone had received a little grass man. People liked to say terrible things and think they were the center of the town's concerns, so the girl was confident she would hear something. But no one spoke about any gloomy little grass men on the windowsills. No one. And every day, the stream at the Ferryman stone continued in its old, ancient ways, but without the girl's favorite person to corrupt the currents.

Two weeks passed, but every day, the girl still went to the stream banks and weaved grass and waited. On the seventeenth day, she sat quietly, attempting to whistle Zippidy-do-da, Zippidy-a, but she kept forgetting the tune and returning to the bluebird on her shoulder, over and over again. Soon she became upset with the bluebird and quit whistling. She noticed three of her cuticles were bleeding, perhaps torn by the grass. She tried to weave a small thimble, but the grass wouldn't keep its shape. She waited and waited until the sun descended and the stars emerged, blanketing her with memories of Thady. She pointed up and said, "There, Thady, right there. What do you think lives in the space between those two stars?" She waited and waited, with her arm dangling in the night air, but only the laced drone of June bug wings and cricket legs replied. With her arm still hanging in the air, pointing to the blackness, she began to cry.

I watched her, Dream, my Dream, from above and also began to cry. That night it rained.

The next morning she woke up late. She claimed to be sick and stayed home from school. True or not, she believed her heart to be sick and couldn't face another day of no one complaining about little grass men on their windowsill. She moped back to her room and, mustering the last of her faith, looked out her window. To her surprise and delight, there sat something green upon her windowsill. She flung open her window and delicately picked up three tiny grass thimbles. She placed them on her fingers with the torn cuticles. The coolness from the tender young grass held a healing strength that affected far more than just her torn skin. She ran outside, directly to the stream bank at Ferryman stone.

There he was. Thady sat on his side of the stream bank, chewing on a piece of long, tender grass. She ran to him and stood opposite. He smiled up at her. He could see that she clearly wanted to leap into his arms, as he felt the same. But he controlled himself and remained on his side of the stream, calmly chewing his piece of grass.

"This is a fine, tender strand of grass. Perhaps a tall lemon grass, I reckon'."

"Thady, where have you been? I've been worried sick! Come here."

"Nope."

"Thady!"

"Nope. Sorry, Dream, you need to come here."

"But you always come to my side of the stream."

"That's exactly why I think you should come to my side. But be careful in those little shoes of yours. The streambed is slippery. So make sure you hold onto the Ferryman."

"Are you really going to make me come over—wait, what's the Ferryman holding?" the girl said as she peered more closely at the stone's pointy top in the center of the stream. "What is that?" She leaned forward so far that she slipped and one foot landed in the stream. "Well, there's nothing for it now, is there?" She carefully took two steps, the small rushing current dancing past her ankles at the deepest footfall. Just as the stream bounced up fiercely, threatening to weigh down and tangle her long skirts, she reached for the Ferryman and then gasped. "It's a ring. A little grass ring." She plucked it off the rock tip and placed it on her left ring finger. She looked up, eyes flowing like the stream she stood in, and said, "Yes."

Thady reached out his hand and took hers. She crossed the last two steps of the stream in a dreamy state. She arrived safely on the other side of the stream bank, a side she had never stood on, never explored, never picked grass from.

All she wanted to do was throw her arms around me. All I wanted to do was throw my arms around her. And so we did.

"I love you Thady Grassman."

"I love you Dream Thimbles."

And we kissed.

It was the first kiss for both the boy and the girl; so needless to say, it was a little messy, sloppy, and needed practice. But the sentiment was honest and the desire to practice plentiful.

When the sun set and the stars emerged, they lay on their backs and pondered the blackness in the sky. With his finger pointing to a star, Dream noticed that Thady's hands didn't seem so large anymore.

"You look different from this side of the stream. Even the stars look different from this side of the stream," Dream said.

"Everything is different from this side of the stream."

Dream looked forward to spending many more days discovering why everything was to be different, now that she was brave enough to explore Thady's realm.

"What's in that space, there?" Dream held Thady's hand, now an easy fit, and pointed it at a particular spot. "Between those three belted stars and the bright soloist."

"There? There sits a space station," Thady said with a mischievous grin. "Like a train station for the stars. It's where you put things that you want to send elsewhere."

"Like my torn cuticles?"

"Like your cuticles. There, in that spot, between those three belted stars and the bright soloist is a cuticle in the space station. It's boarding the train and it won't ever bother you again."

I left a grass man, the prettiest one I ever wove, on the doorstep of Dream's home. I didn't want her parents to worry when they realized their precious Dottie was gone. And she is precious.

I am Orion, and mortals view my belt of stars every night. From Artemis, I learned the art of temptation, the weaving of lures, and to never fall in love. As Artemis loves me, I love Dream. I fear nothin' now, not Scorpio who chases me, not Hades, who stole Dream's mortal life, but I do fear the loss of my love, my Dream. This fear is my weakness. Artemis is wise. A hunter must have no weaknesses. In day, Dream is with me always. But in night she wanders to those who need her. Without her, fear consumes me, forcing me to look skyward at the blackness between the three belted stars next to the bright soloist. There, there is where I place my fear, on a train in the space station. And I let it find another destination, on another windowsill.

SARA MCBRIDE has participated in NaNoWriMo since 2003 and has been a Los Angeles municipal liaison since 2011. She is the host and founder of the Los Angeles Improv for Writers group, which created this anthology. By day, Sara is a research scientist and manager for a biological lab at The California Institute of Technology; however, her first degree is in Theater (Playwriting) from UCLA. By night, she trains in long form narrative improv with Impro Theater, where she learns to improvise entire plays. Her publications can be read in peer reviewed scientific journals (*Cell, Immunity, Journal of Immunology, PNAS*), scientific magazines, like *The Scientist,* and her other writing topics include whisky, travel, and literary reviews (*Fine Expressions, Solo Travelist, East Jasmine Review*). She is obsessed with Jane Austen and obscure mythological figures. She would like to thank her Wednesday night Impro group for inspiring this particular story and Noah Bennett for creating Thady Grassman. You can contact her at Lemur-Publishing.com or smcbride@caltech.edu.

That Delicate Touch

Faith Dincolo

MY LASER BEAM eyes penetrate the darkness of the medical bay as I search for any spare skin pieces or nail clippings. Even something as small and as delicate as a cuticle in the space station surgery center might suffice for my needs. The cuticle of a pinky toe, as the humans call it, should be suitable. A cuticle from a human would be even better, as long as it is female and still attached to the nail. I do not have the hardened horny matter that helps humans dig and scratch with their hands. My fingertips are a blend of rusted metals that are forged into a single vise grip to resemble a hand. My appendages are intended to dig dirt, plant seeds and harvest produce. I am an enviro-bot, one that works in the agricultural land dome attached to the space station.

The sound pattern of the working bees resonates inside my metal body and causes my hearing receptors to vibrate. The bees hum and whir as they fly from flower to flower, in sync with my motors. The shared mechanical harmonization with their hive calls to me and we are one. However, I am unable to hold one or pick one up in order to establish communication with it. This is because I have no fingertips, nails or cuticles. The bees explode under the pressure of my metal fingertips, and their songs stop when their black and yellow fuzzy bodies terminate as I connect with them. In fact, I am not able to communicate with them at all.

Three days ago, I saw a human lift her small hand up to a flower and a bee landed on her fingernail. She held the tiny bee up and as they connected, the bee drove his hardened tail barb into the softness of her cuticle, just under her nail. They danced with her hand waving and swirling in such glory as the bee hung on to her with his stinger! They were one! The human female harmonized with the bee, her vocal tones a high-pitched sound that reminded me of metal rubbing against metal, the first sound I heard as I was created. My need to be one with the bee, to connect in such a unity, is the driving force of my search. If I had even one fingernail and cuticle as the human female did, I could hold a bee too!

The biggest problem is how to find a nail and cuticle that is not being used by the humans. They are a leaky, liquid-filled form that bleeds when their parts are removed. If I could find one human that I could remove a single cuticle and nail from, then I could replicate it and make a softer finger that is more functional. The medical bay is useless. The cleaning bots are efficient and keep the area sanitized. They are not equipped with inter-robot communications. Their orders are all programmed into them by their manufacturer. It is a waste of my battery time to attempt to ask for their help.

I go into the animal bay and stop in front of a white

monkey's cage. Monkeys are very much like humans, but with more hair. This female primate is a tiny creature with a big mouth.

"Let me see your hands," I say. My voice agitates the monkey. She throws her stuffed lemur at me, and it hits the bars of her cage. Lights and bells ring out as I attempt to open the cage door. A female human in a white coat pushes the cage door shut just as I open it.

"How did you get in here? You belong in the agricultural field bay. You should be out planting seeds!" She turns me around, her delicate pinky finger and cuticle pressing against my ocular lenses as she rolls my rounded frame towards the door. The female human continues to push me down the series of hallways and through the doors of the space station to the field door. I keep my closest eye on her hand. She opens the bay doors and pushes me onto a patch of dirt.

I see it. The way to get my cuticle and nail is right in front of me. A small trebuchet that humans test watermelons with by flinging them at the walls of the glass dome, thus measuring how far the fruit can travel, stands beside me. The humans make great noise, shouting and running as the watermelon splats over their heads. The female human walks into the plant fields, inspecting the flowering plants. I pick up a small shovel attachment and instead of adding it to my vise hand, I put it in the trebuchet basket. I pull back on the bucket, and with a hard push, I release the traveling shovel of death at the female human.

She looks up at me as the shovel flings towards her; she puts her hands over her face. The red liquid squirts from her arm. I have successfully disconnected her hand from her arm.

I race over to her, and there, lying in the dirt, below the flowering *Allium tuberosum*, is an entire selection of nails and cuticles. I am careful to choose the smallest, most delicate one on her pinky finger. I carefully pick up the hand and, with great care, remove the nail and cuticle. The female human is a mess; she does not move, but fluids continue to leak out of her body. I carefully cut off her small finger. I cannot get the fingernail and cuticle on my vise hand. I struggle with my wedged shaped hand to affix it to my other hand. I can hear the bees; they are everywhere, but not harmonizing like the day I saw the dance. I must hurry; I do not want to miss my chance to communicate as one with the bees. They are now swarming the female human and attracted to the pollens on her arm. I put the nail and cuticle on my metal hand. Three different bees come to it. The whirring sounds of their little wings as they bathe in the dark liquid of the human female cuticle and nail stir a small motor inside of me. I am communicating with all three of them! I wave my arm to dance with them, but the nail and cuticle fling off my vise grip hand.

I bend over to pick it back up where it has landed in the dirt under the flowering Allium Tuberorsum, and I see the human female reach at me with her other hand. It appears that she wants her nail and cuticle back.

"No, you can't have it; it's mine now."

The bees take off as I speak, and I wave the cuticle and nail at them. The female human grabs again for her parts, and I hold my metal hand away from her. She continues stretching her other hand towards me and I see a single finger reach toward the sleep switch on my body.

"Stupid damn machine, you're getting junked!"

I hear the click. The same click I had heard when the manufacturers turned me on. My eyes dim as the last bee flies off, over the white flowers of the ...

FAITH DINCOLO, MFA, has published poetry and shorts stories in *Ghost Town*, *Pacific Review*, *Fresh Ink*, e-zine *Women's Horror 2013*, and online. She has produced and written over 800 cable TV magazine episodes of Local Matters. Her screenplays have won awards and have been optioned. She has produced, directed, and written short films. She is the author of *Images of America, Saline County*, by Arcadia Publishing. Her poetry collection, *Me and Him Married* was released in May 2014. She dabbles in stand-up comedy and gardening.

The Amazon Adventure

Henry Barker

Chapter 1

I HAD BEEN FOLLOWING them for about two hours straight.

Emma sighed. "Do you really think we'll get to the center?"

Her dad answered, "We're almost there. Don't worry."

Ben called out, "Oh boy, I think this is cool. Wow, look!" The leaves on the ground were rustling and moving toward the family!

Martha pulled out her Amazon booklet, glossy and green with a photograph of a snake with red, beady eyes on it, and was looking for a reference as to what was happening. She found it finally.

"Run! These are army ants. They come in really big groups. They destroy whatever gets in their way." She was very busy running away from the army. With their feet twisting and turning, it was hard to get away. The army ants then got ahold of Frank's leg and then Emma's. Soon after they were all obscured by a spout of blackness.

Chapter 2

HA! JUST KIDDING. It's not the end of the story—as you will definitely see.

The exhausted family was walking normally now, and all of them except Ben said, "Could you get the compass out, Ben?" But Martha added, "Please."

"Yes ..." I whispered.

"Well ... um ... there isn't one in my pocket," Ben said.

"Then where is it?" Emma asked.

"I really couldn't see it when it fell out," Ben exclaimed.

"We need to get him glasses, Frank," said Martha. I knew Martha was the mother, Frank was the father, Ben was the son, and Emma was the daughter. I had seen Ben lose the compass that he had been keeping in his pocket, but it had fallen out and gotten trampled by the army ants—and now I, as well as they, were lost in the Amazon. Everyone in the family was so sad (which was why I was so glad). After a while, I heard constant hissing.

"Maybe it's the leaves we're stepping on," Frank said after a long period of the hissing.

"No, it is not," Martha said consulting her booklet. "There are no hissing leaves listed in the index."

I saw Emma shiver and she said in a shaky voice, "It's very creepy."

I glanced at where the hissing was coming from and saw a sliver of green body. Emma saw it, too. This was starting to get exciting.

"I think that there's something following us," Ben reported. I quickly hid behind a tree, thinking that Ben's "something" was me, but I remembered the slither of green.

"Some*thing*?" Emma said. "We're doomed." Then everybody started arguing about what the "something" might be, and then the something struck everyone except for me. In front of me were four dead bodies, not moving at all.

Chapter 3

I DID IT again. Sorry, I'm a tricky fellow.

Now, I knew exactly what the something was. In the middle of their conversation *something* long, slimy, and green crawled its way out of the bushes. Emma gave a terrifying scream.

The rest of the family gathered around Emma and started asking questions, "What happened? Did you get hurt?" But by that time the *thing* had gone.

"No, no, I didn't get hurt." Emma quivered as she said this. "But I might be later." And then Emma died. No one knew how it happened, but she must have been right in her fear of being hurt later. She could have just fainted, or it might have been a heart attack?

I totally fooled you again, didn't I? You might be too gullible if you fell for that one. I *promise* I won't do that again.

Emma pointed again to the thing that had just crawled out. It was a big snake curled around a branch like a hose or rope. I didn't know what to do. It looked like the family didn't either. Also, none of us knew anything about snakes.

"We should get out of here!" Martha yelled. Everyone was running away—wait. Except I saw at least two things wrong. The first was that Martha didn't bother to pull out her Amazon booklet, and the second was that not everyone was running away. Ben wasn't moving at all. Martha must have been too terrified to think of her Amazon booklet. I could see it in her eyes.

"Hey, guys!" Ben shouted to the others. "I think you dropped something."

"We didn't, Ben," Emma said, looking around, and then screamed, "Ah!"

Ben was reaching down to what Ben probably thought was his mom's green Amazon booklet. The snake then sprayed venom into his eyes and reared back to strike.

"Wow! That hurts!" he yelled and ran. The snake struck but missed its target, just barely.

Like a bee's sting, the venom caused his eyelids to swell but did not blur his vision. He was already a bit blind from poor eyesight and was now running away from the snake, right past where I was (behind a tree). Quietly, I followed them back from where the snake had been.

"Purr ... Purr ..."

Chapter 4

"WHAT IS THAT noise?" asked Martha.

"Probably something bad," Frank joked.

"I bet you're right, Frank," she agreed. "There are so many bad things in the Amazon." She waved her booklet in the air.

"Wow," Ben said, holding an icepack on his puffy eyes. Martha proudly carried a first aid kit. "I got us all into this. I lost the compass."

"No, it was me, guys. You don't understand. I wish I hadn't asked to come here," Emma said.

"But I'm the one who decided we should go to the center," Frank said. I was very happy they were arguing again.

"Let's all just stop right now!" yelled Martha. A yellow eye peered from behind a tree.

"Purr ... Purr ..."

Everyone looked up and Emma hollered.

"Oh, no," Frank said, protecting his ears from his daughter's horrid noises. "We're in deep trouble."

Martha squeaked with fear, and that's what triggered it.

Chapter 5

FROM THE TREES there leapt a jaguar! He pounced onto the ground. Martha was opening the Amazon booklet, but, before she could, the jaguar gave a warning growl. I was glad I was hiding. You do not want to meet a jaguar. It looked like Ben knew what was happening—by the expression on his face, a terrified look. Maybe he thought there was a leopard in front of him or yellow and black blobs, but he was very aware. The jaguar was staring at them. It looked like the jaguar was having a hard time picking which one to eat first. The jaguar singled out Ben—he *was* the shortest.

The jaguar ate Ben, then started for Emma, smacking its lips. Frank and Martha could not budge. The jaguar ate Martha, then Frank. I took a frantic run for it and was glad the jaguar didn't spot me.

Chapter 6

I WAS WAITING for you to look anxious for a hero move. From Ben. From Frank. From Emma or Martha. Or me.

You got tricked; sorry I broke that promise. I'm no hero.

The jaguar started pacing around Ben. Then, the jaguar swallowed Ben whole.

Aw, just kidding.

Ben slowly picked up a stone from the ground. The jaguar roared a warning, and then Ben threw the stone. He was looking at what he thought was the mouth but instead hit the jaguar's eye. It must've been easy to throw a stone at a pink blur. The jaguar suddenly fell to the floor, pawing its eye with a sorrowful face.

"Run," whispered Martha, and all of them came running past me, as I knelt for cover.

Chapter 7

"YES, A RIVER!" yelled Frank and a few colorful birds flew into the streaked sky.

"Don't shout!" whispered Martha, thumbing the index of her booklet for B. "Now we need to build a *boat*."

So they took branches and tied them with rope and made a boat that looked more like a big box than a boat. Martha and Emma climbed inside, while the men pushed the boat into the water. Frank and Ben quickly jumped in and for oars they used small branches. I quickly did the same as them, building a boat. Except mine was much smaller and it was covered with leaves for disguise. Then the boat in front of mine capsized with the family in it. The family tried to swim to the banks of the river, but it was too late; they drowned. I was terrified. I didn't know where to go. Well, the problem was that the family was really still in the boat drifting forward.

I really made you jump. I'm sorry I broke my promise. Again.

Now, back to the story. After about two minutes, Martha squeaked again and Emma screeched. Birds erupted from tree branches. It was actually not what I was expecting. Two ancient, catlike eyes popped up from out of the water. It was a crocodile.

"What's happening now?" asked Frank, hunched over.

"Look," Martha said pointing at the eyes. Everyone gazed at the eyes except for Ben who was confused—since he couldn't see very well.

Martha pulled out her Amazon booklet and said, "Alligator."

"No, it's a crocodile," said Emma matter-of-factly. "Look at the shape."

"Wait ... Yes, you're right," said Martha laughing. "I never knew you were that smart."

"Mom, why do you say things like that?" Emma said.

"Like what?"

Emma looked really offended, but she couldn't do anything about it. Martha was her mother after all. Ben started rowing, probably getting bored because he couldn't come in on the conversation. He then accidentally poked one of the black eyes, and the crocodile snarled and started smashing into their boat. The jolt sent Ben sprawling to the floor of the raft. He felt cold liquid pouring over his hands.

"It's starting to leak!" warned Ben. "Emma, hand me your handkerchief!"

"Why mine, not Mom's?" she whined.

"Now!"

Emma threw Ben the handkerchief, and Ben stuffed it into the breach. It clogged the leak. The crocodile lowered into the water and swam away, not happy that he didn't get food.

"Look, it's a lemur!" said Ben.

"No, that's a monkey," corrected Emma. She was right, we were surrounded by monkeys swinging everywhere.

"Are they dangerous?" asked Martha, once again impressed by her daughter's taxonomical skills.

"I think they're beautiful," Frank said. That was indeed true. They had silky, brown fur, and some were even carrying babies on their backs. Then, I saw the end; the border of the Amazon Rainforest. The family got out at the end of the river and I secretly got out and started walking behind them, casually.

Frank looked back at me and said confused, "What are *you* doing here?"

"I was about to ask you the same question," I said, lying easily.

"I'll ask you again. What is a teenager like you, doing here in the rainforest?" repeated Frank.

"I was just bird watching," I said. "What about you?"

"Family trip," said Frank, coolly.

"Say bye," Martha demanded. They did.

Chapter 8

AFTER THE PLANE ride, Ben had to go to the optometrist (a sight doctor).

"OK," said the doctor. "Could you sit down and read aloud the letters on that screen, please?"

"Sure," said Ben. "A … cu-ti-cle in … the sp … space sta-tion."

"Sorry, they are just a bunch of different *letters*, not words," said the doctor, making a note. Ben kept getting it wrong.

Finally, the doctor said after a series of tests, "You have 20/350 vision."

"Twenty-three, fifty?!" shouted Ben. "NO!" After a moment, he added, "What does that mean?"

"You need glasses. If you'll come over here to the frames table you can help yourself," said the doctor. So Ben grumpily walked over to the frames table and, since his favorite color was blue, he picked the sky blue, circular frames.

A week later, he sat back down in the chair, put on the new glasses and said, "Wow! This is much better." They went through another series of tests and he passed all of them with his glasses on.

"OK, that will be $250, please," said the assistant.

"Oh, thank you," said Martha as she handed the money over. "Say 'thank you' to the assistant."

"Thank you."

"No, thank *you*," replied the woman. And so I went home, because I knew that later on they would live happily ever after, and that is not what I like.

Born on Easter Sunday, HENRY BARKER is a native of Altadena. His birthday will not be celebrated on Easter again until he is sixty-two years old. Henry is ten years old and already has two years of NaNoWriMo adventures under his belt. An avid Harry Potter fan, he loves reading, school, and math, and enjoys playing the violin, board games, and role-playing games. His favorite Amazonian creature is the snake, so it is not surprising that his favorite food is spaghetti (more worm than snake-like, granted) and meatballs. He has the ability to tense his eye muscles and "shake" his eyeballs from side to side. And,- whereas pink used to be his favorite color, he now favors green.

The Heart of It

Katy Mann

"I SHOULD NEVER have won that Nobel Prize." I stared across the table at my interviewer, waiting for his reaction.

The reporter, Allen something-or-other, was a young man, obviously ambitious. He had been punctual, bringing a tape recorder and notepad, and was clearly a bit in awe of me. I was well aware of my reputation: a genius, considered by many to have made a brilliant contribution to medicine before losing my way. Getting this interview had been quite the coup for him. I didn't usually waste time on such trivialities.

Allen cleared his throat, tapping on his tape recorder before speaking. "You are too modest, Doctor."

"No," I replied. "Jamison's lab received the peer approval, the grants, and the publicity. His proposals were the kind that faculty chairs and review committees could easily understand. He was able to run state-of-the-art laboratories to house his research and his students, whereas we had to make do with the space I was able to obtain."

I waved at our surroundings, deep in the basement of a small industrial building on the west side of town, far from the university. Allen had appeared nervous about coming downstairs to my office, pausing at the top of the dimly lit stairway, but he had followed me. The room we sat in was a combination study and examination room. Half the room was carpeted, a conventional study dominated by a large wooden desk covered with books and papers with a floor lamp providing a warm, if dim, light. In contrast, the other side of the room was lit by bright, harsh overhead lights, which shone down on the exam table at the center of the gray tile floor. Glass-fronted metal cabinets containing medical instruments lined the wall. I had motioned him into the worn leather chair in front of my desk. It had been a good chair, but now its age was showing. He noticed the stains on the seat but had the good grace to seat himself anyway.

"I would disagree about not deserving the Nobel," Allen said as he consulted his notes. "Your work has saved the lives of so many people."

I leaned back in my chair and set my chin in my hand in what I hoped was a thoughtful pose. "Would you like to hear why I feel my Nobel wasn't deserved?"

He nodded, pen poised above the yellow legal pad.

"It was premature," I stated. "They gave me the prize for what was only a piece of my work, just a problem that I solved in order to move to the next step."

Allen scribbled a few notes then looked back up at me.

"Tell me about your real work, then. The problem you were working to solve."

I smiled and watched as he relaxed. His growing confidence meant he thought his interview was going well. He was as young and healthy as I had hoped from my review of his internet profile, a recently graduated college student who had lettered in tennis and majored in journalism. He would make an excellent subject.

"The categories of Physics, Chemistry, and Medicine for the Nobel Prize are inadequate," I stated. "They need to be unified into a single prize; only then can my true vision be seen. The work on hearts that received the Nobel was but a step toward my final goal."

The haunted prize giver, Albert Nobel, would have undoubtedly understood my work. He established the Prize in his name after learning the world's opinion of him when a French newspaper prematurely published his obituary: "The merchant of death is dead." I believe that near the end of his life he was acutely aware of the tension between life and death. Though he had made his fortune in armaments manufacture and held the patent for dynamite, he wished to be remembered as the founder of prestigious prizes for those contributing to the benefit of mankind.

"Your heart machine, the Resuscitator 9000," Allen said, "has been credited with saving many lives."

I waved my hand dismissively.

He shook his head, taking my gesture as modesty. "Your contribution to the field of medicine has been important, Doctor."

"That machine does what many others could do," I replied. "Its use in hospitals has been limited to resuscitating the living, restarting the pulse during a medical crisis. As such, it but provides a slight improvement on other defibrillators on an already crowded market. Once the heart is revived, these practitioners of modern medicine work to heal the patient's other infirmities. My work goes beyond what these technicians of medicine pursue."

The autoclave beeped on the laboratory side of the room, so I rose to check it. After releasing the seal and inspecting the concentric circles of test tubes inside the machine, I smiled at the sound of scratching at the door and opened it. Molecule had managed to unhook his leash again, and he peered around the door at Allen, then looked back up at me. I held out my arms and the small lemur bounded into them, dragging his leash behind.

"Got loose again, did you?" I said. "You know where the treats are kept." I put him on my shoulder and carried him to the small fridge, pulling out a box of chopped fruit. He lunged for the pineapple, and I grabbed his chain.

"Our lab mascot, Molecule," I said to Allen. "He was sent to me as an experimental animal, but one of the techs got attached to him. He's proven quite difficult to keep contained," I added with an indulgent smile. I brought Molecule to my desk and set him in the small bed I had made on one of the lower shelves of the book case, locking his leash securely into a hook mounted in the floor. He sat peacefully devouring his fruit as I turned back to my interviewer.

Allen smiled at the furry animal. It was a moment before he moved to his next question. "About your demonstration four years ago …."

"The demonstration that brought both accolades and

censure to my work involved restoring life to a dove," I continued. "I broke its neck then waited four hours to restart its heart using the Resuscitator 9000."

"I have watched that video many times," Allen remarked.

"The public demonstration only showed part of the work necessary to create life from death. The critics were to some degree correct in commenting on the unsteadiness of the revived bird—but only because they saw a limited demonstration. The reanimated dove, whose heart was started hours after its death, ate a beetle but couldn't fly. To fully regain his nature, the dove had to be fed life, to be fed a still-beating heart from another dove. But only after the conclusion of the televised demonstration. I thought that the public reaction to a full demonstration might be unmanageable."

Imagine the public reaction if I had released the dove with a bloody beak to fly above the crowd.

"The revolutionary nature of my discovery could easily be misunderstood by weaker minds swayed by sentiment," I concluded.

Allen began to look nervous and quickly skimmed his notes, making a move to conclude the interview. I wasn't done.

"You said you were curious about meeting Rupert Hancock, one of my students, correct?"

"Yes. I haven't been able to reach Dr. Hancock at his lab," Allen replied, looking up from his notepad, probably unaware that he was nervously jiggling his right foot. He was a careful young man, I observed once again, taking notes as well as recording our conversation. I would be curious to read them after we were done.

"Rupert. My most famous student and defector," I said.

"He made some disparaging remarks about my research, characterizing it as dabbling in alchemy. His comment about my work's application possibly being used to create life from cuticles in a space station was most unworthy of him."

Allen nodded. "I think many would agree that his statement was unprofessional."

"It is true that I pursue the alchemists' inquiries into life and immortality, as their studies were more all-encompassing than the fractured goals of our modern science," I said. "By reuniting the fields of modern science with alchemy, I have achieved one of the alchemists' dreams. Ironically, the elusive Elixir of Life has been within us all along, in our beating hearts. And yet, Rupert has returned. He is in one of the neighboring labs."

Allen looked around, as if he would see him behind us. *Not yet, my young friend, not yet.*

"I had not heard of his return to your lab," Allen said, his excitement at getting a scoop overcoming his uneasiness at the recent subject matter. "He just received a Genius Grant from the MacArthur Foundation."

My lips curled at hearing Rupert's work deemed genius by anyone. The sound of plastic hitting the desk by my feet drew my attention as Molecule tossed the empty Tupperware past my legs. The lemur had been spared because I no longer needed experimental animals. I remember Rupert's reaction the day he came to my labs and saw the prosimian waiting by my office door. I had invited my former student to visit, luring him with a request that he give his opinion on a tricky issue we had encountered. His curiosity and vanity overcame any reluctance he might have had, and he came downstairs to my office just has Allen had, his intelligent, greedy eyes taking in everything.

"Let me call him for you," I said, pressing the buzzer on my desk. "Rupert has contributed to my research, which moved from lower mammals to human subjects upon his return. But to be successful, the process has the same basic requirement. The Resuscitator 9000 can restart the heart hours after mortal death, but the restoration of life still requires the ingestion of a beating heart of the same species."

Allen blanched but tried to cover it. He gathered up his notes and stood up to leave.

Shadows fell on the frosted glass window of the door, signaling my staff's approach. "Rupert is being brought to us."

Allen looked at the door, watching as the doorknob began to turn.

"My goal has been realized," I continued. "I can create life from death. I am pleased to inform you that you will play a role in my research. You will be granted the privilege of transforming from an observer into part of the science."

Allen had turned back toward me when I spoke, but looked behind him as Rupert's swaying body filled the open doorway, his dull eyes unfocused. My assistant held him by an elbow to keep him upright.

"Right now, he only has mobility," I commented. "For consciousness, more is needed."

Allen rose from his chair and backed away from the group at the door toward my desk. I surprised him by grabbing and holding him firmly. He struggled, but I had him in a secure neck lock.

"You think me mad," I whispered into his ear, "but you

are about to become part of history, not just an observer and reporter. You will give my creation life, not just mobility."

My assistant took the struggling man from me, and I donned my lab coat. While Allen began to scream, I leaned over to turn off the tape recorder. The interview was over.

KATY MANN grew up in the Midwest where she attended the University of Chicago. She moved to California with her tabby cat, Gus, in 1995. A life-long reader, her first novel *Prey* was published in 2014. She divides her time between the real world, when necessary, and the worlds created in books and her imagination, when possible. Visit her at www.KatyMann.com.

The Mother That I Lost

Maya Watanabe

I REMEMBER THE DAY my mom died. That day, I had the worst nightmare ever. The second my head hit the pillow, I was transported into outer space, or you can think of it as a galaxy. In front of me, there stood a purple and bluish alien who looked surprisingly pretty, despite having sixteen eyes. Of course I was stunned, but after seeing her cuticles, I jumped! *WOW!* They were jagged, with blood seeping through the skin of her five fingers, and the cuticles were bitten and torn into a mess of raw flesh. She told me that her name was Joanne and, yes, she spoke fluent English. I asked her, "How am I here, and why?"

Joanne replied, "You'll know once you're transported back to your real life."

Yes, that phrase did leave me curious and

confused. Joanne told me that before I went back, I should have some fun there in the alien world. We went to a gelato place, but it wasn't normal gelato; it had creepy *alien eyes* in it. I told Joanne, "Ummm ... I'm not so sure I can eat this."

She laughed carelessly. "Don't worry, sweetie, they are just gummy eyeballs."

I laughed myself, and decided to get strawberry-orange. Joanne with the horrible cuticles and fingers was right: the gummy eyeballs were delicious! They were nothing like anything I've ever tried before, but they were probably the best tasting candy I've ever eaten in a dream. When you bit down, they squirted you with a sour lemon liquid. Right that second, I gave Joanne a nickname, A Cuticle In A Space Station, because she literally was a cuticle in a space station.

With a hesitant look she said, "You have to go home to your room now, Julia." At first I wondered, how did she know my name? I didn't remember telling her my name, but I quickly got over it.

We reached the train station in space–we were still in space–and Joanne told me to jump in the train while IT WAS STILL MOVING! She told me the reason the train was moving so fast was so that I could be transported back to planet Earth faster. Impossible, right? I listened to her instructions anyway and thanked her for the midnight snack. Jumping onto one of the train cars, the wind punched my face and sucked me in. The moment I was in the train car, I remembered everything: Joanne and her bleeding cuticles. Joanne was someone very important in my life, and that person just died. She had depression, which caused her to bite her fingernails until they weren't even on her fingers anymore.

It was my mother.

But then again, why would my mother come to me in a dream as an alien with sixteen eyes? I felt empty-headed afterwards, forgetting how much I missed her, even though it was only just a day since her death. Realizing the condition of "my mom's" nails and cuticles in my dream made me wonder if I didn't really pay much attention to her when she was alive. Maybe I didn't pay *any* attention to her. I will never be able to answer those questions in my life, ever, because I probably won't be getting another dream like that one soon.

MAYA WATANABE is twelve years old and in sixth grade. She does ballet at Classical Ballet Theater. Her favorite subjects are math and science, but she loves to freewrite and write fictional stories. Although she loves school, she also loves to cook and bake for family and friends, and she loves to dance. She attends an afterschool program where she has many friends. This is her very first piece of writing to be published, and she is very excited and joyful to see the result of her story.

A Dwindling Supply of Bleach

Renée Jessica Tan

I FIND MYSELF AGGRIEVED to have to write yet another incident report. Not aggrieved over the incident, mind you, but resentful of the time and resources dedicated to a problem that I forecasted with scant regard. In short, due to unfortunate circumstances beyond my control, Ms. Candy Vilapandi (*née* LeAnn Smythe of the Cleveland Smythes) has met a premature end. Indeed, I am alone in the bio-dome once again, and our mission to create a human colony on Mars has been greatly compromised, to say the least.

Fear not about my mental state. Solitude has never troubled me, even in a place as remote as Mars. Indeed, many of the greatest minds in history have been self-isolated, and so I find myself in good company. I also have my companions in the greenhouse. My solanum lycopersicum ("tomato plants" to those unversed in binomial nomenclature) have yielded a phenomenal crop this season, especially now that Ms. Vilapandi's fluorescent stilettos are no longer perforating the soil. While some may argue it was that very aeration that contributed to the bounty, I would instead credit the mineral-rich Martian dirt and the extra half hour of northerly sun.

Truly, I have cultivated enough nutritious vegetation to sustain a whole city, disproving those many naysayers who said nothing could grow on the red planet. Of course, none of my detractors possessed my multiple doctorates in horticulture, botany, and experimental agriculture, nor the knowledge that comes with such rigorous academic study. Perhaps that is why so many of them championed individuals such as Ms. Vilapandi, perhaps in an effort to sabotage our experiment of life off Earth.

Whilst I am enjoying the blissful quiet brought about by Ms. Vilapandi's unfortunate demise, I fully understand the second half of my mission is to propagate our species. I assure you that I am still fully committed to this task. That being said, and mindful not to bite the hand that feeds me, I feel compelled to say that there must be better ways to engage the public and fund our project than resorting to the spectacle of reality television.

While I had no quarrel with the production itself, letting the braying public decide who has the privilege of leaving her genetic stamp in outer space was portentous and ill-conceived. As someone who would be most directly affected by the outcome of this ratings juggernaut, I would have hoped my opinion would bear weight. Instead, the winner chosen by the unsophisticated viewership turned out to be the most vapid, insipid, and lazy person known to mankind.

Sure, Ms. Vilapandi looked great on camera. I cannot

deny the value of handsome DNA when one is trying to build a population, especially when procreation is ideally executed through traditional means. However, considering all her aftermarket upgrades (including rhinoplasty, breast augmentation, injectables, hair extensions, synthetic nails), I must point out that nothing that made her appear beautiful was actually written into her genetic code.

The only authentic qualities Ms. Vilapandi brought to Mars were an utter abhorrence for anything remotely intellectual and an obsession with her physical appearance. She plucked the lemon tree bare in an attempt to maintain the unnatural yellowness of her hair after I was forced to hide our dwindling supply of bleach. She mutilated my aloe plant because she believed it could cure a nonexistent hangnail. Indeed, I have never met someone so obsessed with a cuticle in the space station. The only other tasks she freely dedicated herself to were surfing the internet and watching television, often at a volume so loud as to drown out my conversation.

Despite these annoyances and my significant reservations, ever the consummate professional, I forged ahead with my commitment to growing the colony. But evidently Ms. Vilapandi, a true product of the common class, was neither stimulated by genius nor inspired to fulfill her obligation to science. My repeated attempts towards insemination were rebuffed, with Ms. Vilapandi usually employing the needless use of overdramatic crying jags and absurd screams of terror. I frequently had to remind her there were no more television cameras around to play to and that her histrionics were all for naught.

The final offense before her fortuitous demise was

desecrating my adolescent grapevines in a ludicrous effort to become inebriated. I caught her stomping her bare feet in a pot full of unripe clusters, my favorite pruning shears tucked into her cleavage. When I asked her what on earth she was doing (forgetting momentarily that we were, of course, not on Earth) Ms. Vilapandi, brandished the shears menacingly in my direction, scissoring the blades in the air like a demented lobster. She screamed that being drunk was the only way she could spend an eternity with "an overblown gasbag," along with even more vile utterances, the likes of which I shall spare you.

I beseeched Ms. Vilapandi to calm and collect herself, but she continued her sparring until I had no choice but to try to wrest away my beloved shears. In the ensuing scuffle, Ms. Vilapandi stabbed me below the left elbow. Thankfully, it turned out to be only a minor flesh wound. I have attached a photo herewith for the incident report.

After drawing blood, Ms. Vilapandi dropped the shears and ran from the greenhouse. Despite my injured forearm, I gave chase since I was concerned about her fragile mental condition. I saw her run into the emergency portico. When I got there, she was prying open the porthole to exit the bio-dome.

I tried to warn her that it was imperative she first don a spacesuit before leaving the station, but she simply spat in my direction and dropped into the chute. Moments later, Ms. Vilapandi reappeared outside, cackling hysterically. Her porcelain veneers flashed as she taunted me gleefully, but soon her laughs turned to gasps. Her enormous breasts started heaving as her lungs searched for oxygen. She banged on the glass, importuning me for help. I tried my best, but, alas, due to my injury I could not do much more than watch as Ms. Vilapandi turned first white, then green, then blue. Eventually she came to stillness, slumping forward onto the bio-dome before sliding down dully to the ground, eyes still open.

I have been unable to bring Ms. Vilapandi back inside due to inclement weather these past seventy-two hours. Until conditions improve, perhaps I can write a follow-up report about the decomposition of human remains in the Martian atmosphere.

RENÉE JESSICA TAN is the author of many unpublished masterpieces and rejected queries. While she is not writing, scooping cat litter, or knitting, she is pounding the streets of Los Angeles. You can follow her running exploits at ExposedTanLines.blogspot.com.

Reviewed

Wendy Erich

Chapter 1

THIS WAIF-LIKE CREATURE is all the buzz, deposing a famous celebrity chef, taking over his Los Angeles restaurant, ensuring her new eatery has exclusivity by failing to give it Any Name At All. There are no signs or street numbers outside the joint, just old corrugated metal doors with copper handles, juxtaposed with a sleek limestone wall shimmering with cascading water. Only insiders know the restaurant is there, and passersby might curiously note the stream of mouthwatering luxury cars waiting for a valet, waiting their turn to be recognized under a pretense of not wanting to be seen.

Yet, one word from me about an old New York Department of Health finding, the rat feces found under the bank of refrigerators, the misuse of butcher block for raw tuna, and her career would spiral downward. The crowds would disappear overnight, and no one would remember the restaurant because it never had a name to start with. A farm-to-table illusion.

From across the street, I watch the cognoscenti entering for a while, mostly B-listers in pairs, rarely alone. Sometimes small groups of four meet up, touch each other's shoulders, extend hands, deliver photo-perfect smiles and press their well-designed jaws into acerbic air kisses. I am wearing pressed blue jeans and a white linen shirt, untucked, paired with a crisp black blazer, a scarf looped at my neck, and a fedora. In minutes, I join the fabric of privilege.

There is a small table reserved for me in a corner under the name Willis. I act casually, dark glasses in place, while feverishly checking my phone. This way I am assured no eye contact is made, and everyone can recognize I am too important to acknowledge pleasantries. Technology improves discretion. Online reservations are made under a phony name, inaudible dictations of succinct thoughts automatically format to text, a press of 'send' goes to an editor I have never met.

No one who sees me grasps the secret power a food critic wields. As usual, I disguise myself. I have my favorites: different looks, different hair. Dark glasses and hats are my trademark. And the accents ... how I enjoy the imaginative and fertile springing forth of a new personality.

Once I was Liam Neeson, gruff and to the point, a slightly Irish brogue muffled between the coughs of a bad cold.

"More drink when you can, please,"–*cough cough*–"the food is quite salty." I had nailed him.

Another time I was a version of Elizabeth Taylor. Coy. Coquettish. The slightest trace of a boarding school accent, touching my hair as I look at the menu. Later they would see telltale signs of rejection at the edge of my dinner plate, bits of half-chewed meat that exited my mouth the same way they entered, on my fork.

Today is special, a Bruce Willis kind of day, and I wonder if this skinny ex-New York chef has noted my reservation. The appetizers arrive, lining up before me in odd peculiar geometric dishes, two at a time, coming from the kitchen faster than I care to consume them. The curiously shaped china is just trying too hard, I note. One tiny scallop rides on a leaf of freshly washed kale with strategically placed drops of dressing, appearing like a specimen plant cuticle in a space station. A mound of the tiniest, irregularly shaped breads, sliced wafer-thin, are stacked spirally like steps in a mid-century modern house. A thickened consommé with floating nasturtium and slender chives is served in a clear angular pod without a spoon. How pretentious is this! It is no longer about food, but merely presentation! How am I supposed to eat this? There is no silverware—it is barbarism!

I feel hunger gnawing, and when the toothsome yet tiny entree arrives, I decide to deliver the ultimate insult to this precocious new chef and send the morsel back untouched. Why should I tantalize my palate with potential pleasure only to be denied more bites? It isn't even worth tasting this Lilliputian filet, arranged on three spare leaves of piquant arugula, dressed in a nectarous glaze of fresh mint and apricot. How long did it take her to carve that Buddha face into the skin of the dried apricot, now neatly tucked into a spoonful of quinoa? I salt it once lightly, then inject my irritation as I crossly order the waiter to take it back.

I send her up, throw the little tart under the bus. I leave the restaurant hungry and annoyed. I stop at a diner across town and gobble up a robust, juicy hamburger, heavy with sweet, cooked onions and savory french fries under a blanket of rich cheese sauce. My anger still fresh, I furiously thumb my opinions into text format, unconsciously mentioning the chef by name, along with her flawed health department standing from her previous life. I press send, and she is toast.

Chapter 2

"IS THIS SYDNEY Stanton?"

"Speaking," I said groggily. The phone jars me from a sound sleep. I nearly trip over a tray table on the floor to grab my cell on the fourth ring, sending a tower of leftover Styrofoam flying. It is only eight a.m.

"L.A. Police. Stanton, we would like you to come in for questioning."

"Whatever for?"

"There has been a death ... of a well-known chef."

Now they have my attention. "Who?"

"We won't say her name, but you mentioned her in your Sunday review ... you know, last weekend's paper."

The blood drains from my face. The little raisin-faced wench. My hatred of her is exposed, and now I need a way to hide it from the police?

"Yes sir, sure thing. I'll be there in thirty minutes."

"Not necessary. We have a squad car outside waiting for you."

"Give me ten minutes."

I scramble, quickly peppering my face with water, glaring at my unruly mass of hair in the mirror, and instinctively reach for the olive green fedora with the bright blue piping. Dressed in minutes, sunglasses covering my eyes, I snatch the well-worn canvas messenger bag that holds my laptop, phone and cords. I might be there a while.

I look around the apartment. There is nothing unusual. If they search, they will find nothing. By habit, I load remaining traces of my late-night snack into the dishwasher and the trash, just to tidy up. I hate leaving something undone, something messy, never wanting to leave so much as a crumb behind. Little crawling guilt monkeys would be scratching at my spine.

Chapter 3

A YOUNG MOTHER longed to dress her twins alike but their incongruent sizes made it difficult. Invariably strangers would ask if the heavier child was a boy or a girl, to which the mother would summon her most stinging glare and retort, "Are you referring to my twin girls?" as she marched off. People were incredibly rude.

They were never like other twins. To begin with, they were fraternal, merely two eggs sharing a womb, and the firstborn (by only seven minutes) was so tiny she stayed behind in the hospital for nearly four weeks, while the healthier one, born at near normal weight, flourished at her mother's breast.

When the tinier twin was finally able to join her sister at home, there was intense joy and celebration by their parents, relatives, and neighbors. It required turning the sweet pale pink nursery into a neonatal incubator of tubes, machines, and schedules, but the grateful parents were undaunted. There were machines for measuring sleep and machines for measuring fluids. Tubes that went in and tubes that went out, buttons that flashed and beeped all night long. The fuss, the attention that was given over her tiniest cries!

The twins grew side by side, the firstborn weaker and prone to illness, the younger a product of robust health. When the mother pushed her daughters to the park in their double stroller, she loved to joke that the younger one ate everything in the womb and left nothing for her big sister.

Oddly, the joke played out as the toddlers grew. The more diminutive would wrinkle up her little nose at new foods and push them away with her tiny hands. She learned that if she shoved it nearer to her hungry sister, all would be happily consumed. Occasionally the twins would push their dinner back and forth, and sometimes the smaller one might taste the uneaten food, earning heavy praise from their doting mother just for the few morsels she would swallow. It was a game between the twins.

By the time they were teens, few people recognized the girls as sisters, much less twins. The firstborn was a petite, honey-eyed willow, an athletic gymnast who dipped and swooped atop the narrow balance beam as though she were on a ballroom floor. She was a golden girl who loved to read and got good grades in math and science. Most of all, she loved to bake. Her favorites were exquisitely decorated cupcakes, made with colorful candies that created animal faces or flowers, often too beautiful to eat. She herself was never tempted to taste them unless someone insulted her by refusing to eat her masterpiece. Only then would she insolently take a large central bite to destroy her creation, thereby proving its transient vanitas.

Her huskier twin sister did not have as many gifts. She was neither athletic nor studious, and early on adopted tomboyish ways that distinguished her from her delicate twin. They didn't even shop for school clothes together as the heavier sister opted for the Men's department rather than Juniors, happier sporting unshapely jeans, black tee shirts, and always a hat. She too loved to read, but her sole interest was a lowbrow celebrity magazine. She loved Michael Jackson and covered her side of the room with his photos and memorabilia. Her joy was being alone when the entire family was at her twin's gym meets and the house was gloriously empty. Then she would come alive, posing in front of the mirror, practicing dance moves and lip-synching to Beat It.

Chapter 4

"MS. STANTON? RIGHT this way please."

I sit down in the worn-out chair and glance around me. I pull my hat down a bit lower and look at my phone for distraction. I check my email, delete a few bits of store sales junk, see there are no messages from friends, no texts. Battery at 57 percent. I ask for a tissue, and they hand me an entire box.

"Ms. Stanton. We would like to advise you of your rights."

"What the heck for? I have done nothing!"

"Do you know Sandra Huntington?"

"She just opened a new restaurant. You obviously saw my review."

"She never got to read your review. She was found dead Sunday morning in her home. She was poisoned."

"My God! That's terrible!" I shift my weight. "Certainly you are not accusing me? I don't even know her."

"Can you explain why your newspaper columns from the last ten years had all been kept neatly in a scrapbook found in her bedroom?"

"Perhaps she was a fan. I have fans who follow my reviews. She was obviously in the business." I have to be careful. I begin to worry about perspiring in an already gamey shirt.

"Ms. Stanton. You are her sister."

"That is preposterous!" Beads of sweat are now sliding down my spine.

"Will you come with me? You may call a lawyer if you like. I would advise it."

Chapter 5

I ALWAYS USE my own salt shaker. I abhor the tasteless, flakey grains one finds in restaurant shakers. I prefer a Himalayan pink salt, how it adds pure crystalized sunshine to food, enhancing it without detracting from tender flavors. I travel with it.

But the night I ate at my shriveled-up twin's restaurant, I made a point to use a 'special salt' on food I planned to never touch. I knew Sandra all right. I could visualize her outrage over a patron insinuating that the starters were too salty and then, more insultingly, sending a main course back to the kitchen untouched. I would offend her to the core.

And she would take her slender little pinky and swoop it along the sauce that she worked so hard to prepare, touch it to her tongue while insisting the taste is perfect. In her rage, she might even take a large succulent bite, childishly insinuating the patron must be insane, that her food is divine and to die for.

I picture Sandra in my mind's eye that night; just as restaurant orders are crushing down on top of her scrawny frame, and the heat and tension are at its peak, my twin would blow her cork. She would be livid. She would shout and point a spoon with indignation and make her little scooping motion to prove something to her staff, and then, eight hours later she would be dead. It is pure luck I reached the right target.

Of course, that night I left her restaurant immediately and hit the street. I carefully wiped my fingerprints from the tiny salt shaker filled with poison, crammed the evidence into a littered Starbucks cup, and threw it into a trash can in West Hollywood. There is no way to find it, no way to trace it to me. I didn't realize in my angry written disclosure of L.A.'s newest celebrity chef that my critical words might send some eager inquisitive detective to fine comb her lousy apartment. The words lead him to me.

Perhaps the anorexic little prune did love me. I stopped speaking to her years ago, after our parents were gone. I actually feel flattered in a bitter sort of way, how she collected my review columns and saved them to a scrapbook. It adds a dulcified sweetness, yes, it makes my arrest more palatable.

WENDY ERICH is a writer and professional calligrapher who has moved twenty-six times, lived in eleven states and four countries, married, raised kids, survived cancer, holds a BA in English and an MA in art history, and kept a journal since she was ten. Since few, aside from Carolingian monks, immerse themselves in an Illuminated Book of Hours, she is retiring her calligraphy pens to concentrate on writing fiction.

Mr. Mungo's Shop of Oddities

Alexandr Bond

IT WAS A warm summer's day and Mr. Grey was enjoying his routine stroll through the park. The sounds of life were all about him as he made his way, taking a minute to watch a pair of doves flitter to and fro while a nearby organ grinder played a merry tune despite his monkey acting so sullen, perhaps feeling guilty because it had stolen an apple moments before. Smiling to himself, Mr. Grey continued on his way until he saw something that caused him to pause again.

In front of Mr. Grey sat a young man lounging on a bench, a bottle of spirits in his hand and the most self-pitying look upon his unshaven face. It wasn't the first time he had seen this young man; in fact, he had always been in the park, here and there. Mr. Grey remembered the first time he noticed him, but he found it strange to recall, for the young man had a presence to overlook even if he had a face to remember. As he thought back, it occurred to him that he had never witnessed the young man in such a deplorable state. Decision made, he stepped lively, and before the lad had a chance to protest, Mr. Grey planted himself right beside him.

"Can I help you?" The young man asked in a not-very-friendly tone.

"Are you all right?" Mr. Grey asked. The young man gave him a rueful look. "You look to be down on your luck, if you don't mind me saying." It looked as though he did in fact mind, but he said nothing, until Mr. Grey urged him to speak. After a few minutes the young man obliged and spoke of his woes: no job and no love, without friends, and soon no roof to call his own. He continued on and on, his desperation cutting to the marrow even as resentment tempered his sorrow.

"And that's my story and I'm sticking to it, no matter what the doctors say," he announced, laughing bitterly and taking a chug from his bottle as if to say that was that.

Mr. Grey made no move to reply, but took off his top hat and glanced down at it. It was old and frayed, a once-crimson belt wrapped around it. Though the buckle, as well as the hue of the strap, had long since faded, the knowledge of how the hat came into his possession remained ever present in his mind; a pleasant reminder like a lighthouse beacon that purges away all shadows.

"I've seen you around," the young man said. "And I got to ask, what is the deal with that stupid hat?" Mr. Grey chuckled jovially at the young man's words and turned to gaze at his dour companion.

"Well, you see, that is a story to tell, and perhaps one you should hear. Some years ago I was like you; my world gone all achromatic, downtrodden and bleak." He gave a quick bark of a laugh. "A pen that ran out of ink after writing only 1,667 words a day had more to live for than me." The young man gave a puzzled look and Mr. Grey smiled. "Hear me out, my young friend, and you'll see." And with that the man with the top hat began his tale.

* * * *

So there I was, three and a half decades old, over the hill and staring down old age. But I would not be stopped in my quest, a simple mission: to find some luck. It was a cold winter's morn in February and I found myself standing on the corner of a forgotten boulevard while snowflakes danced gleefully on my head, mocking me. I had tried in vain for the last week or three, but still no luck had I found. I had but one stop left, a secluded shop at the end of a steam-flanked alley. But luck called to me in a susurrant tone through a partially open ornate door. From behind the thick wood wafted soft scents of nutmeg and old hickory. I mustered up what little courage I had, flung the door open wide, and bounded through.

    I was struck at once, as though I had stepped into an entirely new world. The walls were hidden by clutter. From top to bottom and side to side, shelves and cabinets and boxes and plaques all filled the spaces around me. For a moment I wondered if my claustrophobia would set in, but as I looked up toward the ceiling, it seemed to disappear into darkness, my fears swallowed up by the night's sky. A breeze crawled down me then and I let out a sigh. Surely this place had what I was looking for.

    "Welcome! Welcome!" a voice boomed and I turned to

find a man descending a flight of circular stairs that I swear hadn't been there a moment ago. It took him six or seven minutes to finally reach the bottom floor, an arduous task in appearance, and yet he was not bothered by it at all. Older than I; he held a cane and wore a brown top hat encircled by a red belt with a silver buckle.

"Let me get a good look at you," he said as he approached. I noticed that he wore two monocles, one over each eye. "Just as I expected," he added once his inspection was done, his rust colored handlebar mustache moving as he spoke. "You're a man in search of something," he declared. I nodded fervently.

"Yes, how did you know?" I asked and he grinned.

"Why, anyone who comes here is looking for something." He pointed to his left and I followed his finger. On the far wall was a sign that read:

Mr. Mungo's Shop of Oddities

"That is me, or should I say, I." He tipped his hat. "But I should add it's pronounced like *bongo*." I opened my mouth to inquire but he spun away and quickly strode over to a display case. "I have many things, as you can well tell. So, I am certain that I have what you are looking for."

"Oh, that would be glorious," I exclaimed, feeling that the tables had turned. But before I could tell him what I wanted, the man suddenly broke into a song and dance that lasted a good six or five minutes ending with a bow and him tossing his cane over his shoulder. I raised an eyebrow and intended to interrupt but balked when he dipped his hand behind the cabinet and pulled out a glass eye.

"Is this what you want, m'boy?" he asked, his voice suddenly British. "I got this in '78 off an actor who liked to play Macbeth. Very funny bloke. And quite a gent: he once was thrown out of parliament."

I blinked and stared at the old cloudy thing. It smelled of pus and strawberries. I shook my head, my revulsion clear. Mr. Mungo-whose-name-rhymed-with-*bongo* frowned deeply.

"Very well, what about this beauty?" His voice changed back to what it had been when I first arrived and part of me wondered if I imagined the British accent. He placed a white-gloved hand on my back and led me past a stuffed snake-woman wearing sunglasses. I fought the urge to look beneath them.

"Wouldn't it help if I told—?" I began, but he clamped his other hand over my mouth; the taste of licorice teased my lips.

"Now, now, my dear friend. Questions like that are for people out there." He pointed past my head toward a door that wasn't there, but as I turned to look he ushered me away.

"But—" My words were lost as he blathered on about nothing important until finally he stopped in front of a wooden box stained a deep wine color. Charcoal iron links encircled it and I could just barely make out the faded image of a skull and crossbones upon its surface. As I was about to touch it, the box rumbled, its motion from within. I jumped back and Mr. Mungo cackled at the startled look upon my face.

"Inside is a shovel, a wanderer of places. He's buried many and more I'm sure. If you touch it once, you'll be gone, my friend, and for that there is no cure." The box quaked once more, its chains rattling like Old Marley's ghost. I backed away ten or nine feet.

"That's not what I want!" I shouted, my voice echoing like a howl in a cave. The monocled man dropped his gaze, his mustache twitching.

"I know!" He declared, his tone a loud whisper. "Follow me!"

He moved like a shadow; I followed like a stone.

"Happiness is here," he said, finally stopping before a large object under a tarp. I was about to tell him that was not what I was after, but he silenced me with a finger. I made a face, then stared up at the tall and oddly shaped thing in front of me.

"Voici!" He shouted, his accent changing again, this time to French. He pulled off the tarp, and my jaw dropped at the sight of a medieval trebuchet. It occupied so much room, I began to seriously question the size of the place. "It's broken in three places but quite a steal. Said to have belonged to Louis XIII but you didn't hear that from *me*, mon ami."

"No! I don't want this either!" His expression soured at my refusal, then he sighed.

"All right, all right; what about this?" He disappeared and reappeared only eight or seven minutes later. "I found this in an ancient pyramid in Madagascar!" Like water flowing over glass, his accent shifted again, this time to something akin to Middle Eastern with a strange hint of South African. In his hands was a long crate, the writing upon it in some eldritch language. He set it on a triangular table beside an upturned Viking helmet being used as a lamp and proceeded to open it. I groaned, my hopes beginning to fall. Stepping forward, I glanced inside.

"What is it?" I asked, completely unsure of what I was seeing. Mr. Mungo shook his head. With steady brown-gloved hands, he withdrew the bizarre object.

"This, boyo, is Classgo. A great Pharaoh." It looked like a mummified lemur. I told him as much and he waggled a finger in front of me. "To the untrained eye perhaps, but here is, in fact, the emperor of the great lemur empire. Circa 1910." My frustrations had grown, swarming around me like locusts, but still he went on to speak of an expedition that had lasted fifteen or eleven months and was fraught with danger at every turn. It would have been quite compelling if I cared, but I didn't. I had reached my limit.

"I don't want cursed shovels, or lemurs, *or* broken catapults!" I snatched the long dead mammal and flung it so far that the sound of it crashing into something was barely audible. The man spat on the floor angrily, then glared at me through the two monocles.

"Now, see here." Mr. Mungo started, his voice reverting, "if you didn't want it, you could have simply said so. That was going to be my lunch."

"Luck!" I shouted. "I simply want *luck*!" He stared at me for a moment, then threw up his arms.

"Well, my boy, you should have said something earlier. I have a very lucky find over here." He gestured for me to follow and I did, silently hoping that it wouldn't be another useless item. One to three hours passed as we trekked around more strange things: painted-over windows, a headless scarecrow, a man in a cage typing fervently at an old typewriter, as well as a dozen derelict ships.

Finally he halted before a single glass display, a light from above encircling it. Inside sat a royal blue satin pillow and upon it was a speck of white.

"This will bring me luck?" I questioned. Mr. Mungo laughed.

"Oh, heavens no." His guffaw became a soft chuckle as his accent became Russian. "This, comrade, is a cuticle."

"A cuticle?" I asked, dumbfounded.

"Da, from the space station." He turned back to the object in the case. "Can you believe it? I found a cuticle in the space station." I placed my hands on my head as he marveled over his trophy all the while humming a song from *The Nutcracker*.

"Let me be perfectly clear." I started, my voice low, my tone devoid of emotion. "I do not want a lucky find; I want something that will bring me luck." Mr. Mungo stared at me for a second or four.

"Oh, well, in that case, I have a rabbit's foot you could have. It's still attached to the beast, so if you don't mind taking the whole thing off my hands, that would be great." The shift in his accents no longer surprised me and I just shook my head and sunk to the floor as hopelessness filled me.

At that moment, a woman appeared, her heels clicking like claws on stone. I gave her little attention for my eyes were mostly fixed on the marble floor. All I saw as she glided past me was her hair, a flowing river of scarlet. Mr. Mungo excused himself then and attended the woman, his accent becoming thick Italian as he offered her an oar from a sunken gondola. I half listened, not really caring as I fretted internally. My quest had come to nothing; my luck was not there. Hours seemed to pass before the woman left, and I was again alone with the man whose name rhymed with *bongo*. The mustached fellow with his two monocles frowned and grew quiet and still. Ages passed before he spoke and when he did it was filled with sadness.

"I'm afraid, old gent, that I haven't a thing in my shop that could bring you luck, as those who have owned them before could probably attest. But you are in such a state, such a spot of bother, that I offer you this in hopes that it serves you well." With that he took off his hat and set it upon my head.

* * * *

When Mr. Grey finished his tale, the young man gazed at him dubiously as Mr. Grey looked back with all seriousness. A moment passed with neither of them speaking and in that span, the older man made a decision. He stood up, the creak of the bench as well as the young man's eyes following in his wake. The old top hat was still in his hands and without hesitating, he placed it on the young man's head. The young man's skepticism became confusion as he set down the bottle of spirits and lightly touched the hat, his fingers gliding over the rim, then the old leather strap.

"As he said to me, all those years ago, 'May it serve you well.'"

"And this will bring me luck?" There was hope in the young man's tone, but before Mr. Grey could answer, another voice sounded.

"Darling! Over here!" They both turned to see a beautiful woman in elegant dress with long cascading scarlet hair. He smiled and glanced back at his young friend.

"It did for me." Mr. Grey winked at the young man, adjusted his tie, and patted his black pants before linking arms with the woman. After one last glance back, they made their way past the organ grinder with his guilty monkey, past the flittering doves, and into the waiting limousine.

ALEXANDR BOND first began writing when he was nine years old. His first story was for a contest held by Disney. He didn't win, but that is beside the point. Ever since, he has been writing stories and successfully completed the NaNoWriMo 50,000 word challenge in 2012. When not writing, he enjoys traveling and has journeyed throughout the continental United States. Alexandr has studied Cinema Production, the French language, the Russian language, and Parapsychology. Like Mr. Mungo, he too collects oddities including a "genuine" dragon's skull, the bust of a werewolf, a dozen medieval weapons, a Shih Tzu, and a seventeen-year-old Himalayan.

Sasha and Derek

Alana Saltz

H E'S DYING.
It doesn't matter what I do. I sing to him. I give him sips of water. I stroke his skin. I tell him stories. But nothing's helping. He's going to die soon, and I really don't want him to die.

I sit with him all day long, watching him slowly lose everything that makes him who and what he is. Mom doesn't understand. She tells me to get off the floor and go read or watch TV in the break room. She asks why I care so much about him, and I don't know what to say, because I don't know why she doesn't care at all.

My mom is the manager of Canaveral Space Station in Cape Canaveral, Florida. We just call it Space Station. Space Station is the place where they keep some of the parts and equipment for space ships and shuttles. Stuff for NASA and NASA projects. The warehouse is stocked with sleek, shiny equipment. Rows and rows of heavy metals and twisting pipes and tools.

It's summer break now, and my mom can't afford a babysitter, and she says seven is too young to stay at home alone. So I've been coming to work with her almost every day for a few weeks. I don't want to stay at home anyway, because he's here. And he needs me. He's dying without me.

It's because Mom is so busy that Derek is dying. You would think in a building full of metallic and gray that you would notice his green leaves turning yellow, then brown. You would notice him drooping and dropping. But she doesn't notice. She's always on the phone or talking to engineers and the occasional astronaut. They come to talk to me sometimes when they see me sitting near her desk.

"What's your name?" they ask, kneeling down beside me and Derek.

"Sasha," I say. "And this is Derek."

"She's beautiful," they tell my mom.

"Thank you," Mom replies.

Everyone always says I'm beautiful. It's weird, because I don't think I'm beautiful. My eyes are the color of Derek's leaves when they were healthy, my skin is very light, and my hair is so long it reaches my waist. I'm thin and tiny so people usually think I'm younger than I am. Mom says I act young too, but when she says it, it doesn't sound like a good thing.

But I don't really care about the astronauts or the engineers or even Mom right now. I care about Derek. I've known him since I was three years old. Back then, he was taller than I was. His bright green leaves and brown bark arms stretched up high above me. Now, we're almost the same height, but his wilting makes him a little bit shorter.

As I got older, I got interested in plants because of Derek. I learned that he's a ficus tree. I also learned that the waxy film on his leaves is called a cuticle. I keep telling my mom that his cuticle is going away.

"See," I say. "Derek's really going to die. The cuticle on his leaves is gone!"

"Sweetie," Mom says. "I'm sorry. But you're a little too old to be this upset about a plant."

She's getting tired of me talking about Derek and plants and cuticles. I bother her about Derek when we go home in the evenings and she orders delivery for dinner.

"He needs our help," I say one night. "His cuticle is almost gone now."

"Stop talking about the plant in the warehouse!" she yells. "I don't care that the ficus is losing its cuticle in the Space Station warehouse. It's just a plant! I'm throwing it away tomorrow."

I start to cry, and she gets sad too.

"I'm sorry, Sasha," she says. "I don't mean to yell. But it's not healthy, how much you care about that plant."

"Derek," I say through my sniffles and sobs.

"Derek," she says.

"It's your fault he's dying," I tell her.

She shakes her head. "Everything and everyone dies. It's no one's fault. I liked the plant ... Derek ... too. I did. But we'll get a new plant. It's Derek's time to go."

I cry harder, and she hugs me.

"It'll be OK, sweetie," she says. "I promise."

I want to give Derek a funeral, but Mom says people don't bury plants like they do people or animals. She says people throw them away.

I sit with Derek on our last day together, tears running down my cheeks. I remember how much I loved watering him with his blue plastic bucket. I remember reading my books beside him, happy to be near a little bit of life and color in a cold, bland place. I keep imagining him all alone in the giant trashcan behind the warehouse. I picture myself in there and think about how I'd feel if someone threw me away like that once I was dead.

I can't handle it. It's too terrible a place to go.

Later that day, an astronaut notices me crying while he's talking to my mom about getting a tool for his upcoming space trip.

"What's wrong?" he asks me. He's a handsome man with dusty blonde hair and a muscular body. He looks like a superhero without the costume.

"My plant is dead," I say, pointing to Derek. "My mom says we can't bury him, so I'm saying goodbye before we have to put him in the trash."

"I'm so sorry," he says. He seems like he means it.

Then, he turns to my mom. "Hey, we're going on a mission in a few weeks. How about I take the plant with me, and we'll give it a space burial?"

Mom looks like she's trying not to laugh, and I'm not sure why. It makes me mad.

"What's a space burial?" I ask.

"We can cremate the plant and send it off into space from the station. People do it with people and pet ashes sometimes."

"Yes!" I say. "I want Derek to go to space!"

It's the perfect way to honor Derek. It's the perfect place for him to go. He's spent his life staring at all the equipment, hearing about adventures. Now he'll finally get to take one of his own.

The astronaut smiles and glances at my mom, who shrugs.

"Thank you," I say. I stand up and hug the astronaut.

He hugs me back and says, "No problem."

The astronaut takes Derek with him when he leaves Space Station. I wipe away my tears. I'm still sad that Derek is gone, but I'm happy that he'll get to spend his afterlife in space. Maybe when I die they can send me there too, and we'll be together again, our ashes mingling together as we float through the universe.

ALANA SALTZ is a writer, editor, and occasional ukulele rocker residing in smoggy Los Angeles, California. Her writing has been published in lit journals including *vox poetica*, *Feast Arts & Literary Magazine*, *The Occidental Review*, and the *East Jasmine Review*. She will soon receive her MFA in Writing from Antioch University, Los Angeles. Like Sasha, she also hopes her ashes will be launched into space after she dies. Check out Alana's blog at alanasaltz.com and/or follow her on Twitter @alanasaltz.

A Moon of a Problem

Fiona Yang

I'LL START WITH introductions. My name is Bevolinn, but call me Bev. The other person in this story is my— Wait! I can't spoil the fun for you! You'll have to find out for yourself who else is in this story.

Well duh! Everyone hates it when someone spoils the story!

Obviously someone wants to make her own introduction, but not yet, OK?

Anyway, let me start from the beginning. My dad is *rich*, amazing, fantastical, *rich*, kind, fatherly, *rich*, and did I mention *rich*? So of course he owns space stations; seven actually, because he is obsessed with space. (Which is kind of weird because I hate anything that has to do with science, including space.)

One day, I wanted to give him a surprise visit,

but he was on one of his space stations, so I had to ride on a rocket ship with twenty-five passengers (it was expensive). On my way there I got bored, so I started painting my nails with a nail polish called "Shades of Prophecy." As I was painting my nails, I accidentally painted my cuticles, and the creepiest thing happened next. The nail polish turned crimson, then blood red, then it just peeled off. I shuddered, because blood red meant *really* bad fortune, and it had never peeled off on its own. Shades of Prophecy has always led me right, so it was kind of hard to ignore what I'd just seen.

I absent-mindedly stared at it, lost in my thoughts. My best friend had just moved away, and all my other friends went to public school. I attended private school, and public school was forbidden in my household. In other words, life was not in my favor. My goal for the summer was to try to get a new best friend, but no one was qualified for it. Who would've thought my wish would come true.

Aw. Thanks, Sis.

Um, I wasn't talking about you. I was talking about Flame.

Hey!

Just kidding.

Back to the story. While I was finishing up my "thinking session"–which is kind of ironic, because I don't like to think–a girl came up to me and said, "Wow, that's nice nail polish you've got there." I was startled, because she just started talking to me. Before I could respond she asked, "What's your name? Wanna be friends? If we're friends, can I have your nail polish?"

I was irritated because she was so nosy. "I'm not going to tell you my name," I said. "No and no. Quit bugging me!

You're acting like a little child! In fact, you don't even know me!" I looked at her, and was surprised because she looked close to my age and also had raven hair, blue eyes with a hint of green–just like mine!–and tanned skin. She was also a bit tall.

"Fine then. At least tell me your name. I'm Levy," she said.

"Um, no. Stranger Danger!" I said.

"I just want to be friends with you. I mean, we are the only people on this rocket ship under the age of fifty," she said.

"Um, I don't care! Do you even know who you're talking to? I can have security take you to space jail!" All right, I admit. I sounded a bit spoiled.

"You're less fun than my dead grandma."

"If your grandma is dead, then how do you talk to her? She's dead."

"Exactly. If you're dead, you're boring because you can't talk or do anything. Wow, we actually had a real conversation."

"Um, excuse me? I'm not the weirdo trying to ask people about their personal information! Stalker."

"Well at least I'm fun. If you're more boring than the dead, now that is just sad."

"Why you little—" I got cut off by a flight attendant announcing that we had reached Daddy's space station.

I ran off the wretched ship, away from that nightmare of a girl and found Daddy waiting for someone. "Daddy!" I shouted with glee.

He looked up and appeared shocked as he saw me running towards him. Then, I heard that girl Levy call out "Dad." She was running toward us. I prayed to God that she wasn't talking to my dad. She stopped in her tracks with her mouth wide open when she saw me. We gave each other glares and looked at our dad.

He fidgeted nervously, and said, "Wow. Never expected you two to ever run into each other. Uhhhh ... Since you guys met ... Ummm, I have a confession to make. Guess what? You two are twin sisters! Yay!"

We just stood there speechless. It's funny how a simple statement can shatter a girl's world. It took me about three minutes to process what he had just said, but then again, we did look really similar. As I was about to pester my dad for answers, an explosion interrupted me.

* * * *

Ok. First, let me clear things up. My name is Levilonn, but call me Levy. Also, my sister is the annoying one. Not me. Got it? Now I'll tell you the rest of the story. Correctly, and from my side of the whole crazy adventure. Which is also known as "The Correct Story." Anyway, we were still in shock when the explosion happened. I mean, what kind of dad tells his twin daughters they are sisters after fourteen years? I trusted my dad all the time, even when he told little lies, but this had to be his biggest lie of all. Who would've thought she and I were sisters? Well, we look identical, but our personalities are worlds apart.

I was shaken out of my shock when people started screaming, and the smell of something burning filled the entire space station. I turned around and found myself face to face with a ten-foot-tall, silvery-red ... Dragon? It had huge, blood red wings and golden horns. It was deadly and beautiful all in one big package deal. One of the tour guides was trying to calm down the tourists, saying it was just a mechanical robot, when it breathed fire on the guide. All that was left of the poor man were ashes. The dragon turned around and looked at my sister and me with its huge, orange-yellow eyes. I was mesmerized by its whole appearance when it suddenly blew fire at us!

I rolled to one side out of pure reflex, and so did my sister and dad. The dragon stomped away. I turned around to congratulate myself when my dad, the traitor, said, "I'm sorry. It only fits one person." We were both confused about why he was saying sorry when he suddenly twirled around in the other direction and ran off. Later on, I learned he ran to the last escape pod. He saved himself and left us there to die. "Sorry" didn't cut it. I'm ashamed to even call him my dad.

Even if the dragon left us alone, we were the only ones left in the space station—the only ones.

When we recovered from the shock of our dad ditching us—well, not completely recovered—Bev sat up and stared off into space. Then she suddenly looked at me and said, "Get me water."

I fetched a bucket of water. The only reason I did as she ordered was because I knew she was shocked that our very own dad had ditched us. I mean, I was kind of traumatized too. But then her orders became more and more demanding and obviously had nothing to do with the dragon. At last, I was beginning to see her scheme when she put her feet in the bucket of water and asked me to give her a foot massage.

I realized she was just bossing me for fun. For fun! "I will gladly give you a foot massage!" I muttered to myself. I grabbed the bucket and poured it all over her face.

It was absolutely revolting to touch where her feet had been.

Hey!

Bev, your feet smell.

Well, you have—

Back to the story!

"How dare you?!" shouted Bev. "Come over here right now!" She must have thought I was going to listen, but there was a lesson she needed to learn: don't ever make me angry. I'm a nice person who doesn't get mad easily, but I was tired of her voice, her mouth, her everything.

I smiled through gritted teeth and said, "I. AM. NOT. AN. IDIOT! Get it?" It took all my willpower not to give her a concussion with my fists. "Don't you see? We have a very good chance of dying and you're ordering me around to play maid! Do I look like I'm playing around?" I think I sounded a bit hysterical, but who can blame me?

She may be spoiled and think everything is fixed with money, but I didn't care. I actually had a life with friends, schools, teachers, parents, and a good chance of being an awesome student, but this one incident ruined my too-short life.

Then she did the most unexpected thing ever. She started laughing like an insane person, like she didn't care what was going to happen to us. She started jabbering, "My cuticle. The nail polish. This is why it was blood red. The bad omen. It all makes sense now. A cuticle in the space station. Of course. I knew Shades of Prophesy would never lie to me." Then she pulled out her nail polish.

That was it! This girl had gotten on my last nerve. I went

blind with rage and almost made a decision to leave her on the Moon to die. Almost, but I didn't. Instead, I stomped up to her and slapped her face. It felt so good to let out my anger on something—particularly her face. I slapped her and I knew it hurt. When she looked back at me, she had a murderous expression on her face. But not only did I see her contempt towards me, I also saw her fears and hopes of getting out of there alive. In that awkward moment, I understood my sister and her feelings. But, all good things come to an end, and so did that moment.

"So what's the plan?" she asked, totally normal. I guess the slap did both of us good.

"Well, first of all, we need to see if we have a connection to Earth. Do you have a cell phone?"

"That's like asking if I have two eyes. Of course I have a cell phone. But I can't call anyone. No connection. If we did, we wou—" She was cut off when we heard the dragon coming in our direction. It spotted us and started going haywire.

"Run!" I yelled. We ran without a sense of direction and found ourselves in a dead end.

* * * *

My turn. You know, me, Bev. And let me just state for the record that I never laughed like an insane person. I simply had a moment of clarity, thank you very much.

Anyway, as we were running away from the dragon, we ran into a dead end. We frantically looked for an escape route, but the dragon cornered us. I stood as still as a statue and closed my eyes, waiting for death. Instead, I felt myself getting tickled. I opened my eyes, and found the dragon tugging at my bag. Levy was just staring at the dragon like it might suddenly turn around and blow fire at us, which was likely.

But it kept rummaging through my bag, until it found my nail polish. The dragon grabbed it with his little arms and held it in his tiny hands and sniffed the bottle. Then, the dragon cracked it open and drank the nail polish. The weirdest thing happened next. The dragon shrank and shrank until it was the size of a horse. We stared at it and found a little collar attached to it that read "Flame."

"Huh. It must be its name. Here, Flame, here boy." We treated the small dragon like a dog, and then another weird thing happened. It started talking. "I'm not a dog, by the way. I was just visiting Rambulen, but now, I've shrunk! It's all your fault!" We just stood there dumbstruck. A dragon that could talk? Our lives could not possibly get more messed up. Then, Levy started asking the dragon a thousand questions. "Where are you from?" "Why do you call the moon Rambulen?" "Why did you attack us?" "What were you saying back there?" "Do you want to come to Earth with us? I mean, we would have to ride on your back, but can we?" Etc., etc.

Extremely annoyed-looking, the dragon said, "I am a dragon from Ulapian, or as you humans call it, 'Jupiter.' I got confused and accidentally harmed those useless humans. And I have a question for you."

"Anything," Levy answered dreamily. Later on, she told me she had wanted to see a dragon her entire life. I guess her coming to the Moon was a great idea.

"Do you have an off button or a mute? Because you're making me highly agitated," said the dragon with a puff of smoke coming out his nose. Levy took a step back and simply nodded. "Hey you, the twin of the annoying child, is she always this ... pesky?"

"I know how you feel, only a hundred times worse, because I am going to have to go back to our planet and deal with her every single day," I answered.

"Yikes," the dragon said. "Well, you seem pleasant enough. I will let you take me to this place you call 'Earth,' and see if I like it."

During our chat, Levy had fallen silent.

"Who knew a dragon would hate me?" she muttered.

I tried to hold in my laughter, but it came out. She glared murderously at me.

"I'll get you back," she mouthed.

Then, the dragon said, "Climb on my back; you should find a pouch there. Open it, take out the saddle, and strap it on me. We'll ride to Earth."

I have to admit riding on a dragon is cool, especially if you're in space. And the best part was that when we entered Earth for good, Flame started looking like fire. I guess that's how he got his na—

And while we were there, we were attacked by aliens and they had UFOs and—

Whoa. Wait a second. What do you think you're doing? This is not and will never be part of the story. I said I never thought my life could get more messed up, but you're making it confusing! Stop making up stories!

Sometimes, you're still no fun! Like our dead grandma.

Anyway, you must be wondering what happened afterward. Well, Daddy welcomed us when we came home, but we knew why he was making such a big deal: we had a dragon with us and we were alive. When he tried to act all worried, I yelled, "Oh don't you even start with your lame EXCUSES! You are the worst father of all humanity and I will never forgive YOU!" Pretty dramatic, right?

It would have been even better if you actually meant it. Right after he gave you fifty bucks, you forgave him.

I'm ignoring you, and will pretend you never said that. Even after he apologized to us a million times, we still didn't forgive him. Actually, I didn't forgive him. I'm the kind of person who holds a grudge forever.

After that scenario was kind of solved, we wondered how we were even twins, and asked Dad. He said he got divorced from our mom when we were just born, and he took me and Mom took Levy, but we still knew our parents. They didn't remarry or anything. So even though we knew our parents, we didn't know each other because Mom and Dad wanted us separated. It's complicated. At least we got to keep Flame as a pet.

Excuse me, he's not even a pet. He is actually like a person who is demanding and annoying. Kind of like you, Bev.

He is an awesome dragon, and we love the same nail polish. It's a happy ending right?

I guess so if you consider "alive" a happy ending.

Now let's end the story. Let's say it together. One ...

Two ...

Thre—

WAIT! I need to tell the readers something before this story ends.

Ugh! Get on with it Levy. I'm sleepy.

Remember when I said I would get you back, Bev, dear? Well,

I'm doing it now. My sister is a big, fat liar so do not believe what she says about me.

Umm, excuse me? Did I hear you right?

Yes, you heard me and I will tell you why she is a liar. Bev lied 2,395 times so far in her life, 2,405 including this book and I'm still counting. She—

Okay! We're ending the story now before you say anything else that you're not supposed to say! Bye! And by the way, you are so dead, Levy!

Ah. The sound of a happy ending of a story. Goodbye people and have a Merry Christmas and a Happy New Year!

Um, Levy? It's nowhere near Christmas or New Year's.

Oh. Then, well, just ... bye. BYE!

FIONA YANG is an eleven-year-old 5th grader. She lives in Torrance, and has a mom, dad, and an older brother who is sixteen years old. She is American Korean, but her parents are from Korea. She is learning art, violin, ballet, and Chinese at the moment; she also goes to church on Sundays. Fiona enjoys reading books, especially in the genres of fantasy, adventure, and comedy. Her favorite author is Rick Riordan, and her favorite book written by him is *The Mark of Athena*. She considers herself a nerd with a lot of good friends from her after school program. She wrote this story so she could make readers laugh and smile as they're reading it.

I Cordially Accept

Kate Findley

Alex

AT FIRST, I thought nothing of the clicking in my ear. A minor annoyance, that's all. After a day, I hardly noticed it was there. When I had to leave work early because my head hurt so badly, I failed to make the connection. After all, I'd suffered from migraines since I was a kid.

Then, one night, the itching started: first in my ear, rapidly spreading to every portion of my body. In the bathroom, I lodged a Q-tip into my ear, twisting it around until the itching faded away.

That's when I saw the trail of ants marching across the floor and scaling the side of the wastebasket. There must have been at least fifty of them. One of them was carrying a termite on his back, its legs feebly kicking in the air like a wild boar being toppled by a gang of feral cats. The trail started at the edge of the bathtub. I searched every corner of the room, but there were no visible food sources.

A roach appeared at the top of the wastebasket. It was at least as long as a rat. Since we had moved to Arizona, we had not seen a single roach. In Texas, we had seen many, but none of this scale.

The roach descended the side of the wastebasket, tromping over the ants. They scattered in all directions. The roach's wings separated from its body and lifted in the air. It emanated an odd smell, a cross between bacon and ammonia.

I looked for a weapon, but all I could find were Jade's Hello Kitty flip-flops and Margaret's fuzzy pink slippers, hardly suitable for the job. Fumbling through the cabinets, I discovered a lighter. I drew the flame up to the roach and it caught fire. It continued crawling. At last, right before it reached the bathtub, it collapsed, vanishing into a pile of ash.

The bathroom walls stared at me, the pink-and-green-flowered wallpaper soaking up all my nervousness. I felt so calm that I could have gone to sleep right there.

JEB

When we moved to the city, Gill's behavior changed drastically. Once a loving, affectionate child, he was suddenly given to rages and violent sobbing fits, crying so hard he couldn't breathe and slamming his head against the table.

In the country he had been a different person entirely. He'd sit on the porch for hours watching the dragonflies, or walk to the creek with his bucket, collecting turtles for our pond. Now, hardly a dinner went by without an outburst.

"He's only eight," Helen would say whenever I suggested that Gill's behavior was out of line.

Or: "It's a big change in environment for a young child. It's going to take him a while to get used to his new home."

I learned not to bring it up.

"Still," I said one evening, feeling braver after a few drinks, "I keep thinking. We know nothing about his origins."

"Stop!" said Helen, hurling the plate to the floor. "Don't talk about him as if he were a specimen!"

Then I noticed that the door to Gill's room had been open the whole time.

Alex

The sense of calm I felt in the bathroom that night was short-lived.

At work the next day the copier jammed. I kicked it, and a high-pitched ringing echoed down the hallway. People dashed in all directions, shouting. My boss took me into his office. The fluorescent lighting panel bore into me like a probe, my ears clicking incessantly. He explained to me that there had been lots of complaints about my attitude lately, and this incident sealed the deal: if my behavior continued, I would be receiving a reprimand, hand-delivered from the regional manager.

"That's it?" I said.

"Do you need me to repeat myself?" he said.

Right then his face, sitting atop his thick, puffy neck,

looked so big and dumb it made me nauseous. I did my best to smile at my boss, to think of happier things like that time Margaret and I were sitting on the back porch eating shish-kabobs and Jade was running around in the sprinklers pretending she was at Raging Waters and the sun grew all bleary in the sprinkler mist and I felt like I was floating down a river, forever, turtles lazily drifting by.

The clicking grew louder, furiously erasing the image. In its place was a white, throbbing rage. I felt an incredible urge to punch my boss in the face.

No, I instructed myself, *think of Jade and Margaret, think what'll happen to them if you lose this job.*

I slowly backed out of the office, mumbling something about being sick and needing to go home. In the hallway, I sprinted for the elevator.

As I pushed open the door to the lobby, the sun blasted me in the face. Once again, I experienced that same sense of calm that I had felt in the bathroom.

A school bus passed me and a gust of wind sprung up, emptying the trashcan outside the office building. Cans and water bottles rolled down the curb. A swarm of roaches spilled out with the mess, scurrying into gutters. The smell of bacon and ammonia filled the air.

An enormous roach ran apart from the bunch, headed straight for a half-eaten link of sausage. I reached in my pocket for my lighter, only to have it come up empty.

Wait, what was I thinking? Margaret made me quit smoking over a year ago.

Across the street, two women were talking, and one of them was clutching her green visor. The other woman was nervously tugging at her ear. Directly above them was a small blue plane, flying very low.

JEB

We had found Gill at 4:00 a.m. walking along the side of the road. Helen and I had been lost for hours, no hotel in sight. The unlined country road bled into the black of the night. We could only see a few feet ahead of us. We both cried out in surprise when the headlights picked up Gill, then only four.

The boy did not seem upset, only dazed. He had wispy skin, pale grey eyes and a voice barely above a whisper. When Helen asked him repeatedly where his parents were, he would not answer.

In the car, he began to show signs of life. His eyes grew brighter and he spoke in loud, excited tones. When we stopped at a roadside diner, he ate ravenously, downing his milkshake in seconds. Still, he would not speak of his parents. We figured he had been abandoned, so we took him in as our own. Since we had tried unsuccessfully to have a baby for years, we viewed that night we got lost as a blessing in disguise.

ALEX

I walked for two hours. Everything looked different on foot. I passed nail salons, sushi bars and entire shopping centers I had never noticed before driving by in my car. My only objective was to get as far away from my office building as possible. Plus, walking helped to clear my head and made the clicking grow quieter.

At some point I looked up and the blue plane was still there, flying so low I could make eye contact with the co-pilot. He looked straight at me and waved.

JEB

At first Gill was unquestioningly obedient. While Helen showered him with praise, I could not help but think that Gill's behavior was a lingering effect of abuse.

The day we announced that we were moving to the city, Gill refused to go to school. We had to drag him, kicking and screaming, into the car. Two hours later, we found him at our front door. I had no idea how such a young boy could have made the four-mile walk on his own.

"He must have gotten a ride," said Helen.

"Where's the person who gave the ride?" I asked. "Wouldn't she want to talk to us, see if everything was OK?"

The next day, I found five dollars missing from my wallet. I didn't tell Helen. No sense in alarming her. What could possibly prompt an eight-year-old to steal?

Gill, once a lover of all food, now refused to eat his vegetables. When Helen tried to coerce him, he hurled a chunk of broccoli at her face.

"No dessert for you tonight," she said. The next morning, we found a whole gallon of ice cream gone, save for one scoop.

"Maybe we shouldn't move," Helen said.

"No," I said. "We have to. There's no work for me here anymore. Besides, he hasn't even seen the city yet. He's just scared of what he doesn't know. Once he sees it, he'll love it, I'm sure."

I was wrong. Gill did not adjust well to the city. Every day he'd come home with migraines. The kids at school kicked him, called him horrible names, and always stole the brownie from his lunch tray in the cafeteria. He complained of itchy ears and a clicking sound in his head.

We tried acupuncture, therapy, holistic nutrition experts. Nothing seemed to make Gill better.

His behavior at home grew worse. He barely ate. One night, when I tried to coerce Gill into eating his salad, he stabbed himself in the hand with his fork. Another night I woke up to find the boy standing next to my bed, holding a screwdriver up to his head.

Alex

I stopped at a diner. The waiters all paused to stare at me, one by one.

I checked myself in the bathroom mirror. My clothes were drenched with sweat, skin clammy.

My head was filled with scratching sounds, like thousands of tiny feet scurrying across tile. My vision split into twos, then threes and fours. The clicking had burrowed deep within my skull.

I tried to reason with it.

Please, I said as I sunk to my knees, *I'll do anything you want. Just make it stop.*

Slowly, the noise seeped out of me like a deflating balloon. My head became crowded with flowing ribbons of color and all sorts of things I had forgotten were in it, like when Jade decided to ride her bike the whole four miles to the store and buy me an ice cream cake for my birthday and when she got home she was coated with blue and green; even her hair was sticky. Margaret laughed and told Jade to go rinse off in the pool.

No, that couldn't be right. Margaret refused to let any of us go in the pool without taking a shower first, even me. Maybe this time she was feeling lenient ....

A black bar spread across the memory, like static, blurred and smudged.

Gill

Halfway through math I started to feel sick and tried to hold it in, but soon I couldn't take it anymore. I asked Mrs. Stagmire if I could leave.

"Good lord, you're pale as a ghost!" she said.

I threw up in the hallway. The vomit looked like something out of a cartoon, glowing with Kool-Aid reds and greens and radioactive oranges.

In the bathroom, I stumbled around and my head felt all dizzy. I crawled into one of the stalls.

Stop! I screamed at the noise, grabbing onto my head. Maybe if I squeezed hard enough I would kill the thing that was making the clicking and then it would shut up forever.

From under the stall door I saw a roach the size of my hand wiggle out from the sink faucet, crawling across the wall.

It started flicking its wings, making the clicking grow louder. It smelled like a Denny's breakfast combo and the house right after Helen had mopped.

I closed my eyes and pretended that I was in my neighbor's bathroom with the patch of pink-and-green-flowered wallpaper on the wall. There was a painting of a yellow leaf, falling, that always looked peaceful. I tried to fill in every detail, to lock it in place, so I could go back there if I needed to. On the floor by the shower I saw the girl's slippers. I started to feel queasy. Curtains appeared, billowing like a jellyfish, tentacled tips reaching out to me; *Come in, come in, it's all ready now*, they smiled.

Ronnie kicked open the door to my stall.

"How was breakfast?" Ronnie asked.

"Shut up, Ronnie," I said. "You're nothing but a specimen."

"What?" Ronnie said.

"You heard me."

Ronnie's hi-top sneaker moved toward my face. I clutched it and shoved Ronnie across the room, his head making contact with the sink.

The bell rang. The hallway swelled with laughter. The words melted into one big ball, though barely I could hear Mrs. Stagmire saying, "Now class, you be sure and study."

JEB

On my way to work, I took a detour. I drove for two hours. The phone poles on the sides of the road turned into trees. The lines on the roads disappeared, the smooth pavement giving birth to potholes. Eventually I pulled over. It was this spot where I first found Gill.

Even before I saw the small blue plane, I knew that it was coming. It tore through a cluster of trees, branches breaking off, birds frantically scattering. It landed in a burst of sparks.

My phone rang. Helen. I ignored it. It rang again. I listened to the voicemail. Helen was hysterical: "Jeb, are you there? Please call me. It's an emergency. Gill's in trouble. He ... they said he hurt a boy at the school, and now the boy's going to the hospital, and his parents want to sue. But I don't believe it! Gill would never do something like that. You need to get him; I'm still at work. Jeb, where are you? Pick up!"

I tucked the phone in my pocket. What I had to do right now was more important.

Gill

I sat in a hard white room with black bars of shadow stretching across the walls. The AC huffed out Antarctic-style air. Through the slats in the blinds, I saw a blue plane flying in circles around the flagpole in the courtyard. All my teachers were at the front of the room, sitting at a long table. They were scribbling things on pieces of paper. I closed my eyes so I could go back to my neighbor's living room. The whole house smelled like blueberry muffins and there was the mirror with rabbits and flowers and butterflies carved into the frame. I stared at the spiral on the butterfly's wing and it gave me a happy feeling. The clicking got louder. I opened my eyes. A teacher was talking to me, but I couldn't hear what she was saying. My ears felt like someone was sharpening pencils in them.

Alex

I was seated at a booth when a woman approached.

"Alex!" she said, taking a seat across from me.

Was that my name? It was startling to hear someone else say it, but also comforting, bringing me back into my body.

She had aqua eyes, shimmery burgundy hair, and feathery eyelashes. Wearing a slim emerald gown, she was a mannequin in a Macy's diner display.

"Douglas called," she said. I could tell from her face that this was not a good thing.

"Well," I said, "what did you say to him?"

She looked at me apologetically. I scanned the room. Everyone was staring at us. It felt wrong talking to this woman.

"I know what you're going to say, Alex," she said. "I should have hung up on him. But I at least owed him the time of day. Eight years together, that's no joke."

Eight years. That's how long I had been married to M—. I couldn't remember her name. I tried to put a face on her, but everything came up blank.

The woman's eyes darted back and forth, her hands fidgeting. I had a sudden urge to reach out and clasp her hand and gently stroke her arm, but I restrained myself.

The clicking in my ears had died down to a faint murmur, and the itching was all but gone. The diner clanged with the sounds of forks and knives scraping on plates, air quivering with a syrupy film. My skin felt tacky.

"Hey," I said. "How about somewhere quieter?"

JEB

I climbed on board the plane. The seats were empty. At the back of the plane was a man standing in front of a projector. He had an indistinct face, the type you forget the instant you turn away.

On the screen was a pulsating mass of white, larva-like bugs. Some of them were beginning to sprout wings.

"What you are looking at is Gill's brain," the man said.

"What have you done to him?" I asked.

"No," he said. "The proper question is: what has Gill done for us? When Gill first caught our attention, we knew he had potential as a host. His mind was a fertile environment, receptive to new ideas, open to new ways. It made the perfect breeding ground for us."

"Breeding ground?"

"Yes, you heard right. Right now we thrive in the city, but soon we will have colonies in every building, in every tree. To people like you we may look primitive. But our technology is far more sophisticated than anything you can imagine."

He paused for a second, registering my confusion.

"I took on a human form so I could better communicate with you," he said. "But normally, we look similar to what your species calls a roach. We can transmit thoughts from one mind to another like you transport goods. Our technology has become so efficient that we now only take up inches of space and can plug into any source to survive. We don't need infrastructure and can survive on scant resources. We feed on human memories."

"Gill hospitalized a kid today," I said. "Soon he might end up in the hospital too. He tries to hurt himself."

"How so?" the man pandered, mock concern on his face.

"One night, he stabbed himself with a fork. Another night, he held a screwdriver up to his head. He barely eats anything."

"You know we can't have this," said the man. "Child protective services could always make a visit. Either you handle this or we handle you."

"How can I when you won't leave him alone?"

The man did not like my question, but he deliberated for a moment.

"Very well, then," he said. "It is time for our little ones to hatch."

He pulled out a map.

"You need to bring your son to the Source," he said.

GILL

Jeb (he kept telling me to call him "Dad" but it felt weird) was waiting for me in the hallway. The principal must have told him everything, and I knew I was in big, big trouble. I wondered what he was going to do to me. He didn't look mad or anything, though, so that was good.

He drove past the road with the red barn next to it where he usually turned to go home. I opened my mouth to tell him he forgot to turn but then I thought, *No, that wouldn't be a good idea.* We passed things I had never seen before—auto repair shops with rust-speckled signs sitting atop spindly poles like dandelions, hollowed out warehouses with crows pecking at garbage in the empty parking lots, burger and shake stands with half-lit neon signs flickering against the purple of the setting sun.

    At last, we pulled over. I waited for Jeb to open his door, but instead he just sat there in a trance. I wished he would say something–anything–or that somebody else would come and start talking to us. Finally, he opened the door.

ALEX

The woman's house looked squat and diminutive from the outside, but on the inside it was surprisingly spacious, almost like a space station. Walking through the hallway, I felt like I was floating, disconnected from time. The walls were curved and pinkish, with shadows in the crevices that seemed to extend to immeasurable depths.

    "I'll be right back, Alex," she said, turning into the bathroom. "Make yourself comfortable."

    I searched for clues to her identity and hopefully, her name. The fridge was plastered with photos, secured with magnets designed like pieces of fruit. One photo featured a freckled blonde girl proudly clutching a tooth. Underneath it the words "Jade" were scrawled in crayon, each letter a different color. Next to it was a photo of a woman with a headful of windblown curls and a ruddy face sitting on a doorstep. This was "Margaret." Both the girl and the woman looked uncannily familiar, but I couldn't place them.

    The floor was scattered with Frito crumbs, surprising given

how thin she was. I bent down closer and saw that they were actually the slivered ends of toenails and fingernails, dozens of them. In the middle of the pile was a cuticle, which gleamed like a sliver of wet sponge in the sunlight. A cuticle in the space station. I looked out the window and saw the blue plane. It was spinning in sweeping, haphazard loops like a kid learning to drive in the school parking lot.

"Would you like a drink?" asked the woman.

How long had she been standing behind me?

She handed me a martini glass filled with a chameleon-green liquid. We sat on a couch with the kind of soft, worn cushions that make you feel as if they're taking you hostage. I was relieved to find that I had sunk low enough that I was below the frame of the window, out of the plane's eyeshot.

She took off my shoes and began to massage my feet. The drink was pure Smarties and maraschino cherries. My head felt heavy, and I sunk backwards until the whole room seemed to sway with me, as if I were on a boat. On the wall hung a painting of a Del Taco. That's odd, I thought, her kid must have painted it. In the yellow sun that's featured in the Del Taco sign, I saw a brown figure quiver. It was a roach, a big one.

"You saw my mess back there, didn't you?" she said apologetically.

I feigned ignorance, though I knew she was referring to the pile of nails.

"I'm sorry you had to see that," she said. "It's just that these parts get so uncomfortable. And this time of year, you know, is prime molting season."

With her right hand, she took her left fingers and began to peel them backwards as if she were removing a glove.

Gill

We walked to an empty Del Taco with a "For Sale" sign. Jeb kicked open the door. As he turned on the light, the ceiling seemed to shift. Hundreds of tiny bodies appeared, flickering like salmon in a stream.

We went into the bathroom. The wallpaper was peeling, the floor soft and saggy. I was afraid my shoe would break all the way through. Paint chips crunched under me.

"Wash your hair," Jeb said, pointing to the sink, which was covered with brown and yellow spots.

"I don't know," I said.

"It's OK," he said. "There's nothing to be afraid of. Pretty soon they're going to leave your head, and everything's going to be quiet again. All the clicking will be gone forever."

"They?" I asked.

He didn't answer.

"I'll be waiting in the kitchen," he said.

I turned on the water. It spit out sharp ribbons.

"Make sure you wash your hair really good now!" Jeb shouted from outside the door.

I picked up the soap bottle, squeezed-in and dented, a big sticky square where the label used to be. I shook it and only a tiny bit of soap came out. It smelled like rubber cement glue.

As I scrubbed my hair, I heard a noise like ten eggs cracking and felt a splitting in my head.

A roach moved across the mirror. At least, that's what I thought it was. It looked like it was from the dinosaur age, with mandibles capable of crushing a hamster. It was even bigger than the one I had seen in the school bathroom.

What do you want from me? I asked.

I felt something crawl out my ear and down my face. It was a tiny baby roach. Another one came out and then another and another. Each one jumped off of my face and landed on the sink. They lined up in a row behind the big roach. After the fifteenth baby roach jumped out, my head felt like an empty room.

You've done your job for now, the big roach said. *We'll be back in a few years, when you're old enough to appreciate the nature of your work.*

Why can't you leave me alone? I asked.

Your task is much too important, the roach said. *You are helping to give birth to a new species, one infinitely superior to man. We are not ungrateful for your efforts. When the human race eats up everything on Earth—we have calculated that this will happen in approximately twenty-five years—famine and warfare will result. But you will be safe. We have reserved for you a golden throne in our kingdom, where you will rule over the universe.*

I don't care about a stupid throne, I said. *I'm staying with my people.*

I'm afraid you don't have a say in the matter, said the roach. *You're our domain now.*

I closed my eyes and pretended I was in the bathroom with the flowered wallpaper and pink fuzzy slippers and that Hello Kitty face. Then, a man appeared in my imaginary bathroom, and a big roach just like this one raced across the floor. The man took out a lighter and burned up the roach.

You see that? said the roach, bringing me back to the ugly, grimy bathroom I was actually standing in. *That man. We tried to play fair with him. He gave us you and his memories of you, and we gave him a fresh wife, a model life. But he played dirty. So now we're eating up all his memories. Pretty soon he won't know his own name.*

ALEX

The clicking began again, rapidly escalating into a din, each twitch of the woman's roach leg turning up the dial.

"I have to go now," I said, standing. "It's almost six o'clock. Soon, everyone's going to wonder where I am."

I wasn't sure whom "everyone" referred to, but it sounded like a convincing enough reason.

"Silly," she said. "It's way past six. But go along, babe."

Outside it was so dark I couldn't read the street signs. Yet a path lit up before me like a lightning bug lantern.

Eventually I arrived at an empty Del Taco, windows covered in dust. Crawling with roaches, I bet. Hatred seethed through me.

A warmth emanated from my pocket. I reached in and there was the lighter, just like I knew it would be.

JEB

The Del Taco filled with the smell of gasoline.

"Gill!" I called out. "You OK in there?"

No answer. Fingers of heat grabbed onto my neck. Flames swallowed up the floorboards. The walls were melting.

I ran into the bathroom. Gill's eyes were open, but nothing registered. I picked him up and fled out the door.

Across the street, I watched the Del Taco dissolve into flames. It was then that I noticed the man holding an empty gasoline can.

ALEX

My head felt like ten car doors screeching against curbs.

"You crazy or what!" a man shouted at me, holding a boy in his arms. "You trying to get us killed in there?"

I tried to tell him that he had way more to worry about from the roaches than some stupid fire, but the clamoring in my head was so intense I couldn't hear myself think.

Then the blue plane appeared in the sky, illuminated by the fire. Flames skirted off the wings, like it was in a cartoon. Finally landing, the plane's cabin door opened and a ladder descended.

JEB

The man who greeted us on board the plane was different than the man I spoke with the last time. While that man was imposingly calm, this man was scrambling, nervous. He spoke in clipped phrases, swinging his stubby little arms as he spoke as if trying to propel his words forward.

"Look what you did, Alex," he said dramatically to the man with the lighter, gesticulating at the fire. "Four years of breeding.

Erased. You think the clicking's bad now? You got one thing coming."

"Your threats mean nothing," said Alex. "All your minions are shriveled up to a crisp. Soon there'll only be one of you left. And then, like a Bigfoot putting its big foot down, there won't be none of you left."

Chuckling, the man said, "Imagine how many others are already hatching around the planet …."

"But we've destroyed the Source," I said.

"The source is the source is the source … we have sources like you have fingernails. They fall off, they grow, they live forever."

"They won't," said Alex, waving his lighter menacingly. "I don't care if I have to burn down every building in existence."

"We're not going to let you take over this planet," I said.

"Even if it weren't hopeless?" said the man, shaking his head. "It'd still be hopeless."

ALEX

My head felt like it was being flattened in the jaws of a giant hole-puncher. The back of my throat throbbed and I remembered when I was no older than six or seven and my mother stuck a popsicle stick way back in my throat, thrusting it forcefully. But no, that wasn't right; my mother wouldn't do something like that.

Jeb offered me a ride home, but I didn't know where to direct him. He said I could stay in their guest room, and we'd figure things out in the morning.

His wife made me a grilled cheese sandwich. Afterwards the boy brought me a fun-sized Hershey's bar, and everything in my head felt like that calm, quiet bathroom.

Roach

I laughed as Jeb, Gill and Alex deplaned. Alex waving his lighter around like he was a comic book crusader out to torch the world of its evil influences; Jeb puffing out his scrawny chest. What a pathetic bunch they were. The whole lot of them from shape to sound. We're not even on their register. We only need a small amount of resources to survive. Eventually, the planet would be ours.

KATE FINDLEY grew up in Port Aransas, TX, and now lives in Los Angeles. She received her BA from the University of Southern California and her MFA from Otis College of Art and Design. You can read excerpts from her short story collection, *Tilt-A-Whirl,* at katefindley.wordpress.com/.

Ghost in the Machine
Melora Sundt

"Despite all the neurological evidence, we are no closer to understanding the complexity of the human mind, its capacity for invention and reasoning, than was Descartes. We might as well be studying a ghost in a machine."

Dr. Rosie Kenedia, Ph.D.
(The Mind vs. the Body.
Old Order Text, Date not verified, p. 1).

* * * *

"The notion of a 'soul' independent of the neurologically controlled brain, the proverbial 'ghost' hidden within the body, or the 'machine,' has about as much evidence in its support as does the myth of God hidden amongst the stars. Many people live in space, and not one has witnessed God."

Dr. Kenesaw Zuruckhaltend, Ph.D.
(Review of The Mind vs. the Body.
Old Order Text. Date not verified, p. 14).

SHE WANTED ME to think she lived on the street. Everyone knows the kind. Clothes are dirty; hair looks stringy, matted, unwashed; shoes are worn through and the wrong size. Clothes are an indistinct gray, baggy, torn in places. Smells like piss. I wanted to hold my breath as she walked by. She was talking to herself, but I couldn't catch what she was saying. She began twirling in circles, sometimes balancing on the curb, like a tightrope walker, threatening to tip into the road, laughing, yet never actually falling.

She was my target. I could pretend that I didn't recognize her and move on to interview the patrons in the coffee shop, but I *did* recognize her—I was the only one who would—and so she was mine. I took a breath and moved in as close as I could without getting clocked by her flailing arms—no, "flailing" isn't quite right. She was actually quite graceful as she played on the curb's edge. Another giveaway.

She'd made a mistake the previous morning. She'd threatened my charge, the Prince Regent. She failed, but that wasn't her mistake. No, her mistake was that she believed no one had seen her face. But I had. And here she was, an assassin hiding in plain sight. Just another street urchin. Biding her time for her next opportunity, which I'd make sure would never come. I'd seen her that morning, and now I was going to bring her in.

"Time to go," I said, reaching to grab her hand.

Time slowed down. She stopped chattering, stopped moving and looked down at my hand holding her wrist. I looked down, too, and saw what looked like tattoos on her fingers: delicate, tiny drawings adorning the space at the base of her nails, edging her cuticles. I'd never seen the like.

I brought her hand up closer to my face. Each finger was the canvas for a different inked line drawing, mostly patterns, but one was clearly tiny ivy leaves twisting around her thumb. Extraordinary. It reminded me of something, and for a second, I was in a perfumed room, soft pink, a silk curtain blowing against my face. I blinked.

Back in the present, I slapped the first restraint on the wrist I gripped.

"You are confusing me with someone else," she said between clenched teeth, and she wrenched back against my grip, then tried to punch with her free arm and kick my legs out from under me with her foot.

I expected as much. I slapped the second half of the restraint across the arm that had nearly cracked my nose, completing the security link. Her legs were still a threat so I pulled the stunner from my belt, zapped her in the abdomen, and held on to the restraints as she crumpled at my feet. I secured her ankles, then pulled up the chain attached to my belt and clipped it onto the restraints, tethering her to me.

As I tapped my ear to signal the transport team, she gave a last attempt to pull away, hissing, "You're making a mistake. Get these off before they see!" I was surprised she could talk, let alone move, given the jolt that had passed through her. I'd been lucky. She was much stronger than I had estimated, and that miscalculation scared me.

I could feel a shift in the air behind me, signaling the arrival of the transport team.

"Good work, Officer. We'll take it from here." Three uniformed women stepped forward, each armed with two weapons that I could see, and another two I knew to be embedded in their belts and helmets. The first officer unclipped the chain from my belt and attached it to her own, pulling the woman to her feet. "You want to catch a ride with us?" she asked, looking at me.

"Sure. Thanks." A relatively uneventful interdiction. Not much left but the report to file. And we were back in the space station before I had loaded another chain onto my belt. I still didn't like or understand transport. It left me with a slight headache every time.

At that moment, I couldn't remember the first time I'd transported, must have been at least thirteen years ago or so. Funny how you forget things like that, something that was monumental the first time it happened.

I got buzzed in through security, found my room, and went for the bed. The hours on my feet were taking their toll. I yanked off my boots, grabbed a light blanket and set the timer for forty-five minutes, a short nap to fight off the headache and the too-many consecutive shifts on the job. Not standard protocol, I know, but it was worth it. It was a relief to have brought this case to closure.

The timer went off, but it was too loud, too soon, too … urgent. A voice in the hallway, giving commands, carried through the door.

"It's time."

"For my report? But I just got back. I haven't had time to write it," I yelled back. "Give me a break. I just laid down."

"Doesn't matter. You're up." The door swung open and a uniformed officer stood, backlit by the light in the hallway. She held out a cup and a pill. "For the headache. You have a headache, don't you?" She thrust the cup and pill at me.

"Yeah." I swung my legs over the side of the bed, pushed off and took the offered cup and pill. Gone in one gulp. Instant relief. "Just let me put on my uniform, and I'll be out in a sec."

"Not necessary. Just come with me." The officer stood to the side and beckoned out the door.

No uniform? Well, all right; I can adapt. I shoved my feet in my boots and followed the officer down the hall. She showed me into the C.O.'s office, sparse as always. The C.O. stood as I came in, and gestured to the chair across the desk.

"Sit, Ms. Carpenter."

Huh. *No reference to title.* I began to feel a bit uneasy. I didn't think I'd done anything wrong but with the C.O. you never knew.

"You know why we're here?" The C.O. flipped open the folder on her desk, searched through a few pages inside it, stopped on one and looked over her reading glasses at me.

A paper copy? This C.O. is obviously nostalgic for the old order. I wonder if she's even a supporter of the Prince Regent?

"I assume you want my report?"

"Ms. Carpenter, we go through this every week. No, I do not want your report. There is no report. I want to know why you insist on refusing treatment. This treatment is painless, and it *will* clear up the dreams and sleepwalking. You want that, don't you, to be productive again?" She sat back in her chair and waited.

I didn't know what to say. Was this a prank? "I don't know what you mean. I *am* productive. I just brought in the most elusive assassin of our time."

The C.O. sighed. "I'm afraid not. You were sleepwalking

and you left the hospital. We had to send officers out to retrieve you last night." The C.O. took off her glasses and rubbed her eyes. "Let's try it from the top, again, OK? Do you know where you are, Ms. Carpenter?" She cocked her head.

"Of course. I'm on the space station. As is my prisoner with her grimy clothes and tattooed cuticles, in the space station, awaiting booking, unless you've done that already." I folded my arms and sat back hard in my chair. Really, this was nuts. And I still needed that nap.

"No and no. You are in a psychiatric hospital–involuntarily I need to say–as the result of trauma from your job. Do you remember what you do for work?" The C.O. set the file aside and waited.

"Is this a trick? You know what I do for work."

"I need to hear you explain it to me."

"I run a security force for the royal family. I protect the Prince Regent. And I'm the best at it, but you know that." I could tell she was watching me carefully, not blinking, but I couldn't figure out why.

"Good, that's correct. And do you know what precipitated your hospitalization?" She actually raised her eyebrows expectantly at me.

"I don't understand what you mean by hospitalization. We're here at the space station. It's where the Regent and his body guards are based."

"See, that's where you fall apart every time. I'm going to give you some bad news. I regret to inform you that the Regent was killed three weeks ago by an unknown assassin."

"That's not true." I stood up. "That's completely untrue.

The Regent is in his suite." As I said this, I saw in my head the pink billowing curtain again. *Where was that?*

"Sit down, Ms. Carpenter." The C.O. didn't raise her voice but the command was unmistakable. I sat, slowly.

She continued, "You were on duty. You took the first bullet; it grazed your skull. Your hair graft is taking nicely, by the way." I automatically reached my hand to the right side of my head. I felt a wide swath where the hair wasn't quite right.

"That shot dropped you and gave the assassin a clear shot at the Regent. He was not as lucky as you. Ever since, you've been delusional and sleepwalking at night. You have disabling headaches from the wound. You've been here for exactly twenty-one days, and you've attempted to leave the facility seven times so far." She paused, clearly gauging my reaction.

"Look, there's an easy way to end this foolishness. Call the Prince Regent." I reached for the communicator on my belt, and, not locating it, tried my other side, still not finding it. *Fell off on the bed?* I rubbed my face, trying to remember. "There was an attack, and it was aborted. I was there. I saw her face," I began, but she cut me off.

"You didn't see her, or his, face. There were witnesses. The assassin wore a hood. She or he attacked through the parlor window. Only their hands holding the gun were visible. The person fired and fled. You got really close, you tried your best. We all agreed that no one could have moved fast enough." She paused. Again with the sympathetic look. "We can continue to do this, night after night, or you can cooperate. I don't know about you but I'm getting exhausted by this cycle. Aren't you tired?"

"I work until the job is done. I don't have time to be tired." My headache was returning.

"But you're not working, that's the point. You were sleepwalking, and the hallucinations are getting worse, probably because you aren't getting enough real sleep. And neither are we, I might add." We looked at each other.

I wanted to grab the pen out of her hand. *Sleepwalking? Hospitalization?* We were wasting time. I needed to question the prisoner. I was about to lay in to this paper pusher *(and if she really is a C.O., I'll be violating Directive 12—not for the first time!)* when a breath-stealing thought dawned on me: there could be another explanation. Something had gone terribly wrong while I was away. I didn't actually recognize the C.O., but that wasn't unusual. They rotated. *Could this be a trick? Could we have lost control of the space station? Has there been an uprising from the old order? They might want me to think I've gone psycho so they can subdue me. The hair graft is a nice detail. I'm impressed. Maybe I'm the only one of the team left.* I needed a moment to think, so I willed on a poker face and just looked at her. Inside my head, though, I sped through the emergency protocol: *Were the other crew OK? And if they weren't, who could I signal?*

"All right," the ersatz C.O. began. "I'm clearly not getting through. Why don't you return to your room, get that nap, and we'll try again when you've rested." She closed the file and waved to the officer standing in the hall. "She's going back to her room," the C.O. informed the officer.

"I know the way, thanks." I stood, needing to get out of sight. I knew I had to play the compliant psych patient. It might buy me some time while I checked on the rest of the team. I knew I also had to find the prisoner, and check with the team guarding the Prince Regent. If this really was a takeover of the space station, I hoped they'd had enough time to evacuate—*but who are these people?*

I snuck back out of my room and headed to booking, passing one unfamiliar face after another. I thought I'd try a little test and ask for my prisoner. The booking officer flipped through papers *(Paper files again. Didn't we computerize decades ago?)* and came up empty. Not good.

"Sweetheart, no one like that is going to show up in these files, I assure you." The booking officer looked up sympathetically from the desk.

"I brought her in myself last night, with three other agents." I took a breath. *If it's a takeover, assume all staff has been taken and replaced.*

"Ms. Carpenter. You were the one brought in last night with three of our security guards. You were sleepwalking again."

Crap! She's one of them, too. I hated the sympathetic, knowing look in her eyes. "Fine," I said, back in the psych patient role. "Thank you for your time." I walked away, forcing myself to walk normally until I could duck down a side passage and head toward the holding cell area. The almost-assassin had to be somewhere on the space station. I wasn't sure how much longer I'd be allowed to roam free. I had to assume the hallway cameras were tracking me.

I moved methodically from cell to cell, all empty. I tried taking even, deep breaths to keep the panic at bay. *Was the Regent safe?* I'd seen no way to access the comm devices; every station was staffed. *Did Command know the trouble the space station was in?* I checked the interview rooms—all empty.

I sat at one of the interview tables, retracing the previous night. *Keep it together! Think. What was I doing before I saw her?* I couldn't recall. I couldn't recall! I grabbed at the table. *No restraints! What interview table doesn't have restraints?* I looked around. There was a two-way mirror. *Good sign, right? Stop. Don't doubt yourself. They want you to think you're crazy. You know you brought the prisoner in.*

The C.O. eased into the chair across the table from me. I hadn't even heard her come in.

"Is it becoming clearer to you?" She patted my hand, then gestured to the room. "These are counseling rooms. You've spent a good deal of time in here." She paused. "Come on, come with me back to your room. Let me help you. There really is no assassin here." She patted my arm.

I tried to recollect the assassin's face, her height. Even what she had said to me: "You're making a mistake," or something like that? *Could I possibly have dreamed the whole thing?* But I saw her. I smelled her. *You don't do that in dreams, do you?*

The fatigue was becoming crippling. The headache was back.

"Ms. Carpenter, I'm getting more than a little concerned." I raised my eyes to look at the C.O. as she spoke. Old habits die hard. "We expected to see shorter 'hangovers' from these nocturnal wanderings of yours. If you won't cooperate, we do have the authority to administer medication. Your condition is serious. I wish you would trust us."

I could see the curtain blowing in my mind. I tried to tune the C.O. out and focus on it. I closed my eyes and saw the curtain move, saw myself running towards it, then a pair of hands came from behind the curtain, holding a gun. No face, just the hands. And they were tattooed—little ivy leaves running up the thumb. *Not the face,* I realized, *the hands! I had seen the assassin's hands!*

I bolted back from the table. "She's here on the space station. I have to find her!"

"Officer!" The C.O. called. "I'm sorry to do this, Ms. Carpenter, but it's for your own welfare."

I turned to run from the room but two large officers stepped in my way, one carrying a stunner. Cursing, I couldn't stop in time and ran right into it. The effect was instantaneous. I collapsed to the ground, with one of the officers catching me under the arms. I had full consciousness but couldn't move. *Shit! Colossal mistake. Literally right into their hands.* I tried to move my mouth to speak but couldn't get coordinated.

"Ms. Carpenter. I'm sorry about this. The officers will take you to your room, and then we'll give you a sedative and some antipsychotic meds. You'll feel better soon. Don't panic." The C.O. walked alongside me as the two officers carried me to my room, and my bed. Once I was situated, she left, shutting my door gently.

Almost instantly, the door reopened and a masked nurse came in, bearing a syringe in her gloved hands. One of the officers rolled up my sleeve and the nurse stepped up to prep my arm. Unwelcomed tears spilled from my eyes as my frustration at being unable to move or speak overwhelmed me.

I watched the nurse move the syringe into place and press the plunger. It was fast acting. I could feel my muscles relaxing immediately—a fuzzy, all-is-right-with-the-world feeling. As the nurse stepped back and pulled off her latex gloves, I caught a glimpse of dirt on her hands. *Sloppy*, I thought. *Dirty hands giving me an injection.* It was getting more difficult to think about anything. *It's not dirt; it's tattoos.*

MELORA SUNDT is a faculty member at the University of Southern California's Rossier School of Education. Melora, her husband, two daughters, four dogs, five rabbits, and Miss America, the chicken, live in Los Angeles. She has the best job ever—allowing her to teach in L.A., Hawaii, and online, with some of the most creative colleagues anywhere. She has been making up stories since she was a kid.

Situational Gravity

Brad Ray

Two hundred and seventy miles above the surface of the Earth floats a collection of pods, parts, and people. Collectively it is know as a space station, but to the astronauts currently residing inside, it's simply known as home.

Astronaut Mike Andrews eyed his fellow 'nauts. Jessy was leaning up against the lockers to his left, arms crossed over her chest. He still needed to figure out how she managed to casually lean in zero-gee and not become a human pinball.

In contrast to her, there was the Russian. Saurus, as Mike called him, was oriented with his head to the "floor." Why he did this, no one could figure out. Maybe since he was from Russia while Mike and Jessy were from America, he just wanted to remind them that America was beneath him. On a globe, at least.

The three spacemen formed a loose triangle, in the middle of which floated an object most dangerous: a cuticle. The obnoxiously offending offing lazily spun in place, mocking Mike. He would remove it, but he needed it there as a lesson to them all.

"So, who did it?" he asked.

"Who did what?" Saurus responded. He gripped the floor and started himself spinning in place.

"Who let a cuticle run free in here?" When no one answered, he tried again. "There's a cuticle in the space station, people. Focus!"

Jessy examined the nails on her left hand. "It wasn't me. I haven't cut mine in several days. Plus, that's not a cuticle, it's a hangnail."

Mike pointed to the object as it slowly spun. "That's a cuticle."

She cleared her throat. "A cuticle, which is sometimes confused with the eponychium, actually refers to several different structures. It can mean the keratinocytes that produce horn protein keratin, or the cuticula pila within a follicle." She rotated her wrist, the nail following suit. "In this case, what we have here is the keratin which would ostensibly be covering the tip of a finger." She smiled at him. "In other words, a common hangnail."

"Whatever," Mike snorted. "It could still be yours. It could have been here for days, hiding, waiting," he challenged her. "Or you could have kept it hidden only to unleash it upon us now."

"Or it could be his," she said, pointing at Saurus.

The Russian was facing away from them, but slowly spinning back around. "It was not mine. That nail is thin, weak. Mine are strong, Russian nails."

Mike peered closer at the cuticle. It was a nail; there was nothing special about it. "When's the last time you clipped, Saurus?"

"This morning, after I exercise. Over in habitat module."

The habitat module was three over and one up from where they currently were. For the piece to have traveled all that way on its own was unlikely. It had help, or one of them was lying.

"Why do you care so much?" Jessy asked. "Beyond the danger of the object floating into your face as you sleep."

"It's disgusting! It's hideous and revolting and disgusting!"

The biologist rolled her eyes. "Whatever."

"Show me your hands, both of you," he commanded.

"Really, Mike?" Jessy asked.

"Yes, really. Hands. Now."

She held out her hands, wrists bent, fingers pointing down. "See? Nothing."

Mike pushed off the floor, floating closer to her. He used one hand to grip her wrist, the other to spread her fingers, moving them around so he could inspect them. Her left hand was clean, no sign of any recent damage to her nails.

He dropped her left hand, reaching for the right. She jerked it back for a moment, before slowly presenting it. A grin spread across his face as he caught what she didn't want him to see. Her right ring finger had a jagged nail.

"Aha!" he cried. "A broken nail. Tell me, when did it break?"

She grimaced. "This morning. I was working on something in the botanical module when I chipped a nail. But I caught the piece that came off and disposed of it!" she scrambled to add.

"Apparently not all of it."

"No, I swear, I got rid of the evidence. That nail can't be mine, and I can prove it."

"How?"

She pulled her hand away from him. "Give me a moment and I'll show you." She turned around, opened one of the lockers and pulled out a pair of tweezers. Several other instruments attempted to escape, but she pushed them back and sealed them in the locker.

Carefully, she plucked the cuticle out of the air, clamping it down with the tweezers. Floating over to the workbench, she lit up the magnifying lamp. She thrust the nail under the light. "See?"

Mike joined his head to hers. "What am I looking at?"

She held her finger with the broken nail under the light right next to the cuticle. "See the scab on my finger? When the nail broke off, my finger bled. If the cuticle was mine, it would show signs of blood on it. But since there is no blood, the cuticle cannot possibly be mine."

Guiding the tweezers, she held the offending object over her broken nail. "Look at the edges, they don't even come close to matching up."

With a hard squeeze, she locked the tweezers down on the nail, letting them go. She held both her hands under the light. "As further evidence of my innocence, I provide this. Look at my nails. There are no jagged edges or points as there would be if I had cut them recently."

Her hands slammed into the table. "With that, you have a perfect trifecta of evidence." Placing a hand over her chest, she bowed. "I rest my case."

"Alright, fine. It wasn't you," he admitted. Her gloating smile said it all. "Which just leaves you, Saurus."

"Какого черта вы собираетесь о чем? Это некоторые серьезные дерьмо. Этот чертов гвоздь не мое!" Saurus spat out.

Mike blinked a few times, before turning to face Jessy. She just shook her head and shrugged. Neither of them knew Russian, a fact that Saurus exploited constantly. For all they knew, he had just cursed them out or been remarking about the weather.

Saurus had finally stopped spinning. With a burly arm he pointed at Mike. "And what about you? You accuse me, but you are not so exempt from accusation." He waved his hand. "Go on, show biologist your hands. I trust her word." With that, he crossed his arms across his chest, glaring up at them from the floor.

"Hey, yeah!" Jessy said. "How do we know it's not yours?"

"Because I haven't clipped my nails in a week!" Mike said.

Jessy put her hands on her hips. "Well then. Prove it."

Mike's face lost his grin. "Uh, I don't see the need for that."

"Why not? You курица?" Saurus asked with a smile.

Mike set his face into a hard look. "No. I am simply above reproach. My cleaning habits are meticulous."

"фигня. None above reproach."

Mike's hands went behind his back. "You have all seen me," he said, sticking out his chin. "I am the cleanest one aboard this vessel."

"Cleanest, yes," Jessy said. "But that doesn't mean you

can't make mistakes." She reached out, grasping his arms. "Sasha, help me out here."

The Russian grinned. Pushing off the floor with his hands, he flipped over in the air, wrapping Mike in an embrace. Mike squirmed and struggled, but he couldn't escape the grasp of Saurus.

"Стой смирно червь!" Saurus shouted. "Jessy, grab hands."

He felt Jessy's hands clamp over his wrists. No matter how much he struggled, he was no match for her iron will. Slowly, inexorably, she drew his hands under the light. "No! I won't submit!" he shouted. "I am above reproach, you filthy animals!"

It took several minutes of struggling and shouting, but finally, Jessy released him. "He's clean, literally. His nails are cleaner than any woman's I've seen, and they definitely haven't been clipped lately. Unless he used a nail file."

"There aren't any of those aboard. We can't risk nail dust getting into the instruments and equipment," Mike said.

"I dunno, prissypants," Jessy said. "Someone like you? You'd try and sneak one on board."

Saurus finally let him go. With as much dignity as he could muster, Mike oriented himself upright, smoothing down his flightsuit. "I would never try something so heinous." Once he was sure his suit was wrinkle free, he turned on Saurus. "Now, what about your nails?"

Saurus shrugged. "I already said my nails are Russian." He held his large hands under the light.

Jessy peered down at them. "He's clean." She grimaced. "Well, not clean, but they are certainly in one piece."

Mike took one look at the Russian's nails and blanched. They were horribly filthy. "How can you stand that?" he asked.

Saurus laughed. "Is easy. Dirt makes Russian nails strong. Makes Russian stomachs even stronger. Also makes my wife's borscht close to edible."

"Ah, you found my nail," a tinny voice said. Mike looked around, but didn't see anyone else in the room besides the three of them. In fact, other than the three of them, there was no one else on the station.

A whirring sound drew their attention as a panel in the wall slid aside, revealing a robotic claw. "Thank you, I've been scanning for that pesky thing ever since I lost it during my morning cleaning." The claw gripped the nail, drawing it back into the panel, which closed once more.

Mike blinked his eyes. "Did the computer just say it lost a nail?"

A writer by day, chef by night, BRAD RAY enjoys the little things in life. A good plate of food is the ultimate quest reward. Just as the pen is mightier than the sword. Astronauts should never have to eat freeze-dried food. That sort of thing puts anyone in a bad mood. To rescue them from that cruel fate, is Brad's idea of the perfect date. For more whimsical musings and bad poetry, you can find Brad on Twitter @BradRay44.

Second Sunrise

K. Andrew Turner

THERE'S NOT MUCH to tell. The first people aboard the space station Second Sunrise, after the rich like the Umbersteens, were the Vietnamese. There were always house personnel: chefs and butlers to run the daily household. But manicurists, no. To avoid spending a fortune to send their wives back to Earth, a few husbands brought up salon workers—the cheapest they could find. There had been parties and balls, but none of the ladies had thought to bring along a maid, and the butlers did not know how to style hair or fix broken nails. Though it was meant for the rich to escape the poor, Second Sunrise was less than it was dreamed to be. There would always have to be workers.

After a few years, Second required maintenance. All space stations do. The small staff they had aboard in the beginning–Rodrigo, Shelly and François–wasn't sensitive enough to the residents' needs. I came during the clandestine call, badly in need of work after mastering engineering at Beta Numatics, to help with Life Support Systems as a Waste Removal Specialist. I cleaned up shit and ended up fixing more plumbing ducts than I ever thought I would have to. But it paid. Second always paid on time and just slightly more than anywhere else. I've seen their salons and parlors and fancy, real-wood furniture, wallpaper and enormous, hand-woven rugs from Tibet; I'm not sure they miss the money.

Second was built differently than the rest of the stations. Sphere-like in concept, the station housed large complexes that each had a view of the stars. Much of the machinery necessary to life was within the center with no access to spectacular, vertiginous views. Whoever designed Second should win an award for foresight. While there were no "apartments" per se, like Alpha Numatics–those rather small, tight spaces with only a bed, washbasin/waste remover, and tiny refrigeration unit–Second had the space and hookups for basic life support within the heart; we didn't have the luxury of separate space like in most stations. Someone knew rich people.

It was in one of these Cubbies, as we call them, that I used to share my life with Dolores. We happened to have been assigned the same Cubby—think tiny cramped space with barely room for a bedroll, and pipes overhead. I rarely saw her, except on Sundays, and then only for a few moments before and after she returned from the small chapel a few of the religious Catholics set up—they are still looking for a priest or whatever they call them, from what I understand.

Unlike Alpha Numatics, Second is not as hard and metallic. Each Cubby has cardcloth dividing the Cubbies –mostly recycled cardboard and castoff cloth blended together—painted a pale yellow the ladies call Daffodil Spring. I have a Single Standard bed: six feet lengthwise, three feet across, and two inches high. I brought my aquamarine sheets with me when I moved. They don't clash at least. There were two lights above the bed and a short box that usually has my reader on it. I generally have an extra pair of clothes inside—which I never work in.

Mrs. Umbersteen gave a small screen of painted swans to Dolores that serves as our bathroom and sleep divider. We are one of the few lucky for such privacy. I think it's because Dolores doesn't like to see me naked.

I've been to the Umbersteen's twice. They have a slightly larger complex of rooms that face the moon. Mr. Umbersteen, drunk the second night I'd been there, told me that was because he and his wife are night owls. I had been summoned. Both Chesapeake and Jamal, the two other guys on duty for the shift, had been called to other residencies. I didn't mind the Umbersteens. Not many ask for me by name, but Mr. Umbersteen said he would again next time they had an incident. I suppose it might mean something to another person, but me? I'm waiting on something better.

I dislike Mr. Wrigley most of all. He owns two residences on Second, side-by-side, and demanded a door from one to the other be put in. Apparently this had been going on for a while, and I was, unfortunately, assigned to be on the installation team—something I had never done before. I was assigned cut-out duty, a rather nasty process. The initial stages of installation, which require some knowledge of opening mechanisms—standard protocol for residence to public area doors be a certain material and dimension. One of the reasons that Mr. Wrigley was annoyed was because he wanted wooden doors, but Second firmly stood by that the door was private-to-public-to-private and thus required a standard door or no door at all.

Mr. Wrigley asked me if I knew about wooden doors.

"No," I told him.

"Nobody knows how to hang a god-damn door on this station. Worthless."

I remember the bookcases—three of them, floor to ceiling—filled with books of all colors and topics that we had to move so as not to catch a fire and kill us all. There weren't enough workers to have a first crew move everything. So I heaved and shoved and lifted until the room was clear.

Turning on the Operations Laser is like suddenly becoming a god. I could have destroyed all the life in that room if I had wanted.

"Jeremy, you know how to use one of these, right?" Jamal had asked.

"Of course," I said. "I have a *degree*."

Jamal rolled his eyes. What did he know of such things? What difference did it make if I had used one or not before? How different could it be than fixing plumbing?

The stupid old man watched the entire time. I'm not sure why, but he just stood there, arms crossed over his chest, scowling. It was a good job as far as I could tell. Surely it was good enough for regulation!

But Jamal told me, "Go take a break. And eat or something." Then he gave me this severe look. My mother used to give me those same looks when I'd done something wrong. When I came back, it smelled like fresh electrical destruction, a burning ozone and metal that only cutting walls made. Jamal hadn't trusted me enough to do it by myself.

"He's a good kid," I overheard Jamal say. "But he's got some wrong notions about his education."

"I don't care about damn degrees! I came to this damn station to get away from idiots!"

Jamal shrugged but said nothing more when he saw me. What was that all about?

I almost walked away, but I just shook my head instead. I was used to such treatment from people. The old man gave us an extra frown for good measure before we left. When I asked Jamal later, he only shrugged. We rarely spoke after that.

Dolores once told me that Mr. Wrigley didn't have a wife but managed to see little Dolores anyway for all his nail needs. She was one of the few manicurists not Vietnamese. Beauty school graduate.

"We have education in common," I said when she told me.

She only gave me this really weird look, glancing at the paper affixed to my wall.

"Did you print that out?"

"Of course, Beta Numatics Schools always let you print them out."

Whenever I mentioned it afterward, she held my hand and said, "Oh, sweet mijo." There was something about the sadness in her eyes.

Anyway, she told me she would trim Mr. Wrigley's nails and clear away the gross stuff to avoid infection and ingrown nails. She once said that his feet were like lumpy potatoes, dry and rough and wrinkly. In this rare conversation, she gesticulated wildly to show the nails flying everywhere. Then she shook her head, "He can't even do it himself. Most of the other guys do, but he can't even reach his toes. They all think we are," and this is where she giggled and grabbed her rosary, "making love. But it's really just about cuticles in the space station." I laughed with her.

I used to hang out with Chesapeake, before the whole Mr. Wrigley thing, as we came on the same shuttle, but he stopped talking to me after we had sex that one time. He loved drinking, and I liked hanging out with him. He was fun and easy-going, even Dolores liked him, and she didn't like a lot of people. I remember that night more clearly than I do most others.

We were in my Cubby and Ches had brought along a bottle of vodka. It was the first time we really hung out alone, outside of our work shifts.

"Stole it from that fucker, Mr. Chiddester, last shift. He won't even know it's gone."

He gave it to me to sample, generously, before asking for it back and sampling it just as much. We talked about all the people we knew on the station, we talked about its short history, we talked about the workers and employers, we talked of politics on Earth.

The bottle was half empty by then. He smiled, and that's when I felt the urge to kiss him. It wasn't a shock, I don't think, to him. We were on my bed, the lights adjusted to mimic late evening.

"So, where did you go to engineering school?" he asked me, his hand on my leg, after we'd made love.

"Beta substation on Alpha Numatics," I said.

Ches leaned back for a moment and then tilted his head. "Didn't think they had schools there. Isn't it just more slums?"

I shrugged. Hey, I am proud to have gone there, to have graduated and left for some place better. "Where did you go?"

He laughed, "I went to Hap Hazard."

I wasn't sure what he meant, so I raised the bottle to our achievements. "To us. We did good."

He removed his hand and gave me this weird smile. We finished the bottle and disposed of it. He said goodbye shortly thereafter, and we haven't spoken since.

I still see him in the Uniform Distribution Room. He looks at me occasionally, but I don't think he sees me. I don't know what went wrong. Jamal wouldn't say much, but he said he talked to Ches a few times, but Ches told him to stop asking for me. Jamal said once he thinks I make stuff up in my head. Jamal says a lot of things, mostly that I should mind my own business.

"Chesapeake? Jeremy, you should leave him alone. If he's not talking to you, respect the man's decision."

"But he used to talk to me. We used to hang out."

"Leave it."

Then, after the whole Mr. Wrigley thing, Jamal will only acknowledge me. He won't say much else anymore. I probably pressed him too far about being friends with Chesapeake, and he told me, "You used to go to school, too. Did you used to know the President?" Dolores, before she left, was the only one who talked to me on a regular basis. She'd always roll her beads in her hands when talking to me as if she were praying for me. I don't know where she went. Maybe it was that I used to drink? I haven't seen her, but the other girls say she's around, still working. Maybe it was the whole co-ed thing. I don't know if I'll get a new Cubbymate or not, but I'm hoping I do. It's lonely, much like it was back at Beta substation.

K. ANDREW TURNER writes literary and speculative fiction, poetry, and nonfiction. He teaches and mentors creative writers with traditional and meditative techniques. He is a freelance editor and also the Editor-in-Chief of *East Jasmine Review*—a literary publication. He lives, works, and writes in the San Gabriel Valley, just east of Los Angeles. Andrew would like to remind everyone to eat their fruits and veggies, as they are a good source of vitamins and help fight viruses, space aliens, and a mother's constant nagging—really. You can find more about him and his work at www.kandrewturner.com. Follow him on Twitter @kandrewturner.

A Magical Trip to the Moon

Irene Kang, Ben Kang, and Matthew Kang

Jessica

I WAS WALKING AROUND my neighborhood when I felt my phone ring. I took it out of my pocket and read the text message from my best friend, Jeannie.

Jeannie had been an orphan until she was adopted. However, her parents (not the real ones) barely knew her.

The message said: "Meet me at Wilson Park." When I got there, Jeannie was glaring at me furiously and smiling wickedly. *Wait. What did I do? Is it because of the shortcake I ate or that I beat her in a game?* I thought deeply.

I walked to her and said, "Sorry."
She looked at me and replied, "What for?"

MICHAEL

"Michael, tell Jeannie that I made sandwiches and I'm inviting her over for lunch," said my mom.

"OK," I said as I walked out the door to find my cousin, Jeannie. Her adoptive parents were nice and all, but Jeannie preferred hanging out with my mom and me most afternoons.

I walked to the park, where Jeannie said she would be. Once I got there, I saw Jeannie talking to another girl. "Hey Jeannie!" I started to walk over to her, and then suddenly an object or animal fell out of the bush and landed right in front of my feet. I didn't know what it was, but it looked like a small mouse or rat. I reached down to touch it, but at that moment, it jumped up and bit my finger. Before I fell unconscious, I heard Jeannie scream my name and saw her and the other girl running towards me. I fell down hard on the grass.

JEANNIE

We ran to Michael, my cousin, and I saw a strange creature. *Weird*, I thought as it looked at us then ran away into a bush.

I called my auntie, who called 911. They took Michael to the hospital and I left Jessica behind at the park because my auntie and I had to follow the ambulance.

Michael

When I woke up, I didn't know what time it was, where I was, or what had just happened to me. I was inside a small, cozy hospital room, with comforting blue light and a soft bed. There was someone in the room next to me, but I didn't know who it was. As I groaned with pain, I asked, "Who's there?"

"How do you feel, son?" my mom asked with a shaky, yet relieved, voice.

"My body hurts everywhere. Where am I and what just happened?"

"Well, it's sort of hard to explain, but I guess I'll try. The nurse just said that you've been diagnosed with a very rare disease called astronomical hemophilia.

"What's that?" I asked.

"It's a very rare disease, and the only cure for it is to drink moon rock tea. However, most people die from the disease because they won't risk going to the moon," my mom said as she tried to hold down her sobs.

Jessica

The next day, I went outside and walked to the park, coincidently seeing Jeannie.

"Uh ... hi!" I said.

Jeannie snorted and gave me a devil-eye look, then knocked me out.

When I woke up, I found myself tied to an enormous

rocket targeted at the moon. I was wearing a space suit. Suddenly Jeannie, now my nemesis, appeared in front of me, standing on the roof of the rocket.

"Hey! You will go to outer space and bring moon rocks back. You must complete this mission or you'll be stuck in space. Also, *gravitydaboo*! There, now you're space trained so that you know how to stay in one place and won't fly off into the galaxy," Jeannie said. "Oh, and don't worry—I'll be able to watch you and will teleport you back to Earth when your mission is complete."

"Wait, you're a wizard! Oh, and … WHAT! How can you see me that far away?" I asked.

"There is a camera glued to your helmet," Jeannie said.

"Oh. But … Why do I need to go?"

"I am afraid of space, but I LOVE rocks! Duh! Why else do you think I'd send you there? Oh, and Michael needs the moon rocks." Jeannie said this like it was obvious, that I should have naturally assumed this, instead of thinking she just enjoyed torturing me.

"Why can't you just teleport me to the moon?" I asked.

"Because it's *so* much more fun to see you stuck to a rocket. Oh, and don't worry, the rocket won't explode. It's the latest model and super safe. The pilot is very good at his job. I'm sure it's not his first mission or anything."

MR. KANG

On March 15th, I was given a degree in rocket studies, and became an astronaut. On that night, I was invited to a celebration in honor of my graduation at Mesoamerica's biggest university. At the party, however, I met Neil Armstrong Jr. Jr., and we had a conversation about astronomy. I was going to die from too much information when he suddenly gave me a folder. There was a paper inside. The paper gave me my first ever assignment: to pilot a rocket to the moon along with 1,000 people to observe the moon's shape, size, and surface.

Three Months Later ...

1,000 passengers sat patiently on an enormous rocket, all of them waiting for me, their captain, Captain Kang, to arrive. I quickly changed into my airtight suit and walked up to the rocket. While walking, I realized how dangerous the flight would be if I made a mistake. The flight was 384,400 kilometers and I was piloting a rocket the size of three regular ones. However, this was a four million dollar offer, so I couldn't turn it down, even if I was scared. I really needed the money to save an endangered troop of lemurs in Madagascar. I walked in and warmed up the boosters.

JESSICA

The engine was starting so I figured there were only ten seconds before the rocket launched into space and I might possibly die.

What if Jeannie isn't really a wizard? What if she's only a mediocre wizard? What if her space breathing spell doesn't work?

I closed my eyes as the countdown started.

10 ... 9 ... 8 ... 7 ... 6 ... 5 ... 4 ... 3 ... 2 ... 1

When the rocket landed on the moon, I opened my eyes

and the rope untied itself—*CREEPY*. *I guess Jeannie is a pretty good wizard,* I thought.

I observed the galaxy and saw many space stations near Jupiter. But I didn't see Pluto since it wasn't a planet anymore.

WOW! I was amazed to see so many comets. But they were so big and scary I wanted to go home. I quickly looked around to gather something ... what was it? I thought ... I thought ... *MOON ROCKS*! *Huh! I remembered!*

MR. KANG

"We have now arrived. You may unbuckle your seat belts and observe." I unbuckled and looked through the window onto the moon's surface and saw something totally unexpected: a girl outside collecting moon rocks!

"Hello everyone, this is an emergency. Please sit down in your seats until I come back into the rocket. I will have to go outside to investigate. Just stay here," I said with a nervous and scared voice. I quickly put on my space suit and walked out onto the moon's surface.

JESSICA

I gathered a few rocks and held them in my hand, in front of my helmet camera. As I turned around, I saw an astronaut walking towards me, but my body was flickering at the same time.

MR. KANG

"That's strange! I know I saw a girl. I'm sure I saw a girl, right there." But the girl with long dark hair and glasses was gone, and I realized I was talking to the moon.

Suddenly, I heard an alarm ring out, and I rushed back to the rocket to investigate. I looked at the cockpit window and quickly saw a thin crack. I opened my emergency pocket, and in it, there was a nail clipper and tape. "What the heck are these for?"

I looked at my hands and suddenly came up with a crazy but genius idea. I grabbed the clipper and started to clip my nails. The passengers looked at me in confusion. I tried to put a fingernail in the crack, but it wouldn't fit. It was too big and curved. The crack needed something even smaller, thinner, and more flexible. So I cut my cuticle. It fit perfectly! The cuticle didn't fall out of the crack and secured the window. I used the tape to seal the crack.

"Yeah! A cuticle in a space station saves the day!" one of the passengers screamed out.

Neil Armstrong Jr. Jr. might have said that technically it was a rocket and not a space station, but I'm a practical man.

I enjoyed my hero status and flew everyone safely back to Earth. "My first job rocked!"

JESSICA

After I saw my body flickering, I closed my eyes and soon opened them again, seeing Jeannie in the park. I handed her the rocks, then walked home. Suddenly she appeared in front of me and said, "*Memorylosedebrada.*"

I forgot everything except my best friend Jeannie, my family, my everyday routines, and my other important things.

"Um, Jessica. I have to go. Bye!" Jeannie said nicely.

After that, I went back home.

JEANNIE

I walked to my favorite cousin's house and went in. I gave the moon rocks to my aunt for her to make cold moon rock tea for Michael. I really wanted him to live.

MICHAEL

I woke up in the morning and saw my mom standing next to me holding a glass cup with cold moon rock tea. She said, "Here you go. This is the cure to your disease. Enjoy."

I grabbed the cup and gulped it down at once. All of a sudden, I started feeling weird. My stomach and throat were hurting and within a few minutes, I was lying unconscious.

A few hours later, I was on a hospital bed again, but this time, it wasn't as bad as before. The nurse told us that I had been cured of my disease, and I was healthy again. My mom hugged me, and Jeannie was there. Jeannie said a funny word and then I forgot all about being sick. I walked out and went to the park to play.

Mr. Kang

I went to the park after flying my first space mission. I stopped to blink my eyes. I couldn't believe it. I saw *the* girl. She had the same hair, the same glasses, and I knew it must be the same girl from the moon's surface. I walked up to her and asked if she had visited the moon recently. She looked at me like I was crazy.

Jessica

This man started to walk up to me, and he asked me something. I gave him a strange look that said, *what are you talking about?* He looked familiar, but I didn't really know who he was. He was babbling something about the moon. I had absolutely *no* idea what he was talking about.

Mr. Kang

She didn't understand me, and as I tried to solve what was going on, another boy approached. He asked who I was and why I was badgering the girl. I explained everything I saw on the moon, and they both didn't seem to understand what I was saying.

Michael

When I saw the man, whatever he said to me made no sense at all. Then, I saw Jeannie, who I asked about the situation. She hesitated and tried to look away. I forced her to explain what happened, and she told us the truth.

Jeannie

I wished I'd never gone to the park to meet Michael and Jessica. Because of that little "coincidence," I had to tell everybody what had happened. However, I left some parts out of the story, such as the part where Jessica was teleported from the moon back to Earth.

Jessica

After Jeannie's confession, I didn't even know what to think. I scratched my eyebrows. *Hmm. How come I can't feel anything?* "Hey, why does it feel like my eyebrows are gone, and where did they go? Jeannie, is there something you need to tell me?"

JEANNIE

When Jessica asked me about her eyebrows, I started stuttering. *Uhh, what should I say? What should I say?* "Umm ... well, it's just that ... it's just that I'm still practicing my teleporting skills and sometime pieces don't always .... Well, things go missing on occasion and I think that your eyebrows ... MEMORYLOSEDABRA!"

All three of them, Mr. Kang, Jessica, and Michael lost their memories of what happened on the moon and carried on with their lives. I eventually learned how to fix Jessica's eyebrows and in the process discovered that when a spell goes wrong, it creates a strange little creature that can cause astronomical hemophilia if it bites you. *Isn't that weird?*

IRENE KANG is a fifth grader. She has a dog that she loves and cares a lot for. Her dog is her best companion when she is at home. She has two brothers and worked on this story with them. Irene loves to watch television and likes to read mythical books like the *Percy Jackson* series. She also likes to ice skate on hot days.

BEN KANG is a bright and enthusiastic seventh grader who loves reading books and doing math. His hobby is reading, and he also enjoys out-of-state vacations. When he graduated from elementary school, he received the Presidential Award signed by President Obama, and he also boasts several music trophies and basketball memorabilia.

Currently, he resides in Torrance with his family and his loyal dog Choco.

MATTHEW KANG is an upcoming eighth grader. His greatest interest is music; he has performed in many concerts and won several music awards. In the Southern California School Band and Orchestra Association (SCSBOA), he and his advanced middle school band earned the second highest rank. He hopes to one day become a professional musician. As a bonus, his love of music encourages him to earn high grades at school, thus he is a straight-A-student. He also thinks it would be really fun to stand on the moon someday.

The Olopa Bean

Dan Nowell

I HAD BEEN WORKING for nearly four months in southern Guatemala when I heard the news that my former colleague and current adversary, Gabby Dominguez, had publicly and professionally dispelled the legend of the Olopa bean, the object of my arduous expedition and the sole reason for my being in this part of the world. And no, she didn't contact me directly to inform me of her supposed findings. I found out while watching the local evening news while drinking some over-caffeinated coffee out of a triangle paper cup. There was no internet access in this remote part of the highlands, so my only connection to the rest of the world was through the one news channel my little television set received when the weather was decent.

There was no way I could convince my employers back home, who had been financing my expedition up until then, that Gabby was lying. See, I was working for a large restaurant operator based in the

U.S. that was in the process of opening up a specialty coffee division. And, like I tell everyone who will listen, it was a super-secret project among the corporate restaurant world that was designed to blow the lids off coffeehouse chains and coffee distributors across the nation. It was so secret, in fact, that they didn't tell me much else about it. BG Concepts, the company that contracted me, said they had strategically purchased thousands of acres in Guatemala in hopes of finding the legendary Olopa bean, thought to be the most distinguished and complex coffee bean ever known to man. Or at least to the white man, that is, because it was rumored to have been drunk only by a local indigenous tribe and was virtually unknown to the rest of the world.

From unverifiable accounts, rumors, and twice-translated stories, the legend goes that it had a complexity of spice, smoke, flowers, and a tiny bit of chocolate thrown in for good measure. And because this Strictly Hard Bean-grade coffee was found in a mountain-protected basin, it was impervious to the wet ocean weather. In theory, it was the perfect bean if it really existed. And the first company that could get its greedy hands on it and put it in front of coffee snobs from Seattle to Boston could control the entire U.S. coffee market. Now, how I came to find out about this Olopa bean is a whole other story.

But it's good, so I'll tell you anyway.

My psycho ex-wife, or should I say *loco* because she was Spanish, was born and raised in the region I was holed up in. And despite all my preconceived notions, she didn't cook or clean, nor do much else for that matter, but she did know one thing and one thing only: coffee. She immigrated to the U.S. for reasons other than being poor, and I met her in Miami when I was involved in a very different type of business. Her family had run a huge coffee estate ever since her great-grandparents crossed the ocean from Spain and started spreading the language, among other things, to the natives. Her family thinks I married her for her money, and my family thinks she married me for the green card, although neither was true. It was old-fashioned love, if short lived.

Her first language was Spanish and her second was English, which she learned from a private school. But more important than Spanish or English, she spoke Ch'orti', the language spoken by the local indigenous Maya people that worked the fields. This connection allowed her incredible access to the world of the Ch'orti' Maya, an unlikely feat for someone who wasn't even Maya.

When she ran the estate, she found it odd that the Ch'orti' would never drink the coffee they harvested except for when it was offered to them, just to be polite. In the five years she ran it, she never caught a single employee stealing coffee beans or even asking to bring some home to his family. And the coffee the estate produced was of the highest caliber—so good that it would make a pacifist from Portland want to stab someone over a cup of it. It was that good, if you believe the legend.

She set off to investigate by snooping around a Ch'orti' village until she discovered that they did, in fact, drink coffee, and a lot of it. How my ex-wife got one of them to talk is still a touchy subject, so let me just gloss over it by saying it may or may not have involved her, a bottle of *aguardiente*, and a peasant farmer named Candino who finally blabbed. His story goes that after the Guatemalan army scorched to death every living thing in a small mountainside village in the

1960's—and by every living thing I mean plants, animals, and humans—the land was left infertile for decades. The Ch'orti' tried planting all kinds of seeds to no avail. Finally, one rainy spring morning, a farmer looking for the machete he dropped the night before happened upon a tiny green leaf sprouting through the earth. He couldn't believe his eyes at the sight of this because as far as everyone knew, no one had attempted to plant a seed in the ground for decades. Of course, the Ch'orti' probably have some story of a magic bird that dropped the seed from its mouth while soaring over the village, but all you need to take from it is that this sprouting was special, and no matter what grew from it, be it a weed, a flower, or a coffee tree, it was sacred to them and not to be touched by outsiders.

I, on the other hand, knew better than to believe a *Jack and the Magic Beanstalk* story and determined that there had to be more of these trees growing in at least a hundred-mile radius of this supposed sacred coffee tree. It was ecologically inevitable. I figured if it were possible for one unique tree to have sprouted from this infertile soil, then there had to be others just like it, and I was determined not to come home until I found one. I didn't care what I had to do to get it.

It was about my third month in Guatemala when Raul, my Spanish translator, informed me that some locals spotted a woman with a team of assistants going from village to village inquiring about the bean. They assumed she was from the U.S. because she wore sunglasses and jeans, something practically forbidden in these parts of town. Just from that description, I surmised that it was Gabby Dominguez. I also surmised what she was doing so far from home. We both worked together a few years back at Hal Restaurant Brands' beverage division because of our unique knowledge of the coffee industry. I may have mentioned the Olopa bean story to her in a drunken stupor trying to impress her with my knowledge, or it might have slipped while we were intimate, but I'm sure I mentioned it to her at least once, and I knew she was trying to beat me to it. She and the company both hated me for reasons I can't talk about because of a court order, but trust me when I say they had several reasons for finding the bean first.

In my mind, the whole world was waiting for me to discover this bean. I felt like Christopher Columbus. If I had come back with anything but the Olopa bean, even if I came back with something that could loosely be defined as the Olopa bean and tried to convince people that it was special, it would have been analogous to an astronaut arguing that he found extraterrestrial life when all he found was a cuticle in the space station. Sure, it might have technically fit the definition, but it definitely wasn't the big breakthrough that would forever change humanity.

But once Gabby made the public announcement and laughingly dismissed the legend of the Olopa bean, I knew my financing was finished and my paid journey was over. She had destroyed me professionally. No one would respect me anymore. Of course, BG Concepts would believe her lies over me because she put herself up as some coffee expert and me as some nut looking for a unicorn. At that point, even if I were to have found it, she would argue that it wasn't the Olopa bean and that it was just another bean that had already been discovered. And to make matters worse, it was all a lie. She *knew* the Olopa bean existed. But if it were to be found, she wanted to be the one to find it. Or at least give the credit to the Ch'orti' people. She was born in Florida but was of Guatemalan descent, so there was no way she wanted another white man to make yet another discovery in Mesoamerica. It was your typical case of textbook racism, but I didn't care anymore. I was no longer going to get paid either way. But I really wanted to taste that coffee.

Upon hearing Gabby's report, I decided to skip town for a while to decide my next move. While Raul studied a map of Guatemala that looked like it was from 1980, I threw our backpacks and empty water jugs into the back seat. We sped off in the Jeep, and I flicked my cigarette over the cliff so I could firmly grab the wheel with both hands as we drove down a muddy, mountainous road. It rained hard the previous night so the roads were a wreck. I glanced up for a second, and among the dense trees I could make out a pack of monkeys swinging quickly from tree branch to tree branch, almost as if they were trying to keep up with us. I wanted to get off that mountain as fast as I could to get away from those monkeys while avoiding mudslides and whatever else Mother Nature had in store for us. I stomped on the gas pedal with my muddy sandal, and we hightailed it down and around the mountain.

We stopped at the first village we encountered on flat land in order to fill our water jugs and eat some breakfast before I was to leave the country. I was going to go to El Salvador for a while to figure out my next move. There was a girl that I used to see who had invited me to stay at a small house her family owned. I didn't mind staying there for a while because I enjoyed being in this region of the world, and Central Americans seemed to embrace me. Plus, my knowledge of local cultures and knack for languages tend to open doors, which makes it easy for me to get around.

The server brought to our table a plate of scrambled eggs with tomatoes and onions, a thin piece of *carne asada*, black beans with tortilla chips, and a couple of fresh, handmade tortillas. It didn't look appetizing to me at all so I just stuck with coffee, which was pretty gross but not as bad as what I had been drinking earlier. Raul kept on pestering me to try the food, so I took a bite of the tortilla and said it was good before even tasting it, just to placate him. My mind was still focused on the Olopa bean, and I couldn't get over the fact that I still hadn't tasted that coffee.

I looked over the map Raul was studying to see how far from the border we were when I saw something that stopped my heart for a moment. I don't know where he found this map, or how old it was, but it appeared that we were in the village of Quezaltepeque, about a couple hours from the border. Now this wasn't exciting in and of itself, but what was incredible was that this particular map showed something that no other map I had ever seen showed: a small village called Olopa, and it was about thirty miles away from where we were.

Upon confirming with the waitress that the village of Olopa actually existed, and after a few minutes of me screaming at Raul for not knowing about this place before, we ran back to the Jeep so fast he forgot to pay the bill. It dawned on me that that was why Gabby was in this part of the country, and that she dispelled the legend of the bean just to throw me off and to buy her and her crew some time to find it in Olopa. I knew I was within thirty miles of the bean, but time was running out. She could have already found it. I realized that I had been given a second chance, and I wasn't about to let it pass me by.

After a bumpy and twisty hour-and-a-half drive through the mountains, we arrived at the small village of Olopa where we saw hundreds—no, make that *thousands*—of villagers parading through the streets, carrying floats of Jesus and some saints who were unfamiliar to me. I plugged my nose because the village was encompassed with an omnipresent burning smell, which Raul told me was from the wood stoves inside the villagers' homes. Raul neglected to inform me that it was Holy Week, meaning the streets were packed with pedestrians. Gabby was probably already there and I was desperate to beat her to the bean. I started punching the horn like a New York cabbie to get these people out of the way, but I kept getting lost driving up and down the steep concrete streets. I knew I was getting closer to the main plaza because in between buildings I could see a mass of people gathering. I figured that's where the main festivities were taking place, and if they were celebrating Holy Week in Olopa style, they had to have been drinking that coffee.

These people were not moving fast enough, so I pointed my pistol in the air and fired off a few rounds to let them know I meant business. To my surprise they didn't even flinch, as if it were common to hear gunfire during religious ceremonies. I kept my hand pressed firmly on the horn to signal that it was an emergency while Raul stood up in the Jeep and shouted commands in Spanish to the crowd.

Our ride through the village took a turn for the worse when I made a hard left around a tight corner onto a narrow street and smashed right into another float on wheels that was being prepped. The impact sent it rolling down the steep street while villagers dived out of the way. It ended up crashing through a storefront. I looked behind me and noticed I had effectively halted the parade, which was good, but I now had thousands of angry villagers running toward me. I drove down the same street because it was now clear of pedestrians and veered right to access the village's lowest streets.

Through some scrawny trees, and at a distance of a few hundred yards, I finally saw the main plaza! Thousands of villagers were gathered around an old church, but I couldn't make out much more than that. I swear I thought I saw them drinking from elaborate Maya coffee cups, but I only caught a glimpse because I had to keep my eyes on the road. I shifted gears and turned toward the plaza, but to my surprise we were driving straight toward a National Civil Police vehicle filled with armed agents pointing shotguns at our heads. I looked behind us to see if I could back up and escape, but I saw half the village chasing after us with machetes. Raul had already put his hands up and begun to exit the Jeep. There was nothing else I could do but sit there and catch my breath and let them arrest me. After all, I could have just acted like a lost tourist and blamed the reckless driving on a dropped contact lens. I'm a good liar.

While being transported to the police station, the agents screamed a litany of charges against me, none of which had anything to do with my actions in Olopa. It turns out that the cigarette I flicked off the cliff landed on a straw hut and burned down half a village. At least that's what they claimed. It had been a rainy week so I don't see how my cigarette could have hit anything dry. But I had already come to the conclusion that the whole country was out to get me, probably initiated by my ex-wife or Gabby, who blabbed to the authorities that I was in the country for reasons other than finding the Olopa bean. I just kept my mouth shut and waited for an attorney who never arrived.

I was found guilty of a lot of stuff I didn't understand because I wasn't provided with a translator. They didn't even notify the U.S. Embassy of my arrest. I was furious, and I begged and pleaded for them to let me go, but no one would listen to me. I told them all about Gabby, and how she set me up, but they didn't seem to believe me. The country simply didn't respect me. I started smashing my chair over the desk and putting my fists through walls, all the while vehemently denying all charges against me. Someone hit me over the head with a stone statue, and the next thing I remember is waking up in some remote jail. I spent my first night there wide awake because there were these Guatemalan howler monkeys outside my cell that kept wailing all night, scaring the death out of me. They reminded me of the Madagascar lemurs I encountered on another mission, only these were ten times scarier and seemed hell-bent on psychologically torturing me day and night. I had no contact with the outside world, so I could only imagine Gabby being featured on the cover of every coffee trade publication known to man due to her supposed discovery of the Olopa bean.

I was never told how long I was to remain incarcerated in this hellhole or how I could gain my freedom. I've begun to lose track of the days and months and years. If only I could go back in time, I would have done things a lot different. I never would have let them arrest me in Olopa. I would have shot those agents and ran over to the main plaza to grab a bag of Olopa beans to bring back home. If Gabby were there, I would have thrown a handful of them in her face. But hindsight is twenty-twenty. I haven't accepted my fate just yet, but there's not much I can currently do about it. One day my story will be heard, and I'm sure somebody will come looking for me.

Until that day arrives, I'm destined to remain locked up alone. Aside from the howler monkeys, the only other sign of life I encounter in my cell is the gloved hand of an anonymous person who slips a tray of food under my door every morning at the exact same time the monkeys outside start to laugh and manically pound on my cell walls. It's always the same meal, too: a cup of lukewarm oatmeal, an overripe plantain, and a hot, steaming cup of the most complex, spice and chocolate-infused, Strictly Hard Bean-grade coffee that I have ever tasted in all of my life.

DAN NOWELL is a senior writer at a Los Angeles financial services firm. His writing credits include a quarterly financial publication titled *The Capital Connector*, and this author bio. Before writing commercial nonfiction, he received his bachelor's degree in English from UCLA while taking the bus from Koreatown and back. If you like liquor stores, panhandlers, or the occasional hangover-curing street taco, you will love his unique collection of Koreatown short stories. Start reading at www.dannowell.com.

I Spy True Love

Susie Tex

WHO IS THAT? Just play it cool.
   Five seconds later, a whoosh of air entered the room and a man emerged from the mist. He stalked across the room and boldly, confidently, headed to the scented antibacterial lotion section.

OK, slowly make your way over to him …. Oops, too fast …. Oh, these loofahs look interesting …. OK, he's looking down again. What to say? What to say? Think fast.

The man, looking down, furrowed his perfect forehead as he compared Guilt Monkey Nectar and Parkway Earth Delight.

Oh, perfect hands …. Look at his concentration. He's handsome and a thoughtful consumer. Let me run my fingers through my hair. Nice, classic flirt move. Ah, fingers stuck—did I brush my hair this morning?

"Hey … um, Guilt Monkey Nectar?" she squeaked. He looked up and met her eyes. And smiled.

* * * *

Once in a while, Joanna has a very good day.

Despite it being four months ago, that day was a very good day and Joanna often replayed the scene in her mind. She remembered how he showed her both bottles and asked what she preferred. And she may have slightly fumbled in real life, but in her memory she perfectly quipped that it's the guilt that makes monkeys smell so sweet. And he laughed. A perfect musical laugh that made her sweat a little and smile a lot.

Ever since that day, Joanna visited the lotion store, hoping to see him again. She couldn't catch his name because he had to leave so quickly, but she flashed her half-full loyalty card hoping he'd see it and come back to find her there. Never mind that there were thousands of chain stores in Southern California. He was so observant about the lotion that she knew he caught a glance at her driver's license with the very prominent zip code.

And ever since that day, Joanna had been practicing for the perfect follow-up. She was not going to be caught off guard again. She knew that next time, she really could show him how wonderful she was. And then, he would never leave.

So she made a list:

Operation Mr. Shower Factory

1. Dress cute.
2. Be memorable.
3. Work in a unique and unexpected talent, like Dance Dance Revolution or _____.
4. Develop more unique and unexpected talents.

And then she burned her list and said a little prayer. She rolled up her sleeves and got to work.

Every day, she woke up an hour early to choose her clothes and accessories carefully, incorporating color, texture, pattern and shine. She was glad her weekends binge-watching *What Not to Wear* were paying off.

Then, in an effort to be memorable she decided she was going to be funny on purpose. She spent two hours a day collecting funny things to say or do. Because she couldn't glean from lotion what kind of humor he had, she spent time learning everything. Just in case. If it was pop culture, she learned to imitate Lisa Simpson teaching Maggie: "Lemur." In case he liked physical comedy, she perfected a stumble that landed squarely between clumsy-silly and awkward-endearing. She even went so far as to learn jive from *Airplane!*, impersonate Goat Boy from *Saturday Night Live*, and rant like George Carlin. The last few were a bit rough on her vocal cords.

She practiced Dance Dance Revolution (DDR, she'd say, all casual-like) to the point that she could do all the moves without looking. And she quietly sat sometimes and thought about what else she could learn.

She was ready. She knew he would just have to love her. Who wouldn't want a girlfriend who could do Goat Boy speaking Jive while dancing some sweet sexy moves? Exactly, she thought. She would be so fun at parties, and everyone would laugh with her and talk to her.

And like the saying goes, good things happen when you least expect it. Joanna woke up late one morning, tired from a binge evening of "clothes fitting the smallest part of the waist" and the possibility of being "comfortable and put together." She hurriedly dressed and ran out the door with a funny feeling that she forgot something.

She greeted all the Shower Factory employees as she assumed her position at the back of the store, with a perfect view of the entrance from behind the spinning tower of sample sizes. She came at a different hour each day, knowing that her methodical methods would eventually pay off.

Before she knew it, the hairs on the back of her neck stood up. As if in a daze, she looked around, disoriented and distracted, before she realized that he was in the store and heading towards her.

There he is! Oh quick, look at all these samples. Ohmigosh, he looks so cute! I really must look at these samples because I'm going on an exotic trip ....

The man made a sudden turn before he reached the samples tower, and walked briskly to the aromatherapy section.

What's wrong with him? Poor thing. I can help him! I have strong, well-trained hands that can massage his sore shoulders from all the ... whatever he does.

She ran her fingers through her hair to boost her flirting confidence, and remembered she did forget to brush her hair that morning. But undaunted, she walked over to the aromatherapy section.

"Hey."

He looked up. "Hey," he replied with the briefest of lingering smiles.

She glanced at the jar in his hand, and silently congratulating herself, said, "Ah, have a headache? Jus hang loose, blood. There's a great coffee shop that catch ya up on da rebound on da med side."

His look of surprise turned to a genuine smile as he nodded, setting down the bath salts. "Wow, you like *Airplane!* too?"

This. Is. Happening!

"Shoooot," she replied.

Joanna and the man laughed, and it was magic. They headed towards the coffee shop and before heading in, he told her he needed to make a call and would meet her inside.

* * * *

George rounded the corner, and pulled a piece of a paper from his jacket. It was wrinkled, but *Operation Cuticle in the Space Station* was clearly written across the top. He couldn't believe his luck. He'd been feigning an interest in lotions for months. He knew the odds were astronomical, but he hoped he'd run into her again.

He got out a lighter, and lit the paper on fire while saying a short prayer. After frantically trying to put out the small trash can fire he started, he smoothed his hair and entered the coffee shop to go and get his endearingly awkward dream girl. He had found her.

SUSIE TEX is an exciting new self-acclaimed short story author, unpublished novelist, and formerly anonymous blogger. She participated in 2012's National Novel Writing Month, and is so excited to be part of this anthology. When she's not writing or being confused for a quarter horse, she is working, taking classes, stress-snacking, and trying to be funny on purpose. Visit her at tasteslikeonion.wordpress.com.

Not Hansel and Gretel

Jamie Park

I MYSELF HAVEN'T *seen the murder. I just happen to know the story, but if you don't trust me, might as well stop reading the tale I'm going to tell.*

There was a kind lady who lived down the street. Gentle, compassionate, loving: all the characteristics a good neighbor would have. However, she had a deep, dark secret.

You might be thinking that having a deep, dark secret is not what a good neighbor would have. Well, you're wrong! Everybody has a secret they keep to themselves. This kind lady is like any other with a secret.

Her name was Gretel.

Yes, just like the character from Hansel and Gretel.

As nice as she was, every kid in the block thought of her as a witch: a cruel, selfish, broom-riding witch. There is a story to how she got this ridiculous title, and it all started with a little boy named Hans.

THIS STORY IS NOT LIKE HANSEL AND GRETEL. *Hans is not the shortened version of Hansel, nor is he the character from the movie* Frozen.

About twenty or thirty years ago, a little boy moved into the neighborhood of Memoirville—an ordinary seven-year-old boy with an annoying little sister, Elma. Like all boys, ranging from age two to when they die, he was curious about his new home and decided to explore. During this time, Gretel, who was probably about thirty-four, baked a pie for her new neighbor. While she was walking over to Hans' house, she forgot to close the door to her very own house. Hans was just walking around and somehow got himself inside Gretel's home without raising any suspicion. To his shock, Gretel's house was nothing like the other houses in the neighborhood. The rows of shelves were filled with sweets, from cookies to cakes. Hans found his mouth watering as the aroma filled his nostrils. Distracted from all the sweets surrounding him, Hans did not notice Gretel closing the front door and standing right behind him. All Gretel whispered was, "Go ahead."

That was all it took for Hans to dash from shelf to shelf, cupboard to cupboard, trying each and every tasty morsel. In the middle of gobbling down a chocolate glazed doughnut, Hans realized that someone had said to him, "Go ahead." He was suddenly very frightened, for the last time he had checked, he was alone in the house. Hans' fork slowly came to a stop as the floorboard behind him creaked under the weight of something obviously larger than a bread box. He slowly turned his head to see—

Now, this is getting pretty interesting, isn't it? Well, I'm going to be honest with you. I completely forgot the next part. So, I'll leave it up to you to fill in the blank. It could be sweet Gretel with more plates of cookies, or a smirking Gretel holding a thick rope and some duct tape. It also could've been some flower goblins dropping by to ask if they should plant tulips or roses. I really don't know. Sorry.

Hans somehow ended up outside Gretel's house with a full stomach, completely unharmed.

When Hans went home, he quickly ran to the bathroom to wash his face. Right then, Elma walked in.

"What're you doing?" Elma asked.

"Nothing. It's none of your business," Hans sneered.

"What's that on your face? IS THAT CHOCOLATE? YOU DIDN'T BRING ME ANY?" exclaimed Elma.

Hans quickly denied the fact, washed his face, and went straight to his room. He lay awake wondering what had happened at the house. He finally decided that he would have to return.

The next day, Hans snuck out of his house early, so Elma wouldn't see him. He went up to Gretel's home and knocked urgently on the door.

"Hello," Hans called.

The door slowly creaked open, and Gretel was there with a face mask on.

For those who don't know what a face mask is, it's scary. It makes a normal person look like an alien from another planet. However, people say it makes your skin softer.

Gretel replied, "Yes? Oh Hans! What brings you here"–there was a short pause–"at seven o'clock in the morning?"

Hans hesitated, but mustered enough courage to mutter, "Were you the one giving me permission to eat all those sweets?"

Gretel, as if expecting this question, smiled.

It wasn't one of those gentle smiles. It was one of those creepy "I know what you do at night" kind of smiles.

Then, she motioned Hans in.

You're probably wondering why Hans went in. To be honest, I don't know either. He was a pretty stupid kid.

Hans went inside and felt the exact same feeling as when he first came in. As he was looking around, his eyes landed on his shadow. Hans' eyes got as big as a full moon, for what he saw was the last thing he'd ever see.

You're curious about what he saw, aren't you? As a storyteller, I shouldn't exactly tell you. It might ruin your brains, and that's the last thing I want to do. Just kidding. I'll tell you because I couldn't care less about how this affects you. After all, you're the one who chose to read this.

Behind Hans' own shadow was a taller one. It belonged to Gretel! She was holding a knife over her head, swinging it down into Hans' back. The reason for this is unknown. Gretel was never suspected of killing anyone, and the police closed the case by saying Hans ran away from home.

Years later (after Gretel died), the house was abandoned. More importantly, a girl named Cinderella came by, and found a way into the house.

NO. IT IS ABSOLUTELY NOT CINDERELLA FROM THAT WRETCHED GRIMM'S FAIRY TALE.

Cinderella didn't find anything unusual, until she came by

a small station in the house. It was a very bizarre station. A small space of a room decorated with mini rocket models.

It's somewhat like a ... hmm ... a space station!

What she found could've solved the disappearance of Hans and given Gretel the punishment she deserved, albeit retroactively since she was already dead. Cinderella found a cuticle in the space station. It was Hans' cuticle! DNA evidence of Hans' fate at the brutal hands of Gretel! However, Cinderella found this very insignificant, so she left.

If no one suspected Gretel, how do I know this? Well, that's a good question. It's also the end of this story. I think it's time you should know how I know this horrible, sad story. Don't be shocked. I know the story because I am Hans. The next question that's probably in your mind is, if I died, how do I know about Cinderella? Well, most of you don't believe in ghosts, but I died a very sad death. For those who know about ghosts, when they die and leave part of their soul on earth, they can't move on. That's exactly what happened to me. As a soul roaming around, waiting for someone to notice that I haven't run away, I saw every person who entered Gretel's house, including Cinderella. I was murdered. The only hint—my cuticle—was ignored.

If nobody knows about my death, how is Gretel known to be a witch because of me? Well, long before Cinderella, and a few minutes before my death, someone saw me sneaking inside Gretel's house. Someone I never noticed: Elma. She followed me to Gretel's house that morning because she was jealous of all the chocolate I'd eaten. For once, I was glad I couldn't escape my little sister. After my "disappearance" she tried telling my parents, but they wouldn't listen. Who would listen to a five-year-old? It just seemed like she was blabbering about a kind lady because losing her older brother traumatized her. One thing though, is that her friends, her five-year-old friends, believed her. They spread the word to people they met, but like every rumor the story grew and changed with each telling. The story evolved over time into Gretel being a witch, all thanks to my little sister Elma. But my death is still unknown.

My soul will forever be trapped until this case is solved. Now that you know my story, spread it to the world so that I can finally rest.

JAMIE PARK is a fourteen-year-old girl attending middle school in Torrance, California. She enjoys reading books, researching cancer, and free writing. During her free time, she is usually with her friends. She is very outgoing and active. Her favorite subjects are science, math, and language arts. She mainly excels in science and her goal is to be a Crime Scene Investigator (CSI), hence the reason her story is about a murder. Although Jamie isn't very imaginative, with the right inspiration she can be creative.

In the Event of a Migraine Take a Snot

Lillith Black

My head felt like it was cracking in two, and I tried to blink my eyes one at a time, as blinking both at once caused indescribable pain by lemur language. I deserved every ounce of that pain. What was I thinking, downing seven shots of that nasty ombrian drink? Or was it eleven shots? Now that I thought of it, more like eighteen. Drinking alone, what an idiot. Formel was right when he had tried to stop me from drinking shot number thirteen.

Wait, Formel had been there? Oh, of course, that ombrian jerk, always finding his way to other people's alcohol. No wonder Allen was making fun of him joining us as soon as we downed two first shots. Yep, Allen, Sonji, and I were drinking and Formel just had to barge in. It was as if he just wasn't getting that we didn't want his ombrian face in our tight lemur group. Three bottles of "A Cuticle," that nasty, nasty ombrian drink. The bitter taste that hits your mouth as soon as you down it is revolting, but what does one do if A Cuticle in the space station is the only buzz-inducing beverage we have left? We would down it and then chase it with "An Earwax," a cheese snack we hoped was made out of cheese.

As another wave of pain hit me, I remembered that Allen hadn't been there last night. I must have been thinking of the drinking contest we held on Monday. At least I *thought* it was on Monday. Boredom on the space station was omnipresent and after two lemur years in open space, we'd consumed every mind-numbing beverage on board, leaving us only with "A Cuticle," a drink as revolting as its name.

At last, I crawled my way to the medical bay, searching for a dose of pain reducer. Allen, our med specialist, was nowhere to be found. Maybe he drank with me after all and now was hurting in his room just like I was earlier. Allen was a good guy, lemur like me and naturally we got along. It was always nice to have a buddy in the medical bay especially when cut off from civilization for months on end. Finally, I found a bottle of "A Snot," a painkiller, with another unfortunate name given by ombrians. Lemurs should have never outsourced all the vessel supply contracts to them. At times I wasn't sure if I was ingesting a product or a by-product of a product. I downed the pills and closed my eyes, waiting for the pounding to stop.

An eternity later, with my head feeling as one again, I stumbled my way into the main hallway. I needed to check on my drinking buddies, however many there might have been. The only way to find out was to ask them.

Allen's door was closed and even though I pounded for at least two minutes, he didn't open.

"Forget you!" I screamed. "No A Cuticle for you tonight!"

Formel's and Sonji's rooms were further down and I dragged my feet there. One at a time, I pounded on their doors and received the same lack of response. I yelled at them, too, and headed back to my room, determined not to share my bottle of A Cuticle with any of these jerks. I might have made an exception for Sonji—he *had* saved my butt during our last repair run when my harness broke. But Formel? No way. He was an ombrian through and through, and never cared for a single soul.

On the way to my quarters, I stopped by the captain's room to check up on the station's course. We didn't have a captain per se. Collectively we took care of steering our space station through the endless nothingness of the universe. Since my teammates were passed out drunk in their rooms, I figured it was my turn.

I walked in to the captain's room and almost tripped in the darkness that filled it.

"Great! These drunks killed all the lights, what gives?!" I cursed out loud to shake off the surprise and headed carefully to the other side of the room to light up the instruments. I tried to push a few buttons and pain ran across my fingertips. The buttons were sharp, as if the tops were broken off.

"What is going on in here?" I mumbled to myself, slowly moving along the wall to the main light switch. When I got there, I found the switch in the off position. I flipped it, cursing under my breath and squinted my eyes. A flood of light filled the room. The room looked like a hurricane ran through it; buttons on the control panel were smashed, the broken off pieces scattered everywhere, joysticks yanked out and laying on their sides, the cover on the captain's chair was slashed and the stuffing exposed.

I was about to ask myself another question when I glanced on the floor to see what I almost tripped over. There by the door laid Allen, face down, the back of his head cracked and blood spilled on the floor. I felt vomit making its way up my esophagus. I turned away. I searched for something to hang onto. My gaze fell to the left of my foot and I saw something under the right control panel. I squinted my eyes and realized that I was staring at someone's hand. Like a madman, I pulled on the hand and dragged out what appeared to be Sonji, cold and lifeless, his neck broken by some violent force. Right there on the spot I spilled my guts. And then I spilled them some more.

Two of our four-person crew were dead. It was just Formel and me left on the whole space station.

Formel! It must have been him who killed Allen and Sonji; what else to expect from an ombrian? He was always such a loner, too good to be hanging with us unless we were drinking mind-numbing beverages. He was always jealous of our tight crew. We didn't oust him on purpose but he always acted as if his race was superior to ours. Sure, they built the best ships, but we had the best crews in the universe. I had to protect myself. Looking around I found a neck of a broken bottle. It still had Allen's blood and some hair on it, but it was better than nothing. Formel had to pay for what he'd done to my lemur brothers.

Trying not to look at the bloody bottleneck I was squeezing in my hand, I made my way quietly to Formel's room. I didn't knock, but instead quietly snuck in. I made my way along the wall. All the rooms on the station were designed identically, so I could find my way to his bed in complete dark, no problem. I got to it and stood there, waiting for my eyes to adjust to the darkness. I began to recognize contours of his body resting on the bed. I raised my hand with the broken bottleneck.

"Formel, I know what you've done and you will answer for it!" I yelled, ready to strike him if he attacked. He didn't move. I couldn't believe it. He killed two people and slept like a baby.

"Formel, you ombrian jerk. You have killed two lemurs and you will be subjected to the strictest punishment!" I tried to sound thunderous with authority. Still he slept.

"Formel!" I yelled, now shaking his shoulder. My hand felt wet. I realized when I touched him that he was ice-cold. I yanked my hand back, stumbled and tripped over his lamp. Light flooded the room and I saw him. He lay there, blood soaking most of his sheets.

I screamed and ran out of the room. I ran down the empty hallways, screaming and leaving bloody handprints as I grabbed onto the doorways to turn the corners. When I ran into the drinking room, as we lovingly named our dining area, my eyes fell onto the bottle of A Cuticle. Slowly I made my way to the table and picked the bottle up. Turning it around, I read the back label. "For consumption by an ombrian only. May cause uncontrolled violent behavior in other species, especially lemur."

I lowered myself onto the couch, still staring at the label and my bloody hand holding it. As though on autopilot, I twisted open the cap and poured some into a glass.

"Shot number one." A Cuticle went down my throat, as revolting as its name.

LILLITH BLACK is an American writer who lives in Southern California with her husband and daughters. By day she works as an information analyst, and by night, or whenever time permits, writes fantasy and paranormal stories. She is currently working on paranormal YA novel *Sleepwalker Chronicles* and fantasy vampire romance *Love Me or Bite Me*. Read more at LillithBlack.com

A Regular Saturday Night

Dan Portnoy

ROUTINE IS VERY important.

- Wake up promptly at 2:30 p.m.
- Drink 8 oz. of water.
- Do 100 push-ups & 100 sit-ups.
- Complete a two-mile run in less than twelve minutes.
- Alternate between fifteen power cleans with 135 lbs. and thirty pull-ups every other day.

Your body is a tool and must be bent and broken to comply with the will. I had a wrestling coach tell me, "Pain is just weakness leaving the body." It turns out he's right.

- Shower, shave and eat 6 oz. of yogurt and 3 oz. of fruit for breakfast.

Journal for twenty minutes, any pertinent thoughts

on the previous day's activities. Include any lessons or insights learned. Perhaps a new discovery about our process. Next is the need to sharpen the mind. Read sixty minutes from one of the classics by Plato, Nietzsche, Dickens, or Milton.

Then thirty minutes of meditation. Oh no, it's not for a higher power. It's time that I use to strengthen my resolve in the course of my life. If we don't have commitment to a cause or an idea, then what are we doing? We'd be no better than a pack of wild dogs barking at traffic.

Then it's time to get out on the town.

At 4:00 p.m. in Los Angeles, the working class is headed home and the working stiffs are just starting to move to the night shift. I make my way into the city promptly at 5:30 p.m. All the cars stuck in traffic. Why would they do this to themselves? Scurrying to and fro because they want to measure up. Judging each other by the emblem on their cars and the number of bedrooms in their palatial estates. I don't blame them. I used to be the same way, but I have long since abandoned such trivial concerns.

At 6:00 p.m. my first stop is the 76 gas station on Sunset and North Alvarado. Pick up the paper and a coffee for the nightly scouting; staying up on current events is crucial when evaluating prospects.

Over the next several hours, I hit up the usual spots. Hang out at seedy bars, take in a midnight movie, or cruise to an all night diner. Subways, bus stops, and Union Station. Watching. Listening. Always evaluating.

When I began, I looked throughout the city, but I've come to find that west siders with their entitlement and spare cash are much too likely to break for my purposes. They just lay down and die. Much sturdier stock comes from neighborhoods like South LA, Boyle Heights, and, of course, the war zone of Skid Row.

These neighborhoods are a phenomena to me. No one gives a shit about them, and for my intentions, it's shooting fish in a barrel. Nonsensical ramblings about the state of America paired with the desire to score drugs makes as much sense as trying to trim a cuticle in the space station. There's no place of reference for those on this sane side of the spectrum. Besides the stale smell of marijuana being one of the better olfactory experiences of the neighborhoods, it's the most feral form of humanity I've encountered. I dare you to walk through 7th and San Pedro at 2:00 a.m. and listen to the commentary of today's America. Between the gang activity and junkies looking to score some crank, crack, or heroin—whole crops of people are free to mold as I see fit.

Which brings us to you.

The hazy cloud you're experiencing should start to clear. Chloroform, although not very elegant, is terribly effective.

"But why is it important to have a routine?" you ask. It's not a terribly smart question, but I will answer it.

It started three years ago. I was suffering through my snoring, boring life. Each day my priorities were centered on my nine-to-five job. My life had a routine but there was no purpose and no end game. None other than to get through the humdrum as best as I could and hope for a comfortable retirement. Marking time in a socially acceptable manner. If I could manage to save up a few dollars and take a few modest trips to see the world, that would be a bonus.

My awakening started one evening. It was 11:43 p.m.

and I had just completed my nightly routine of hygiene and shutting off the lights and checking the doors. I was settling in for sleep when I heard a ruckus outside the house. For climates with mild winters, like here in Southern California, louvered windows were the standard for decorative window fixtures. Builders and architects in the 1950's thought it would be a great idea to bring natural ventilation. Unfortunately, not every choice made for aesthetic purposes also makes a great choice for security. So the ruckus outside my house was near the louvered windows. One of the three men reached his hand in through the window and unlocked my deadbolt. They gained entry to my house in a startling seven seconds. I tried to leave, but there wasn't an opportunity. When they entered my bedroom, try as I did to overcome them, they were too powerful.

In retrospect, I don't think they expected to find me at home. There weren't any signs of life, and I hadn't left any lights on. There was a time when I wished I had been a gun owner that night and took them out like Dirty Harry, but I've come to understand that I needed to be cleansed.

To be purified.

Ultimately they provided me with a gift; I no longer have many of the trappings holding me back in my worldview. I'm now free from fear. A fear that haunted me my entire adult life. Significance.

One of the darker sides of humanity relies on our dominance. Once we have it in our head that someone isn't important, we can convince ourselves to do just about anything. My attackers Terry, Keith and Darryl–yes, I was able to find out their names–must've gone down that road and watched a few movies too many. They beat me unmercifully and there were a few times where I didn't think I was going to make it, but in the moment, I didn't care.

A fractured skull, most of my teeth knocked out, a ruptured spleen, four broken ribs, a broken tibia and two fractured femurs from where they drove the nails into my thighs. Darryl must've seen a few movies about modern day torture and wanted to see if it was true about a car battery and the right amount of force. Time was lost to me as I was in and out of consciousness. The police report and my doctors told me that I endured fifty-seven hours of suffering before paramedics found me and I was hospitalized for my wounds. Due to my extremely wounded state, I was placed in a medically induced coma for two months so my body would heal itself. They said I was lucky to be alive.

That's the funny thing. It was only through this consuming fire, this trauma, that I was able to see the new world that lay right before my eyes. Three blunt instruments shaped me. It was an outcome that they couldn't have known. I was becoming something other than human.

First the occupational therapy and then physical therapy; after that much time unconscious I had to learn how to walk again and so started my routine. With each new step I plotted to reunite with my immersers. They brought me to a new place of consciousness and I would return the favor, just without the benefits. Their cleansing would be my gift to them.

Of course there was psychotherapy. It was like *Tuesdays with Morrie* if Morrie was an obtuse degenerate, incapable of seeing all that was really happening in the world.

As for Terry, Keith and Darryl, they were never caught

for the felony burglary and malicious wounding. I know it's gruesome, but we must boldly summon our gumption if we are to bring to bear all of our power. It was nearly a year before I finally caught up with them.

Terry had turned a new leaf and was working hard as a parking lot attendant to support his family. You can imagine his look of surprise that late Wednesday evening when he opened the door to find me. His wife was a spitfire and put up quite a fight. I can only assume that was for the children's sake. However, Terry was incredibly docile, like a sheep about to be sheared or a cat playing possum. He knew the debt that he owed was coming and knew he couldn't escape it. He now stood in the shadow of his own creation and knew that the reckoning would consume him.

Keith was much quicker; no family to speak of, but he knew he was a worthless piece of shit. He pleaded with me for some time and at one point soiled himself. He met God with a clear conscience. The same couldn't be said of his pants.

Darryl was a much slower burn. After I finally tracked him down, I had to wait until he was released from prison. Misdemeanor burglary was his preferred vice and was now testing the limits of the prison system. Fortunately for me, he's not a criminal mastermind and never saw me coming.

Revenge is somewhat satisfying, but it's also very base. Conceiving a plan that ends in murder now lacks luster and I no longer have a zeal for it. However, trailblazing a path toward enlightenment would be a much higher reward. To help others see their importance—just imagine. And so began my calling as a higher functioning person and grand inquisitor in the refinement of human behavior.

Darryl, while not a great addition to the human race, did provide some great data in the journey to purification. Many of those insights I'll be sharing with you tonight.

As for our time together, I've been able to improve upon the process and streamline it a bit. The cleansing that you'll receive tonight is adjusted for maximum effectiveness, but I won't kid you, the pain you're about to experience is quite sickening.

One more thing before we get started. Your hands and feet are quite secure and, since it's not my first time, I'd like to give you a mantra over the next several days and certainly the next few hours. Yes, they will be the worst. A sentence for you to repeat in your darkest times. Remember this, "Through pain, weakness leaves my body. My body is a tool. This tool is my salvation." Say it with me. "Through pain, weakness leaves my body. My body is a tool. This tool is my salvation." Yes. Yes, you've got it.

This is the seventy-fourth time I've recited this benediction to a qualified candidate. May you embrace what you could become as I have. Sadly, I can only control half of the equation. The rest is up to you. Welcome to my anvil. Your body is to become a crucible and in the end you'll join my army or we'll learn what you're made of. Feel free to yell out if you need to; your screams will be a testament to the purification.

We've got a long road ahead of us. Let's get underway.

DAN PORTNOY is the author of *The Nonprofit Narrative: How Stories Can Save the World*. He loves helping passionate people strive for the impossible and on several occasions, he's seen it happen. When not writing scary fiction, Dan loves whimsy, *Adventure Time*, and The Muppets. He lives in Pasadena, CA. You can find him at portnoymediagroup.com where he writes about connection, engagement and fun things on the internet.

A Sunlight Symphony

Anna A. Chen

"THIS PINE TREE is a portal," the dwarf says, tugging at my sleeve. "The tree will dip you in the morning sun, and you will be free!"

Yes! A sunlight baptism is all I need. The trees will plant me in the earth as a seed. And I will climb from the cracked lips of our Mother Earth and flower with the sweetest pollen the bees will ever taste. I am ready.

"This pine tree is a portal. You will be free," the dwarf repeats. And he waters me with his whispers.

I hear people, the laughter of leaves, the quick yelps of fallen twigs losing the war against rubber soles in the distance. Crunch, crunch, crunch. Louder as people march nearer. But my feet are rooted near the dwarf, near the tree, near the portal as it sings above me. Time is sluggish today, her two hands inching along in carefully calculated monotony. She says she's ready for mutiny, and I cheer her on. "You are ready, Time! Break free with me."

"You've captured the sky in your azure eyes," sings the pine tree, interrupting me. He looks down at me as the breeze plays music through his leaves. "The azure I see is power in you, power from all the sky and the sea." His boughs bow to the ground, and I am his king. "Climb upon me," says the tree. "Let me be your ship, Captain. I steer toward the sun."

I climb up his torso and ride his back. His gnarled limbs stretch like the corners of a yawning cat's mouth. He sighs and strains through syrupy warmth toward the sun.

"You are tender now. The sun is ready to receive you, Captain," the tree says.

"Hey you! What are you doing up in that tree?" says a woman with a skirt like a lampshade.

"K-I-S-S-I-N-G!" the dwarf speaks for me. I notice a group of people has gathered below, including a man with a solemn face. I remain perched in the tree as they stare and wait for me to speak.

"O Captain! My Captain! You can't abandon ship!" screams the tree.

I bend until my lips almost touch his chapped limb. "Don't worry, Tree, the captain is the last to leave," I say quietly, and his bark softens.

"Who are you talking to? Come down, mister!" Lampshade says worriedly. I hear someone below whisper a code, "Call 911."

"You can't go down." The dwarf redirects me back to the world above. "You can't leave the leaves and me. Look to the portal. Look to the tree. Look up at heaven, not down to misery."

"Yes, look up toward the sky," the tree chimes in. "I see in your eyes a piece of the sky. See the blue? You are ready to come home."

"Let me try something," Solemn Face says to the others. He turns to me, "Hey, I have a gift for you. Come down here, and I will give it to you."

Ah, yes! A gift. It must be his blessing. Solemn Face is handing me off to the sun. In his eyes, I see a flicker of understanding. He is a candle in the darkness, but sometimes he quivers and bends my way. My heart is pounding.

Solemn Face and the group of people with him silently watch me. I take a breath in. For a second, the world forgets to spin. A second of silence.

But then the dwarf advises me, "You can't trust this man. Inside his left breast is a stone that beats all alone. It's black and cold and covered with a heavy moss and old cobwebs. Look at it decay! Decay!"

"Decode! Decode! The message is here. In my bark, there's a code. It's a song. It's an ode to the sun—"

"Stone! There's nothing in his chest but a stone. And it's black, and it groans with a hunger for your soul! Trust the heart, the one true heart, that beats in us all." The dwarf's voice dies down and the tree falls silent. The world around me crescendos in a hurricane of sound. Leaves begin to howl. Bark begins to crumble. The branch upon which I sit grows ten feet long, roaring, stretching toward the sun. The tree and the dwarf hum an eerie, triumphant song. "To the sun! To the sky! Burn in a glorious hue! Feel all weight dissipate in silent, sapphire blue!"

I am ready to be dipped in the sun, head first into the warmth, into the womb of the earth. Butterflies exit my mouth and nod their heads in agreement. Their antennae point not north, not east, or south, or west, but up to the smiling sky. They whisper, "Fly!"

I stand with my wings outstretched. Sunlight licks my raw face as my body shrivels in understanding. I am enlightened. I am an insignificant piece of this infinite, breathing world. I am a pebble in a plantation. I am a cuticle in a space station. A seed in this ocean of sunlight.

Lampshade and Solemn Face take aim with their eyes. Envious looks fling like arrows from their eyes and sting as they find their way to my heart. My heel is hit, and like Achilles I am defeated.

My wings crumble. Their feathers become leaves that fall in swirling motions to the ground, to the feet of Lampshade and Solemn Face. The dwarf's voice grows thin with the wind until remnants of words are barely audible, "K-I-S-S-I-N-G ...."

Sirens are calling to me. The tree loses to airy waves that crash and thrash the hull. The pine ship overturns in this sea. The sun walks away from me.

I lose my balance. I sink. I fall to the ground. The sound of Lampshade's feet draw near. Solemn Face and more men appear. Fallen, dead leaves scream under their feet.

And I am held down, my ear pressed to the dry dirt as our Mother Earth whispers through her cracked lips, "Hush, my warm sun. You are never alone."

Darkness. And I am home.

ANNA A. CHEN is a young poet and future physician interested in mental health. A recent graduate from UCLA with a B.S. in Psychobiology, a B.A. in English, and two baby turtles. A lover of frogs, flip flops, and sentence fragments. whitecoatpoet.blogspot.com

The People of the Apples

Jasmine Chung

CAST: James, Peter, Sharon, Lauren, Joanna, and Justine

LAUREN: (Alone on stage.) This story takes place at school in the music room. It shows the different complications that six friends could have.

JAMES: (At the round table, yelling.) All Naked Apple Group Members! I'm calling an emergency meeting!

SHARON: (Walks over.) Hey honestly, I never really understood why we're called the *Naked* Apple Group. It's just weird.

JAMES: (Face to palm.) Really? How many times do I have to tell you the story?

SHARON: (Shrugs.) I honestly don't remember. But I'd love for you to tell me again.

JAMES: (Rolls eyes.) Well, to make things short, we got it from the Naked Juice brand. Aaaand everyone just so happened to like apples. At that time we really had zero inspiration.

SHARON: Eww, honestly, who would want to drink something called Naked Juice? (Holds up hand.) Nope. Don't explain. I honestly *don't* want to know.

JAMES: Hello?! *You* were the one that wanted to know!

SHARON: Whatever. So what's all the fuss?

JAMES: You'll see. Can you call everyone over? It seems like nobody really heard me.

SHARON: Of course. (Leans over to JAMES.) But how about a little alone time? (Holds out hands.) How are my cuticles? Feel my hands. (She grabs JAMES's hands and tries to make him touch them.) Aren't they soft?

JAMES: (Pulls away hands.) Ummmm, no I'm OK. (Puts elbow on desk, daydreaming.) But I need to talk to Lauren ....

SHARON: (Rolls eyes.) Why do you care so much about that girl anyway? She already likes Sammy.

JAMES: Well …. (Blushes.) It's just that—

SHARON: (Frustrated.) Ugh, whatever! (Holds up hand.) I don't care. I'll call everyone over, OK? (Goes off stage to get everyone else.)

JAMES: (Murmuring.) Goodness, that girl *cannot* leave me alone!

SHARON: (Enters with jazz hands.) I have everyone here.

(PETER and LAUREN enter stage.)

JAMES: Oh good, everyone's here. You guys couldn't hear me, or something?

PETER: Oh no, we heard you. We just didn't think that you were as important as what we were doing.

JAMES: (Glares at PETER.)

PETER: (Shrugs.)

(Everyone gathers around the table and sits down.)

JAMES: OK, so as you all know, Sharon is leaving for the summer.

PETER: (Over-exaggerating.) Yeah? So what?

LAUREN: (Teasing.) Aren't you even going to miss her?

PETER: (Stuttering.) Well yeah, but I'm a girl and she's a guy .... No wait, I'm a guy and she's a girl. So yeah, people might get the wrong idea if I show, you know—

LAUREN: All right now, we all know that you like Sharon so there's no use in lying.

PETER: (Slouches.) Geez, it was worth a shot though.

SHARON: (Holds hand out at JAMES.) He's right. It's not a big deal anyways. (Flips hair.) I'm coming back next year, so you don't have to cry about it.

JAMES: Anyways! You heard about the phone call, right?

SHARON: (Jumps up, covers mouth and gasps.) Are you talking about the creepy stalker one?

JAMES: That's the one.

SHARON: I thought it was Sammy at first, but then later, I realized that he wouldn't do such a thing, even if he were to try to pull a prank on me. And besides, it didn't sound like him after a while. Well, not over the phone anyways. (Flips hair.) I just find it sooo annoying how everyone's attracted to me. It's just like, like I'm a celebrity.

PETER: What? I didn't hear about any of this.

SHARON: What? I thought it was obvious that everyone liked me!

PETER: (Waves hands.) No. No. No. It's not that!

JAMES: (To SHARON.) Not *you* dumb butt! He's talking about the phone call. You know! Ugh, how could you be so stupid?

SHARON: What? So … you *don't* think I'm pretty? Well! (Flips hair.) That's probably a lie. You're probably too shy to say anything. (Crosses arms.) And it's easier to be totally mean to me than to be the nice guy you want to be. I know. (Hands to chin.) You just can't help yourself.

JAMES: (Ignoring SHARON. To PETER.) You should've paid attention during the last meeting over the phone.

PETER: (Slaps hands on table.) Not nice. You hogged the phone!

JAMES: I called you over; you didn't come. (Shrugs, holds up hands.) What else could I do?

PETER: OK! Well technically it's not even my fault because you were taking over the phone, and besides, (beats chest) I'm a busy man!

JAMES: (Crosses arms.) Oh yeah? What were you doing?

PETER: Some stuff that's none of your business.

JAMES: (Folds hands over table.) Oh yeah, probably mooning over a certain someone's yearbook picture?

PETER: (Stands up suddenly.) You wanna go, bro?

JAMES: (Stands up calmly.) Challenge accepted.

(The boys tackle each other.)

LAUREN: (Holds out arms trying to break them up.) Boys! You can do that at home all you want, but this is a serious place! And besides, I thought this was an *emergency!*

JAMES: (Sits down. To LAUREN, sweetly.) OK. Whatever you say. (To PETER, glaring and gritting his teeth.) We'll settle this later.

LAUREN: (Puts down arms.) No, that's not how men do it! And I promise you I *will* plant you on the space station with Sharon if I have to.

SHARON: Does that mean he's going to be with me, alone, in the space station?

JAMES: NOnononono. (Whimpering, begging eyes to LAUREN) Please no—

SHARON: You can look at my lovely cuticles.

JAMES: NOnononoooo! Anything but Sharon's cuticles in the space station!

LAUREN: (Evil look. Taps fingers together.) Sharon, should we drag him to the space—

JAMES: (Holds up hand.) OK, sorry …. Back on track! (Folds hands on table.) The truth is, it really was a call from Sammy, or at least from his phone.

SHARON: What? So are you saying that his dad was calling me, or something?

LAUREN: (Palm to face.) No, he's saying that there might've been a possibility that there was someone else at his house using his phone. Whether it was (left hand up) a friend or (right hand up) not, it could be dangerous to you. Come to think of it, it's pretty harmful to Sammy too, assuming that he doesn't know a thing about it.

PETER: (Holds up hand.) Wait, wait. Tell me from the beginning. What happened?

LAUREN: (Takes a deep breath.) In the middle of the night, someone on Sammy's phone called Sharon.

(JOANNA enters.)

JOANNA: Whatcha guys talkin' about?

JAMES: You're not a part of this, so I'm going to have to ask you to leave.

LAUREN: Sharon's got a stalker.

JOANNA: (Slaps hand on table and collapses in a chair.) *What?!*

SHARON: (Puts head down.) It's nothing serious.

JOANNA: Oh yeah, so you're going to just say that having a stalker is nothing serious? I mean, I know you're attractive and all, but seriously, you have to tell me this stuff!

PETER: (Crosses arms.) I agree! It's more than serious! I mean, you don't deserve a jerky guy like that! You need some one intellectual. (Pushes his glasses up. To JOANNA.) According to James, this stuff is confidential, meaning—

LAUREN: (Slaps table.) Sammy's not jerky! (Points at PETER.) You are!

JOANNA: (Annoyed tone, waves PETER away.) Yeah, yeah, I know what it means Mr. Know-It-All! (To SHARON.) So what are you going to do about it?

JAMES: We're not sure if it's a stranger or not.

JOANNA: (Crosses arms.) Even if he's not, what if he kills her?

PETER: (Points fingers up.) I second that!

LAUREN: (Palm to face, shakes head.) Sammy's not that kind of guy!

(JUSTINE enters and sits at table.)

JUSTINE: What? Killing? I wanna hear!

JOANNA: Someone's gonna kill Sharon.

PETER: And it's super serious.

LAUREN: (Rolls eyes.) You're over-exaggerating.

JUSTINE: (Taps fingers together.) Hehehehehehehe! Not before I kill them first! (Cracks fingers.)

SHARON: Joanna! Shut up!

JOANNA: (Holds hands up.) Whoa there!

PETER: Yeah! Go get Sammy, Justine! And shut up, Joanna! Nobody wants to listen to you!

LAUREN: (Crosses arms.) But Sharon's right. Others shouldn't know about this stuff. It could get serious. And Sammy could get in trouble for doing something that he didn't do.

PETER: (Leans forward.) But we never know! He probably did it, seeing the kind of person he is. I mean, what kind of person would do such a thing besides him?

JOANNA: OK fine, let's—

LAUREN: What do you know about him?

JUSTINE: (Frustrated.) What happened?

PETER: Sharon got a call from Sammy's number in the middle of the night, but it wasn't really Sammy at all, so we gotta figure out who the caller was. Even though I personally think that he probably did it, making him a big fat jerk.

LAUREN: He's not a big fat jerk! Good grief, you don't even know anything about him!

JUSTINE: OK, first of all, (To Sharon.) why the heck do *you* have Sammy's phone number?

JOANNA: (Points at JUSTINE with wide eyes.) That's *exactly* what I was wondering! (High fives with JUSTINE.) (To SHARON.) Hey, going out with him could be dangerous. He's got stalkers ready to get you at every corner. (To everyone else.) Who knows what'll happen? Maybe he could get his stalker friends to kidnap her and stuff ....

JAMES: (Holds head.) Joanna! Why would that happen?

JOANNA: (Shrugs.) It's possible! (To JUSTINE.) Right Justine?

JUSTINE: (Thinking.) I guess it's possible—

PETER: Disgusting! That's why you should probably go out with someone else—

SHARON: Like James!

JAMES and PETER: (Begging.) Noooo, please, please, please—

LAUREN: Guys, let's not go there. We have to think logically. First, why would a stranger be at Sammy's house? I mean, let's face it. I'm sure he has some weird friends that say, you know, some weird stuff, but we can't really do anything about that. We shouldn't let paranoid thoughts get to us. Let's use some common sense and be sensible. And guys, it's almost time to go.

JOANNA: (Ignoring LAUREN.) What did the person even say?

SHARON: Something about Sammy wanting to go to the mall with me?

JOANNA: (Slams table and jumps up.) What? What if what I was saying is right? The mall is a dangerous place!

SHARON: No, he was talking about this Saturday. You know how we were planning to go to the mall all together?

JAMES: What are you guys talking about?

JUSTINE: Oh, the one where we were planning to buy jeans and stuff? Why would Sammy wanna come along? It's kinda weird. Even if he's used to hanging out with us girls, I bet he would enjoy playing Minecraft all day more than going to the mall.

LAUREN: I actually bumped into Sammy the other day—I waved hi, but ... I don't know, he was acting all weird. But guys, time's almost up.

PETER: How weird? (Makes the OK sign with his fingers.) I know all about Sammy. Every flaw. Just tell me, and I'll know why. (To SHARON.) Even though I still think that you deserve someone obviously better. From what I can tell, he's up to no good.

LAUREN: Oh good grief, for the billionth time, he's not that kind of person! You know, you're really suspicious. What if *you* are the one who made that phone call?

JAMES: Yeah, just shut up dude! You don't know everything about him!

SHARON: Guys, don't get into another fight. This is serious. (To JAMES in a flirty tone.) Thanks for sticking up for me.

JAMES: No. I wasn't sticking up for you! I was sticking up for Lauren, you stupid—!

LAUREN: (Ignoring JAMES.) I'm guessing Sammy's involved with the phone call somehow. And guys, we're running out of time.

JUSTINE: Well, he has to have *something* to do with it. It's his phone.

JOANNA: Sharon, this is what you get for going out with that weirdo.

SHARON: I'm not going out with him! (Quieter voice, talking behind her hand.) I'm secretly going out with James!

PETER: (Palm to face.) No you're not!

SHARON: (Stands up, stomps feet.) Yes I am!

JAMES: (Rubs hands together.) Noooo, please, please don't … I don't like you! I like someone else!

PETER: Get a clue! There are people that appreciate you more than stupid James does!

(The bell rings. PETER walks off stage.)

LAUREN: (Stands up.) I told you guys, we didn't have much time! What are we going to do with the audience now? (Points at audience.) We can't just leave them hanging!

JUSTINE: (Shrugs.) Oh well. I guess we just have to save it for another time. (JUSTINE exits.)

LAUREN: (Making an X mark with hands.) No! That's so rude! We have to finish it.

SHARON: Why? It's going to get too long.

LAUREN: Fine. I'll just tell them what happens.

JAMES: No, no, no, no, no, no! That's not the proper way to do it!

LAUREN: Well, we can't just leave them hanging! (Points to the audience.) They'll be itching to know what happened to everyone! I'll just tell them the part about how Sharon gets kidnapped and—

(JAMES exits. SHARON follows, reaching for his hand.)

JOANNA: No! Whatever! They'll just have to bear with it! It's not the end of the world.

LAUREN: Mmmmm ... (Looks at audience, then at friends, then audience, then friends, hesitating.)

JOANNA: (Puts up hand.) Are you coming with us or not?

LAUREN: (Looking back and forth between friends and audience.) Ugh ... Well ... I guess I'll ... But who will warn the audience about—

JOANNA: (Barges in front of LAUREN, to audience.) Hey guys! Let's play a game! It's called, "Make up your own ending to our little story!" (To LAUREN.) There! Now let's go! We'll be late for class! (Pulls LAUREN by the arm.) (To audience, waves.) Bye guys!

(JOANNA exits, dragging LAUREN with her.)

(Lights out.)

JASMINE CHUNG is an eighth grader in Torrance, CA. She was born in California, but spent about half of her life in Illinois. Jasmine lives in a family of four, with a mother, father, and a little sister. Her parents encourage her to study, and she attends an after-school learning academy. She wishes to be a judge because a courtroom is so theatrical. She enjoys reading and writing fiction and plays. *The People of Apples* is her first published play and her first performed theatrical work. She would like to thank the actors who brought her words to life.

Prince of Persian

June Low

"W-WHA-WHERE AM I?"

I'm barely awake before a huge yawn overtakes me. When it passes, I blink back the tears and look around. I am on a very large bed. It is so wide the ground is impossible to see from where I am. Rolling onto my back, I see the ceiling soar high above my head. The purple and grey pattern on the bedspread looks vaguely familiar. This giant bed, this giant room—it all looks familiar. I've been here before. I bolt upright as I realize I've been here forever! The giant's castle! Memories of last night come flooding back. How she betrayed me with a promise. Left me on this giant bed. In this room, this prison cell! The door was slammed shut and locked. No hope of escape. Nothing I could do but wait for her return. I must have fallen asleep.

Curse this sleeping curse! It might have been longer than last night. I have to get out of here!

Moving to the edge of the bed, I peer over the side.

The door of my prison now stands ajar, a most unexpected and suspicious development. I must proceed with caution. I listen, straining for any sound from my captor. The air is calm and dead silent. It looks like a two-story drop to the ground. I vault off the bed onto the floor then pause. No one comes. I inch towards the doorway. Flattening myself against the doorframe, I peek around the corner. The coast looks completely clear, and it is still completely silent. The giant's castle has been completely deserted overnight. This is not a good sign. I walk down the hallway, hugging the walls. I am still keeping alert but there seems to be no one else about.

I proceed further down the hallway when suddenly there is a loud flapping of wings. I shrink back into the shadows on the opposite wall and look in the direction of the sound. Through a large open doorway, giant windows look out to a blue sky. A grey speckled bird with a tiny beak and round eye just landed on a wire strung outside. It seems to be looking right at me, trying to tell me something.

Crossing the hallway, I enter the giant Library. Enormous bookcases line the wall, each filled with massive tomes and various artifacts. I walk up to the nearest one and mentally chart my route to the top, the closest point I can get to the bird. Bracing with my knees, I jump and grab on to the edge of the first shelf. I'm able to leap from shelf to shelf easily despite the doodads that litter my path. Close to the top, I misjudge an attempt to squeeze past an interesting-looking thingamabob. My foot slips and knocks it off the shelf. It falls a long way and smashes onto the ground below me, bursting into a thousand glittering shards. I climb the last shelf and take a moment to catch my breath. The bird makes a "groo-groo" noise and slowly the sounds begin to form words.

"Keep up your strength. Find the way."

"How? The way to what?" I ask, standing up against the window. When the bird does not respond, I shout and bang on the glass. "Do you mean the way out?" The bird appears unperturbed.

"Keep up your strength. Find the way," it repeats, without any change in tone or emotion. And with that, it hops around on the wire and flies away.

Stupid bird.

Disgusted, I jump down from the bookcase and leave the Library. The end of the hallway brings me to a giant flight of stairs. Flattening myself on my stomach, I slide up to the edge and look over. The stairs spiral downward, obscuring any view I might have of what lies below. My eyelids begin to droop. I'd better find a safe place before the curse takes hold of me again, perhaps down there.

I descend the staircase and find myself having to squint against the flood of lights. This must be the Great Room. Immense glass-paneled doors lead out to a balcony beyond. Luxurious drapes hang from floor to ceiling on either side. Plush furnishings are arranged throughout. As I take in the enormous proportions of this room, the hairs on the back of my neck begin to prickle. A sinister presence is stalking me. Out of the corner of my eye, I see a ringed-tail swish from behind a curtain. The lemur!

I race to the door and whip back the curtain, my daggers drawn. The giant lemur looks at me wide-eyed. Obviously it thought itself well-hidden. I set upon it at once while I have the element of surprise. It lunges aside and hisses, baring its fangs, claws at the ready. I scowl, my daggers crossed defensively in front of me.

"I thought I killed you!" I said.

"As if it's that easy to kill a lemur!"

I feint left and thrust right. The lemur buys my feint and is caught off-balance as I slam against it, knocking it to the ground. We roll across the cold, hard floor as I struggle to keep its claws from my eyes. Then in a flash, it is gone. I cast quick glances about, but it seems to have vanished into thin air. I check myself for injuries, thankfully finding none. I will have to be careful from now on. I'm not as alone in the castle as I had thought.

I prowl the room in a slow circle, looking under furniture and around the potted plants. No sign of that darn lemur. I notice another bit of movement towards the middle of the room. The corner of a piece of paper flapping up in an ever-so-gentle breeze. Ah, the giant left one of her books! It lies open, spread out and inviting perusal. Perhaps this will provide some clues to what has transpired here. I lean in to read the large type on the top of the first page.

"A cuticle in the space station."

What? That makes no sense. I scan further down the page and find another line.

"Borage makes new jam gains."

Furrowing my brow, I squint at the text. The sentence changes before my eyes.

"Ultimate daytime for gypsum lane."

What sorcery is this? I turn the page, skimming the black text but the words appear to swim before my eyes. Frantically,

I turn page after page, searching for something, anything that makes some sense. The desperation causes my fingers to shake and grip too hard, ripping the thin paper to shreds. Soon, there is nothing left but a pile of finely shredded bits of black and white. Exhausted, I give myself over to the sleep that has been repeatedly dogging me.

I feel refreshed when I awake moments later. There are whiffs of a delicious aroma wafting towards me. I follow the smell into the main Kitchen. There is a large bowl on the floor. It is overflowing with food. Remembering the words of the grey speckled bird, my stomach begins to growl. I have to eat to keep up my strength. But what if it is a trap? The growling in my stomach grows more insistent.

I put my nose low to the bowl and inhale deeply. It doesn't smell foul. I select a morsel and eat it. Feeling no ill effects after a few moments, I decide it is probably safe to consume. I am careful to only eat from the middle, because if the food is poisoned, it would be around the edges. I must be careful to stay away from the rim.

I am cleaning up after the meal when my stomach begins to sour. Damn! It must have been poisoned! I dash out of the Kitchen, down the hallway towards the Great Room. One of the plants there, I'd recognized it earlier as an emetic. It might not be too late to make myself eject the poison.

The plant is perched on a high platform on a single spindly column. I can almost reach a leaf. The pot begins to teeter and tip over. I jump out of the way just in time as the heavy planter comes crashing over the edge. And then I hear that sinister hissing laugh. The lemur leans over the edge, grinning its wide fang-filled grin.

"You again!" I snarl.

"Banzai!"

The lemur makes a flying leap off the top of the platform. Daggers at the ready, I brace for the impact. At the last moment, it twists and flips over my head, landing behind me. I swivel around but it grabs me in a bear hug. Reaching behind me, I wrench as hard as I can, pulling it off my back. It wriggles out of my grasp, the slippery fiend. I run towards the fallen plant, reaching out to close my hand around two leaves. The waxy fronds slip through my grasp just as my feet are yanked out from under me. Twisting onto my back, I kick out hard, dislodging its grabby claws from around my ankles. Scrambling to my feet, I pounce, knocking it to the ground. Springing onto its chest, I press all my weight through my knees. I close my hands around its neck and wring it with all my might. The lemur grabs at my wrists ineffectually and I feel its grip weaken within seconds. Its eyes roll back in its head and its tongue begins to protrude grotesquely from its open mouth. I roll off its limp form, breathing a deep sigh of relief.

I go over to the fallen plant and gather a couple of leaves. Cramming them into my mouth, I chew furiously. Ignoring the bitter taste, I force myself to swallow. The effects are almost immediate. Already, I feel the wave of nausea rise up from my stomach to the back of my throat. I gag and gag again. I'm on all fours, unable to hold my head up as the convulsions grow stronger. I heave onto the floor a small mountain of undigested food.

"Ugh."

I move away from the mess, feeling slightly better but weakened. So much for keeping up my strength. My eyes won't stay open as the curse easily catches up with me. I crawl under an enormous sofa in the corner. This should keep me hidden from that lemur's friends while I catch a quick nap.

A sudden noise jars me awake. It is a mixed sound, clinking and rattling and a muffled voice. I am immediately alert. The sound seems to be coming from outside the Great Room. Scrambling out from under the sofa, I rush across the Great Room to an enormous door. Staring up at it, I think it must be twenty men tall. How had I not seen this before? The ornate knob halfway up the massive wooden panel is rattling, as if some giant on the other side were attempting to dismantle it.

I cast a quick glance left and right. There is nowhere to hide. Every muscle in my body tenses as I prepare for the inevitable.

* * * *

Sophie pushed the door open slowly, expecting a little grey-striped head to come poking through the opening. She smiled down at the tabby cat sniffing at the tips of her shoes.

"Why, hello there, Aubrey. Did you miss me, kitty-kins?"

She pushed the door open wider to let herself in, blocking the opening with her body and gently forcing the cat to step back into the entryway.

"Did you have awesome adventures while I was gone?" She crouched down to scratch between his ears. Instantly, she was rewarded with the low "rrr-rrr" rumble of a purr. The cat pushed its fuzzy head against her hand, then past it to rub against her legs as Sophie straightened up and surveyed the living room.

The potted plant on the corner side table had been overturned onto the floor, dirt from the pot scattered around it, the leaves chewed up. Last Friday's newspaper lay in shreds on the carpet next to a tattered soft toy lemur. Close by was a small pile of cat vomit. Aubrey arched his back against her shins, purring. He brushed insistently against the bottoms of her jeans, leaving a mat of white hairs on them.

"I guess that's the last time I go away for a weekend," she grumbled to herself.

Aubrey looked up at her with green eyes and let out a big yawn. "Mrreow?"

JUNE LOW is an ex-software engineer living her nerd dream of becoming a writer. She grew up in Malaysia, lived most of her adult life on the west coast of the United States, and is currently gathering inspiration as an expatriate in the Middle East. Her first passion (after writing, of course) is food, with travel coming in a close second. She spends most of her days wrestling recalcitrant muses and cooking up an ethnically-diverse storm. Her non-fiction food writings can be found at www.twosaucytomatoes.com.

Morning, Baby

Sophie McLachlan-O'Hara

A RTHUR IS A good baby. Arthur doesn't cry.
It sounds arrogant of me, but I think it has to be said: I know that all the other mothers in the neighborhood are secretly a little jealous of me. I see them in the morning with eyes like swollen tea bags, stumbling out the door and into their sticky SUVs to drop their kids off at school. They obviously didn't catch a minute of sleep. They never do. I always notice them eyeing me up as I stride out of the house, pushing Arthur along in his stroller, with my hair ironed, nails painted, eyebrows plucked. I can sometimes even catch a glint of a glare as they shove sunglasses onto their faces or into their haggard hair, buckle up, and reverse out of their driveways. It's wrong of me, I know, but I can't just help but smile. I really got lucky with Arthur. He's such a perfect little boy.

Normally, Arthur and I like to go to the library in the morning, but today I have decided to take a walk to the park because it's started to get warm again.

Even with the sun shining, though, I've swaddled Arthur up in two blankets. You can never be too careful. At two months old, Arthur is still susceptible to fatal colds and flus. Call me overly cautious, but Arthur is far too important.

I arrive at the park and it's relatively quiet. A few toddlers gurgle and giggle at the far end, near the playground. I stroll towards them and pass by the small community flowerbed. A lot of the plants are still in hiding. Some came out too early and were killed by a February snowstorm, their wilted little corpses slumping in the soil. It's a shame that no one has cleaned them up yet.

I reach the playground and settle down on a bench, content in the sunshine. A few boys and girls tumble around the equipment, squeaking down plastic slides, bobbing up and down like Jell-O on the swings. They're all a little grimy, with sand flecking their hair and chocolate stains freckling their shirts. I don't mean to judge their mothers, who are suspended there next to their children, half-dead, because I am sure they're overworked and tired, but I can't help it. I would *never* let Arthur get into such a state.

I turn to Arthur now and gaze at him as he snoozes silently in his stroller. I wonder if he notices that I spend most of my time staring at him. I lightly dust my fingertips over his rosy cheeks, round and red, as if he were holding two apples in his mouth.

"Is that your baby?"

A little girl with disgruntled ponytails and freshly scraped elbows waddles up in front of me, waggling her body like a marionette.

"Yes, his name is Arthur," I tell her.

She teeters closer, pushing her snout into the stroller. She comes up after her examination. "He's kinda ugly."

Children have this peculiar way of being brutally honest. Their words are undiluted. Hearing her is like eating Kool-Aid mix straight from the packet.

"He's beautiful. Most babies look like him, you know," I tell her.

"Well, I've seen lotsa babies and I've never seen one that looked like that. He has too much hair."

It's true. Arthur's head is slathered with thick, black curls. He came out that way, with that mop on his head. It makes him look like his father and I think it's beautiful. But, before I can speak again:

"Well. OK, goodbye now," says the little girl.

She scuttles away.

* * * *

At night, I always bathe Arthur. It has almost become a ritual. Right before dinner, at 6:00 p.m., I draw up water into the baby tub and test it with a thermometer. Arthur prefers it at 75 degrees Fahrenheit.

When I bathed him the first few times, I was terrified that he would thrash and drown himself, but Arthur is a very docile thing. He sits very still in the water and never cries when I start to lather his skin with soap. That's probably because I'm exceedingly careful with him. When I scrub him down, I pretend that I'm feather dusting Edgar Allan Poe's tombstone, or slowly pushing back a cuticle in zero gravity at a space station. I never let any soap get in his eyes and he never wiggles. We work as a perfect team, he and I.

It isn't always a private ceremony, however. Usually, I see Ben, wispy like charcoal, lurking in the doorway. He always floats there, his eyes translucent, unspeaking. Just watching. I used to notice tears, silent and sloppy, drooling down his face and dripping off his nose, but now he just hovers there, dried out and exhausted.

I know why he's upset: I spend too much time with Arthur and not enough time with him. Ben thinks that it's because I dislike him, but really, he just doesn't understand. I don't join him in bed anymore because I prefer to sleep on the floor next to Arthur's crib, in case he needs me. I don't have time to talk to him anymore because I'm busy checking up on Arthur, or making him clothes, or arranging his room. Every second with Arthur is precious. After three miscarriages, Arthur is a miracle and I intend to invest myself fully into him. That's why it sometimes makes me a little resentful how Ben just hangs there, moping, not letting me enjoy motherhood in peace.

* * * *

I'll let you in on a secret: I'm not the perfect mother. I can't breastfeed.

Research says that breast milk is the best food for your new baby because it is the most nutritious and because it forges a bond between mother and baby. Try as I might, though, nothing will come. Sometimes, it makes me cry thinking that Arthur is hungry, maybe even starving, and I can't provide for him.

Enough is enough, though. I am done with formula milk. I won't let my body reject motherhood like this. I'm going to see the doctor tomorrow to resolve this problem and that will be that.

* * * *

It's morning, bright and early, and I feel refreshed after another peaceful night with my perfect little boy. I get him ready for the day and push his soft limbs into a new outfit: a handmade onesie. In preparation for Arthur's birth, I sewed together twelve tiny outfits based on the patterns for Cabbage Patch Kids' clothes. Luckily, everything fit him perfectly. I tap him on the nose, my precious little Cabbage Patch baby.

I head out the door and place a blanket over his stroller so that he can nap.

In the waiting room of the doctor's office, I sit far away from the other patients. In the sterile light, they all look like death: there are withering, pregnant teenage girls, bloated women heaving into plastic bags, and women gasping from pain, or nausea, or both. I remember how jealous I used to be of them and how their bodies allowed them to carry a child.

My name is called and Arthur and I wheel away from all those poor souls.

* * * *

"It's a little embarrassing. I haven't been able to produce any breast milk."

I sit there opposite the doctor, a round ball of sweet cookie dough. On shelves, models of female anatomy loom over us. The doctor smiles softly.

"That's not uncommon," she says. "And it's nothing to worry about. Hang on just one moment, and I'll pull up your file. When did you give birth?"

"January fifth" I tell her immediately. It's a reflex response now, those happy two words.

"Here, I think I found you."

She double clicks her mouse. She scrolls. She stops.

"January fifth, you said?"

"Yes."

She draws her eyes over to Arthur's stroller, as if they were being tugged and yanked by a puppeteer.

"Do you have another child?"

"No, I just have the one." I pause, uncomfortable from the heaviness in the air. "Born January fifth. His name is Arthur. He's sleeping at the moment, but would you like to see him?"

There's another pause, but at the doctor's end this time, so I pull Arthur's blanket back anyway. There he is, sleeping soundly. I glance up at the doctor's face, anxious for her praise, anxious for her to say anything.

But she says nothing. Instead, she just swallows and raises a hand to her lips. I look back down at Arthur, trying to understand the problem, but he appears healthy.

The doctor turns back to me, her eyes sullen and gaping.

"I know how hard it must be," she says. "I lost one, too. Several, actually."

I blink.

She continues: "I didn't leave the house for two months. I lost thirty pounds. Everyone copes differently, they say—"

"I don't know what this has to do with breast milk," I interrupt.

She swivels over to her computer, hiding her face from me. "Have you considered looking for a surrogate mother? Or, and I realize that it might be a little early for this, maybe adoption?"

She clicks her mouse, eyes consumed by the monitor. "I'd be happy to talk to you about this; like I said, I went through something similar and I ended up adopting a beautiful little girl, but let me refer you to someone better equipped for this discussion. Have you ever seen a therapist?"

I don't know what she's implying. But I don't like it. My mouth tastes metallic. My eyes ache. My throat is raw. "I came here to talk about my breast milk problems. If you're not going to help me, I'll just go see someone else."

Another uncomfortable pause.

I stand up. She doesn't protest.

Not quite breathing, I push Arthur out of there and down the hallways and through the waiting room, where there is a commotion over a deathly sick woman, but Arthur is a good boy and he doesn't make a sound. Finally, I burst outside, and tears bung up my nose and leak down my cheeks, but I don't know why.

SOPHIE MCLACHLAN-O'HARA is a recent graduate from the UCLA School of Theater, Film, and Television. While she spends most of her time working on her novels and screenplays, she also enjoys traveling to weird and wonderful places, spending too much time on Tumblr, and drinking an unhealthy amount of tea.

Beginnings

Nita Lieu

IT'S HAPPENING. IT'S actually happening. I've waited my entire life for this journey. I've prepared, I've trained, I've suffered through hibernation, and now I'm finally ready.

I couldn't move, but a gloved hand passed me to another gloved hand, which carried me into the sterile shuttle. Warmth. The hand laid me gently onto a cushion, and a domed lid slid shut. The air around me rumbled, sending a shiver of fear through me. I felt the weight of a dozen planets press down on me as we accelerated into space. I couldn't breathe.

And then I was weightless, contained only by the dome over my body. I sighed with freedom. Liberation. Intense pressure returned as we decelerated, and I stiffened, this time in anticipation of what was to come. As we docked, a door slid open metallically with a rush of air. The dome retracted, and a gloved hand enveloped me once more.

I took a deep breath. Here was the final test. As we approached the glowing structure, my training kicked in, and I started to glow in response. For an endless amount of time I lay dormant on a frozen planet, but now I was awake, glowing, the heat from the others stimulating my heat. Perfect. I was ready to join this life form. It was time.

"All right," said the captain. "Let's get this cuticle into the space station."

NITA LIEU is a former Los Angeles resident who likes eating dessert, singing karaoke, visiting libraries and museums, going to amusement parks, watching plays and musicals, wearing Uniqlo clothes, hanging out with friends, laughing at Japanese variety shows, listening to the radio, riding trains, playing puzzle games, having tall bookshelves, reading at the beach, and keeping track of word counts, among other things. She doesn't like bugs, spicy foods, horror movies, bright lights, overpriced amusement park food, waking up with an alarm, batteries that run out too fast, and other things she can't think of right now. She lives in Texas.

Patient Zero

Dara McGarry

"I CAN'T BREATHE! I can't breathe!" Those were my first words as I climbed out of the claustrophobic capsule and into the choppy waters of the Atlantic. After spending 426 days, most of them alone, as Chief Logistics Manager in orbiters, the space station, and finally Mars, all I could think about was breathing real air, no matter how polluted. Finally, I wasn't tethered to a tank or constantly looking at a meter to make sure I returned inside the Command Center before the oxygen ran low.

They always told me I could get by on 10 percent, but those dials were optimistic and the one time I allowed myself to stay out with less (I was obsessed with digging a formation of igneous rock out of the red planet's surface), I started to get woozy and bad decisions were made. Specifically, staying out even longer, until I became unconscious from lack of oxygen and had to be rescued by Dr. Simonson, who was perturbed that not only did I break protocol, but that I also interrupted the perfectly decent chat he was having with the new intern, Bridget. He made it very clear after giving me mouth-to-mouth that I was an infinitely worse kisser than the intern. And besides, my beard tickled.

I left the intern fascination behind ages ago when it started to make me uncomfortable—being nice to them, seducing them, pretending everything was all fun and games when we knew full well that once they had completed the program, they would never make it back home. But that's another story.

I somehow managed to swim 500 meters in the deliciously warm ocean before the Marine helicopter arrived. Hell, I would have swum back to Cape Kennedy if they hadn't stopped me. Primarily because it soothed the annoying tingling I'd had in my lower back for what seemed like forever. And I just wanted to be on land, walking with normal gravity, breathing my precious air, and generally going about my business free of any space gear. The moment I was pulled inside the chopper, I started to quickly undress.

"Whoa, Captain Mulloy, there will be a debriefing session at base. You will have the opportunity to shower and dress there, sir." The young corporal looked slightly concerned and for a split second, I wondered if my face had somehow been transformed into something hideous and alien from my time in space. Then I realized that I was still poised to peel off the suit. Smiling broadly, I zipped back up and tried to set the young man at ease. "These suits are itchy. Especially after wearing the same one for over a year." I laughed and tried to remember what it felt like to wear a t-shirt and jeans. Honestly, I couldn't.

Settling down into my jump seat for the noisy ride back to

base, my thoughts turned to those I left behind. The mission had started out as a lot of hard work, coupled with a lot of fun. Undoubtedly, it was the best crew I had worked for. We met as mere voices and grainy images transmitted from the Command Center on Mars to the Space Station where I worked alone. But after almost a year of virtual partnership, we were the closest of friends. Then everything changed when I got to Mars. That's when we found out about the virus.

Bridget was the first to go. I suspected that the night Dr. Simonson saved me from suffocating, he became intimate with the intern. He was probably a carrier and she, being young, overworked and underfed, had no immunity. And of course the good doctor was in denial of his symptoms for some time, not wanting to give up his penchant for young girls.

"That blonde intern seems to have bonked a little early, don't you think? She's only been here five weeks," he whispered to me in between logging data. Bonking was the term we had given to the complete shut-down the interns experienced when they became useless from lack of sleep and lack of contact with anyone other than the seventeen people in the Command Center. Years ago, when the crews were larger, it was almost like a small town. But with the latest budget cuts, it was all about working efficiently with disposable labor like the interns.

"Yeah, they aren't as robust as they used to be. I mean where are they getting these people? Art school?" We chuckled like a couple of goofy kids and went about our work. But I wondered if he was onto something. Bridget certainly was less energetic. It must have been bad if he was complaining about her. Simonson never turned down a good make-out session, no matter how sickly and pathetic. Then I remembered seeing her heading back to her quarters from the toilet facilities the week before. Her sweats were slung low on her hips, and sure, I was checking her out. But I saw a mark at the base of her spine. At first I thought it might be a birthmark, which was kind of sexy, but then I realized it was moving.

The next day, Simonson seemed under the weather so despite his protestations, I dragged him to sickbay. Bridget was already there, having been found unconscious near her desk. She now had a fever of 103 and was delirious, mumbling something about missing faces. It didn't mean much to me at the time. Dr. Aimee Denham, with her unnaturally long fingers, quickly shuffled between typing in the database and adjusting an IV drip. Her quick, startled head movements reminded me of a lemur and those elongated, prosimian hands did nothing to dispel the image.

She quickly assessed Simonson; then, as she went back to Bridget, motioned to the supply cabinet in the corner.

"Hook Simonson up to an IV; he's dehydrated. I need to figure out what's killing the intern." Everyone on the project had medical training and we were all expected to help in case of medical emergency. But Denham's micro-management meant that rarely happened. I stared in disbelief that she was allowing me to touch her equipment.

"Just do it, Mulloy," she snapped. I meekly reached for an 18-gauge needle as she looked back at some readings on the monitor. "This is bad. Really bad."

Denham realized that there was a potential situation if this was in fact contagious. She summoned for Mission Specialist McCall to head up to sickbay. The intern's fever was unchanged in spite of the numerous techniques used to reduce it. And the cold packs seemed to have made her other symptoms worse. Her eyes started to swell, then the rest of her face followed.

McCall arrived just as Bridget's temp reached 104. By the looks of her swollen face, McCall was hoping it was simply an allergic reaction to some of the foodstuffs. After all, the intern had been tasked with setting up and breaking down the staff meals the previous week. Hopefully, this was nothing more than a nut allergy gone wrong.

"Just stick to the standard protocol. We can't waste any more resources on an intern," McCall said flippantly as he strutted out of sickbay, adjusting his hair after the air lock puffed his pompadour out of place. Our eyes darted to each other in disbelief. Did he really just disregard the life of our friend? I mean, sure Bridget was just an intern, and we don't regard interns very highly. In fact, the entire intern program was designed to work these kids to death, as it was cheaper to dispose of bodies into space than to ship them back to Earth. But we actually liked Bridget. That had to account for something.

She moaned a deep, guttural sound and twisted slightly so the ice packs fell away from her face, revealing a horrible, disfigured mess. Denham leaned in to inspect, then recoiled.

"Her lips are fused! Oh, god, so are her eyes!" She gasped with what I thought might be compassion or concern. Whichever it was, it was fleeting.

The young intern turned her head in my direction. Even though she no longer had eyes, I felt her staring right at me. She started to pull herself off the table as if reaching right for me when Denham quickly went into Contagion Code 2 mode. She was nothing if not efficient, and managing the work force to operate at 100 percent, 24/7, was her primary objective. A potential virus loose on the crew would be catastrophic, and it was not going to happen on her watch.

"Code 2!" Denham slapped the alarm button and pushed the intern back down on the table then quickly distributed HAZMAT gear to Simonson and me. I put on the sweat-inducing suit and rolled my eyes, not only because it aggravated my claustrophobia but also because I knew it was futile.

"How are you going to explain this to McCall?" I groaned as I helped Simonson untangle the IV line from the suit. "He's going to stick with his nut allergy story and Corporate is going to pitch a fit over the downtime." It was standard procedure for the crew to stop whatever they are doing during a Code 2 alarm. It could take hours to clear the Command Center and during that time all operations were required to cease.

"By law we have to have bi-annual drills. This might have been one of them," she smiled slyly as she slipped her helmet on then deftly grabbed a long HAZMAT bag and started to pull it over Bridget, feet first.

"What are you doing?" Simonson was near panic, partly because of his affection for the intern and partly because he knew he was also infected. His glassy eyes told me it was only a matter of hours before he'd be on that table, lips fused.

"We're ejecting her into the trash orbit," Denham said with a shrug. "She'll be dead soon anyway. Look, her nostrils are nearly fused—she can't breathe. Whatever this is, I can't lose any more crew. We have to get it out now." She forced the bag over Bridget's now featureless face and zipped it up with determination. I glanced over to Simonson who was increasingly delirious. Despite his foibles, he was my best friend. Unsure of whether Denham had determined that he was infected, I put myself at great risk and ushered him into my quarters while the doctor was rolling Bridget to the ejector system, which was nothing more than a high-tech trebuchet. I knew I couldn't help him, but I vowed to do my best to keep him comfortable while the virus ran its course.

Interplanetary diversification was the Vandermere Corporation's secondary objective for the mission, behind maximizing profits in mineral mining, of course. After the discovery that niobium could replace fossil fuels in 2052, the Earth was quickly depleted of its cache and Mars, which had been eyed for potential colonization for years, became the primary source.

It was a universally accepted approach for nearly a decade until it became evident that the radioactive fallout from niobium processing, which was still done on Earth, was slowly killing the population. That's why Vandermere moved the processing operation to Mars, with a strategic ten year plan to build more processing plants of all types all over the red planet, thus cleaning up the industrial sites polluting the Earth.

It was a genius idea, tapping into funding sources from both sides of the political fence. Environmentalists were eager to relocate the toxic waste makers, and utility corporations were paying big bucks for "clean fuel." Auto manufacturers were back to making over-sized vehicles that you could practically live in, since fuel cells were cheap and abundant. The operation had been running for two generations with no major introduction of alien germs or viruses, and the shuttling of processed fuel cells back to Earth had been generally considered to be quite safe.

Raising the alarm that there was a potentially face-melting virus contaminating the fuel cells would instill instant panic in the population and have severe consequences for the stockholders of Vandermere. In other words, no one could know. It needed to be carefully–and quietly–contained.

When Denham cornered me that evening in the canteen, I calmly told her that Simonson was fine. He was just a little upset about the intern since he had stupidly fallen in love with her and that it was nothing a bottle of Jack and a hangover couldn't cure. She bought the story and gave me her usual glare just to make sure I was sufficiently scared so as not to report the truth.

Since Simonson and I had been working on a side project to optimize the payload capacity of the fuel cell shuttles, no one noticed he was missing for days. I made excuses for him— he's napping, he's got a cold, he's shagging an intern. His presence was missed but not mourned.

Finally, after a particularly unsatisfying dinner of beets and cottage cheese (the Martian soil turns beets an unnatural and unappetizing shade of gray), I returned to my quarters to find Simonson standing there next to what appeared to be a large puddle of sewage. The sulfurous stench was so thick, I had to concentrate to keep my barely digested dinner down.

"Howdy, stranger!" Simonson was checking himself out in the mirror. He looked the same and I noticed his ego was certainly intact as he admired his reflection. "I think I have fewer wrinkles."

"What?!" I wanted to back out of the room and run. But

I had no place to run to. "You were dead this morning. I was just going to drag you out to the trash ejector after curfew. I don't .... How is it possible?"

"It's fine! It's like a snake shedding its skin. See?" He held up what looked like a soiled bodysuit and waved it around. "You just have a snooze and come out a little younger, certainly stronger." Simonson effortlessly lifted a couple of my dusty kettle bells from the corner. "It's just a DNA sequencing thing. Genius program, really. It makes a carbon copy of you except the aging switch it set to 'off.'"

"I don't understand. How do you know all this? You are you, right? Dr. Adam Simonson," I said, backing away. I was still confused and frightened.

"Relax! Of course I'm me," he said, trying in vain to offer some comfort. "Some idiot in HR accidentally emailed me the confidential brief last year, so I read it. I never thought they'd actually do it though. They were going to send a virus through somebody, Patient Zero they called him, to infect all of us here. Then, if it worked, they'd take it back to Earth."

I sat on the edge of the bed, stunned.

"Everyone in Command Central is a test subject. Even Bridget." His voiced trailed off as if he really felt something for her.

"So, it is in fact contagious?" I already knew the answer but needed to hear it anyway.

"Don't worry. It's only passed through saliva. I already kissed you once, I'm not doing it again. Supposedly, the virus can even replicate dead people—if you have their DNA, of course. It takes longer and you have to have a Petri dish, but you can do it. I was thinking about finding something from Bridget … maybe a toothbrush. I really liked her." He mindlessly dragged his skin suit across the floor, leaving a small trail of goo.

"Her quarters were completely cleaned, Adam. Denham had the whole place scrubbed while you were, um, out of commission," I offered. "She told McCall it was all part of the drill. He has no idea."

"Right. I'd think he was the virus if it weren't for the fact that the only thing he's kissed is his own butt." He used the skin suit as a morbid marionette, gesticulating wildly. He suddenly grinned. "Hey, remember when we picked up Bridget and that group of interns?"

"I think so. Why?"

"I'll bet we can find something from her in the shuttle. Doesn't matter how small. Anything. A hair, an eyelash …." His face was incandescent with hope.

"A hair? An eyelash? How about a cuticle on the space station? You're insane, Adam." I caught myself before launching into a tirade. "Look, I know she meant a lot to you, for some reason, but let her go. You're not going to find her DNA. Besides, how would you know it belonged to her? You might accidentally replicate that horrid kid from Oklahoma, remember?"

"Oh god, I forgot. That guy was so irritating with his constant narrating of everything he was doing." Simonson sat down on the edge of the bed next to me and laughed. "And he was lactose intolerant."

"He was everything intolerant. Almost overloaded the air filtering system because we had to keep it on high all the time." I fell back on the bed behind him, laughing. Simonson leaned forward, putting his now unwrinkled head in his hands with a sigh.

"Yeah, we should get back to writing up that report. I hope you finished it for me," he joked. I was just about to playfully kick him when I saw it. On the base of his spine, where I had seen the moving patch on Bridget. It was small, but legible. Vandermere.

As Simonson cleaned up his puddle (he tried to make me do it as penance for almost sticking him in the trash ejector), I went directly to McCall and requested a holiday. I'd been out for over a year, and despite the corporate policy allowing two weeks back on Earth per year, no one ever takes them. "You know, taking a vacation will ruin your career," they'd say.

McCall was strangely understanding and logged the request. He never liked me anyway, so I assumed it was his way of sabotaging the promotion I was due. I opted to leave the next day. I'd get back to Earth in a week, then figure out what to do next. By then, more people would be infected, so maybe I wouldn't have to go back. I loved that job, but I couldn't face a future being stuck in a building with a bunch of faceless, corporate zombies.

A week and a day later, the senior Project Manager, the VP of Production, and a whole group of people from Corporate greeted me at Cape Kennedy. My estranged wife, Jen, was standing at the back. After so much time away, I had forgotten why I hated her. I looked into her eyes and for the first time in ages, really thought about making a go of it back in Florida. Why not? We had a great life together before, although as hard as I tried, I couldn't remember much about it except for the photos I'd pasted inside my locker. Funny, I couldn't remember any of those photos being taken.

After the debrief, I took my first real, hot shower since I left. I think I must have stood under the water for forty-five minutes or more. It felt like magic, washing away the past. I thought about Jen and that house I'd seen in an issue of *Architectural Design* that McCall had on his desk back at Command Center. It was a modern, A-frame glass building set into a verdant hill. I bet we could find something like that, with a pool. We'd get a dog and have barbeques with our friends. But like a zap, my lower back tingled again and those thoughts were gone, replaced by a sudden sense of urgency to get back to the Command Center and back to the optimization project with Simonson. I panicked when I remembered we'd never filed our report. Images suddenly came pouring into my head at a frenetic pace about my first day on the mission: the "Vitamin D" injections corporate gave me for my time alone on the Space Station; the day I felt weak and slipped off for a quick nap before an important conference call back to Earth; the waking up in my own puddle of sewage, floating in zero gravity. Then, running my fingers over the base of my spine, I felt it. Tiny, raised letters: Vandermere.

A native Nashvillian, DARA MCGARRY has lived in Chicago, London, and Los Angeles. Raised on a diet of Shakespeare, *Twilight Zone,* and Johnny Cash, she prefers to explore a variety of genres. After many years working in theatre, comedy, animation, and film, she is currently enjoying the literary pub scene in London and can usually be found poking at her iPad somewhere in Fitzrovia. Any visitors from the states should please bring Tapatio Sauce. Follow Dara at www.tumblr.com/blog/daradactylworld and cowbird.com/dara-macgarry/stories/.

And To Think It All Happened Over a Box of Cookies

Kayla Delie

IF IT HADN'T been for my boyfriend Jemmy and my two twin cousins Danny and Davy, we might have been able to avoid this whole great big mess. But it wasn't *my* fault Jemmy was going to Hawaii for vacation without even telling me, and it *certainly* wasn't *my* fault that Auntie Jen and Uncle Job were coming to spend the summer with us– again!–and bringing their two boys with them. And if you think it was *my* fault Mom and Dad came up with their "great idea" about spending a week at Space Station Camp, well, that's a plain lie.

My idea of a perfect summer is spending all my time with my friends. Half the time you would find me loaded down with shopping bags at the mall, and the other half of the summer you would find me with Jemmy. Maybe we would hang out at the beach or see a movie. But when I phoned my friends, each and every one of them turned me down because of their plans. I was really bummed about that, but I thought for sure that Jemmy wouldn't turn me down. So I made one last call. One of his friends picked up to say that Jemmy would be going to Hawaii for the summer. Just like that, all my hopes of a perfect summer were dashed. How could he just leave me like that? Some boyfriend!

Mom must have seen this as her opportunity to drag me along to someplace boring, because when I told her that I had nothing to do this summer, she said, "How about camping at the Space Station?" as if it were the most brilliant idea of the century. I should have known something was up, because Mom hates camping. She's the type of mom who loves fancy dinners and five-star hotels, and she hates picnics and camping because they're so "inconvenient." But then again, it figures she'd take us somewhere like the Space Station Camp Resort. It's a camping site in the middle of the woods, though it actually resembles a small town with a minimarket, a gas station, and an electronics store—all things I think really shouldn't be in the woods.

Anyway, Mom wouldn't take no for an answer, so we loaded up the pickup and were ready to go the next day. Mom didn't want us to take any luxuries, including my phone or computer, which I thought was pretty silly considering we would be camping within a mile of the electronics store. I stuffed a week's worth of clothes into my backpack next to my pajamas and books.

"Liiiiizzy!" Mom called from the car.

"Coming!" I hollered back. I quickly scanned my bookcase for things I might have left out. I grabbed my iPod and slipped it between two shirts. As I did, something clattered onto the floor. I bent to pick it up. It was the golden charm bracelet Jemmy had made me as a gift. In a split decision, I stuffed it into my pocket. I wasn't ready to forgive Jemmy yet, but just because he was being a jerk didn't mean I had to be a jerk back. I shouldered my backpack and headed downstairs with a sigh.

Now, the only part I really hated about the whole camping experience was the car trip. Trust me, spending hours on end in a cramped car between two of the noisiest, peskiest boys on the planet is enough to drive anyone nuts. If only one of the boys were Jemmy, it would have been a different matter, but of course, *he* was probably on his way to Hawaii by now. I still couldn't believe he could just leave me like that. I was so angry and hurt that I spent the entire car trip wallowing in self-pity with the twins' voices ringing in my ears like the raucous cries of crows. I was at my wit's end when suddenly the little crows quit squawking and fell asleep.

My mom's sing-song voice woke me up with an overly enthusiastic, "We're here!" I stepped out of the car, eyes closed, eager to escape the penetrating aroma of five-year-olds, and took a deep breath of fresh air. But what I saw when I opened my eyes knocked the air out of me like a punch in the gut.

The cabin right in front of me was made of roughly stacked logs that were still full of splinters. Flakes of paint were peeling off the walls the way you might peel a cuticle off your finger. The whole cabin was in desperate need of repair. I felt sick just looking at it.

Gee, thanks a lot, Jemmy, I thought to myself for about the hundredth time. *Just fly off to Hawaii and leave me all alone in the woods, why don't you?* I was just starting to get worked up again when Mom came up beside me.

"Well, what do you think?" Mom asked, snapping me out of my reverie.

"Mom. Please don't tell me that's where we're sleeping in for the next six nights."

"Yup, all you kids are," she replied cheerfully. "But Dad and I and your aunt and uncle have rented a different place to stay."

"Wait, wait. You," I said, my voice rising in sheer disbelief, "you won't be with us? You're just going to leave us in that ...." I searched for a word to describe the shack and came up with none. I noticed again the peeling paint. "You're going to leave us in that cuticle in the Space Station."

"Oh, it's bigger than a cubicle. You'll be all right," Mom said dismissively, in that tone she uses when she knows she's won an argument. "We'll spend all day and afternoon together. Besides, it builds character to spend some time alone in the woods."

That's Mom for you. It's perfectly fine for her kid to build character in the woods, but for herself, she books a spa and hotel.

"Well, we've planned out dinner so you can watch the twins. There's mac-and-cheese and cookies on the counter. Don't forget to save some cookies, because that's all I brought. They're homemade. See you in three hours. Remember, don't let the kids have more than three cookies each–you know how hyper they get–and don't let them stay up after 9:00 p.m. Don't disappoint me, or I'll never hear the end of it from your Aunt Jen. Bye, Lizzy!"

I shook my head. Any other mom would have said something like "Love you, Lizzy!" or "Is there anything you need before I leave?" or *at least* "Watch out for bears!" but nope, *my* mom never said a word more to me than she had to.

So unlike Jemmy. I bet he'd feel sorry for me if he were here. I sighed.

In a way, I was pleased that she thought I was old enough to be by myself. At the same time, however, I was speechless at what she was doing. I mean, what kind of mom leaves her twelve-year-old daughter in the woods in charge of two five-year-olds? Everything suddenly seemed so ridiculous, I couldn't help but laugh. I headed into the cabin. At least we had homemade cookies to pass the time.

But in a moment I wasn't laughing anymore, because just then, Danny toddled out of the cabin with his hands behind his back. I hadn't seen him walk in, which just went to show how irresponsible I was. The twins could have jumped off a cliff and I probably wouldn't have noticed because I was too busy daydreaming about Jemmy.

"Hey there, Danny, what's that you've got?" I sang half-heartedly, because I'd long since learned the hard way that sudden movements would send Danny speeding away.

"Nooothing," he sang back, which was just about the only word I'd ever heard him say (the only other word he'd ever said was something so rude, I could get spanked for repeating it). You could ask him anything and all you'd ever hear is, "Nooothing."

"What have you got, Danny?"

"Nooothing."

"What else is new, Danny?"

"Nooothing."

"Hey Danny, if I socked you in the stomach right now, what would you do?"

"Nooothing."

"Come on, Danny, how about just a quick peek, huh? Just once? Come on, how about it?" I coaxed, all the while edging closer until I had him cornered. Suddenly, I lunged and wrested his hand open. Danny grinned broader. My jaw dropped. He had a cookie in each hand.

I threw open the cabin door. Just as I expected, Davy was there too, leaning over a nearly empty plate, stuffing the only homemade cookies I'd ever seen into his mouth, one after the other, like a machine. They must have been good, too, judging by the way he was plowing through them.

"DAVY!" I hollered, so loudly I surprised myself. Davy dropped the cookies he was holding and turned two wide, innocent eyes on me. He smiled.

"Hi, Libzy," he mumbled, spitting crumbs, and held out a cookie. "Libzy wav uh coogy?"

"No!" I shouted. "No, no, no!" I picked up the now-empty plate and waved it high above my head. Mom never notices when I'm good, but she always catches me when I slip up. Mom would throw a fit when she found out about this. I narrowed my eyes. That is, *if* she found out. There must be *some* way I could cover up this mess. Davy and Danny were watching me with wide eyes. All the hollering must have gotten to the twins, who were usually as dopey as dough, because Davy blinked and said, "It's all right. There's a bakery."

Those were the longest two sentences I'd ever heard either of the twins say, but I was in no mood to be surprised. "Bakery? There is no bakery! We're in the middle of the woods!" I shouted, then stopped to think. "Wait a minute. Mom has never baked anything before. Come to think of it, she's never cooked anything before, either." Realization dawned on me.

"Come on!" I grabbed one boy in each hand and ran outside. I followed the road. The place I was looking for couldn't be far.

And there it was: "Ed's Bakery and Pasta" in huge neon letters. I must have dozed off for the last few minutes before we arrived, and Mom suddenly remembered she'd be going out so we wouldn't have anything to eat, and slipped out to ...

Well, anyway, we entered the bakery. Cartons of instant macaroni lined a whole shelf. Mom must have reached for the first thing she saw.

And there were the cookies! The exact same cookies that were on the plate back in the cabin. I picked up a box and handed it to the clerk. "There's no tax, is there?" I asked.

The clerk gave a bored shake of his head. "That'll be five dollars and eighteen cents, miss," he said, then peered over his thick-rimmed glasses curiously, as if he'd never seen a twelve-year-old girl with two squirming boys walk into his store to buy a box of cookies.

I dug everything out my pockets: a rubber band, a key, my charm bracelet that slipped between my fingers, and a bunch of coins which clinked as I counted them hurriedly. Danny flipped around and shrieked to be put down. Davy did the same. The clerk's eyebrows rose.

"Here." I dumped fifteen quarters, nine dimes, a half-dollar, twelve nickels, and ten pennies on the counter. I knew it wasn't quite the right amount, but it's hard to count and hold onto a wriggling kid at the same time. I felt a tug at my hand. "Danny, quit it," I muttered, and then to the clerk, "Keep the change. Receipt, please."

The clerk thumbed his cash register, his eyes still on

me. Just then, as I reached for the receipt, Danny twisted. I grabbed him by the sleeve, and in a second, I was holding an empty shirt and a topless boy was hightailing it out of the store. In his hand he clutched something shiny ....

My charm bracelet from Jemmy!

"Augh!" I hollered. "Dannyyyyyyy! Come back here! That's my bracelet from—" I stopped myself abruptly before I finished the sentence and started pounding after him, a shirt in one hand and Davy in the other. Then I ran back to the counter to grab the cookies. The clerk's eyebrows shot so high up that they disappeared into his bushy hair. Say, Jemmy had beautiful blond hair just like that ...

Davy squirmed out of my grasp. As I turned back to grab him, I looked up and saw that the clerk was staring right at me in undisguised shock. He'd probably never seen anything so ridiculous in his life. "Well, *you're* rude," I muttered under my breath. "If Jemmy were here, you wouldn't dare look at me like that." I turned to flee out of the store, huffing indignantly.

"L ... Lizzy?" I heard a voice behind me say. Oh my gosh, that sounded *just like—*

"Jemmy?" I breathed in disbelief. "What in the ... what are you *doing* here? You work at a bakery? Why aren't you ... in—" I stammered as the boy stepped out from behind the counter and came towards me. Then I got over my surprise and looked away.

"You lied to me! I thought you were in Hawaii, when you were here all along! If I'd known, we could have–oh, I don't know–gone someplace fun, or something. I can't believe you were planning to leave me alone all summer, without any—"

"Lizz. Lizz! Hey, I can explain, it's OK, it's all right," Jemmy soothed. He hugged me to calm me down, and all my anger drained away as I looked into those luminous deep eyes ...

Suddenly, shrill screams shattered the moment. Danny! I had completely forgotten about him. Trust Danny to ruin the moment, I thought as I dashed outside, gripping Davy's arm in one hand and an embarrassed boyfriend in the other. Jemmy was blushing as red as a cherry. But my dreamy smile slid right off my face when I saw Danny.

Not twenty yards away was a great pine, and Danny was clinging to its branches a few feet above the ground. A huge grizzly was rooting about underneath, apparently unconcerned about the boy right above his head, who was waving and screaming his head off.

The grizzly looked straight at us. I breathed in sharply, but Jemmy just burst out laughing. He laughed his childish, unrestrained laugh which I had been missing, and despite myself, I felt calmer. "Kid!" he called to Danny between giggles. "You can let go of that branch now. That teddy bear's harmless. He visits us all the time to eat our daily leftovers. Come on, you can come down now. Look, you can even feed him out of your hand, see?"

Jemmy swiped a loaf of bread from the store and tore off a piece. The bear shook his head and ambled over, then promptly wolfed down the treat. Danny slowly edged off his perch, whimpering, but as soon as his shoes touched the pine needles, he was off like a rocket in the direction of our cabin. Davy, who hadn't made a sound until now, yelled and fussed until I let him go. He sped off after his brother. Jemmy tossed the rest of the bread away, and the bear lumbered off in pursuit of the snack. Jemmy walked over to the foot of the great pine and picked up something. Then came back to me and with a heartfelt smile attached my charm bracelet to my wrist. He locked the bakery and I glowed as Jemmy and I started towards the cabin after my cousins. He explained everything on the way—how his parents had made him take a summer job, but he had made up that big fib about going to Hawaii so that I wouldn't find out. I thought that was a silly thing to be embarrassed about, and I made him promise never to lie to me again.

After I got the twins into bed, which was easy because they were already exhausted, Jemmy left.

Of course, I never told Mom any of this; I set up everything so that the place looked just as she'd left it. Some things are just meant to be kept secret. But as I watched my bracelet twinkle in the moonlight one last time before I closed my eyes, I thought to myself that maybe camping wouldn't be too unbearable after all.

Kayla Delie is fourteen years old and an eighth grader. She likes to spend time with her friends, watching dramas, and daydreaming. She also likes to sketch and play basketball—even though she isn't very good at it! Her favorite season is winter and she loves animals, especially horses and bunnies. She loves playing with her friends, whom she considers her second family. Her characters Davy and Danny were inspired by her two cousins, though they are actually way nicer than in the story.

A Job's a Job

Stephen Buehler

FRANK STOOD IN front of Big Larry's desk. Next to him was Junior, someone he had grown fond of during the last three years. They worked well together and their boss sure seemed to have a lot of confidence in them.

Frank watched Big Larry open his desk drawer, rummage past a Heckler & Koch P-7 pistol, a pint of bourbon, and a box of Cuban cigars before removing an 8" x 11" piece of note paper.

"Can I have a Cuban?" asked Junior.

"Forget it," Frank said. "Those things will kill you."

"Listen up knuckleheads," Big Larry said. "Seems like someone's been talking to cops. I can't have loose lips in my organization. Bad for business."

Frank knew what their assignment would be. They'd had clean-up jobs before.

Big Larry read over the paper one more time. "Frank, take this list. I'm not sure if all them talked or just one, but we've gotta clean house. Make sure they never talk again."

He handed the list to Frank. He slowly read it over and then read it again.

Frank asked, "Everyone on this list? All four?"

"Everyone," Big Larry said. "You got a problem with that?"

"No, sir," Frank said. "Junior, are you up for this? It could get messy."

Junior replied immediately. "To me, a job's a job. You don't squawk about it; you just do it."

"I'm just asking," Frank said.

"I'm just telling you," Junior replied. "You drove last time; we'll take my car."

"Naw," Frank said. "That thing's ready for the junk yard. We'll take mine but you drive."

Outside of their boss' office, Junior asked, "Think Big Larry will ever give me the list?"

"I'll tell you what: next job, you ask him yourself," Frank said.

* * * *

Sammy D., the local loan shark, threw the fractured bar door open and staggered outside, taking a deep breath. Fresh air would do him good. His bloodshot eyes searched the street, no sign of trouble.

Wrong again, as usual. Four hands grabbed Sammy's shoulders, jerked him backwards into the alley, and slammed him against the wall. A cold barrel of a gun pressed to his head.

Sammy shifted his eyes to the left finally getting a look at

A Job's a Job

the guys that grabbed him: Frank Basso and "Junior" Naducci. Two bad guys working for Big Larry. *This ain't good.*

"Speaking of loan sharks," Frank said to Junior, "you still owe me twenty."

"*Now?* Wait until we're done here, OK?" Junior said.

Frank nodded and then removed the crumbling piece of paper from his coat pocket and double-checked it.

Junior grabbed Sammy's throat with his free hand and squeezed. "What number is he on the list?"

"Number one. Right here it says, Sammy Dimaggio," Frank said.

The gun pressed tighter to Sammy's head. "What have you got to say for yourself, Sammy? Can't keep your big mouth shut, huh?" said Junior.

"I didn't talk," Sammy said, closing his eyes. "Why you guys doing this?"

Junior smiled at the frightened man. "A job's a job, Sammy. Frank, get ready to cross the first name off that list."

Before Sammy could protest or even make a last minute plea for his life, a loud bang emanated from the alley, followed shortly by the thud of Sammy's body hitting the ground.

Walking away from the alley, Junior handed over twenty bucks to Frank.

* * * *

"Mad Dog" Burke closed the door to his bookie's office carrying fifteen grand. He thanked the lord that Little Princess placed first at the track that day. Tonight was his night. He'd have enough for the big poker game later. Even the best cheat in town needed some start-up money. He pushed the button for the elevator. Immediately the doors opened. It wasn't empty.

Frank and Junior grabbed Mad Dog and yanked him inside. Mad Dog's newly-won bundle slipped out of his greedy hands decorating the carpet with green. Before Mad Dog knew it, a blur of glinted metal smacked the side of his head. He dropped to one knee.

"Big Larry don't like jerks that talk to the cops," said Junior.

"I didn't, I swear," Mad Dog protested weakly.

"Cry all you want, Dog, but your name's second on the list," Frank said.

"Yeah, a job's a job," Junior added.

Frank nodded at Junior; it was time. A cannon blast filled the small elevator. Frank crossed the second name off the list. The job was half over.

"Dinner after we're done with the list?" Junior asked.

"Sure, but no sushi. I hate that stuff," Frank said. "And if you want Mad Dog's cash," he said, looking at the floor, "take it; it's yours."

Bending over, Junior said, "I love the perks of this job."

"Don't get used to them," Frank said.

* * * *

Buddy crawled through his apartment window. After climbing the fire escape five floors, he was beat. He'd finally have enough money to pay his landlord and then he'd be able to come through the front door like everyone else. He dropped the bag of newly acquired items he swiped from some rich guy's uptown house. After such a bountiful score, he envisioned a nice hot bubble bath, a glass of wine, and Mozart.

The small lamp by his favorite reading chair clicked on. Buddy lived alone. *What the hell is going on?*

"Doing some night work?" Frank said.

Buddy recognized the two figures sitting in the big cushiony chairs in his living room. *This isn't good.*

"You jawed to the cops," Frank said. "Big Larry don't like that."

"No, I didn't, I swear," said Buddy. "It wasn't me. I think I heard Mad Dog Burke was being a stool pigeon. I've been as quiet as a cuticle in the space station."

"What the hell does that mean?" Junior asked.

"I don't know," Buddy replied. "It's just something my Grandpa used to say. But then again, at that time he was crazy as a guilt monkey."

"And what the hell does *that* mean?" Junior asked.

Frank interrupted. "Buddy, we have a piece of paper with four names on it. Maybe you talked, maybe you didn't, but you're the third name on this list," Frank said, waving it in the air.

Buddy heaved a defeated sigh. "OK boys, do what you got to do. I know a job's a job for you two. That's one thing I always admired about you: you always followed orders."

"That's right," Junior said, pulling the trigger, ending another life. Junior loved his job. He tucked his gun back in its holster.

Frank looked over the list, only one more kill for that night.

"Where next?" Junior asked, standing up.

"Nowhere," Frank said, still seated.

Junior was confused. "What do you mean 'nowhere'? There's another name on the list, right? We told Big Larry we'd finish them all."

"Oh, we will," Frank said, whipping out his pistol.

Junior went for his gun, knowing he was the one who talked.

"Don't," Frank said, pulling the trigger three times. Afterwards, he sat in the chair for a couple minutes thinking about what he had just done. He left the apartment without taking the fifteen grand.

* * * *

Frank stood alone in front of Big Larry.

"Where you been?" his boss asked.

"Had to take a cab over," Frank said.

"Any problems?" Big Larry asked.

Frank handed him the list with four names crossed off it.

"No sir, no problems at all," Frank said. "You know what Junior used to say: 'a job's a job.'"

Stephen Buehler started life as a suburbanite living outside Philadelphia but eventually moved to the big city of Los Angeles. He dabbled in television before enduring a long stint in advertising. Along the way, Stephen pursued stand-up comedy and now enjoys performing magic. With his own company, ReWriteDr, Stephen helps other writers achieve their dreams. His Derringer nominated story,

"Not My Day" was published in the anthology, *Last Exit to Murder*. He has completed a mystery/comedy P.I. novel, *Detective Rules*. His current project, "The Mindreading Murders" is for the Stark Raving Group. For more information about Stephen Buehler: www.stephenbuehler.com.

Mushrooms are an Acquired Taste

R. Hadlock-Piltz

I'M AN EPICUREAN, though you'd never expect it. Looking at me, you'd think: there's an Aljauzanian of Betelgeuse stock if ever I saw one, and like all Betelgeusians, all those sons of Bast, I'll bet he's as ignorant of food and fine dining as a Fomalhaut ice-worm, that he has the underdeveloped taste buds of the rest of his race. But you'd be wrong. We may not have taste buds, but we do have taste. Take myself for instance. It's not a lack of taste buds that keeps me lean. I'm a tramaddict; a shroom-head; an amateur mycologist with the emphasis placed on the ama. Oh, now, don't look shocked. You can read it all over my face and don't pretend otherwise: see my puffy, bloodshot eyes and thinning hair? But I have brains under these stringy locks, and I knew, I just *knew* something was wrong when those three jumpers walked into the Bar Nova on Bast Orbital Station IV: it was because they hadn't any taste.

Picture it: I'm at my usual place at the bar, and I spot the couple and their "friend" right off. Most people coming into Bar Nova have credits, but most Betelgeusians have the taste to not look as if they spend them on their duds. I look like I haven't spent any because I haven't. Being a spore-head means Carcassonne takes my precious credits, never mind how I earned them in the first place. But these three, especially the two lovebirds, look as if they bought their clothes yesterday, and they probably did. Flashy. The male lovebird opens his beak and out comes this low, basso profundo squawk that is like no lingo I've ever heard, but then the smaller man, in the delicate gray suit, snaps to a waiter and orders up a table in too-perfect International Orionese. I can hear by his nasal accent that he's Epsilonian, with that arrogance they have that comes from circling a class-five star. Smug.

Since we mostly get ex-pat Aljauzanians and Carcassonnians as the L2s in the Betelgeuse system, I get interested in the two foreign birds with the funny squawks. I ask to move over to a table. The bartender knows me really well; he does me a favor and soon I'm seated next to the trio, facing the other way. The lady-bird hasn't squawked up yet, but she's a match to the male and soon enough, once Graysuit has read them the menu, this not-so-basso but low voice comes out of her, talking that strange lingo. And coming out of *her*, it sounds good. Sexy. She's a looker, too. Thick white-blond hair, like a polar-bear's pelt. Her partner has a thick blond mane too, covering most of the facial region. They look like typical ice-worlders, I think. So Graysuit, the Epsilonian translator, helps them order, and then they start talking in a pidgin sort of Orionese with the waiter.

"We've must practice Betelgeusian Orionese. We've are the

Fomal ambassador," says the mane-man in his basso voice. They all give him an indulgent smile. I'm smiling myself because I've just realized these really are a couple of hicks just off the jump, credits or no: Fomalhaut folk. Permafrosters. They've come a mighty long way, with a minimum of three space-time jumps between here and the frozen Fomalhaut homeworld. And then my drink comes. I get distracted for a bit because it is Denebian brandy, and the waiter forgot to chill the snifter. Then I listen in again, and they're still talking in broken Orionese.

"When we're going to Betelgeuse-Bast?" asks the woman.

"Soon enough, once you've met the Betelgeusian ambassador to Deneb tonight at the party."

The lady pouts a bit, and I'm guessing she's eager to feel real gravity under her feet again down on Bast, but what she probably doesn't know is that even with their diplomat status they might never set foot there; the translator is just massaging her ego. There's a famous Betelgeusian saying: "High caste, low orbit." Only the highest get lowest; that is to say, closest to feeling real dirt between their toes instead of moon dust. I'm an Aljauzanian-Betelgeuse loyalist and BOS IV is likely as close as I'll ever get to Bast, and I've got contacts real high up in the government. No, I can't tell you who they are.

I stop the waiter as he's passing by. They hear everything and if anything is happening on BOS IV it goes through Bar Nova. Sure enough, he tells me there is a real prime-line party happening, an exclusive affair in one of the station wings where all the diplomats, ambassadors, and nouveau-riche live. Party equals booze, pills and, with Carcasses there, guaranteed trama, the real deal shrooms. Now, I happen to know this old-time Aljauzanian dame who made her credits in the colonies, never mind how, and she lives in that wing, so I'm thinking how can I walk this to my advantage? So I call her up, and she springs the trap for me.

"Oh darlin', of course I can get you to that party," she says. "It wouldn't be a party without you there!"

I demur. She tells me to knock it off and asks if I am going to escort her or not. I say I wouldn't miss it for Bast. I'm dreaming of trama-visions already.

"But," she says, "there won't be any of the Carcassonne stuff to be had, seeing as this party is being hosted by the Betelgeusian ambassador to Deneb. Everyone knows he never indulges."

"Why not?" I ask, not ready to give up the hope of a score.

"Because, silly, he's a dyed-in-the-Fomalhaut-worm-wool patriot! He's supposed to hobnob with the Carcasses, be friendly to them, but not buy whatever psychedelics they're selling."

No trama. No luck. But I can't beg off now since I promised to be her date, so I have to go through with the space-walk. Now I'm starting to resent my nosiness. A dry, dull evening will be had by all. But then the Fomal bird at the next table keeps talking; she says something interesting, and I realize she will be there at the party. So if my date doesn't cling too close to me maybe I can swing my luck in another direction.

I know what you're thinking: tsk tsk. I am planning to seduce the Fomal ambassador's wife! But it's not what you're thinking. It isn't that at all! It is something I overhear when the Fomal ambassador gets up to ask which way to the gentlemen's head. Then the lady and her translator have a moment to put their heads together, and that gets me really intrigued. I am practically leaning out of my chair, and not because of the Denebian brandy. I can see what's happening because I am watching her reflection in the snifter, which I am now glad hasn't been chilled as it gives a nice upside-down, convex reflection of the pair at the table behind me.

She leans in real close to Graysuit, and I am expecting something racy: maybe a love triangle by the way she keeps looking at him. Her eyes kept darting up to see if her husband is gone and then back down to stare hungrily into Graysuit's eyes.

Then she says, in that low sexy voice, "A cuticle in the space station."

I am sure she's made some kind of verbal mistake—it just doesn't translate. But Graysuit's face stays in a steady orbit, as if she's said nothing unusual at all. He takes a sip of his cream-of-mushroom soup and says, "This Betelgeusian food is terrible! It's true what they say. They have no taste buds!"

Well, he makes me want to stop listening then and there, so I do. I finish my drink and leave. It only really hits me what the ambassador's bird meant when I'm getting ready for the party that evening. Which is why, at the first opportunity, I plan on trying to get the Fomal bird alone.

I don't have much luck at the party at first; my date clings to me like an Epsilonian sewage-leech. We make the formal glad-handing rounds, and I shake paws with the tee-totaling Betelgeusian ambassador to Deneb. Then, as luck would have it, just after we are presented to the Betelgeusian ambassador, the Fomal couple is waiting their turn in line to glad-hand him too, and right bang between them is Graysuit, with his nasal, perfect Orionese introducing them as "Mr. and Mrs. Fomal Ambassador."

I take my chance. Once the ambassadors are done pawing each other and blond-beard is yammering away in pidgin, I make sure my date finagles the teetotaler into introducing us, and believe me, she knows how to do it! Aljauzanian women are real diplomats. She could talk the pants off a ... well, I won't go into that now.

"May I introduce the Fomalhaut Ambassador and his wife, and their translator Mr. Nilam," says the ambassador to Deneb. Well, Mr. Nilam, *née* Graysuit, looks me up and down, pegging me for an Aljauzanian right off, but Mr. and Mrs. Fomal Ambassador are nice enough, mostly because they don't know any better. I share a significant look with Mrs. Fomal Ambassador. Real significant. Then I give my date the eye, telling her in unspoken terms to "get these gentlemen out of my hair while I talk to this woman," but she won't take the hint.

In fact, she yammers away about the bird's flashy dress and how she bought one just like it last season, and it turns out the two ladies have a lot in common and wouldn't you know it *but she* goes off with the bird! Betrayed by my own date! Well I'm flummoxed. I'm standing around with the other men, and soon enough the two ambassadors are off yammering away with each other because, wouldn't you know it, the Deneb ambassador majored in Conversational Fomal in college!

So polar-bear-beard waves off Graysuit, saying in so many words he isn't wanted, and it's just Mr. Nilam and myself staring awkwardly at each other. Soon enough he's clearing his throat.

"Erm ... I think I saw you earlier today. In the Bar Nova. You were seated at the next table."

I allow that was me. "I hope you don't think I was eavesdropping," I say. "But we don't get many Fomals in the B.N."

His pale skin flushes a bit, but he rallies and says, "Not at all. And I hope you didn't take my comments about Betelgeusian cuisine personally."

"Not at all," I lie.

"Well, pleasure having met you," he says and wanders off to the punch bowl. There's a line for the punch. For a teetotaler's party it's a long line, and I rather hope someone's spiked the brew with some "space station special" if nothing more worldly. Well, that kills it for me. I storm off to the coatroom; date or no, I'm not going to score anything at this shindig and I remember some pills, some "blue lumies" I think are in my coat pocket. I'm rooting around in the coat pocket, sure I put the pills in there and getting angrier and angrier I can't find them when it hits me like a solar wind: Mrs. Ambassador told Mr. Nilam, "a cuticle in the space station."

She told Mr. Nilam!

Quicker than I've ever run in my life I'm out of the coat room and flying at warp-speed to the punch bowl, and I haven't even tasted the "blue lumies" this evening! I find Mr. Nilam with his hand up over the bowl, as if he's about to pour himself some punch. So I give him some. I knock him clean into the punch bowl! It tips over and then the translator, the bowl and the punch are spilling to the floor together, and there's a shockwave of shrieking and gasps and "see here's!" around the room.

"What is this meaning?" yells the Fomal ambassador's wife.

I yell right back, "Ditch the phony accent, lady! I'm wise to your game!" Mr. Nilam is trying to find his feet to get up and run, but I grab his wrist, hard, and his fist is balled up. I make him drop what he's holding in it. It falls to the ground.

Since my hands are occupied by Mr. Nilam's attempts to break loose, the ambassador to Deneb stoops and picks up the packet.

"Why ... what is this?" His glasses adjust to micro-scale,

and he fingers the packet in his hand. "It looks and feels like some sort of porous membrane."

"I assure you, Mr. Ambassador," I say, "it most certainly isn't as porous as you'd think. If you analyze it, I think you'll find that membrane contains 'cuticlins,' specialized insoluble proteins often found in certain plants, of the sort grown in the Carcassonne garden worlds. And ... ahem ... I've just remembered, 'cuticle' is the common term for the 'pileipellis' layer of a certain kind of fungus known for its special psychoactive properties."

"You don't mean ... trama?" He holds the membrane out at arm's length, as if it might suddenly bite him.

I nod. "Sort of. This is probably the cuticle. The trama contains the psychoactive part—and even then I can't say for sure. It's a secret how exactly the Carcassonnians process it to bring out its psychoactive properties. I don't know if what you hold in your hand is botanical or artificial, or would have any effect at all."

Mr. Nilam stops struggling, seeing he's lost the game, so I reach out and gently take the membrane from the ambassador. "But I can say what I do know. Mr. Nilam is undoubtedly from Epsilon sector, and the Epsilonians have long chafed under the 'special status' relationship that Carcassonne enjoys with Betelgeuse. You yourself have spoken highly of that 'special status.' It would certainly reflect badly on you if this," I finger the membrane, "were to be found in the punch bowl. Might make some people think you weren't entirely on the up and up when spouting your opinions."

The ambassador to Deneb, always a sallow man, turns an even more papery shade of pale. I press on.

"I overheard the Fomal ambassador's wife speaking to Mr. Nilam this morning. She said, 'a cuticle in the space station.' He's a translator, but he didn't bat an eye at hearing such strange words, which was very odd. Especially as she hardly had any accent at all when she said it. And then he replied to her and made a disparaging remark about Betelgeusian cooking which I forbear to repeat. But the germ of it is that he spoke it to her in good old International Orionese. Not that heathen tongue they speak in Fomalhaut."

What I don't mention is that when getting ready for the party I guessed that "cuticle" was also slang for "trama," which is slang for something chemical and unpronounceable. I had meant to confront Mrs. Ambassador for a taste or two, if my date and the nattering ambassadors hadn't gotten in the way.

But I don't need to say any of that, for at my first words Mrs. Fomal Ambassador turns pale and starts to run for the door. I notice now that her blond hair has mighty dark roots for a Fomal lady, and that her big, expressive eyes are bloodshot behind her contact lenses. But her husband grabs her before she can run far, and she collapses into sobs and slumps in his arms.

"Yes, my wife is Epsilonian, what make you of it?" he says. "It is not her fault; her problem's with the drugs." But he is blushing mightily as he says it and his basso is a tad less profundo than before. Maybe he was duped, or maybe he isn't the real ambassador; either way, his diplomatic mission has been a failure.

Over near the overturned punch bowl, my own hooked fish starts laughing.

"Caught! By a colonial Aljauzanian!" Mr. Nilam laughs. I laugh right back, only mine is nastier.

"Yeah! And by an Aljauzanian mycologist at that! The next time you try to plant evidence on a Betelgeusian ambassador, take care whose food you criticize!"

I leave Mr. Nilam, the Fomal Ambassador and his wife in the hands of the BOS IV security officers and excuse myself to attend a private party of my own. The membrane turns out to be non-psych when I test it. I return it to BOS security as evidence. I may be a spore-head, beholden to the Carcass by chains of proteins, but my heart belongs to Betelgeuse. Like I said, I am a patriot. And a true epicurean. In fact, the ambassador to Deneb is planning a banquet in my honor. There's sure to be a lot of courses. I don't suppose you could lend a friend some "blue lumies" to tide him over?

R. HADLOCK-PILTZ currently lives in the Milky Way Galaxy, somewhere along a spiral arm, in a solar system comprising nine planets (sometimes fewer, as *h. sapiens sapiens* lacks a rigorous and exacting planetary taxonomy). She would like to visit Fomalhaut someday. She does not intend to disparage Fomal folk in *Mushrooms Are an Acquired Taste*, nor does she share or endorse the views of the narrator. Any resemblance to people living, dead, or otherwise defined, in any galaxy, is purely coincidental.

The Test

Viannah E. Duncan

"You can't get in unless you know the password," I said.

"Do you know the password?" she asked. I could tell she was anxious by the way she paced back and forth over the well-worn Persian rug. I watched her from my seat on the stool like I was watching a tennis match, but I felt much less enthusiasm about her performance than I would about sitting in the stands at Wimbledon watching Ladies' Singles.

"I do right now," I said, "but it changes every two or three days."

"Which is why we have to go tonight," she surmised.

I nodded. "Yes."

She frowned. "And the password was expensive?"

"Very."

"Is it something we could afford again?" she asked.

"Are you *kidding* me?" I shot back, leaning forward on my stool, the wood creaking as I shifted my weight.

"Right, right," she said, raising her hands in placating surrender. "OK; tonight, then."

"Take a deep breath, Beth," I said. I wanted to make her stop pacing, but I knew if I did that, she'd just start tapping her fingernails against the counter or chewing on the end of a pencil or something. I continued, "It's not the end of the world."

"It could be if we fail."

"One thing at a time," I said slowly, forcing myself to be calm so as not to make her bolt. "Do you trust me?"

She ignored my question, chewing on her bottom lip while she paced.

"Beth, stop."

She stopped and looked at me.

"Do you trust me?" I asked again.

She was silent for a moment and then said, "Yes."

"Then it will be fine," I said, letting her moment of uncertainty pass. "We'll go in, rescue the undercover agent, and get out. OK? Stick to the plan and everything will be fine."

She nodded, trying to convince herself more than me. "I just … I really need this."

"And I *don't?*" I asked.

She ran a shaking hand through her long dark hair. "No, no, I know. We're in this together. Let's go over it one more time."

"We get in the car provided for us," I started.

"With the database information," Beth interrupted.

"Yes," I agreed. "We get in the undercover agency car with

the information to trade and then have the driver let us out a few blocks from the door."

"And the driver doesn't know anything?"

"Yes," I confirmed, "that's correct."

"All right, we get out, and from there we walk."

"Yes. And I have the password. We should be able to get in, if we go tonight."

"I'm just worried that it won't work out the way we want it to. There are so many things that could go wrong. What if our agent is compromised?"

"He won't be. We'll get him out. We've got the stuff to trade, right?"

Beth nodded, pulling a standard coded message ring from underneath her dark blue a-shirt. A long chain had been threaded through the ring, and she wore it as a necklace, the information never leaving her possession.

"Let me do what you've asked me to do," I finally said. She nodded. "Go lie down and rest, OK? Your anxiety is catching, and I can't afford to be off my game."

"But what if—"

"Now."

"All right." She turned toward the back room, where she kept her meager belongings next to the cot she had chosen when we'd been assigned this excuse for a safe house.

"If you really can't handle it," I said after her, "take one of the light green pills in the cabinet behind the mirror in the bathroom. It'll help you relax."

"I think I'll be OK," she said, waving off my concern. I knew she'd take one of the pills, though. She was as predictable as ever.

"I'll wake you up when it's time to go."

She nodded but didn't look back. Then, she passed the threshold into the next room, turned to the right, and left my field of vision.

The next few hours passed in a blur. I prepared my outfit, trashed the entire thing, and then decided on something else and something else again. I called to double check when the black car service would arrive and made sure to request the most discreet of drivers. I went over and over again in my head the part I was going to play and the lines I had been given. No matter how many times I played this role, it seemed, I still got butterflies in my stomach. Beth was rubbing off on me.

We had extracted agents and hostiles before; we were the best at this type of delicate negotiation, and we complimented each other's weaknesses with the other's strengths. Where Beth saw the forest, I saw the trees, so to speak, and visa versa.

This time, however, was completely the same and completely different. I had to decide whose life was worth more—mine or hers. I hadn't told Beth what the entire trade would involve. It was true; they wanted information, but they also wanted someone who could *interpret* said information. That was Beth or me. This undercover informant we were supposed to be busting out was apparently a high priority for our organization while Beth and I were ... well, we were less so.

"You may decide however you like," the director had told me during the briefing, "but one of you must stay behind to interpret the information. That's the trade. Your service to the organization will not go unrecognized."

I frowned, remembering that conversation. I had kept that part of the mission to myself, still unsure whether I would give up myself ... or give up Beth. I knew she would volunteer if I explained, but she had a family. She had people counting on her, waiting for her to come home; I didn't.

The trade wasn't going to be a vacation, no matter how I played it. Afterward, *one* of us was going to have to find a new partner.

I dressed slowly and checked the mirrored cabinet before waking up Beth; yep, one of the pills was missing. Perfect. I headed into the back room with my neutral expression firmly in place, shaking the sleeping woman by one shoulder.

When she looked up at me, her gaze bleary, I said, "It's time."

She nodded, rolled out of bed, pulled her hair into a ponytail, shrugged into her jacket, and grabbed her knapsack on the way out the door, following my lead.

We walked down the steps in silence, and the driver waiting for us in the black car made no comment about our ragged appearance or choice of destination that late at night. Beth slid into the back seat; I slid in beside her and closed the door. The ride was smooth and quiet, and before I had a final chance to wrap my head around what I was about to do, we had arrived.

I got out first and held the door for Beth. After she was beside me on the road, I leaned in and tipped the driver. "Can I trust your discretion?"

"Of course, ma'am," the man said, taking the wad of cash from my hand and putting it in his jacket pocket. I closed the door and watched him drive away; he didn't look back. Finally, I turned to Beth.

"You ready?"

She smiled a weak smile. "Yeah, as ready as I'll ever be." She took my hand and squeezed it tightly before dropping it again. Her worried eyes followed my movements.

I turned and led us through a maze of dark side streets and back alleys before coming upon a plain oak door in the side of a brick wall. The door had an elaborate knocker depicting the Roman god Janus, but was otherwise unadorned. I nodded to Beth, and she reached up, lifted the knocker, and struck the door three or four times before letting it go.

After a moment, a panel I hadn't noticed just above the knocker slid to the side and I could see the shadowed face of an old woman looking out at us.

"What's worse than finding a hair in your linguini?" she asked, her voice scratching with apparent disuse.

"Finding a cuticle in a space station," I replied, working to keep my voice steady.

The panel slid shut, and, for a single moment, I thought I'd ruined it for both of us. Had the password already been changed? But then the door creaked open and the old woman beckoned us inside.

We stepped through the doorframe and the door swung shut behind us, obviously heavier than either of us could handle by ourselves. The entryway was dimly lit, and the brocade wallpaper offered little in the way of comfort.

Beth was standing about a step behind me, and when the old woman asked, "Have you the payment?" I nodded to my partner. Beth pulled the chain from under her military-issue jacket and off over her head. The coded message ring swung in the low light, glinting as it turned on the chain.

The old woman held out one wrinkled hand, and Beth

dropped the entire necklace into the woman's palm. She held it close to her face to verify its authenticity and then, apparently satisfied that the ring held the requested information, enfolded it into the recesses of her heavy, layered clothing.

"And the rest?" she asked, her gaze moving from me to Beth and back again.

Beth looked at me, alarmed. "What?"

I paused for a split second, frowning.

"Her," I told the woman.

"What do you mean?" Beth asked me, suspicion in her voice clear.

The woman's eyes narrowed. "This girl is the rest of your trade?" she asked, ignoring Beth's obvious distress.

My partner gasped, looking to me to deny the charge, but I couldn't meet her eyes.

"Yes," I told the old woman.

"You're *sure*?" Beth asked me, her voice rising with emotion. My frown deepened.

"Yes," I said, half-glancing at her. "I'm sorry. I knew you would've volunteered anyway, so I thought ...." I trailed off, surprised by her expression.

She wasn't at all shocked or frightened. She just looked sad. "I'm sorry, too," she said.

The old woman was shaking her head. "You have failed again," she said, and it was unclear whether she was speaking to Beth or me.

I furrowed my brow in confusion, but it was Beth who responded. "Give me one more chance. Please. I can help her!"

"What are you talking about?" I asked, and it was my turn

to look suspiciously from the old woman to Beth and back again.

"She *still* has not learned self sacrifice, Agent," the old woman said, ignoring me completely. "I'm sorry. We cannot risk it in a real time situation."

"No!" Beth said, stepping in front of me as if to stop the old woman from attacking me. "I can still save her. I know she's good inside. I *know* it."

"Agent," the old woman said patiently, "this is the tenth time in a row that the candidate has literally traded *you* with the data instead of herself, even though you both know that *you're* human and she isn't."

"*What?*" I sputtered angrily. "What in the hell is going *on?* Are you *insane?*" I asked the matron, my speech growing noticeably louder in order to force them to listen to me. "What are you even *talking* about? Not *human?*"

"Agent," the woman said to Beth, her voice stern. She looked at me sympathetically, as though I was a child who didn't understand the rule I had just broken and yet still had to be punished for breaking it.

Beth turned to me, tears in her eyes. "I'm so sorry. I tried so hard. I tried to save you. You're worth so much more than scrap metal, and you don't deserve deactivation."

"What?" I asked again, still bewildered at this sudden change in my partner's demeanor.

"I'm sorry," she repeated. "I believe in android humanity. I do. Please believe me when I say that, but I can't let you sacrifice a human over yourself. Again. After all we've been through." She wiped the tears from her face with the back of her hand.

"Wait. What are you—" I began, but Beth leaned forward and pressed something against my arm. I felt a pinching sensation, and then I was tumbling forward into darkness.

VIANNAH E. DUNCAN hails from the Los Angeles area and writes nonfiction by compulsion, poetry by inspiration, and reviews when the mood strikes. She holds a Master of Fine Arts in Creative Writing and has been published in several small literary journals and anthologies. She's *almost* certain that she's not an android, and she has a cantankerous cat named Cleopatra. For more, visit her online at duncanheights.com.

Charles Oleson Maverick Anderson

Jedidiah Shank

CHARLES OLESON MAVERICK ANDERSON, otherwise known as "Coma," dwelt on the planet known as Lupa Minor until a series of events changed his life drastically. Coma sat down on the couch and took up the newspaper next to him.

"Well, well, well," said a voice behind him. "If it isn't my big bro back home from the war."

Coma turned around and saw Ronin, his little brother. Ronin had a wicked grin on his face and a strange remote looking object in both of his hands.

"I came home expecting you to be here waiting, but then I found out you went on some 'errands,'" Coma replied.

"Yeah, and I came home from work yesterday expecting you to arrive when you said you would, but no, your flight was delayed." Ronin said. "But anyways, here. Check this out."

Ronin handed the remote to Coma. Coma observed the device and turned it on. It made a projection of a full colored screen showing the news in three dimensions.

"Whoa!" Coma said surprised, "How did you get your hands on this? Only the government has a hold of the latest hologram technology."

"Well, let's just say I had a few hours to spend by myself, waiting for you, so I built one."

"How did you—"

Coma was interrupted mid-sentence when there was a knock on the door. The brothers turned their heads toward the door. Coma finally answered it. Outside was a man wearing a Marine Corps uniform decorated with many different medals. He stepped inside and looked at Coma.

"I am sorry to come on such short notice," he started to say to Coma, "but there has been a catastrophe. We need all the soldiers we can find whether they are active or not. For your cooperation, we will promote you to Sergeant. If you would, I would like to discuss the details with you in private."

Coma stared at the officer, nodded, then turned towards Ronin and passed him back the holographic remote. "I'm sorry, Ronin," Coma said softly and then closed the door behind him.

Several months passed and Coma was now riding in a space shuttle. He had a grumpy look on his face, which warded off the other soldiers. He was sent to Lupa Major to be transferred from the 422nd to the 221st Marine division as Sergeant in the Lupan Armada. Coma looked around the shuttle. It was half empty due to several M.I.A.s from Coma's squad. He was told that when they landed on Lupa Major they would fill in the gaps of Coma's squad. Two Marines were having a conversation, but the only phrases Coma could make out were "Came from nowhere ... Lupa Minor ... destroyed ...." Coma was stunned. Curious, he leaned forward to listen more carefully, but his grumpy look silenced the marines. Before Coma could inquire about what he had just heard, the doors opened. They had arrived at Lupa Major.

When they landed on Lupa Major, Coma was surprised at what he saw. There wasn't much to look at except for a big desert of white sand and several military bases in the distance. He had always been told how magnificent Lupa Major was with its huge cities and its beautiful plains. Based on what he saw, he decided that they were all lies. Even if it had been beautiful, all Coma wanted to see was his home on Lupa Minor.

Out of nowhere the officer in charge of Coma's platoon approached.

"All right, Marines!" the officer said. "My name is Lt. Jones, but that is 'Sir' to you! There are strange things happening to space stations around our galaxy and the government wants to send the Marines in ASAP! These space stations are being crumpled up and torn to shreds by an unknown force. As some of you may know, Lupa Minor has also been destroyed along with countless battleships protecting it from space."

Coma's eyes widened as he stared at the officer in shock.

The Marines inside the shuttle must have been right. Could that mean that Ronin is ... dead? Before Coma could succumb to devastation, he shook the news from his head and continued to listen to the officer.

"This could be the doing of the Resistance," the officer continued, "or it could be our first contact with alien life-forms! Whatever it is, we have our orders to put a stop to it! Do you understand, Marines!?"

"SIR, YES SIR!" replied all of the recruits.

"Good, because that is the last time I am going to say it. Now get into your five-man squads and get to a transportation shuttle in 0200 hours! Let's roll out, Marines!" On that note, he left.

When the transportation shuttles took off, Coma could already feel something strange. It felt like the air around him was slowly tightening and squishing him. Right when he felt like he couldn't breathe anymore, the feeling went away and everything was back to normal. He put his hands to his face and whispered his brother's name, "Ronin."

Once the shuttle landed at a different, but still ugly and barren part of Lupa Major, Coma looked around to see if he could spot his new men when an officer from the military base came up to him with six new recruits. Coma spotted a familiar face in the small crowd. His brother Ronin was standing there with a wicked grin.

"These are your new soldiers, Sarge," the officer said. "Make sure they behave."

Coma smiled and said, "I'll be happy to take these men off your hands, sir."

After the officer left, Coma smiled at Ronin and patted him on the back. Ronin laughed and smiled back.

"I thought you were dead!" Coma told Ronin.

"I thought you would think that," Ronin replied, "so I joined the Armada and asked to be transferred to your unit so you wouldn't cry yourself to death."

"Oh, like I would ever do that."

After they had been assigned roles at the base, Ronin walked up to Coma, leaving the others, and said, "I've been thinking. What if space has a mind of its own? What if empty space is actually Space, an entity, and is causing these weird things to happen?"

"What?" Coma said in disbelief and annoyance, "That doesn't make any sense. Where do you always find your crazy ideas? I mean, how can empty space have a mind of its own?"

"Just hear me out OK?" insisted Ronin, "Lupa Minor had no weapons or anything that could destroy anything. The planet was mostly nothing, just empty space, or Space. That could have caused the destruction of the planet. And ever since we landed on Lupa Major I had a weird feeling. As if the space around me was getting smaller. I thought that it was just my imagination or it was the planet's different atmosphere messing with my brain, but now I'm certain that the same thing that happened back home is going to happen here. You've been feeling it too. I know you have, come on, admit it."

"Fine, I admit that I've had weird feelings too, but that doesn't prove anything. What if it is the atmosphere of Lupa Major?" Coma replied, forgetting that he was now a sergeant and shouldn't be showing favoritism to his little brother.

"There was also this scientist who studied empty space. He realized that all matter is meant to be all in one piece, but the space around us is pushing matter apart. That was his theory of gravity, so it would make sense if Space is what's destroying everything."

"That's absurd, Ronin. Just forget your ideas, the Armada will figure things out."

"Cut the chatter, Marines!" the Lieutenant yelled, "I want all of you to gear up on the double!"

"What's going on, sir?" Coma asked, "We just landed. How come we have to gear up?"

"There has been an attack inside one of the military bases. I have orders to have you guys standing by for combat. Now move!"

Coma led his five-man squad from the shuttle and grabbed a ballistic vest and helmet. He put the helmet on, powered up the HUD, and his view filled with analytical information of the environment. He heard Ronin whisper, "Cool." Coma and his squad put on the rest of their armor and grabbed M12 assault rifles with 30-06 armor-piercing rounds and plasma gunpowder. All the squads took speeders to the neighboring military base where sixty other Marines greeted them.

"What is going on?" asked Coma, "Who attacked? Wha—"

"Stand down, Sergeant." One of the Marines interrupted. "There has been a death at this base and there might be more. We don't know who did it or how, all we know is that some kind of invisible force is killing our Marines."

"An invisible force?" asked Ronin, "Something that the HUD doesn't see?"

"The private who died was doing regular guard duty when he was called by one of his officers. The private said, 'I can't move.' The officer thought the private was being disobedient so he started to yell and walk towards him. When he was five feet away, the private's skull shattered from the inside. The officer said that no trace of any explosive devices appeared in his HUD scanner. There was nothing hidden within his skull, or anything in his skull as a matter of fact. Just empty space. I will answer all of your questions after I get a perimeter sweep, but until then, I want all of you Marines to MOVE OUT!"

"SIR, YES SIR!" the Marines replied.

After several perimeter sweeps, a loud yell could be heard, calling for every Marine available. Coma and Ronin ran as fast as they could and when they arrived they saw a Marine floating in the air as all the other Marines pointed their weapons at him. The Marine couldn't move.

"What is going on, sir?" the Marine asked, "Sir?"

The officer sighed and said, "I'm afraid that there is nothing we can do to help you soldier. I hate to say this but you are going to die. Right now."

"What!? Right now? Can I say my goodbyes to my family?"

"There isn't enough time for that, Private. The only thing we can do is to pay for your funeral."

"I ... I understand sir. It's just that I—" With a violent bang, the Marine's skull shattered and his lifeless body fell to the ground.

Then suddenly, another Marine fell down dead. Then another. And another. One by one the Marines slowly decreased in number until more than twenty Marines lay lifeless on the floor.

"RUN TOWARDS THE MESS HALL! WE CAN REGROUP THERE!" cried one of the remaining Commanding officers as he himself ran away.

Coma and Ronin didn't need to be told twice. They both ran away as fast as they could.

"So you believe me now, Coma?" Ronin asked breathlessly, while running for his life.

"Yeah, yeah," Coma replied, also breathless. "Just how do we solve this situation?"

"I think I have a plan, but first we need to get to a power generator, and fast."

"We have direct orders to go to the mess hall. If we go there, we might have enough man power and fire power to stop Space from doing any more damage."

"You don't get it do you?" Ronin yelled. "You can't destroy Space! We have to divert its power away from us!"

Several officers who were running along side them looked at Coma.

"You have to follow your Commander's orders, Coma," one of them said. "It doesn't matter how risky it is. Orders are orders."

Coma clenched his fists and made a decision.

"We are going to the mess hall, Ronin, whether you like it or not!"

Ronin lowered his head and didn't make eye contact with Coma.

"Fine," he said, "I know you'll regret it."

Coma, Ronin, and the other officers reached the mess hall only to find that the force inside there was completely obliterated. They all dropped their weapons and ran to the nearest runway. When they got to one of the hangars, Ronin stopped to fiddle with the electrical system connected to the hangar.

"Follow me, Ronin!" Coma yelled, "This isn't the time for playing around! Follow my orders and we can get out of here alive!"

"I know what I am doing, Coma!" Ronin yelled back, "Just listen to me for once and get inside the hangar! I know a way to hold off Space."

Coma reluctantly ran inside the hangar as another Marine's head exploded. Ronin ran inside right when Space slammed the door shut.

"What were you doing out there?" asked Coma.

"I programmed the electrical charges to project power to cover the hangar so then the air around the hangar is no longer under Space's control. It's like I cut off a limb from Space, but it won't last for long. I need a generator to hook up to one of the shuttles so then I can make a portable shield, a cuticle if you will.

"A cuticle?"

"Like on a plant leaf. It's that thin protective shield. At Station 112 on Lupa Minor, some scientists made their own cuticle covering the space station. The cuticle doesn't block solid objects. Fortunately, Space isn't solid."

"What in the blazes are you two guys talking about?" asked a Marine.

"We'll explain after we get off Lupa Major," replied Ronin. "But first we have to get to the point where the source of Space is. The Void." Ronin desperately hunted through the hangar for a generator.

"How are you going to defeat Space by going into The Void?" Coma asked as he dodged flying machine parts his brother was throwing. "There is nothing there!"

"Exactly. If I can get in there I can take a modified power generator and throw it into The Void, creating a cuticle that surrounds the source of Space which will limit its power to just the small section inside the cuticle. It will be like cutting off the head."

"We cannot risk all of our lives for an idea that no one understands!" Coma replied angrily. "Our best chance is to get to the nearest space station and get more help."

"That won't do anything! Have you not seen what Space can do? It destroyed Lupa Minor and Lupa Major!" Just then, Ronin stood triumphantly, holding a blue and silver device. "This is what we need. Now follow *my* orders for once and we might even survive."

Suddenly there was a loud crash as the roof of the hangar split open and another Marine exploded.

"Hurry!" yelled Coma, "We have to get out of here!"

Coma looked around as the hangar was collapsing and ordered the other troops onto the shuttle.

Ronin activated the portable generator. "We're now protected in our own power cuticle."

Coma shook his head in disbelief. "We're alive. You saved us, Ronin."

Crackled, fuzzy orders from the shuttle's transmitter

filled the interior. "All forces gathering on Lupa Prime. Fly directly to Lupa Prime."

Coma took the wheel and flew them into space and towards the Void. "I'm sorry about doubting you earlier, Ronin." Coma said.

"It's OK," said Ronin gratefully, "I understand. And I'm sorry about trying to force the idea into your head. It's pretty hard to understand, but we have to remember that we are in this together."

"Sergeant," a distressed marine said, "Lupa Prime is the other direction."

Coma smiled at Ronin and continued to fly towards the Void.

When they entered The Void, the Marines put their space suits on. Right when they opened the door, Marines started to die.

"Come on Ronin!" cried Coma, "Your plan better work! Hand me the generator!"

Ronin gave him the generator and then froze with his face pale. Coma turned around to see what was wrong.

"Come on!"

"Coma ...." Ronin replied in a shaky voice, "I ... I can't move."

Coma stared at him in disbelief, "No, no, no! You have to do this with me!"

"Stop Space, Coma. It is all up to you."

"Come on ... Ronin, don't say things like that."

Ronin smiled and said, "When you are ready, cut the blue wire and connect it to the green wire. That will reverse the power shield, encasing Space in the cuticle. Just remember, there are different Voids inside the galaxy. They are all connected which means there are still openings for Space to attack. Encase them all. Cut off all the heads. Finish this." With those last words, Ronin's eyes rolled back and his body exploded.

Coma couldn't believe his eyes. He had just watched the only person left for him to love die and he couldn't do anything about it. But inside him a spark of courage appeared, and he knew that he had to stop Space. He cut the blue wire and connected it to the green wire, and the generator started to spark.

"So you think you can stop me," said a voice inside Coma's head, "you must realize all your hard work will be in vain. I will find a way to be free and more of your pitiful friends will die. Just let it be. Let yourself die. Save yourself from more suffering."

Coma clenched his teeth and said. "As long as there is still something to fight for, I will not give up. As long as there are people like Ronin and me, the human race shall prevail! I swear that I will stalk you to the ends of the galaxy and beyond, for I am Charles Oleson Maverick Anderson, defender of this galaxy. And you have to get through me to ever be in charge."

With that final word, he threw the generator into The Void. The generator exploded and a sphere of electricity covered the darkest spot of The Void and sealed in Space.

Coma felt his space suit slowly loosen and realized that his chest throbbed with horrible pain. Several of his ribs were broken. Coma had stopped Space just before his body was crushed.

* * * *

From that moment on, my hatred for humans grew and I vowed revenge. I will never give up for I am almighty. I am all knowing. I am everywhere. I. Am. Space.

JEDIDIAH SHANK, or Jed for short, is a thirteen-year-old 8th grader whose favorite thing to do is to play video games in his free time. His other hobby is building or animating with LEGOs. He takes piano lessons weekly and he likes to interact with his friends online. Jed does not order spicy food at restaurants because he cannot handle spice very well.

No Exceptions

Ted Nitschke

MY LAST NOVEL topped out at 1,600 pages, a new record for the publisher. In all telling, it consisted of just over 400,000 words, and to hear from the critics, very little plot whatsoever. The fourth in a planned series of six books, it became my highest selling and most reviled book in a long career of highly selling and mostly reviled books. I was the king of taking people's money and pissing them off. Trademark, patent pending.

I am the exception.

I figured it out decades before–not the secret, no, that came much later–but the trick to building an audience. I was no Hemingway—heck I was no Buffett, but I knew I was at the least a serviceable writer. I had ghostwritten a few of those crap kids' novels, the kind that left you with a cliffhanger at the end of each chapter and immediately resolved them on the next page, surely a legend in my own mind. The characters in the books were flat and one-dimensional; I had very little leeway. I couldn't kill off one of the bastards, even if it made sense. I wished I could've. I would do it with my own bare hands, I imagined; that's how much I hated writing those books. But the checks came in and I kept doing it. I could write these books in my sleep. I did write in my sleep. Increasingly stupid scenarios to put generic characters into and pull out of flooded my dreams. I asked myself, what the hell am I doing? It was writing, yes, I was being paid to write, but it was all well-choreographed bullshit.

I had to write my own books, my own well-choreographed bullshit. Writing has to be one of the vainest forms of expression, that idea that someone out there might want to read something just because you, the "author," wrote it. I needed a solid boost to my ego after years of making some asshole publisher truckloads of money. I might not have been Hemingway, but I knew I could make some decent cash and I probably wouldn't end up like dear old Ernest in the process.

I knew what was out there, what was making money. In those days it was all legal thrillers and terrorist plots. People weren't reading Pulitzer Prize winners or anything written up in the Times—and I should add, still aren't, to my knowledge—but they were reading cheap paperbacks with flashy covers and bold titles. The only thing that's changed since then is that people read them on screens instead of paper. Makes just as much sense as anything I guess.

Science fiction held promise, I thought. It hadn't really broken through mainstream but with enough massaging and bland storylines, it could be up there next to Ludlum and Grisham. I would write a science fiction series—and it would be a series—a never-ending journey into the pseudoscientific world of some shit I would come up with. If the first one was good enough, I could buy myself an island in a couple years.

Now the island waits for the next moment I can tear myself away from this damn promotional tour. It's not that big, but it's mine. No one can take that away from me.

Genius. That's what I'm called when I go to bookstores and sign illegible scribbles on nameplates. It's what I'm called every time my idiot editor phones me up and asks me when the next book's gonna come out. It's what I call myself when I think about the moment I came up with this goddamn neverending book series. I'm not Ernest Hemingway, but I might be a genius and hell, I own an island. Hemingway never owned an island.

Let me reiterate that. I own my own island. My own goddamn island.

The series and the genre came easy, but I had very little idea of what the books should actually be. I made it up on the fly. "A cuticle in the space station." That was the first line of the first book. I was off to the races. "A cuticle in the space station." It wasn't the most original thing in the world, but it got me going. The cuticle floated around, cut off from some careless resident of the station, out of the outstretched hands of our main characters—all pieces of other archetypes out there in the world, a bit of Star Wars here, a little Arthur C. Clarke there, all wrapped up in the easily digestible form of cheap paperback books with creased spines you could find discarded in airport lounges around the world. That single cuticle floated past every single character I could think of, right into the air vent and right into one of the proton stabilizers (what did that even mean?) and our gallant space station crew dove right into action. Adventure, crisis, disaster, the book had it all. Every chapter featured explosions or sexy situations. I even had a well-placed lemur in a spacesuit. I knew the book, a culmination of my experience writing crap for elementary school book sales, would be an instant hit. Feeling confident about my chances, I sent off my first pages to the publisher. They loved it; it was a future classic, the kind of book that would make Dan Brown piss his shorts. All it needed was an ending.

My propensity to kill beloved characters—well-earned, at this point—did not come out of a sadistic streak. In this first novel, it was a necessity if I wanted people to pick up the next one in the series. I needed a cliffhanger, that damn lemur on a space station plummeting towards an altogether alien planet. Pure brilliance, if I say so myself.

I planned on killing off every single character except one. The lemur would live, damn it. I was getting attached the little fellow, and hell, I needed something for the sequel.

Writing an ending always made me nervous. It had to hit, this one especially, it had to work. I sat down and tried to finish my disposable masterpiece and the stress came on in a wave. This was different, something different than usual—chest pain, shortness of breath. I felt like I was having a heart attack.

I killed off the first character the only way I knew how, gruesome and tasteless: I blew him to bits by the vacuum of space. I felt better immediately. My breathing calmed, my heart started pumping again. A trick of the mind, the heart, the glorious written word; whatever it was, I felt a whole lot better.

The symptoms returned a few days later and I tried something. I went back to the novel and killed off another character, this time the chief science officer, eaten by one of his twisted experiments. I felt like a million bucks, like nothing had happened.

I went to the hospital of course, got checked out by the doctors. They patched me up and sent me on my way with a clean bill of health. I had nothing to be worried about. Perhaps it was gas or a Dickensian bit of undigested beef.

But I thought I knew what was going on–not that I ever told anyone about it; they wouldn't believe me anyway. By killing my characters, I was getting life. The Destroyer of Fictional Lives, I would become immortal.

Here is where I give the caveat. This is how I see it and it's always worked for me. It's the only explanation I could come up with. From here on out, you have to take my word for it. Either it's true or not, I don't care which one you pick. Isn't it all just a story anyway?

I didn't think much past that, except I knew my life depended on writing the next book as soon as possible. I sent the manuscript into the publisher and immediately started on the sequel.

Introducing a new set of characters at the beginning of the book, difficult in itself, allowed me a new group to kill off if I needed to. The first book was published—"A massive success! When can we have the sequel?" Soon enough, soon enough, I told them.

The first sequel allowed me to completely stop the heart attack from ever coming, as far as I could tell.

The third book put me through a bad flu season, not a

sniffle in sight, no shots needed. Everyone hacking and coughing, I was the only one immune.

The fourth, my latest, my longest, the most new characters, and if you ask my critics, my worst book. I stopped caring about plot, structure, anything. It meandered, it faded, and nothing ever happened, excluding deaths. The critics, even my beloved fans, hated it. They hated it and asked for another, please. Just because I had roped them in.

The fourth book cured the cancer.

Some people fight cancer with treatments or positivity or whatever Good Morning America blabbers on about every day. I fought my cancer with words. Words that described the most despicable deaths I could imagine. I fought cancer the only way I knew how.

The day the book hit number one on the New York Times Bestseller List, I was declared cancer free. A scientific miracle, the doctors told me. But I knew better.

Everyone has their explanations for the things that happen in their lives; mine was merely a bit more outlandish. I could chalk it up to chance, I could chalk it up to God, but I knew it was killing off those damn characters. Nothing is random, I always believed, and I felt like I finally had proof.

It was greedy, living this way. I let myself go; eating anything I wanted, not doing anything to take care of myself. I wasn't a healthy guy to start with, but I knew as long as I had characters to kill, nothing could happen to me. As long as people wanted more books and I could write them, I would be fine.

Two complaints about my writing permeate the discussion around it, both owing to the fiery passion of my fan base.

Both complaints centered on good old death, that jolly subject to which I owed everything.

First, the complaint that I am likely to die before I finish this series. The second, that I enjoy killing off characters with heartless abandon, that I ruin the fictional lives of beloved characters because I revel in it. Both of these are absolutely true. I have no intention of ever finishing the series at all. I will string it out into eternity, killing your darlings, staining your books with tears.

A single message rings through all my novels. A message of despair and doom. Death comes to all of us. My readers will die, their children will die, and their children's children will die. I will keep writing.

I am the exception that proves the rule, sitting on my private island whiling off toward the end of time.

The fifth and next book in the series might prevent a chronic illness or a hard fall from a ladder—who knows what will happen to me next. I feel the Grim Reaper on my shoulder, breathing hard on my neck. Maybe I'll write him into the next one.

Today is the day I will begin my next novel in the unending series.

I find myself sitting down at the computer to begin the next bestseller piece of crap, feeling like I have never felt before. On top of the world, fingers flying at the keys. This will be my masterpiece, the one that puts me over the edge. The one that cements me in the history books.

The first death will be magical, powerful, electrifying. I reach it with ease. How must I do it, how shall I offer this character to the higher power?

Nothing comes to me.

This is something that has never happened before. I have no idea how to kill her off. My mind races, frantic, but nothing rises to the surface. Die, character, die already. The blank page taunts me, laughing at my delusions of grandeur.

The pain comes quick, like a prick right to my left temple. My hands fall onto the keyboard, limp.

I see them, those I have sacrificed for my immortality. They tell me one thing:

"No exceptions."

TED NITSCHKE gave up a spot on the International Space Station to pursue his dream of becoming a writer, or at least that's what he tells himself. In his short life he has graduated from both UCLA and Pepperdine, married the girl of his dreams, appeared on "Keeping Up with the Kardashians," and eaten a disproportionate amount of Costco hot dogs. His future goals include publishing his first novel, creating a children's television show, and buying his own private island.

Sugarfruit

John Everett

HER ESCAPE FROM the transport prison had been an accident. The whole colony of pregnant females had been pulled from their controlled environment. The portable prison unit, "The Great Box" as they had come to feel about it, was placed into the dark cargo hold in the belly of the vast vessel. She was only attempting to get to the fresh fruit across the way when she had broken free. A hole at the edge of the wire and she had wriggled out, just like that. Now what? Someplace in the black-dark cathedral the fruit was still there. A little food, perhaps some juice and she would have enough energy to reach the far end, the end to which the thick, cold air was moving. She sensed that was where she wanted to go, needed to go. But there was fruit and juice here now. Just a moment for pause and she would seek the room's far end.

The thin waxskin of the apple was nothing she hadn't seen before. But this was different, uncut. It was odd. For as long as she could remember she had possessed the razor edged tools she needed to cut through the waxy skin, but had never used them until just now. It tasted bitter. But the fruit below the waxskin was sweet, high in sugar and energy. There was a collection–another "Great Box"–of apples in the cargo bay. She only needed one, just part of one, just the outer edge of one, single, sweet apple. After eating her fill she left behind a single egg, perhaps a dozen eggs. There were several eggs to be certain, more than enough eggs. It was a good apple, sweet, bitter, waxy. They would be well nourished there, a good nursery.

She was ready. The fruit sugar was already converting into the heat which fired her flight motors. Her paddle wings vibrated then spun and grabbed into that thick, dark, cold air. She arched her hook feet free from the bitter waxskin. Away she lifted into the heavy gelatin gas.

The air pulled her along to the far end of the cargo cathedral, a river of heavy, cool gas moving into the airshaft. She didn't know where she was going. No matter, heat was ahead. That much she could know, or feel, or sense, perhaps predict; it didn't matter. There was more to do. The buzzing wings hurled her into the ductwork of the giant transport's ventilation and recirculation system. This was the pulsing heart of the ship's life support infrastructure. Compressed and warm, the gelatin gas kept the ship's occupants alive whilst they traversed cold space. She was only a meter from the impellor when she perceived the pulsing and the danger of its spinning blades. In less than a thousandth of a second her wings reversed direction and attempted to pull her away from the whirling impellor disk. She was too close. The electric drive was too strong against the rapid and constricting column of air in the duct. In an instant, a minute, an hour, no matter in flytime, she was pulled through the blades. Her multi-facet eyes watched in perfect temporal clarity as each blade rotated past. The thin grey layer of dust at the trailing edge of each silver plate gave her lens eyes the impression of an orange peel surface. There was the sensation of pressure, heat, too much heat, burning heat. Then, an instant, a minute, an hour later, cooling as she shot through the blades, untouched, and into the fully conditioned air at the other side.

This new column of gelatin gas was a pleasure to move through, warm, soft, moist. Her buzzing, humming, swirling wings moved her through the river of gas. Grids of light and movement bounced wild within facet lenses as she propelled herself through the tunnel. Instinct and the smell of more fruit directed her wings into a certain outlet vent. Hook feet found purchase on a smooth plastic surface. Wings stopped. Silence. Non-silence. Stiff gelatin gas pushed against her. There was the din of the impellor, and the still fresh apple scent from the cargo cathedral far down the ventilation duct.

Facet eyes collected motion. Waxskin cutting tools sought food but found only the scent of human-oils and carbon dioxide. She knew all too well the stench of human-oil. The now abandoned colony as well as The Great Box had had this smell. The Human-oils which sat beneath her made odd sounds, just as they had done at the colony. Human-sounds were unnatural, grating. "Don't spill that, Jeffery!" "How much for a vodka?"

The grating vibrations gave her a sense that she should move away. There was more fruit. Her razor tools felt it. Fruit!

Feet unhooked and sugarwings spun and she was zooming over the human-oil heads which lived within the cold walls of the transport vessel, the space station. Individual molecules of a new, delicious fruit bounced off her waxskin sensors. Their intensity made her wings respond, navigating her to the correct location. The human-oil, a galley wench, took no notice of her as hook feet gripped the grape's green skin.

A new surface, soft under hard hooks, tasted as its scent had predicted it should. Razors cut through the thin skin, a cuticle in the space station, without resistance. Sweet sugar. This was a good nursery, sweet and damp. More eggs, a dozen, a hundred, didn't matter. The grape nourishment was better than adequate, better than even the sweet cargo apples. Her motors coughed to life, lifting her back into the viscous air. More human-oiled heads moved above her, below her, past her. There was a slow hand which moved in her direction. Her wings perceived the slow hand and moved away, flytime, without effort. Then, in an instant, razor tools felt the fruit, odd fruit, a new fruit. There was fruit at the surface! Purple Fruit!

Feet hooks found the surface fibers, dense, heavy, and slick. Within the tangled mat of plastic ropes and human-oil smear there was trapped a sweet jelly, a purple-red jam. It was fruit but not quite fruit. Different. Odd. Waxskin tools probed the purple gel and found only sugar, pure, absolute sugar wrapped in the scent of fruit. It was not fruit, only corn sugar. Deception Fruit! Confusion. She left no eggs there. They would not have been nourished in Deception Fruit. Corn sugar would have been a poor nursery. There was no fruit sugar, no egg sugar. Wings pulled her away.

The general movement of gelatin air compelled her to the

front of the giant ship. More smells, more heat was ahead. Instinct navigated her magic, buzzing, swirling wings. It was only a moment to reach the giant bulkhead, perhaps an hour, a marathon of buzzing navigation, an instant, a lifetime is no time in flytime. Warmthlight! Limitless warmthlight was under the hulking bulkhead. Human-oil was there, too. But there was warmthlight. It would be warm. She sensed no fruit there, but it would be a good place to rest after the day's activities.

Passing with hook feet upon plastic ropes under the bulkhead, more warmthlight than she had ever known in the transport prison greeted her facet eyes. Sugarfruit wings pulled her high up into the bridge, the control deck, of the transport ship, the space station. Human-oiled air, thick as grease, moved slowly about her in her resting spot upon a giant plastic toadstool. The pilot of the ship, one of two pilots always on duty when the vast glacier of a machine was in motion, reached across the warmthlight. The giant hand moved, and the wings moved her away, flytime.

She found a bright corner upon the control deck of the space station and hid down deep beneath the edge of a panel there. Warmthlight panels allowed her body to cycle, a nice place to rest. Movement. Non-movement. Confusion. Waiting. Non-waiting. She left no eggs upon the warmthlight panels. There was no nourishment upon the panels. There was noise, some vibration. The human-oils made their screeching sounds, "Ground spoilers! Reverse green! Deceleration!" She felt the meanings of the sounds in the quieting vibrations, the reducing noise and the slowing vibrations of the sun panel. There was stillness. The warmthlight panel was finally, completely still. Non-movement.

The human-oils moved. She did not. She remained fixed upon the panel. The hulking bulkhead swung open and the human-oils moved through the opening. Fresh air and new smells came into the control deck. They were entirely new smells to her. There was fruit for certain, but new fruit, unknown and untried fruit. Her waxskin razor cutter vibrated, tasting the molecules. Magic wings and hot sugar motors pulled her through the bulkhead frame and out into a completely new world. Her hot wings propelled her through the ship's main porthole and high above the green landscape of distant mountains and proximate trees. Razor sensors were again vibrating. A grove of mangos was beneath her. Fruitsugar wings carried her deep into that grove.

The spaceship's journey was complete. Her abandoned transport prison, still pungent and smeared in human oils, was unloaded from the aft cargo bay as was also a crate of fresh Washington apples.

The captain of the space station looked out upon the building at which his ship had docked. The sign read, "Bienvenido al aeropuerto de Cancun." A second sign read, "Gate 31." Unseen by the captain, deep under the skin of a fresh Washington apple, a tiny white dot of DNA began to move.

JOHN EVERETT began telling strange and off-the-cuff short stories about the same time his first child was old enough to understand language. His most requested tales usually involve secret monster caves, mad cow disease, tooty-chip cookies and metal robot fairies. John also enjoys watching classic science fiction movies with his very young children—*Alien*, *Jaws*, *Poltergeist* and *American Werewolf in London* are big favorites. John uses the ethical merits of these well-known films as well as Fox News commentary to form the basis of his general world view.

Not So Ordinary Day

Rebekah Ruther

AFTER WORKING ANOTHER long shift at the botanical gardens, it was finally time to go home. Don't get me wrong, I love caring for the thousands of blooming flowers that appear in the springtime. But with spring comes warmer weather, and it can be tough working in the sun all day. Although I am usually happy with the thought of leaving work, my usual sense of relief wasn't present today. Walking to the car, I dropped my keys out of nervousness. I was concerned with what people would think of me when I got there. God forbid there would actually be someone I knew. As a made the long, awkward drive to my destination, I had to stop myself multiple times from turning back. When I finally arrived, I sat in my car for ten minutes preparing myself for the new experience to come. I took a deep breath and stepped out of my car. Wiping my sweaty palms on my pants reminded me of how bad my nails had gotten from digging in the dirt all day. I was embarrassed. Walking through the door of the nail salon, the bell chimed, alerting the workers that a customer had arrived. To my surprise, the space of the small salon was quite peaceful. Although it did not rid me of my nervousness, it helped a little. I walked past the floor-to-ceiling shelf of nail polish to the lady at the counter and asked her what I should do. She told me that station four was available. Taking the stroll over to the chair seemed like an eternity. As I was walking, people were looking at me. I wondered if there was something wrong with my hair. My thoughts were disrupted by the overpowering smell of what I knew to be nail polish—I knew this because I had three daughters. As I sat down in the massage chair, the lady that would be doing my nails gave me a weird look, and I immediately considered making a run for it. To distract myself from the awkwardness between me and the lady trimming my cuticles, I looked for a magazine that could hopefully take my nervousness away. As I picked up a magazine featuring the NASA space station on the cover, a tiny piece of my freshly trimmed cuticle fell on top. "Hey look," I said to the woman, "A cuticle in the space station." All I received in response to my comment was another weird look. I decided to stop trying to make small talk, and instead entertained myself by looking around the room. A customer with fresh neon pink nails was talking to the lady behind the counter, and there was another woman performing the daunting task of picking out one color from what seemed to be millions. I wondered why the lady doing my nails didn't start a conversation with me, but I blew it off and continued observing the other people present in the tiny room. In a way I hoped they didn't notice me as much as I noticed them; I guess that's what happens when you're a man in a nail salon.

Rebekah Ruther is seventeen years old and starting her senior year. Although writing has not been her favorite subject in the past, with the help from her wonderful mother, she has grown to enjoy it. Her favorite form of writing is poetry. She plans to continue writing poems inspired by her experiences this past summer.

Confined

Andrea Goyan

"IT WAS A joke."

"It doesn't mean I have to be happy about it," I said through gritted teeth.

Dr. Bill shrugged. "This place is boring," he said. "We're stuck here together, and I have a wicked sense of humor."

He belched while I guzzled a second glass of water to wash away the fetid residue of meat in my mouth.

When I chose to serve my time here with humans instead of on a penal colony, the Custodians warned me it wouldn't be easy. *"They are an inelegant species,"* they told me. *"You may wish you'd chosen the Argynt sector labor camps instead."* But, the Custodians of my kind were always doomsayers and I was a risk taker.

Dr. Bill popped a cherry into his mouth.

I heard his teeth pierce the soft fruit and bite onto the pit. He separated the flesh away, chewed, swallowed, and then continued to roll the hard seed around in his mouth, click-clack, against his teeth. He knew it drove me crazy; our misophonia was explained to him, and yet he did it anyway. I watched the pleasure in his dark eyes as I squirmed in my seat. A hint of a smile crept onto his lips.

"Oh, I'm sorry …." Click-click-click. "Does this bother you?"

He stuck out his tongue, displaying the round brown kernel which sat like an egg on a pink nest of flesh.

I took a deep breath. The Custodians taught me that trick during my preparation. The extra oxygen in this atmosphere could be used to calm my limbic system. I needed to stay on task. My success here would open the door for my people to settle on this planet, and our survival depended on it. I would show the humans that we could get along, that we weren't to be feared, despite our size and superior strength.

When they suggested this trial co-habitation, we knew they'd make it as challenging as they could. Criminals from both sides made for odd diplomats. As annoying as he was, Dr. Bill wasn't my enemy. He was a volunteer inmate, and like me, he was expendable should this experiment kill either of us. I crossed my arms and noticed they still ached from the copious inoculations I'd received. There were very real fears on both sides.

"I'm fine," I said.

I looked at my fellow convict and remembered the way his small hand felt in mine when he took it to welcome me here five solar days earlier. His skin was soft like the fuzzy membrane covering the peaches the prison Keepers gave us yesterday.

"When I was a little girl …" I said.

Dr. Bill barked, shooting the seed across the table to hit me in the chest.

"A little girl?" he said. "Oh, that's ripe."

I took another deep inhalation, refusing to let this omnivore rankle me. He snatched another cherry from the bowl on the table between us. As I listened to him devour it, I wondered how he made everything he ate sound like he was a wild animal rending the flesh from its prey. It sickened me.

"You know I am a vegetarian?" I said.

He smiled. "Yep."

"And, you've been told that it's paramount to my species?"

"I've heard that." He snickered and leaned toward me, "Like a *prime directive?*"

How naïve this creature was. He assumed I didn't know the reference, but my people spent decades preparing to make contact. I wondered what discipline he could have possibly completed his doctorate in?

"Then, why would you adulterate my food with the flesh of an animal?" I asked.

Click-click-clack.

I could have overpowered him in an instant, but hurting him went against our convictions. He knew it, his own Custodians would have taught him that, and it was why he dared push me.

"I grew up in a small town," he said, "And the thing I learned there? You can dress a cat in a suit but it's still a cat unless it learns to walk on two legs and shoot a gun. Here you're the outsider, and we do things my way. Your predecessors didn't have a problem with it."

It was a lie, of course. Yliova killed herself. She'd lasted only two weeks into her sentence. The one before her, Rda, made it to three before he went rogue and had to be "reassigned," which we all knew meant he was sent to an asteroid in the Celan Galaxy and would never be heard from again. Something here drove my people crazy faster than an infestation of Pertrolaclyl lice. I looked around; it certainly wasn't the accommodations. The environs were bland but clean. All furnishings were made of a composite material in white, black, or metallic tones. Our food was grown in hydroponic chambers and they'd even imported proper sleep recliners for us. All in all, not a bad place to do my time.

Click-click.

I fixed my gaze on the doctor. The remnants of flesh between my teeth nauseated me. If he'd tainted Yliova and Rda's food too, it was probably what drove them to their respective ends.

Click-click.

"You understand we aren't a violent species?" I said.

"Yep," Dr. Bill said. Click.

The enamel on his teeth was very thin. I wondered how he didn't chip it.

He spoke again and a tiny bubble of spittle puddled at the corner of his mouth.

"She told me you evolved when you became vegetarians."

"Yliova?"

He blew out air between his lips until they vibrated. "An impossible name to pronounce."

"Like mine?"

He threw up his hands. "I don't even bother. It's like a revolving door with you all."

I wasn't going to take his bait, as humans say; I needed to represent the best of my kind.

"That's a shame, Doctor Bill," I said, enunciating his name carefully.

Prior to being shipped here, the Custodians double checked my pronunciation, vocabulary, and knowledge of human customs before they deemed me ready.

"Dr. Beel," he said, imitating my accent. "It's not like you sound like a native."

"Our diets are an important and integral part of both our physical development and our societal structure," I said. "We've been vegetarians for over three and a half centuries."

"So?"

"Even the slightest meat in our diet has dire consequences."

I'd begun to sweat. The liquid leaving my pores smelled like animal flesh.

Rubbing his belly he snorted and said, "Cat-in-a-suit."

"The punishments for dietary indiscretions are severe."

He laughed.

"Look around? Could it be worse than this?"

Cocking my head, a human gesture I'd learned, I said, "Much worse."

"Don't look at me like that, it's creepy."

I attempted to smile. The Custodians worked with me for months on that, a slight upward curling of the lips without any display of teeth. *"Do not threaten them,"* they warned me. What Dr. Bill didn't know was that though I was a vegetarian, my teeth told a different story, an older one. He didn't know that the bits of meat he'd slipped into my rationed breakfast meal as a joke awakened a primal urge I struggled to control.

"Failure can take many forms," I said, thinking about Yliova and Rda.

He put his hands behind his head and kicked his chair back until he balanced on two legs.

"We're not as dumb as your kind seems to believe. You think they'd have put us up here with you if they thought you were a threat? They told me it would be like bunking with a cow."

I shook my head, another learned movement.

"We are nothing like cows," I said.

"Look," he said, leaning forward until his chair legs smacked back onto the floor. He interlaced his hands and put them on the table in front of him. "If I said I was sorry would it make everything better?"

He batted his eyes at me.

This was a smug creature. I glanced up to the overhead monitors. Somewhere in space the Keepers watched, members from both species, each with his own agenda. Dr. Bill popped another piece of fruit into the hole in his head. His lips were bright red with the juice.

Blood. He didn't know I could smell his, a consequence of my tampered meal. My nostrils flared, and I moved my head from side to side, sniffing. It was intoxicating. My jaws ached. My senses so keen I detected the bead of blood drawn from a cuticle in the space station thousands of miles over our heads where our Keepers witnessed.

"Many ways to fail," I said.

Smiling I revealed my long sharp teeth.

Click-click-cl—

I reached across the table and grabbed Dr. Bill around

the throat. Somewhere in the room in space, I imagined the Keepers panicking when my teeth perforated his neck. As his blood filled my mouth, I knew I'd failed my mission. All diplomacy was over; the humans would never allow us to settle here without a fight.

I chewed and swallowed, noting that I was wrong about the human's skin; it was tougher than a peach.

Panels of red lights on the wall began to flash. The shrieking alarm that accompanied them fed my fevered feast and the sound of his bones: click ... click ... crunch.

Dr. Bill was delicious.

A lover of dark comedy, science fiction, fantasy, literature, playwriting, poetry, or really any good story, ANDREA GOYAN is thrilled to be a part of the NaNo Los Angeles Anthology. She's new to the NaNo community, running her first NaNo marathon in November 2013, and loving the supportive environment steeped within the pressure cooker of the thirty-day deadline. Andrea began writing as an adjunct to her performing career. As a playwright, her work has been produced over a dozen times in Los Angeles. She paints, gardens, knits, bakes, has her own business, and is working on her second novel. Andrea lives in Los Angeles with her husband and three cats. Her website is andreagoyan.com.

Mortimer Marchand

D.B. Randall

TO THE EDITOR:
While normally I do not send epistles to the local press and thereby expose myself to judgment on the part of an unlearned and generally insensate audience, and, while I am unfamiliar with the processes by which my text may be left untouched or, on the contrary, altered beyond the intent of my original message, I find myself at wit's end and in need of self-explanation. My lawyer, naturally, has recommended against this course of action; still, my conscience and the fact that I write to you from a rented yacht in international waters compel me to make clear some conclusions rendered rather untidy by spurious logic.

With regard to the motive, some noise had been made early in January hinting at common jealousy: rivalry among geniuses who both strove for attention and fame. (The question of monetary gain was not at that time pursued.) This line of reasoning was, in my humble opinion, the most accurate. Had the detectives made enquiries along these lines among the teaching staff, fingers would have pointed them in my direction. (While I admit to nothing, I cannot let stand sloppy reasoning.) The young and, may I say unreservedly, beautiful detective who had proposed this ancient and apt motive for murder was soon to discover that, within his own ranks at the department, he himself would be vulnerable to the sting of professional backbiting.

The February 8th dismissal of Detective Truly from the case was a blow. News of the reassignment, the case regrettably turned over to the incapable hands of the elder Detective Roberts, rendered me paralyzed for nearly two days. I could not get out of bed, so despondent I had become. Even an offer from a female admirer to see the new French film at the Laemmle–normally irresistible to me (the film, not the admirer)–could not resuscitate my *joie de vivre*.

With regard to the severed digit never recovered, not one forensic specialist was able to determine the time at which the member had left its host. Had anyone reasoned that the finger had been removed *avant la mort*, then Detective Truly's case would have blossomed into a full-fledged, fructified investigation. (Detective Robert's casual and ill-managed inspection was, quite frankly, an insult. His admission to my lawyer that he had failed to take notes during several impromptu "checkups on leads" left me *non-plussed*. After some reflection on the subject, I became acutely embarrassed for the Pasadena Police Department on the whole to have employed an investigator so lacking the skills required in the art of interrogation.)

As to the victim's contract with [a local aerospace firm]

and in all fairness to the victim, he was not an entirely bogus choice in hiring. The director of the underfunded Manned Space Program cannot be faulted for his ignorance. Director Vishwanath had no inkling that it was I, an articulate, if shy interpreter of the theoretical–not the victim–who would be covertly making the glorious theory into a design *vivant*. Before I made the CAD drawings from the victim's germinative notes–hastily scribbled on cocktail napkins from his evening crawls along Colorado Boulevard–the victim had nothing properly to show for his singular approach to human life in deep space. (His defiance of the status quo, and his refusal to allow for only unmanned space and planetary exploration made him extraordinarily popular among the students, if not with his fellow academicians.)

This romantic yearning in him I found undeniably attractive, and thus we began our intense yet short-lived association. Of course, he had no foreknowledge of my specific interest in his cryptic notes. (He left them ever unattended on his desk when he went to piss out the prior evening's quantity of St. Bernardus.) He considered, as did the preponderance of our fellow professors, our mutual interests in falconry and Campari to be the gluten that bound us. So it was that with only a few hours each day apart from his company, my efforts were hampered. Sneaking onto the college's network via a dummy account was, perhaps, more liberating and fulfilling than the actualization of the visual model itself. Nevertheless, such roundabout maneuverings were costly in terms of time and vigilance. Strain had set in. Throughout the holiday season, I became a nervous wreck.

As the deadline approached to make a public unveiling

of my efforts—and I would have given your publication the honor—I was met in our office on the morning of the crime by the victim, wagging his finger ingenuously at me, who asked if I would consider assisting him in the creation of a design for a manned space station. I simply lost it. Snapped in two like a new pair of sushi sticks. I went mad. I believe that once, as a child, I underwent such a transformation while at boarding school. The matron had accused me of setting bed sheets on fire, and I was summarily sent to the headmaster's office. The assumption was that, left to sit for forty-five minutes in the secretary's office, I would cool off and find the words with which to defend myself. Instead, I bit the affable headmaster in the hand the moment that he opened the paneled door for me. (Biting cases got sent home with no review, of course. A fact which I knew before I had even procured the matches.)

It could have been the fact that the victim asked for assistance with a smile on his face. Into that broad smile I could read no ulterior motive in his asking, I could discern no cat-and-mouse agenda. Yet had he asked without the smile, had he asked with a worried frown knitting his brow or even in a deluge of fretted tears, then I may have been moved to share my secret with him and present it to him as a gift, a surprise or, better, as a gesture of faith in his diabolically genius determination to see man extend himself into the universe as gods among the stars.

Again, please understand that I make no admissions here. Perhaps I write a little too closely from the heart or from that which weighs upon it. But it was I who telephoned the handsome Detective Truly in late February when the investigation was put on debilitating hold. Attempting a rough and deeper tone to my voice, I pressed him to "make a QT call in the space station case," which he quietly did. Given my instructions to check the underside of my desk drawer for passwords, he would be able to decipher the pattern before him: to discover the dummy account and to lay bare my designs.

Although Detective Truly would have, I inwardly believe, brought to light the entirety of my genius and that of the victim's (through my conveyance as designer, albeit), the police department (at Detective Robert's insistence) dropped the entire investigation and filed it as a cold case. This broke my heart.

And so, without any confidence in the young detective's ability to extend his reach beyond that which his inept superior will allow, I send to you this letter as both prompt and exorcism. The sea is heaving today, and I am unable to continue this correspondence comfortably. Over the past weeks, my vision has become too sensitive, and I find that only a darkened room with its windows shuttered will afford me ease of mind. This room's walls are pitching to and fro at the moment, so I think a pace around the deck above, even in this horrid weather, will offer a respite from the murmurings I keep hearing here below. There are times when I worry that the walls themselves are speaking to me as they once did in my tiny, shared office at the college campus. *Les murs murmurent.*

As a child, D.B. RANDALL secretly practiced riding a bicycle on a small patch of cement in the backyard of the family home in the Pacific Palisades. A fig tree overhead had altogether purged itself, and the sticky, lumpy fruit–glued to the pavement and rotten in the summer heat–functioned as treacherous obstacles. To this day, the author can ride in circles to the left only and faints at the cloying scent of overripe Brown Turkeys.

D.B. Randall is a *nom de plume*.

Dreaming Magic

Irene Chung

THE FULL MOON was bright and shining through the window. Clara was still awake, staring at the Moon. She couldn't sleep with the noise of the pack of wolves howling on the little cliff that loomed over the orphanage in Connecticut.

But there aren't supposed to be any wolves in town. She got up and looked out the window. Up on the cliff, she saw that it was not a pack of wolves, but only a lone wolf. It looked down at her with its unusually colored sea-green eyes. It seemed to be trying to say something to Clara. She dressed and quietly tiptoed down the long hallway to the lobby of the orphanage.

Clara opened the door and looked to see if the wolf still stood at the edge of the cliff; it was still there. Clara saw the outline of the little black wolf.

She suddenly had a strange urge to climb up after it. So she climbed up the mountain the way her parents had taught her when they were still alive.

They're not actually dead. No one knows for sure if they're really dead or if they're only missing. Clara's parents had been missing for two years and most people thought they were dead or just never coming back.

Clara saw the wolf walk towards the woods. When she got to the top, she saw the tip of the wolf's tail disappear behind the trunk of a thick tree. Clara hesitated, but decided to go after it anyway.

"I must be going insane," Clara muttered to herself. However, when she followed the wolf past a very large oak tree, blinding light filled the woods. When the light faded, Clara found herself in a colossal forest clearing. There were beautiful, brightly colored flowers and bright green bushes. There were also hundreds of different kinds of forest animals. And in the middle of it all, there was a grand palace.

Then the wolf from before came along and barked at Clara, and somehow she understood it. It said: "Please put your fingers into the bowl of water, only up to your cuticles." Clara wondered what was happening and how she could understand the wolf, but Clara put her fingers into the bowl of water up to her cuticles, as she was told. The palace doors opened, and the wolf went in. Clara followed and listened to all the things it said.

Apparently, Clara's parents hadn't actually died; they were the king and queen of all the forests in the world and they finally returned to this palace in order to properly rule all the forests in North America. The reason they left Clara in the orphanage was because she was too young to really experience the magic of nature. Also, the wolf's name was Willow.

"Oh, OK then. Can I see my parents?" asked Clara. She'd missed her mom and dad for almost ten years now, and she wanted to meet them as soon as possible.

"Of course," Willow said. She led Clara through a long but beautifully decorated corridor. They entered a large room with two thrones and sitting upon them were Clara's parents. She ran to them and hugged them.

"I missed you a lot. Can I stay here with you from now on since I'm older?" Clara asked them.

"Yes, you can stay here now. You are older, and you can experience magic. The animals outside can help you use magic," Clara's father said.

"I agree with him. You are the princess of all the forests. You should learn how to care for the forests properly," Clara's mother said.

"Just one question," wondered Clara. "How do you take care of all the forests in the world?"

Her father answered, "There is a space station out in space that tells me if something goes wrong in one of the forests. I simply put my hands in a bowl of water, up to my cuticles, like you did outside, and I can see all the forests. A cuticle in the space station is the great source of our magic. Then I send one of my council members to the troubled forest to deal with the problem."

* * * *

"Well, I doubt you're the princess of a forest, much less that your family has royal blood. Also, no offense, your parents are still dead," said Sophie. Clara was still at the orphanage, and everything was just a story Clara had been making up. Sophie was Clara's best friend.

"My parents aren't dead. They're only missing. Also, just because I'm at an orphanage doesn't mean I have no parents or that they're dead," replied Clara.

"Actually, that's what being an orphan is all about," said a new voice. It was Harry. "And I'm pretty sure your parents *are* actually dead. They've been gone for ten years now!"

"Why are you in the girls' room?!" yelled Sophie and Clara in unison.

Then the door banged open and the lights flicked on. Everyone woke up.

"Clara, Sophie, and Harry!" demanded the orphanage's director, Mr. Anderson. "You three are in big trouble for staying up past your bedtime! Especially you, Harry. You know you're not supposed to be in the girls' room!"

The three kids walked out of the room as all the other girls, except the few still sleeping, laughed and gaped at them. Clara, Sophie, and Harry felt humiliated as they followed the director out of the room.

The next night, Clara couldn't sleep again. So she woke up Sophie and decided to tell her a made up story again. This time, the story was about Clara falling into the ocean while on a boat with her parents and becoming a dolphin. Then Sophie told her, "Well, your parents are still dead, you can't turn into a dolphin suddenly, and how are you ever getting on a ship in the first place anyway?"

Mr. Anderson came in again and told Clara and Sophie to come to his office. "How many times do I need to tell you this? You cannot stay up past your bedtime! At least Harry learned his lesson."

One of the staff came in with Harry behind her. She explained, "This boy was trying to sneak into the girls' room again."

"Guess not," Mr. Anderson sighed.

IRENE CHUNG was born in September and is excited to turn twelve years old. She lives with her parents and a little brother four years younger than her. Her parents moved to America from a small country in Asia, so Irene and her brother were born in America. Irene goes to elementary school near Los Angeles, California. At the end of school everyday, she goes to an after-school program. Irene likes to play with her school friends, and she also is good at math, like her two best friends.

Pyre

Sarah Hawley

I WATCHED THE FIRE blaze in the clearing below me, the flames tinged purple by the leaves used as tinder.

Everything on Garbrax seemed stained purple. The heat of the day dropped fast into violet sunsets; the sun rose again through a lavender haze that left fat dewdrops on the forest leaves. The tree trunks were coated in jewel-bright mosses that crawled up from the forest floor.

Berry had told me that the mosses grew in symbiosis with the most striking characteristic of this rainforest—the *codiaeum garbraxis*. These large, dense bushes clustered around nearly every tree. Their waxy purple leaves were larger than a man's head, and when they burned the smoke smelled like cinnamon and copper.

The flames before me were blindingly bright, but at the edge of the fire I could see a dark, shriveled lump, enclosed within the rapidly burning cremation frame. I inhaled deeply. Beneath the spicy scent of the burning leaves, a new smell rose: a half-savory, half-repulsive stench. Ten years of ethnographic field research had taught me that scent well; that was the smell of a community facing its own mortality.

* * * *

5774 P.N., 1st cycle, 1st day

The expedition began in earnest today. I was dropped off near the village we identified from the satellite imagery to begin my observations. The vegetation is thick in this area, and I have been given strict orders to bring back plant samples for Dr. Berry to analyze, since he refuses to leave the station.

James Martin and Rachel Cho, the Consilium's terraforming and environmental manipulation experts, are also canvassing on foot today. Everyone else remains aboard the colonization launch station.

The Garbraxians are bipedal and clearly intelligent. They look much like we do, although significantly shorter on average. Their village is constructed in a circular formation, centered around a large bonfire. The lack of any centralized structure leads me to wonder if this society is egalitarian.

I have a month to complete this first phase of observation—I am confident more answers are forthcoming.

* * * *

Private communication, Dr. Alice Thompson to Dr. John Morgan, Chair of Anthropology, Univ. of Callifrax. 5774 P.N., 1st cycle, 5th day

Really interesting stuff here, John. Just one village so far, but plenty to study. It's incorporated almost seamlessly into the surrounding jungle—if it weren't for the clearing containing the village fire pit, I wouldn't have been able to spot the settlement at all.

The fire is the most puzzling thing thus far. It burns constantly, no matter the time of day. The villagers feed the flames with the leaves of a local plant. It seems like an extravagant use of resources, but the plants are everywhere, so perhaps there's no danger of running out. No idea what the constant fire symbolizes. The villagers cook and dance around it, and today I saw several of them apparently meditating by staring into the flames. The burning leaves smell like cinnamon. At first the smell made me feel dizzy and lethargic, but now I tolerate it well.

Gina Cole, the Consilium representative, doesn't seem particularly interested in my anthropological observations. I had hoped the rumors of scientific neglect on colonization surveys were exaggerated—perhaps not. Will keep you updated.

Hope the lab is running smoothly in my absence.

* * * *

My field bag clanked as I dropped it on a table in the botany lab.

Berry looked up from his microscope, blinking reddened eyes at me. When I pulled out the first sample vial, he quickly rolled his chair over to paw through the synth-leather bag.

"What did you bring me today?" he asked.

"Flowers, seed pods, and a few more garbraxis leaves."

Berry looked like something that lived in a cave, all long, thin limbs and alabaster skin. The lack of humidity on board the station had dried him out, cracking his face and hands. His sickly pallor was a result of his prolonged tenure in space. Berry traveled from station to station, analyzing the samples researchers brought back from the surfaces of planets and moons and asteroids, but he steadfastly refused to set foot anywhere with a natural atmosphere. No one knew why.

He smiled at the vial of tiny blooms and the skin at the side of his mouth cracked, leaking a drop of blood. His tongue darted out to catch it, and I looked away.

"I saw another cremation today," I said. It was the second I'd witnessed in the last two weeks.

"Is that so?" he asked absently, using a set of tweezers to pry up the edges of a globular seed pod.

"The Garbraxians do some very interesting things with the corpses. They hollow them out like eggshells and burn the organs separately."

Berry was silent, studying the underside of a leaf.

"They fill the empty corpses with garbraxis leaves," I continued, knowing that, at least, would interest him. "It makes the flames burn purple. After the ceremony they take the ashes and dump them in the forest." I paused. "I think it's nice, actually. It's so pure. There's nothing that genuine left in the Consilium."

"How interesting," Berry said. "I wouldn't have thought the leaves would burn well, considering how thick the cuticle is."

"Cuticle?"

"It's the outer coating on the leaves of a plant, a sort of protective layer." He pulled out a sachet of leaves, unwrapping them reverently. "See?" He trailed his fingers along the surface of the uppermost leaf. "It's what gives the leaf its waxy consistency. It protects the plant from outside contaminants and helps it conserve water."

I looked at the leaf, remembering the way it had curled and bubbled in the flames. The smell of cinnamon still seemed to cling to me, and for a head-spinning second I thought I smelled burning cuticle in the space station.

For the first week of the expedition it had felt harsh in my nostrils, muddying my head, but now I had grown accustomed to the omnipresent smoke. I even missed it. The air on the station was sterile, nothing like the spicy, crackling scent of the living world below us.

I rubbed my eyes, pushing back against a growing headache. "I just told you about some very interesting hollow corpses," I said, "and you'd rather discuss plant cuticles?"

"Corpses are common enough," he said softly, stroking the leaf with gentle fingertips. "Imagine being able to repel everything that tried to touch you."

"Be sure to tell Gina how effective it is at repelling others," I said. "I'm sure she'll bring a whole bush up."

* * * *

*Private communication, Dr. Alice Thompson to
Dr. John Morgan. 5774 P.N., 1st cycle, 16th day*

Today Gina told me not to talk so much in meetings. She wants me to stop sharing my anthropological observations and to focus instead on what the Garbraxians are using for sustenance, whether or not they're hostile, and how easy it would be to relocate them.

I know you warned me about this, but I hadn't quite believed it before. I guess I hoped I could be an advocate for indigenous rights during the colonization process, a voice for the native community. The usual wide-eyed nonsense. Your critiques of my savior-complex are noted from afar—I know exactly how problematic this perspective is.

I don't know what to do, John. I'm staying as vocal as I can, making sure it's clear that Garbraxian culture needs to be studied and protected, but no one's listening.

I wish you could see it here. Everything on the surface is so vivid. The lush forest, the brilliant orange bonfire with its pulsing violet heart, the smell of dew and hot copper and the omnipresent cinnamon. I see the fires behind my eyelids at night, sometimes.

* * * *

Meetings happened at the end of every week. A month of meetings so far, each one discussing power sources and terrain management and what resources could be stripped from the soil to feed the hungry machines of the empire.

I was still in my field gear. I'd cut it too close to bathe. It had been just after dark on Garbrax when I'd begrudgingly boarded my shuttle. Today the usual work had continued in the village–resource gathering, food preparation–but the villagers had just begun to build the fire higher again when I'd left. Another death? I would never know.

My stomach ached and my head pounded. In the dry sterility of the room, the odor of my work seemed particularly strong—Berry had already edged his chair back, wrinkling his nose at the rich miasma of sweat and smoke that drifted across the conference table. As I stared at my dirt-encrusted hands, the air above them seemed to ripple, and I felt a sudden vertigo. I blinked hard and focused on the meeting.

Rachel and James were seated on Berry's side of the table. Calliope Brinks, the colonization strategist, sat near me, typing notes in her organizer and ignoring me completely. At the head of the table Gina sat in a heavy synth-leather chair, presiding over us all. Her elaborately styled hair gleamed with layers of wax, and tonight she wore a metallic gray suit that glimmered under the light. Expensive fabric from one of the Consilium's many production moons, no doubt.

"Welcome," Gina said crisply. "The date is 5774 P.N., 1st cycle, 30th day, 1900 hours. This meeting represents the conclusion of the first stage of analysis of Garbrax's colonization potential. Report."

"James and Rachel completed the terrain assessment," Calliope said, scrolling down a page of notes. "The terrain is perfectly suited for environmental manipulation and settlement construction. Few changes in elevation, ample water sources. The vegetation is thick, but we can clear it easily enough."

"Power sources?" Gina asked.

"Hydroelectric is a possibility," James said, "and there's plenty of light for solar."

"Tell me about the plants, Dr. Berry," Gina said, tapping notes into her organizer. "Is there any benefit to keeping them? Are they edible?"

Berry cleared his throat, humming faintly before he spoke. "I haven't yet reached that stage of analysis."

Gina stopped writing, staring at him with cold brown eyes. "Why not?"

"There's, ah, a great variety of plant life. I'm only just beginning to piece together the biology of the most common species. It's, ah, fascinating. The leaves are designed to facilitate rapid water absorption, which—"

"We don't care about their biology," Gina interrupted. "We care whether or not they can be used."

Berry wilted. I watched him for a second, but he said nothing more, dropping his head to stare at the table.

"The local tribe uses the leaves of one of the plants extensively," I said, turning to Gina. "Obsessively, you might say. The garbraxis is used to feed their central fire, cremate their dead, decorate their homes, and spice their food, and I've recently seen them wrapping it as a poultice around wounds."

"Good," Gina said. "Dr. Berry, you will determine if these plants can be used to our advantage before we repurpose the forest."

"Repurpose?" I asked sharply.

"This is the perfect environment for a mining operation,"

Rachel said, pulling up a topographical map from her organizer. The undulating green lines reflected off the table; I felt dizzy again. "The soil profile indicates the presence of an enormous proliferation of heavy metals."

"No." The word echoed in my head, pinging around as my vision oscillated. I blinked the haze away to find that everyone was staring at me.

"That is not an acceptable contribution to this meeting, Dr. Thompson," Gina said. "Please clarify."

I reached for the words to express my visceral horror. "Mining would severely damage this ecosystem, which would directly affect the local population. Their entire way of life is based on their relationship with the forest."

Swaths of plants would disappear beneath the hulls of low-flying terrain modification ships. One sweep of a vaporizer cannon, and the leaves would vanish as if they'd never existed. The color would drain out of the world; soon the lush forest air would smell like steel and poison.

My eyes burned.

"The local population is living in a primitive state, correct?" Gina's long fingernails clicked on the table.

"'Primitive' is a loaded word," I said. "They just live differently than we do."

"We're talking about human progress, shaping this world's future through science and technology. That is a far more important task than preserving the lifestyles of savages."

"Don't use that word."

"What, *savages*?" She stared at me. "You said they lived in wooden huts."

5774 P.N., 1st cycle, 2nd day—Their houses are circular and made of a complicated latticework of woven branches, lashed together with brightly colored leaves.

"You said"–Gina looked down at her papers–"that they paint their bodies and dance around a fire."

The pigment is formed from a glittering concoction of soil, rainwater, and crushed leaves. Their sweat mixes with it as they dance. When they spin, little spatters of light are flung off like liquid constellations.

"And now you tell us that they medicate themselves using leaves. These are savages, Dr. Thompson. They are living in a way humanity left behind thousands of years ago."

"Does that make them irrelevant?" I asked.

"Quite frankly, yes."

My head throbbed. "I have a Ph.D. in Applied Galactic Anthropology," I said carefully. "I am a well-respected anthropologist with multiple publications, and not a single scholar in the universe would dismiss my concerns the way you just did."

"You are only here because of a legal requirement," Gina said. "I do not consider you an expert on the intricacies of the colonization process, and I am uninterested in your personal opinions."

I wanted to hurt her. The flicker of flames was rising to the surface of my skin, and the metallic cinnamon scent intensified. I closed my eyes and took power from it. Where once the scent had muddied my perception, now I felt cool and sharp, like a knife blade, all edges and righteous fury.

I stood, slapping my dirty hands down on the table. "Then you're an idiot."

Across the table, Rachel gasped. Berry moaned and rocked in his chair.

"Don't you dare speak to me that way," Gina snapped. A lock of her waxed hair was quivering. "Who do you think you are?"

"An emissary," I said, grinning madly now. I could hear the pounding of drums below, and I knew they were dancing for me. "I speak for this world."

"Alice," Berry whispered. "You can't do that."

"Are you insane?" Gina was staring at me like I'd transformed into a venomous snake. "Get out of this room before I have you forcibly removed."

I smiled as I left. There was still a dance waiting for me below, and the hot, invigorating scent of the leaves.

* * * *

5774 P.N., 1st cycle, 31st day

> Garbraxian time feels different. It stretches out like warm taffy during the day, slow and languid and hot, and then night falls with a startling swiftness. The mists rise from the woods and blanket everything in cool droplets of water.
>
> I've come to find that abrupt transition to darkness comforting. Sudden and certain. I feel certain here, too.
>
> The Garbraxians threw extra leaves on the fire last night, although it wasn't a funeral. They stared into the flames and meditated instead. I sat with them, hidden just outside the firelight, breathing deeply. In that space of calm I made a choice. It is easy to make

choices when the smoke is inside your lungs—all the distractions of the outside world fade away. You are filled with utter clarity. For so long I have built a life on uncertainty and nuance—now I feel the burn inside, the righteous call to action. My cause is just, my mind clear, my course set.

* * * *

"Try it, Berry," I said, shaping the pile of leaves on his work table the day after my meditation. They seemed to sing under the pads of my fingers, their smooth surfaces vibrating with unheard music.

"I don't think that's a good idea," Berry said hesitantly.

He looked exhausted. The bags under his eyes were bruise-colored against the pallor of his skin, and his lips had cracked again.

"You wanted to know how the leaves burn. This is your chance."

"I don't want to cause any smoke damage to the room."

I pulled a ventilation hood over, fixing it above the pile. "This won't produce enough smoke to matter, and even if it does, we have the hood."

He leaned in, and I could see his yearning curiosity. "What if the smoke is toxic?"

I shook my head. "The Garbraxians breathe it in with no problems. I've inhaled it every day, and I'm totally fine."

Last night I stared into the flames and sucked the smoke into my lungs, as deep as I could get it, until even my veins felt full of smoke. I think I have become something new.

"There are some things a laboratory test will never tell you," I said. "Immersion is the best way to gain understanding."

"You sound like a philosopher."

"Or a priest. That's what science is, after all. An exercise in belief."

He looked at me with sad, weary eyes. "You know that's not true, not any more. Classification is the only true science we have left."

"Is that why you stay in space?" I asked, adding another leaf to the pile. "You think there's nothing left to learn, so you sit up here writing down measurements and pretending that's enough?"

"It's better up here," he whispered, reaching out to touch the leaves as if he couldn't help himself.

Today the freshly risen sun made the dew glint like amethysts. I can't imagine anywhere I'd rather be.

"I think you're afraid." I watched as he stroked a fingernail down the surface of a leaf, his watery, bloodshot eyes blinking rapidly. "That's irrelevant, though. This is nothing but pure scientific analysis. Or has Gina intimidated you so thoroughly that you're afraid of that, too?"

Berry turned then, with a sharp, clumsy motion, and walked to the other side of the room. When he came back he was holding a long, thin lighter.

"Open the hood," he said.

I reached up and flipped the switch that would open the hood's outtake valve.

With a shuddering sigh, Berry flicked the trigger. Soon the leaves were curling at the edges, and a thin trail of smoke began to spiral upwards.

Then, with a crack and a sigh, the entire pile went up at once. I reached up as Berry shielded his eyes, flicking the switch closed again.

"Fascinating," Berry murmured, leaning in to peer at the purple smoke. "What did you say the tribe used this particular type of fire for?"

"Meditation," I said, leaning in to breathe deeply. "They burn it for the acquisition of wisdom and the grace of certainty."

Berry coughed. "That's, ah, quite strong. Are you sure the hood is drawing?"

I could feel the moment stretching out, time becoming elastic and malleable. Berry's face wavered in front of me as I tossed more leaves into the growing blaze.

"How does it make you feel?" I asked.

"Dizzy." Berry leaned heavily on the table.

The smoke danced between us, a veil splitting action and intention. I felt gracious; I would let him know my reasons.

"I'm ending this mission," I said.

"What do you mean?"

"The Consilium doesn't care about science. It doesn't care about this planet or the research that could be done here. You heard them—they're going to level the forests to get to the metals in the soil. They'll destroy all the plants, and then the people will go the same way."

"You don't know that," he said, sitting heavily on a stool. I could see his dizziness, a spinning vortex distorting the air around his skull. I remembered that first potent breath of the smoke on my very first evening on the planet, the way the world had seemed to shift and reorder itself around me.

"The Consilium destroys everything. People like us are just

here as afterthoughts. We sign our names on the report and shuttle off to the next research project, and entire worlds are demolished behind us."

"The plants will be safe here," Berry whispered. "The samples will survive."

"Do you even hear me?" I reached out and grabbed him by the arm, bruising his pale flesh. "Your samples don't matter if the planet is destroyed."

"It's the only thing I can do."

The clarity was aching, piercing. "That's why you don't leave the station," I said. "You know what happens. You just don't want to look."

"I keep the science alive." He looked at me pleadingly. "You understand. You're an official representative of the university. You know how it works."

I knew. Maybe I had always known how it would be, but things were different now.

"I can change it."

"The world never changes," Berry slurred, his chin sinking towards his chest.

He was lethargic and confused, but I felt utterly focused. My clarity of purpose was so diamond hard I imagined I could feel the edges of it scraping the inside of my ribcage. The acquisition of wisdom, the grace of certainty.

"Of course it does," I said. "We breathe in, and the world bends beneath our touch."

I watched him droop further, until his head rested on the table, his eyes closed and his mouth hanging slack as the smoke took him away.

I flicked the switch again, letting the accumulated smoke

filter into the ventilation hood in a rush. The station was spiderwebbed with ventilation shafts like this one. After disabling the botany lab's fire detectors late last night, I had removed a vent cover and crawled inside. It had only taken a few hours' work to drill through the side of the shaft where it passed through the station's main air circulation hub.

I grabbed handfuls of leaves from my field bag, feeding the fire until it burned high. Then I slipped one of Berry's laboratory scalpels into my pocket and went hunting.

* * * *

Private communication, Dr. Alice Thompson to Dr. John Morgan. 5774 P.N., 1st cycle, 31st day

Our textbooks have not been kind to those who chose to shape their worlds through force. We like to believe ourselves enlightened now. We shape through subtler means, under the blazing banner of progress. It's all the same, though. I'm sure you understand.

You once said that I needed to maintain distance in my research in order to stay free of bias, that my savior complex had the potential to be just another form of oppression. You were wrong. I have seen another realm, and I know now that bias and oppression are impossible when intentions are pure. I burn with purpose.

* * * *

I shielded my eyes against the glow of the pyre. The flames were alive with dancing violet spirits that flickered around the bodies, tasting the swiftly blackening flesh. The smoke was heavy and rich, spiced with bitter notes of melting plastic and the sharp tang of wax.

This planet would be safe now.

When I squinted I could just make out the tread of a boot within the flames. The rubber melted and ran in fat drops like the wax of a candle, dripping into the ashy remains of a pristine gray suit.

I needed to gather more leaves. Soon the fire would die down, and my head would spin without the sweet smoke. My chest had already begun to ache.

I headed into the forest, bypassing the twisting path that led back to the shuttle I would never need again. As I walked, the leaves gently caressed my skin.

I'm here to join you, I imagined saying. *We belong to each other, to this forest, to the smoke.* They would understand what I meant. I knew it.

Without the smoke my head buzzed. The path was overgrown, difficult to traverse, and I stumbled. All around me the dark shapes of the forest appeared to move, rushing forward to surround me.

SARAH HAWLEY was raised in Albuquerque, New Mexico. She studied archaeology at USC before completing her MA in Aegean Archaeology at the University of Sheffield. She has excavated at an Inca site in Chile, a Bronze Age palace in Turkey, and a medieval abbey in England. Sarah currently lives in Los Angeles and works in digital marketing. She enjoys adventures, swing dancing, antiheroes, and colorful socks. She primarily writes science fiction and urban fantasy and is working on her first novel. Follow her work at sarahhawley.blogspot.com.

The Factory Job

Jessica Magallanes

IN THE END, it didn't matter which parts really happened and which parts I made up. Of course, lies are easier. Tell enough lies, and the truth fades comfortably like a blurry face in an old photograph.

Sometimes I write my real name just to remember it, scrawling loopy cursive letters over and over on fancy hotel stationery like a bored kid in homeroom. Or I finger the faded crescent-moon scar on my wrist, the one that Benny gave me when he threw my handbag across that motel parking lot in Tucson and shattered my little makeup mirror. The scar is real. Believe that. Glass shards everywhere and Benny snatched one nasty piece off the blacktop and cut my arm, just like that. I didn't even feel it at first. *You wanna die, bitch?* he'd whispered as the blood dripped down my arm. *Next time it'll be worse than glass. And it won't be your wrist.* He grabbed me down low then, and I twisted away and laughed in his face.

Or maybe I slashed my wrist myself. Maybe I've never been to Tucson, or almost passed out while wiping down a shitty motel room with industrial-strength bleach. Never laughed in the face of danger. The story ends the same whichever way I tell it. Benny's still dead. I killed him.

Or I didn't.

Doesn't matter.

* * * *

If the job had gone the way we'd planned it, I wouldn't have been at the factory with Benny that night. But Felix finally trusted me enough; he knew I knew my way around security systems and was tiny enough to slip through an open skylight, which is why I was there when it all went south. Fat Richie usually drove for Felix, but his brother's kid had an asthma attack and he'd had to take him to the emergency earlier that night, so Benny ended up driving.

Fat Richie wasn't really fat. He was actually pretty fit—had to be, since he was Felix's all-around guy. Driver, shooter, delivery boy, fixer—whatever Felix needed, Richie provided. Felix started calling him Fat Richie because of a mistake. Three months ago, Richie was up for murder one but the charge got dropped when the sole witness recanted–the security guard who saw Richie shoot Jasper Maddox caught a case of temporary amnesia–and Richie claimed fate had saved him. Maddox owned the factory and had been Felix's laundry man until things went sour between them.

Of course, Richie could have turned state's and told the DA that Felix ordered the hit on Maddox when Felix caught Maddox skimming, but Richie wasn't a rat—he was a disciple.

Wanted to prove himself, move up the ranks. Richie was always talking about karma and superstitions, like don't step on a crack and don't forget to throw the salt behind you and crazy voodoo like that. Crossing Felix would have been bad fate, he said.

Richie's brother ran a tattoo shop out of his garage. When Richie's case got tossed, he told his brother to ink the word 'FATE' on his bicep. Richie's brother had finished the first three letters when Maddox's boys pulled up, shot a full clip through the open garage door, and sped off. Richie's brother took two in the chest and bled out, but Richie's superstitions must have paid off because they missed him completely. After that, he shot his mouth off all the time about hitting Maddox's boys, but Felix told him to cool it with the payback talk around the bar—you never knew who was listening. *I got a plan. It'll just take some time*, Felix would say. And Richie might have looked like a tough guy, but he was too scared to do anything on his own. Now his arm just says FAT and we try not to rag him about it too much, on account of his brother being dead and all.

* * * *

Like I said, we needed a driver last minute, and Fat Richie vouched for Benny, which was good enough for Felix. Felix didn't care who drove, as long as he was careful and didn't tell nobody after. Felix never came out on the drops anyway. I asked him why one night while I was counting out the tab receipts behind the bar. *Plausible deniability,* he said. He didn't elaborate and I didn't press him. I knew he was slinging meth, but business was slow and the bar couldn't wash as much green as the factory had and make it look legit. I saw the girls slink into the bar around noon on Sundays dropping off grimy envelopes, three inches think, while Richie counted out in the storeroom and Benny stood guard. Every two weeks a black-on-black Range Rover with tinted windows pulled up in front and three men—two of them comically oversized, the third in a tailored suit and barely my height—followed Felix into the back room and emerged an hour or two later, sometimes smiling, sometimes not. Of course I was curious. But Felix paid me to keep my mouth shut, and he threw me a small bonus each week; I didn't ask or complain. All things considered, he wasn't the worst boss I'd ever had.

But Benny? Benny rubbed me the wrong way from the start. When he wasn't guarding the stash, he kept himself busy poolsharking U of A frat boys slumming it in our part of town. He never messed with Felix—he wasn't that stupid—but he didn't know how to keep his eyes to himself when I walked by. He gave me the creeps, the way his lips jerked around after he told a joke, laughing like someone had taught him how. Or how he'd block my way so I had to brush past him when I needed to get behind the bar. I ignored him and minded my own business.

As long as I kept the drinks flowing and the register balanced, Felix was happy. Felix didn't always keep his eyes to himself either, but he was married, and I didn't need the trouble. I'd be lying if I said I didn't think about convincing him to leave his wife, but I always chickened out. I had a plan, too, and like Felix's, it was gonna take some time. We were all pretending back then. Felix pretended he was a respectable business owner, I pretended that I was just a bartender, Fat

Richie pretended he wasn't a cowardly bastard, and Benny pretended to be a human being instead of a big fat turd.

I still feel bad for how things ended with Felix, but like I said, he was never gonna leave his wife and I got sick of waiting. I'd been working at the bar for a few days when I saw her. Felix had sent Richie to drive her to the bar so he could *keep an eye on her*, he said. She was there every night, sitting in the corner booth behind the jukebox. I'd bring her a wine cooler, and she'd nurse it for an hour and then order another while Felix hovered and glared at anyone who tried to talk to her for too long. Even I deliberately ignored her. Ignored that she always wore long sleeve blouses and sunglasses. Ignored the way Felix gripped her arm when they left the bar together. I just kept bringing her fresh napkins and peanuts and kept my mouth shut.

How was I supposed to know she would show up at the bar the night we got back from the factory? That wasn't part of the plan. Her wallet and wedding ring would eventually turn up in the jacket pocket of an ex-con who was wanted for two outstanding Texas felony warrants: kidnapping and murder. The cops labeled her missing, presumed dead.

But that was after.

* * * *

I know you wanna hear about the factory job, but my momma always told me to shut my mouth if I didn't have anything nice to say and the factory job was about as un-nice as you can get. Plus, to really explain what happened that night, I'd have to go back and start at the very beginning.

Until I was fifteen, I lived with my momma and dad

in a suburb outside of Tucson. After they split, I went with momma to California and left my dad and my three brothers behind. Junior was the oldest, then Ollie, then Raymond, who was eleven years older than me. They didn't have time for a sister. Momma and I never got along, but my dad treated me like a princess. I got the perks of being an only child and the youngest all at once.

That last day in Tucson, momma and dad had a big fight, whisper-screaming in the kitchen. I was in my room with Baby, my best friend. We had spent a miserable afternoon pretending that we weren't never going to see each other again. That I wasn't moving 500 miles away in less than an hour.

Baby and I became friends when Miss Tigh paired us up in science class, seventh grade. Baby had a reputation, and I kept my distance until one day I was studying after school and Trent Nichols cornered me in the alcove under the stairs. I hollered when he put his stinky hand over my mouth. Next thing I knew, Trent's whimpering flat on the ground and Baby was standing there with her knuckles split to the bone.

"You OK?" she asked.

"Yeah," I smiled, and kicked Trent in the ribs, hard. Baby crooked her elbow around mine like a debutante's date and whispered in Trent's ear, "That'll teach you to fuck with my friend, asshole." It became her favorite phrase—if you heard those words, you were already on the floor, scrunched up in the fetal position.

After that, we were inseparable and fierce. Boys avoided us; girls ignored us. We only needed each other. We had our lives planned out. Graduation, roommates at State, a year off to travel around Europe, then we'd change our names, marry best friends, and buy mansions next door to each other in Santa Fe.

Back in my room, we were trying not to cry. "You could come live with me," Baby had pleaded, for the millionth time. "My ma won't mind."

"Yeah, and how would I survive?" I twisted the bedspread in my hands. Baby's family lived off food bank groceries and the Methodist clothing donation barrel. Her dad was drunk twice as often as he was sober, and Baby spent most of her time at my house.

"We could get our own place." Baby was grasping. "Just you and me, Nikki."

"With what money? And who'd be dumb enough to rent to two fifteen-year-old girls?"

"I guess this is goodbye, then." She sniffed, tears welling in her eyes.

So while my parents fought one last time, Baby and I hugged and pinky-swore we'd always be there for each other and that we'd write every day. I held my little Instamatic at arm's length and snapped a picture of the two of us.

My voice hitched. "I'll come back, Baby, I promise. Everything we planned."

And then momma and me got in the car and drove to California and that's the last time I saw my dad.

Funny how things work out the opposite of how you plan them.

* * * *

My momma decided to leave because my dad's work had gotten too dangerous. He'd done a turn before I was born, but he never talked about it. He was legit now, he'd tell us, a "family man," but a former associate of his was about to get paroled and he didn't think we'd be safe. Momma wanted to go, but I wanted to stay. I got overruled.

Dad wrote us all the time, and he always remembered to send money. Things didn't work out long distance, though, and their divorce was finalized the same day as my junior prom. I didn't go—I couldn't, since I'd been suspended for fighting. I wasn't into all that high school ritual crap anyway, but prom night guaranteed that the principal wouldn't be home, so I practiced my B&E skills and me and some friends helped ourselves to a little party at her house. Payback for suspending me; the other girl didn't even get a wrist slap 'cause her daddy was on the PTA.

Momma wasn't PTA material. She and I hardly spoke; she was bitter and lonely after the divorce so she jumped at the first guy who asked her out. Gary Detner worked at JPL, where they design the spaceships and all that science crap and oh my god, he talked a big game. He tried to make like he was some genius inventor but when I looked him up on the company directory, turns out he was the assistant to the guy who inspected tools for the astronauts on the space station. All Gary really did was sign purchase orders and make sure the right number of Velcro-patched screwdrivers and nail files were being shipped out.

My momma thought he was hot shit. She barely talked about my dad anymore, and I'd overhear her bragging about Gary like he was Neil friggin' Armstrong or something. *You know, Gary's job is so important*, she'd tell her friend Donna over drinks in our living room. *Imagine having raggedy cuticles up there in the space station! You could snag your spacesuit and die!* Then momma would joke about Gary's perfectly manicured hands and how long his fingers were, and how it would feel to do it in zero-gravity, and Donna would laugh her big horse-laugh and spill her martini on her shirt.

Barf.

I was still writing to Baby every day like I had promised, but by our senior year her letters started to trickle, then drip. By summer after graduation they'd dried up completely. I thought about driving back to see her, visit my dad and my brothers, but something always came up.

That last day photo of us started to fade, best friends looking beautiful and dangerous in our fifteen-year-old bodies. Me smiling bravely through my tears, Baby glancing sidelong at me through downcast lashes. Did she know, then, that my leaving was the beginning of the end for her? And if I'd known, would I have tried harder to stay?

* * * *

I know, I know. The factory job. Fine.

Benny and me left for the factory around ten. We delivered the package to the guard at the front gate and waited for him to give the signal for us to drive around back. The guard at the loading dock in back was one of Felix's; once the package was confirmed, he'd give Benny a backpack with the payment.

The reason I was there? I told you. I knew how to bypass security and Felix asked me to bring him Jasper Maddox's employment file from the factory's records office. The Maddox boys needed to pay for Richie's brother, he'd explained, and the file might give Felix an address, a name, some kind of lead to track them down. While Benny was waiting for the backpack, I slipped in through the skylight and did what I needed to do.

Except when I got back to the loading dock, Benny was standing there with a shotgun in his hands and the dock guard was bleeding out. The guard hadn't even had time to pull his gun.

I yelled at Benny to get in the car. Then I yanked the guard's gun out of its holster and shoved it in my waistband. Before we could open the car doors, the guard from the front gate came sprinting around the side of the loading dock.

Benny wasted him, too. Then he grabbed the backpack and we got the hell out of there.

* * * *

I fumed all the way back to the bar.

What the hell, Benny? It was a simple plan!

Felix was already frantically calling in favors to his bosses, arranging a safe house for Benny.

Fuck you, Benny snarled. *I ain't hiding in some rabbit hole waiting for the cops to bust me. Calm down and quit acting like a girl.*

Calm down? Felix yelled. *The morning shift starts at eight a.m! You think they're just gonna ignore the two dead guards on the loading dock?*

I thought fast. Rearranging my timeline just in case.

What about her? Benny pointed at me.

What about her? She held up her part of the deal. Right, sweetheart?

I nodded and tossed the Maddox file on the bar.

Benny ignored it. *How do we know we can trust her? She's*

only worked here like fifteen minutes. She could be a narc. I ain't going back to prison.

She ain't a narc, you asshole.

What'd you call me? Benny roared.

Felix said *Asshole* and so Benny shot him in the chest, and then we all heard a little voice go *oh* and there was Felix's wife standing in the doorway with Richie.

You know how they say time slows down in moments of stress? Not for me. Everything sped up, like a twelve-inch record playing at seven-inch speed. Richie pulled his piece and fired at Benny, but Benny was faster and dropped Richie with two shots to the head. I grabbed the guard's gun from my waistband and shot Benny in the stomach, then snatched the backpack off the barstool and pulled Felix's wife behind the bar. Felix dragged himself toward the back room, smearing blood across the floor. I pulled the page I'd carefully removed from the file out of my pocket, a copy of the life insurance beneficiary form with the names and addresses of Jasper Maddox's four children. I rolled it up and pushed it into a half-empty bottle of single malt. I stuffed a bar rag in the neck. Then I took a lighter and the keys to the bar from under the cash register.

* * * *

Felix's bar burnt almost to the ground before the fire trucks got there. All that booze, front and back doors locked from the outside, plus the storeroom of chemicals fueled a fire so hot they had to identify Richie and Felix by their dental records.

* * * *

You really wanna know how all this started? Three months ago, I got a phone call out of the blue. The call I'd been expecting and dreading since the day me and momma left.

Nikki?

Ollie?

Dad's dead. Shot. We need you to come home.

I caught the next flight from Burbank to Tucson. Junior filled me in on the drive from the airport to my hotel.

I had a clean look at the shooter, but Ray got antsy; he couldn't hit the side of barn if he was inside it. He iced the wrong guy—got his brother instead.

Figures, I said.

We're laying low 'til the heat's off. When we're ready, we'll take out that punkass and *his boss.*

I stared out the car window as Junior drove. Ten years since I left and everything looked exactly the same. Just dirtier.

We pulled up to the hotel. *You're registered under this,* he said, as he slipped me a New Mexico license with my picture over an unfamiliar name.

I examined the ID. *Ollie does good work.*

Junior nodded. *Dad always wanted you to have a better life, not get involved with the business. Sorry it had to work out this way, but we need someone we can trust. If I send in any of my regular guys, Felix would make them in a minute. Lucky for us, he doesn't even know you exist.*

What's the job? I asked.

How're your bartending skills?

I shrugged. *Passable.*

Good. Your job is to keep an eye on things from the inside. Let us know if he changes his routine. You track when the money comes in and the delivery schedules. We'll decide when and where to make a move. I just need you to promise you won't do anything stupid. Payback for Dad above all, understand? Promise you'll stick to the plan until it's done.

Sure, I said. *Take notes. Pour some drinks. How hard can it be?*

He hesitated.

I gotta tell you something else about Felix—the guy who owns the bar.

Yeah? I grabbed my duffle bag out of the back seat, wondering what could be worse than going to work for the man who had ordered my father's murder. Junior ran his hands through his hair and sighed.

It's about your friend Baby.

* * * *

I stood across the street from the bar, watching thick black smoke escape through the roof. I punched in a number on my phone.

Yeah?

Junior?

Nik?

It's done. Sorry. Tell Ollie I need two relocation packages. Deluxe version.

I never was any good at following directions.

* * * *

I checked us into a motel that took cash and didn't ask questions. It was just after midnight. Felix's wife was still in shock, and she passed out on the bed as soon as we got inside.

I stayed up, looking out the window, trying to make sense of it all. She wasn't supposed to be there. Not yet. That wasn't the plan.

I closed my eyes for only a minute, I swear, but when I woke up she was gone. So were my car and the gun. I went outside to look for her and that's when Benny cold-cocked me and cut my wrist with a shard of glass. He looked really pale, shirt stained brown from the wound in his gut. I must have missed his organs when I shot him. I don't know how he made it out of the bar, but here he was, ugly as ever and bleeding all over the motel parking lot. He grabbed my wrist with one hand and my ass with the other and threatened to kill me. I jerked away and ran back to the open door of my room, expecting to feel the bullet any second. I wondered what he was waiting for, but I didn't have to wonder long because right then my car skidded into the lot and Felix's wife opened the driver's door and shot Benny right between the eyes.

That'll teach you to fuck with my friend, she said, but before she could add her signature epithet, my best friend broke into tears.

* * * *

"I drove back there while you were asleep," she explained. "Nothing but ashes. I needed to make sure the bastard was really dead. Then I noticed Benny's car was gone, so I got worried and raced back here."

"Good timing," I joked.

"When Richie first told me that Felix's new bartender was a girl, I thought it might be you. I figured your brothers might call in that Hail Mary after what happened."

"Thanks for not blowing my cover," I said, wiping Baby's cheek with my sleeve. "It was killing me, watching what he was doing to you. You OK?"

"I'll be OK," she said. "Nikki?" Her voice broke. "I am so sorry about your dad."

For the first time in too long, I wrapped my arms around her.

* * * *

My original plan to get Baby away from Felix, passed back and forth to her on cocktail napkins and torn wine cooler labels for two months, had been shot to shit, but we had always been good at improvising. We just had to work fast.

Benny's blood was spattered all over the doorjamb, so we wrapped him in the shower curtain and loaded his body into the trunk of his car. Then we wiped down the room and drove both cars back to the factory, where we dumped him and his shotgun on the loading dock. I tossed the keys to the bar into the trunk.

"Throw this in the trunk too, OK?" Baby grabbed Benny's jacket off his front seat and handed it to me, stuffing something in the pocket as she did. While I closed the trunk and wiped down Benny's car, Baby wiped our prints from the guard's gun, placed it back in the guard's hand, wrapped her finger on top of his, and pulled the trigger once.

When the day shift arrived in a few hours, they'd see what we wanted them to see: two guards dead by shotgun blast, and Benny dead with two rounds from the guard's gun—one in the stomach, one in the skull. No big loss.

The sun was coming up, so we headed to Junior's to pick

up our packages. Passports, new ID's, and plenty of traveling cash, courtesy of Dad's life insurance payout. That plus the money in the backpack would give us a security blanket for at least a year.

Like I said, maybe Benny would have died from the shot to the stomach. He definitely died from the shot to his head. If Felix and Richie hadn't bought it at the bar, my brothers would've gotten revenge for our dad's death eventually. That part of the story ends the same whichever way I tell it. In the end, it didn't matter.

* * * *

Baby and I are in Europe now, like we'd always planned: five-star hotels, museums, Italian shoes, all that fancy old-world foreign shit. I check in with Junior every few weeks; he says the arson investigators finally turned up my name—only the fake New Mexican one, so I'm not too worried. We're having the time of our lives, Baby and me, even if we are always looking over our shoulders. Never staying any place too long, carefully covering our tracks. I sometimes wonder which side of the law will catch up to me first.

Then, an urgent text this morning from Ray. Three words.
They got Ollie.

It won't be long before they connect the fake name on my passport to my real one.

Annika Maddox. I remember as my pen loops across another sheet of hotel paper. Still my father's daughter. Then I flick Felix's lighter against one thick linen corner and watch the flame erase me again.

We'll leave in the morning; find a new hotel, a new city.

But the money's almost gone.

Richie was right. Fate catches up to us all in the end. All you can do is keep your promises and keep running like hell.

JESSICA MAGALLANES (@jesswritespoems) is a high school English teacher, National Writing Project Fellow, writer, and editor. She has been published in *Statement Magazine*, *The UCLA/Lake Arrowhead Young Writer's Anthology*, and *No Apologies*, the UCLA Writing Project's journal. Her 2013 NaNo novel, *Synth*, is about a young hacker forced to hide in a dystopian New York City after the government shuts down the internet. Her upcoming novel, *Falls Church,* is a YA thriller about a small town hiding a deadly secret. She advises the Garfield High School Creative Writing Club (@GarfieldWriters) and is making progress on eighteen screenplays, a short story collection, and a comic book about a girl and her better-than-average chicken.

The Unauthorized Memoirs of an Anthrophysicist

Sascha Stucky

THE IDEA THAT I would intentionally sneeze in someone's macaroni dish is absurd. Regardless, I'm suspended pending investigation from my busboy job. Busboy is the old, politically incorrect term; now, I'm technically a busser, the way stewardesses are now flight attendants and the cockpit of a plane is now the flight deck. Same turd, different photo filter—as the saying goes. Either way, it's a crap job, but I'm riding it out until I leave for my publicity tour. (That is if I still have the crap job, what with the investigation pending and all.)

Not to dwell on the negative, but I'd like to know how they plan to prove I sneezed in the macaroni. Whatever happened to "innocent until proven guilty?" Regardless, my blog has a lot of hits so I'll undoubtedly be receiving a publishing deal soon. From what I know, publicity tours follow publishing deals pretty quickly, especially for works of great magnitude.

When I think about the macaroni debacle, it feels to me like a witch hunt. It wouldn't be the first time they came after me. My intellect intimidates people. I understand. If I were less intelligent, I too, would be intimidated by an anthrophysicist. Discovering a new branch of science is no small feat, and people are understandably jealous. I actually have a couple of theorems regarding jealousy.

I'd hate to give away anything from my first book, but I'll share one of my theorems with you. It may help you. *Theorem 47: The search for intelligence in others is akin to the search for foreign galaxies.* The evidence there is that it really can't be done. We all assume it exists, but no one has ever seen or found it. For this reason, I lack faith in the criminal justice system, especially that within the restaurant I work. I admit, yelling "only God can judge me" as the security guard dragged me out of the restaurant may have been a poor decision in the grand scheme of things, but I'll be damned if I'm going to let a bunch of plebeian restaurant workers dictate my future. I most certainly did not sneeze on that table's macaroni dish, nor did I stick my finger in it, as they told the management. I know how the misunderstanding occurred; however, I also know the restaurant patrons severely overreacted.

The truth is, I was simply pointing at where in the dish they claimed I'd snotted when someone bumped me from behind and my finger grazed the top of the dish. I mostly only touched the breadcrumbs. Up until that point, things were going well. I was explaining that what they were looking at was not snot, because I had not sneezed. I'd had an amusing thought about one of my theorems while setting their food on the table and laughed. It was a laugh, not a sneeze, and I don't evacuate snot when I laugh. How that thing got on top of their macaroni dish is not for me to say. I'm a busboy, not an expert food waiter.

I should be the one upset; I tried to go above and beyond to help and ended up accidentally touching that slimy thing when I got bumped from behind. I'll send the owners another email with that fact. I could sue them for exposure to an unknown pathogen. What if I end up with a disease? No good deed goes unpunished, you know? When they look at all of the evidential emails I've sent them, they'll see the truth and lift my suspension and welcome me back on staff. They don't know the emails are from me, as I've used another email account and letterhead from my "attorney," Alan Baumsman, Esq. on all communications. From my prior experience, I've learned it's best to communicate via attorneys on serious matters, or to pretend to be one.

That reminds me of one of my other theorems, *Theorem 206: Fear is more powerful than a rocket thruster.* Think about this: people pay to be scared, to attend haunted houses. Fear is powerful. Rocket thrusters are also powerful, but they aren't a threat. When in doubt, I find it's best to make others fearful. Fear is also an aphrodisiac, but I get into that subject with another theorem, and if I told you everything, it wouldn't give you a chance to buy my book. My point is, the best manner to handle unpleasant situations is with fear, and I'm working the fear angle to make the primates I work with see the error of their ways. The job is awful, but I have a grand plan for when I officially quit, so I need to retain employment for that reason.

When I officially quit, I'm going to leave a signed copy

of my book on the manager's desk that says, "Suck my brains, you mortal." It's concise and mature because it will be written inside of my book. Were it just a note, it would simply be uncreative and immature. It's all about presentation, as they say.

The presentation of the macaroni dish was not that great. Someone had forgotten to sprinkle parsley on top and it really lacked the pizzazz of the finishing touch. Honetly, those people were better off not eating it. When you look at the situation, I did them a favor. They certainly did not do me any favors, however, by yelling, "Get your snotty finger out of my plate!" in the middle of the dinner rush. If you want to know how to create a scene, try that. I do not respond well to public ridicule, and in that moment of sheer panic, I picked up the woman's wine glass and doused her with her cabernet sauvignon. It mostly hit her face, and her cardigan set was black, so her dry cleaning complaint is purely selfish. Terrible people attend dinner on Saturday nights before heading to the theater. Pure cretins.

The horrible people for whom I work did not help the situation, either. They swiftly walked up and asked the guests what the problem was. I'm appalled that they'd address the guests and not their own employee, the true victim of the incident. Those lunatic patrons made me burn my finger on their food, caused me emotional distress, and yelled at me. They began recounting their version of things to the restaurant manager and owner, who began apologizing. I find that insane and make it a rule never to apologize, as it implies guilt. I said so at the time and began expounding on the importance of my thoughts, because I live my life by the virtue of *Theorem 2: Without education, humans are useless particulate matter. There is no wrong time for education.* To this, the guests stood up and began yelling, to which I don't react well, as I've mentioned. I did not mean to headbutt the man. I thought he was going to hit me with the macaroni dish and I ducked. It was at this point security showed up.

The benefit of working in a restaurant within a hotel is that security is readily available when people behave poorly. In this case, my feeling of relief at security's arrival proved to be sorely misguided. You can only imagine my shock when the large man put me in a chokehold. Once I began to pass out, he cuffed my wrists with a plastic zip tie and dragged me toward the exit. I've already sent an email courtesy of Mr. Baumsman regarding both the wrist chafing and the public choking.

I'd say it's a surprise that no one came to my defense, but I'm not surprised, which reminds me of another theorem I might share with you. Why not, right? If I can impart some wisdom onto you, I'm making the world that much better. Speaking of, if you are able put me in touch with a book publisher, perhaps I can arrange for you to receive a *Special Thanks* on one of the first few blank pages of one of my future side projects. To stay on subject, though, *Theorem 54: Searching for a true friend is like searching for a cuticle in a space station.* The evidence there is really self-evident. Have you tried to search for a true friend? Have you ever tried to search for a cuticle in a space station? Exactly. You can't hunt for these things. They happen upon you, and rarely, if that.

As I continue to reflect upon the events leading up to my suspension, I can't keep from wondering one thing. Is it possible to associate a manner of walking with a theorem? This is my own branch of science, so, as a pioneer, these decisions are up to me. I take them very seriously. The way my bosses walked towards the table at which I stood victimized was nothing short of scientific. It was as though they each had a yellow no. 2 pencil placed in their buttcrack, parallel with the flow of business, then stood and tried to hold it there as they walked toward the table. Their walk simultaneously expressed panic, fear and despair, but paired with smiles, it created a physical comportment reserved nearly always for those in middle management. There's beauty in the denial of despair, but I'll tell you one thing: Great people never walk that way. Lions never walk as though they're protecting something near their anus. Lions also never have emotions. Yes, this useful rumination brings me to a brand new theorem, *Theorem 292: As evidenced by lions, cold fusion, panthers, black holes, and sharks, greatness and fear are mutually exclusive.* This is how anthrophysics works. It's a merged study of the science of humans and physics.

I am hoping the gentleman with the keys can provide me with another sheet of paper as I have mere inches left on this page. He gave me several sheets and a mediocre pen to use. Some would call it luck that I'm able to have a pen in jail, but this isn't the case. I am alone, so it's not so much that I look non-violent as that I overheard the man say he'd give me a handgun if it meant I'd stop talking to him. For the record, the "letter full of powder" I sent to the owner of the building in which I work was a misunderstanding. The confetti must have disintegrated. Alas, I have spent the majority of my time here fruitfully. I am sure I will be out of this facility within a few hours and eagerly await my return to work. Until then, I'll continue my scientific work to the best of my abilities, which, as this is the last of my available paper, now means writing on myself.

Growing up a military brat in Southern California, SASCHA STUCKY considered being either a spoon maker, author, or a pizza maker when she grew up, until she learned that being an actor was an actual profession, thanks to the Macaulay Culkin/*Home Alone* issue of *Star Magazine*. Besides writing and acting off and on since childhood, Sascha also lives in the real world. She spent years competing in track and field, where she earned over twenty-five medals and awards, placing eighth in the state in high jump, and was inducted into two California college Halls of Fame. Though she proudly attended a nationally recognized party school, she still managed to graduate with honors, earning a Bachelors of Science in Kinesiology. Sascha volunteers politically, performs at Second City Hollywood, vacillates between wanting to be a good person and wanting to be a terrible person, and spends a lot of time trying to stop her dogs and husband from embarrassing her. She hasn't discovered her own branch of science, yet, but there's still time. She likes making new friends on Twitter: @SaschaLorren.

Fallen Grace

Anastasia Barbato

Early 2019

THE SILENCE OF the morning was comforting and serene. No shriek of sirens, no roar of cars driving by outside, no chatter of people walking down the street with their coffees on their way to work. Everything was quiet, the quiet that comes with the absence of sound when you know life should be there but it wasn't. Instead, the steady hum of the city's magnetic circuit board on the solar-paneled roadways and the twittering of birdsong were the only audible sounds. The city practically ran itself these days, since most of its inhabitants were gone.

I slid open the door of my mirrored closet, browsing my clothing options for the day. You'd think working as secretary to the CEO at Graceline Industries for five years would improve my wardrobe, but my black dress pants and navy blazer had yet to fail me, as it was my only 'business chic' outfit; considering that most of my other clothes were sun bleached and screamed shabby, this was the only thing appropriate to wear for the big meeting today. I took out said blazer and dress pants, adding a tight white camisole and a little gold jewelry to at least make it look like I enjoyed my job.

It's not that I didn't want to look the part of working for the most powerful business in the world, but with this job, wearing clothes out of style wasn't necessarily an abomination; well, unless you were meeting with the head honcho himself, as I was today.

Rushing unfed out the door with my makeup half done on my face was a normal occurrence, but today I was on top of things and actually managed to choke down a piece of toast and eggs before starting up my '67 Chevy Impala as it sat black and glistening in my driveway. Working for Graceline, I could buy just about anything I wanted; not that it mattered, anyway. No one owned things anymore. Graceline just permitted you to keep their stuff for a while until they wanted it back. It seemed a reasonable enough agreement, seeing as how their generosity *did* provide the world with so much.

The streets were empty, as they usually were, and I wasn't surprised that mine was the only car driving down the road to work, seeing as how I was one of the last people still living on my block. Nowadays people mostly preferred to plug into one of Graceline Industries' fancy day spas for a refreshing Dreamscape session—and never come back out. I mean, if you could fall into a trance-like state and let your mind soar wherever it wanted, whenever it wanted, wouldn't you stay there, too?

I preferred to keep my thoughts to myself, personally, which is why I was one of the few people who remained Awake, taking care of those in the Dreamscape and tapping my fingers on my desk while Graceline hummed its merry tune into the hearts of millions.

I rolled into the parking lot of Graceline Headquarters, the tallest and most imperial-looking building in the city. It was triangular, a black glass column shooting into the sky and pulsing with the hum of metallic energy; the three silver corners of the building spiraled around it in a braid-like pattern that made the building look like it was being looped by a big infinity sign. The windows were a double mirror, allowing those inside to look out but none to look in. I'd never been authorized to go up to the roof, but I could only imagine what the view must be like on top of the world.

I shoved my hands in the pockets of my blazer and readjusted the satchel strap on my shoulder, drinking in the cool late-winter air and looking up at the greatness of this hulking mass. Little bits of plastic and paper blew in swirls around my feet as I walked briskly to the glass entrance, and with a quick retinal scan I was inside the beast and heading up to my floor.

The air inside was warm and dry, albeit a little stale from the lack of windows as I walked down the spotless, white-walled hallway and down into the building. There was a significant lack of lobby here, just these branching white hallways, which I found odd but unsurprising. Like Starbucks reducing the comfort of the chairs in their shops (when it was still operating, anyway), Graceline wasn't looking to make itself comfortable enough to keep the few Awake people loitering.

On the walls were black picture frames with inlaid frosted glass panels, and as I walked by, pictures of executives shaking hands with important world leaders flicked onto the screens in three-dimensional images. I never really paid much attention to who these world leaders were over the years, but one look at a picture of Butch Graceline shaking hands with the President of the United States spoke a thousand words.

The elevator ride was slow, and I looked out of the glass wall as the silver tube climbed up to my floor. Despite the sprawling city of Los Angeles being a daunting sight to behold from above, the city had long been still as its inhabitants had entered the Dreamscape; the city now operated on automatic timing systems, illuminating the hundreds of empty streets at night and shutting off all of the individual energy systems in homes where people had 'Scaped for more than a week or two to cut down on pollution and excess costs. I didn't really care that the city was sleeping; noise and people bothered me anyway, so it was best that there were only a few Awakened left to take care of the Dreamers. People could be so dramatic sometimes, always ranting about the apocalypse and where this world was headed. I couldn't understand why they didn't just stay quiet and get with the program, until they eventually did. Graceline does that to people.

The elevator came to a smooth stop on the 44th floor, and the doors opened to reveal a small, brightly lit room full to the brim with file cabinets and the three sweaty people I had come to know as my family over the past five years. The other Awakened were just like me: handpicked by Butch Graceline himself to work right on the same floor as his office. We all had special talents that he said separated us from the flock. But boy, he couldn't have chosen a weirder group of people had he chosen the extreme cosplayers at Comic-Con.

The first person I saw as I entered the room was a man, about my age—I was in my late twenties—who had the mind of three supercomputers. The man was lean in his crisp brown pinstripe suit, sleek black glasses perched on his thin nose. and unruly black hair that was constantly falling into his sharp green eyes. He gave me a smirk and leaned back in his chair nonchalantly, but I knew him better than to think that he wasn't analyzing my every move and action. For a guy who was a computer and digital mastermind, he was quite the socialite, and knew just about everything about everyone. He also happened to be my best friend.

"Hey, Rowan," he greeted me, giving me a mischievous smile as I passed him. "Weather's nice for a surf today, isn't it? Just make sure you take a shower before you come in for the meeting this afternoon; we don't want the room crawling with sand crabs from your hair." Todd was referring to the day I took my Graceline ID photo, when I hadn't bothered to clean myself up after surfing before the photographers snapped the picture. This incident had turned into one of many running jokes around our office; I generously served as the butt for most of them.

"Good to see you too, Todd." I replied, breaking into a grin of my own and patting his shoulder good-naturedly. "I'll save all the sand crabs in my hair for you. That way they can nest in *your* unruly locks for a change."

A laugh sounded behind me, and I turned to see a woman with dark brown hair shaking her head at me as she smiled into her coffee cup. She wore a cream turtleneck sweater and silver sun necklace that hung at her collarbone; her gray corduroy pants complimented her curving figure, but the severity of her ice blue eyes would shock any woman away—except those she favored, of course.

"Looking good as always, Monica." I smiled back at her, and she spun back to face her desk in her rolling chair. She took a sip of her coffee as her eyes scanned the algorithms and graphs filling her computer screen. Like Todd, Monica was a technical mastermind, but unlike him, she wasn't very great at starting conversation. However, I believed it was her compassion and understanding that struck a chord with Mr. Graceline and convinced him to choose her as his accountant.

There was a picture of Monica and her girlfriend Francine taped to the right corner of her monitor, and she looked at it occasionally as she replied to me. "Yeah, I bet you say that to everyone—oh, that's right, you don't *know* any other people."

"I know you, Todd, and Francine. You're people," I replied as I headed to the kitchenette to pour my own mug of coffee. Francine and Monica had been going out for nearly three years now, ever since the Dreamscape was still in its early stages of development, and the three of us–and Todd–were an inseparable group here in this room. However, as I looked around the office, I noticed that Francine was nowhere to be found, and her desk had been cleared completely; even the photos of her and Monica's trip to France last summer were gone.

I felt a definite shift in the atmosphere of the room when I returned with my coffee. Monica was sitting and looking at her hands in her lap. "Fran ... she decided to Dreamscape Friday night, and ... she hasn't come out of it yet."

I stopped, my brow furrowing and my heart sinking in my chest. "Oh. What happened?"

Monica sighed. "She hasn't been the same since she came out of it a couple months ago, and we got into a pretty bad argument this time around before she packed up and 'Scaped."

I was quiet for a moment, sipping my coffee in thoughtful silence. "Well, she's probably having wonderful fantasies about vacationing with you in Brazil like you guys were wanting," I said, my tone light and optimistic. "I'm sure she'll come out of it soon and then you guys can go there for real!" I truly believed that what I said would make her feel better. Instead, Todd and Monica just looked at me like I had sprouted wings before shaking their heads, *no*. I blinked at them, puzzled.

"Don't worry about Fran, Monica," Todd said, his voice gentle as he turned to her; they seemed to have ignored my comment. "She'll come out of it when she's ready. In the meantime—" Todd's gaze softened with exhaustion, and he stood up next to me, brushing the creases out of his suit and adjusting his glasses. "Let's just focus on getting through today's meeting with Mr. Graceline, Rowan." We took a breath and simultaneously sighed, which we often found ourselves doing whenever we were together. The price of friendship, I guess.

Todd and I still had plenty of time before the afternoon

meeting, so I headed to my desk to get some work done. Dark mahogany and filled with neat stacks of papers, my desk was like a second home for me. I'd spent more hours at this desk than in my bed at home, and I was excited for the payoff all of my work would receive once Mr. Graceline read my monthly summary report. Unlike Todd and Monica, I didn't have many trinkets or photos on my desk for decoration. However, I kept a picture of my mom, dad, and older brother right beside my monitor, with the words "Much love, 2014" written on it. They had taken this picture in Madagascar, and the sight of a ring-tailed lemur sitting on my dad's shoulder, licking his ear, was one of the only times I had seen my brother laugh. It had been years since I'd actually seen all of their faces in person. They had entered the Dreamscape when it was still new and hadn't emerged yet, but I was just happy they were enjoying their fantasies while I helped to make the world a better place in their absence.

My job for Mr. Graceline, though one of the most important, was often one overlooked. What I slaved over day and night was arranging Mr. Graceline's appointments, dinner parties, outings, family vacations, and, of course, meetings with the President. That last one had been showing up on my calendars for months now, the President conferencing with him via Internet with news on the world economy and Dreamscape's next steps, which was kind of neat. I was also in charge of organizing and filing away all of Mr. Graceline's important documents, which made me quite the bank of knowledge for anyone interested. Not that there were many people left to be interested in the waking world, but still. I took pride in my job.

Work progressed throughout the day without much change besides the rotation of the sun outside the windows. Todd put on his classical music mix to make his monotonous coding work a little more bearable, which I enjoyed listening to as I emailed with Mr. Graceline's business associate in Moscow about the ski trip-slash-conference coming up in the spring. I think one of the reasons Mr. Graceline chose me specifically for this job was the way I could get around, finding communication links with important networking partners and getting him awesome resort locations. While I wasn't too aware of why exactly he needed triple orders of test tubes and lab equipment, employment of dermatologists and scientists, or even his one order of 100 geraniums shipped to the topmost floors, I made sure to get them there. After all, he owned over half of the businesses on the continent; who was I to question his judgment? I was just his secretary.

By the time I had gotten halfway done with my work, my watch read three o'clock in the afternoon. I leaned back in my chair and stretched my arms above my head, sighing contentedly before I stood and patted Todd on the shoulder, signaling it was time for the meeting. He nodded, and together we crossed towards the frosted glass walls of the conference room that spanned from one wall of the fourteen-square-foot floor to the other.

The conference room was nearly empty when we entered it, except for a dark table standing heavy and long in the middle of the floor with Butch Graceline sitting at its head. From the way he sat erect and tall, his broad shoulders adorned in a crisp gray suit and his clean-shaven face smiling with power, he seemed like a king atop his throne looking down on us; he hadn't changed a bit from the first day I met him five years ago, and the sight of him still sent a thrill down my spine.

"Ah, right on time, you two," Mr. Graceline boomed. "Come sit closer to me with your reports, I have some very exciting news to tell you."

I exchanged an excited glance with Todd and rushed over to the seat on Mr. Graceline's right, my heart thumping madly as I took out my monthly summary.

"I'm sure you'll find everything in order, Mr. Graceline," I said, trying to keep my voice from quavering with pride. "Your meeting with the President is scheduled for 4:30 p.m. today as you planned, and the Prime Minister of Russia has informed me that all of your housing arrangements for Moscow have been cleared, and they are setting up your accommodations as we speak. Oh, and your twenty volunteers have Awakened and arrived in the research department, and are approved for work there in improving the Dreamscape."

"Excellent, Miss Waverly. You've done a fantastic job as usual," Mr. Graceline declared. He winked at me. "And please, call me Butch."

I smiled and took my seat, adjusting my papers in front of me while I waited for Todd to make his oral report before we could go over our monthly expense summaries. Mr. Graceline had never told me to call him by his first name before, and his mention of exciting news caught my attention; I thought these must be the first steps towards a promotion, and the idea made my body buzz with contentment.

As I waited for Todd to finish, I looked out the window and admired the light shining off of the skyscrapers of downtown L.A. *The city can really be gorgeous from this height*, I thought as I watched two birds spiral and dance around each other in the sky a little ways off.

Quite suddenly, a fearful shiver rushed up my spine that made my hair stand on end, and I wrinkled my nose slightly as I smelled burning metal in the air. There was a shrill ringing sound, faint at first, but growing louder, and then something shot past the window right in front of me and fell out of sight forty-three stories below.

I heard my chair slam on the ground behind me more than I felt myself stand, and suddenly I was shouting frantically at Todd and Mr. Graceline to come with me downstairs right away, that someone had fallen off of the roof. They looked at me strangely before we all felt the earth pitch and tremble under our feet, and I grabbed a nearby desk to catch my balance as something exploded on the floor below us.

"Mr. Graceline, someone has fallen off the roof!" I repeated anxiously, my eyes wide and my hands sweaty. Mr. Graceline was looking out the window, an expression of surprise mingling with grim certainty in the depth of his dark eyes.

"Rowan and Todd, get Monica and make sure you three get downstairs safely," Mr. Graceline huffed, standing and running his fingers through his thick blond hair. I opened my mouth in protest, but he gave me a hard glare that choked the words in my throat. "Go. I have my own means of getting out of here. There's been a security breach." Even as he was talking, numerous armed guards darted down the hallway toward the conference room, their walkie-talkies squawking incoherently as they came.

"What is going on? What did you see? Where's Mr. Graceline?" Monica demanded, her voice rising in pitch with fright as Todd and I burst out of the conference room and ran toward her. I grabbed her hand and yanked her after me, as Todd grabbed his keys off his desk and led the way to the exit.

Once we had raced down the unending flights of stairs and stumbled into the light of the ground floor, the red alarm lights were pulsating loudly and more armed guards were rushing amid people in disheveled lab coats. I pulled one aside to ask what happened, a mousy woman with ruffled lab scrubs.

"Terrible! Atrocious! One of our humanoid test subjects escaped the labs!" she shrieked. I released her, feeling my heart clench with worry and uncertainty. Since when were there humanoid test subjects at Graceline Industries? People volunteered to participate in revolutionizing the Dreamscape, right? Unless … the realization struck me senseless, and I suddenly doubted how 'Awake' I really was.

I turned to ask this woman for more information but she had already run away, so instead I told Todd and Monica what I suspected.

Before they could respond, another deafening explosion threw us off our feet, and I shouted in alarm as the ceiling caved in above me. Choking on dust and rummaging through debris, I screamed for Todd and Monica but received no replies. I smelled smoke and fire, and having lost my sense of direction completely, felt panic rise in my chest and escape in a wail.

Then, like a guardian angel responding to my anguish, a pair of hands scooped me out of the rubble and hoisted me like a sack of potatoes, carrying me out of the dust and into the white light of the afternoon. My eyes full of dust and soot, I coughed as I squinted in the daylight and looked at my savior.

My eyes widened. A girl who looked barely seventeen stood above me; her entire right half of her body was human, while her left was silvery and cold, and I realized with a jolt what she was.

"You're ... a ..." I choked.

"A cyborg? An experiment? Yeah. You guessed right." The girl's voice was coarse and rough, but filled with confidence. "Man, by the look on your face it seems to me that Mr. Graceline has kept a lot of things from his employees, even his secretary." She shook her head pityingly at me.

I mumbled something incoherent that must've sounded like, "I didn't know, I work in a cuticle in the space station" when I meant, "a cubicle in administration," but she didn't respond either way. As quickly as she had come to rescue me, she dashed away into the city, away from the burning building and from her old life as a guinea pig for the industry. Darkness crept at the edge of my vision, and I lay down on the warm concrete and let the world swirl into blackness around me.

* * * *

I woke up in the hospital a couple of hours later, Todd's and Monica's faces hovering over me. After choking down some gross pudding the nurse had brought me, I dressed in new clothes and told Todd and Monica about how I was rescued by a cyborg girl who said she was escaping from the company.

To my surprise, neither of them looked as astonished as I was about the bio labs at Graceline, let alone experiments on little girls. With further prompting, I got a shrug out of Todd. "I don't know how you couldn't see it, Row. You're the one who organizes all of Butch's imports, aren't you? Couldn't you put the pieces together that he was ordering parts for a cyborg?"

His words stung with truth. How could I have been so naïve to not notice the clues right under my nose? Suddenly, the world's quiet didn't seem so peaceful anymore, and I instead felt the predatory stare in its patience that had used Graceline to swallow up countless human lives.

"It's all right, though, Rowan. You're safe now." Monica patted my pale hand as if sensing my sudden apprehension, and her face expressed sympathy and sadness. "The cyborg experiment that escaped, while she may have … rescued you like you think she did—she caused all of those terrible explosions and the deaths of eight scientists." My other hand flew to my mouth, my eyes wide. "But what I'm trying to say, Row," Monica amended quickly, "is that Graceline has already dispatched a team to track her down and bring her to justice for her crimes. You don't have to worry about any more trouble now, all right? You just focus on getting better. The fugitive will be caught, it's only a matter of time. I just thought you should know what was going on." Monica gave me a tight-lipped smile.

I looked out the window at the dying rosy light on the western horizon, wondering what my life would be now that Graceline Headquarters was damaged, and its image spoiled in my mind as much as it was physically blemished. From what Todd and Monica had told me, Graceline had pulled some workers out of the Dreamscape and was already setting to work repairing the extensive labs that had been damaged by the explosions, but even so I was repulsed at the thought of those labs being rebuilt to turn more innocent people into robot monstrosities.

As I watched the skyline sink into gloomy darkness so unlike the illuminated, life-filled city Los Angeles was before, I finally felt like my eyes were opening to see all of the damage Graceline had done to this city—to the whole world, even. This cyborg, this girl who rescued me from the fire of the building, was out in the city somewhere right now, all alone and being hunted. Heck, it wasn't even her fault that all of those scientists died the way they did. She was a poor, caged animal, desperate for love and freedom.

"No," I said quietly, and Monica stiffened beside me, a questioning movement. I turned to look at her and Todd in turn, my gaze determined. "I won't let this madness continue. For the first time, I … I'm Awake."

Todd blinked at me, and in that moment we had an unspoken conversation with our eyes, and I knew he was backing me on this. He'd known, somehow he'd known of the atrocities here, but now he had someone else on his side.

After a few moments, Monica excused herself and whispered something to the nurse about giving me some extra meds for my delusional behavior, but before the nurse returned with a small bottle of pills I was already gone, my room empty except for the naiveté I'd left behind on the hospital bed.

* * * *

Office-less as I may be, I am determined to let the world know the truth about how Graceline has taken over every aspect of human life. I have to start somewhere, and shutting down the Dreamscape seems like a good place to begin. With new resolve, I've set my course for finding the cyborg girl, who might have the answers I crave to take this business down. With the help of Todd's expert hacking skills, the two of us have been able to let my articles and messages leak into the Dreamscape's very core database, expressing the evils of Graceline directly into people's fantasies and finally giving the people a chance to reclaim their lives anew in this world of corporate greed. The silence of the city will drown in the honking of traffic, suffocate from the sound of motorcycles ripping down the streets, and quiver as people march into life once more.

Safe in my Impala, I turn the key in the ignition, hearing the engine purr and the radio blasting Bon Jovi's "Dead or Alive." Todd sits beside me in the passenger seat, and as he moves to turn down the radio I smile and turn it up louder.

To be continued ...

With a keen eye for discovering the bright side of every situation, ANASTASIA BARBATO's personality is as sunny as her Santa Monica abode, and her temper just as scorching. She enjoys all forms of creative expression, including musical theater, dance, choir, and (of course) novel writing, and her love for British TV shows like *Doctor Who* and *Sherlock* rival her obsession with reading teen mystery and fantasy novels, which she hopes to write one day herself. Her current goal is to publish her working novel before she graduates high school in two years' time, and every step of the way she's contributing as much as she can to her community and peers with her diplomatic and humanitarian insights.

Moving Up

Gabe McClure

"BUT WHY SHOULD I trust you?" Sachar asks me, his beady black eyes staring straight into my soul. You know, if I had a soul.

"Why shouldn't you?" I reply with a wicked grin that probably isn't helping my case. "I haven't done anything to you personally, as far as I know."

"Inadvertently, you have," Sachar says. "Inadvertently, you've wronged a lot of demons down here. Just about everyone, actually."

Nobody trusts a lower class demon in general, and nobody trusts me in particular. It's true, I did make a mess of things a couple hundred years ago. I *may* have accidentally let a small group escape from Hell. It's not entirely my fault though! I had my back turned, and it wasn't my job that night to lock their cages. But people don't ever blame Canaan. *No one* would ever blame *him*, not Alistair's favorite! They only ever blame me. Which more than sucks, but hey. I'm persistent, if nothing else. Slowly, I'll make my comeback. I'm sure of it.

"It was one mistake, one time, a long while back," I wave him off. "I say it's high time we move on from that one little flub up."

"Well, your flub up just about destroyed our organization. Can you imagine if you were to screw up again? Alistair would have my head. And then what if he told Big Red …."

"He's not going to tell Big Red, because he's not going to have your head, because I'm not going to jack this up. Don't worry, Sachar. I can do this." Sachar looks even more worried than before. I give him an encouraging look, eyebrows raised. I'm about to flash him a thumbs up, but he sighs and shakes his head slowly. "Don't make me regret this, Rakkason," he says, handing me a yellow folder.

"You won't, I promise." I bow grandly, hoping it doesn't come off as mocking but deep down knowing that it does, turn on my heel and leave his small office.

Finally! It's all I can do to not jump for joy right here in the middle of Hellion, Inc. I restrain myself only because I know how much of an idiot I'll look like if I give in to such a temptation around so many demons.

However, I can't stop the stupid grin on my face.

I can't help it; I'm excited. I've been working in Hellion's prank department for the last five hundred years—dishing out pink eyes and stomach flus around the holidays, luring flies to swarm around people's food while they're at restaurants. You know, the little things. But now I have a chance to prove myself. I know I can do more than what I've been doing, and actually being assigned to collect a soul is going to really give me a career bump. Or a respect bump. And honestly, I could use both.

I grab my coat off the hook near the front of the office, give a little wink to Deteria, the receptionist I've had my eye on for as long as I can remember. She doesn't wink back, but that doesn't trip me up. Really, I don't think anything could trip me up right now; I'm on such a high.

"Guess who's off to Louisville," I tell her.

"Not you," Deteria replies, never taking her eyes off her cell phone.

"Well not exactly *Louisville*, but I *am* going to Kentucky."

"Have fun," she says, voice lacking any emotion.

"Do you want me to bring you back anything? Keychain, t-shirt, fast food gift card?"

"Why are you talking to me?" She finally looks up to me, her yellow eyes cold and hard.

I look down and then away, a little caught off guard by her bluntness. "All right, then," I mumble before leaving the office, trying not to look or act as awkward as I feel.

I let the short conversation slide, focusing more on the fact that *she talked to me*, and head out toward the subway. It's the fastest route between Hell and Earth that I know of, besides teleportation and summoning. My telecard got revoked back when *all that* happened, and since no one's about to call me to them, I take the subway.

I open up the folder file and read it, since it's in my best interest to know just what type of soul I'm going after right now. It's a girl, around fourteen, named Mack. Tough home life, curiosity in the paranormal, listens to music that causes headaches. Easy target. If the company can get her on our side, then who knows how many people she can influence, and then how many people *they* can influence. It's all about connections, nowadays. And I'm sure this Mack has a few friends she can get on board once Hellion's in control of her soul, of course. And then it'll just trickle down from there, and next thing we know we'll have a greater army on Earth to do our bidding.

It's all very diabolical, very strategic, and, if I play my cards right, then it could very well happen.

The subway pulls to a stop, letting me out in a little town in Kentucky. It's winter, freezing cold around these parts, especially for a demon like me who's used to a certain temperature. We like to keep things hot in Hell, maybe a little humid. I pop up my coat's collar, stow the folder in my inner coat pocket, and button up. I hone in on my internal GPS and start walking in the direction where I know Mack is.

After trekking through the woods for the better part of an hour, I finally make it to her house. It's small, a bit shoddy, with a tiled roof and a yellow front door. I'm about to go up and knock, but that's when I see him.

Darkour. My worst enemy, though that may be more of a one-sided thing. And suddenly, I feel tripped up.

Now, I may be tall, but Darkour is *tall.* Big and imposing, built like a brick wall. He's about as expressive as a brick wall, too. Just being around him makes me feel about as big as a cuticle in a space station.

He doesn't see me, and he's making a beeline for Mack's house. *No!* I will *not* let him ruin this!

"What are you doing here, Darkour?" I ask in a harsh whisper as to not alert Mack or her neighbors of the two demons on the street.

"Rakkason," he greets, voice low and gravelly. I cringe. "What a shock. I didn't expect to see you here."

"I could say the same about you," I say.

"I've been sent to collect this girl's soul."

"Well, that's impossible," I bark a laugh, "because *I've* been sent to collect her soul. So you can scram, bud."

Darkour holds up his hands in defense, the look on his long face sending chills down my spine. "Now, now. No need to be rude. I'm sure this is all a big misunderstanding. Maybe you're just in the wrong place. Shouldn't you be back at Hellion designing whoopee cushions?"

"Excuse me?" I raise an eyebrow. I haven't made a whoopee cushion in three hundred years, thank you.

"Oh, come now, Rakkason," Darkour steps toward me. "You don't honestly believe that you would be sent here over me. Someone like *you* over someone like *me*, the worst over the best. Last I checked, soul collecting isn't even your division."

"I'm moving up," I argue.

"Sure you are," Darkour snorts. "That's why Sachar called me in and ordered me to take over. Because you're moving up."

"Wait. *Sachar* ordered you?" What a no good, two-timing, double-crossing jerk!

"Don't look so surprised, Rakkason. Go home; I got this one. Maybe you can have the next one."

If there even is a next one .... This is my chance, it might be my one and only shot at redemption. I can't let some highly respected, highly lethal, super scary demon stop me!

Without thinking clearly and against my better judgment, fueled by a blind rage and complete determination to get this girl's soul myself, I rush at Darkour and tackle the much bigger demon to the snowy ground. There's a lot of kicking and screaming and a little bit of hair pulling, but then there's silence when we hear a voice.

"What are y'all doing?"

Darkour and I both stop and look over toward the house. Standing in front of the yellow front door is a girl, no taller than five feet, with short black hair and a confused look on her pug face.

"Well?" She asks. She has a thick Southern drawl to her voice, snobby and high pitched.

Mack.

"And what's all this about soul collecting? Is that a new nerd thing? And what kind of a name is Rakkason? Darkour? What are you, elves?"

"You heard all that?" I gulp.

"Y'all ain't exactly quiet."

My eyes go big and I look at Darkour. He looks at me, and we make a silent agreement. We both calmly get to our feet and dust the snow off ourselves. I run a hand through my black hair before Darkour and I bolt off her front lawn, back through the woods, and toward the subway.

Thankfully, Mack doesn't follow us.

"This is all your fault, Rakkason!" Darkour roars once we get on the subway. I sit down and ignore him, feeling betrayed by Sachar, afraid of Darkour, and on pins and needles because Mack has friends that she can tell about us.

But she doesn't know what we are, I remind myself. Then I think back to her file. She has an interest in the paranormal. She might be able to put it together. She might be able to tell those friends, and then they might be able to tell all their friends, and then it'll just trickle down from there and ....

This diabolical plan, I realize, just might have gotten foiled. Say so long to any possibility of an army of teenagers from Kentucky. Hello, prank department. *Again.*

"Don't you ignore me, Rakkason!" Darkour continues. I keep on ignoring him, scooting farther and farther down the subway seat as he continues to yell threats and insults. Eventually, the subway comes to a stop and the doors open. I rush out, dodging Darkour as best I can, and go straight to Sachar's office. Darkour's right behind me.

Sachar's talking to someone on the phone and typing something on the computer, but I don't care. I slam the door to his office behind me, hoping it intensifies my entrance. It would have, had Darkour not reopened the door to follow me inside and then slammed it himself.

"Why?" I ask, not caring that I'm interrupting the liar's business. He holds up a finger, telling me to wait a minute. "*Why?*" I ask again, a little less kindly.

Sachar sighs and tells whoever's on the phone to hold for a minute. "Why what?" He asks me. He's put on the mask of impatience, but I can see beads of sweat forming at his temples, giving away his sudden nervousness.

"Why would you send Darkour out to collect the same soul as me?" I try and keep my voice level, but it's hard. Do they really *not* trust me that much? "I told you I could do it."

"Your word doesn't hold too much stock these days, Rakkason." Sachar shrugs and turns his beady gaze onto Darkour, who's standing behind me. I can feel him huffing down my neck, still angry at me for ignoring him on the subway. And probably for tackling him in the snow, too. "Did you collect the soul, Darkour?"

"I did not," Darkour says, cold voice lower than ever. "Rakkason was more determined than expected."

"I'm standing right here," I remind them, glaring back and forth between the two of them. Sachar shushes me, and that's when I lose my cool. "You know what? If it weren't for you and your dirty scheme with Darkour, then that girl's soul would be in our system. I would have gotten her, no sweat. It would have been a cakewalk. But because you sent Darkour–of *all* demons, knowing how much we hate each other–both of our covers were blown, and—!"

"Your covers were blown?" Sachar cuts in, holding up a chubby hand to silence me.

"Yeah. Because of Darkour."

"I'm not the one who started our brawl," Darkour chimes in. "Besides, you were speaking too loudly. I'm sure more than just Mack heard you."

"What? No I wasn't. I was whispering."

"You call *that* whispering?" Darkour snorts. "I'd hate to hear you yelling then."

I give him an exasperated look, unsure of what he's talking about. I was whispering our whole conversation out in the snow, wasn't I?

"It doesn't matter," Sachar raises his shaky voice, trying to regain control of the situation. "Darkour, you will not be faulted. Everyone will blame Rakkason, so you have no need to worry."

"Again, I am *right here*."

"And again, we do not care," Darkour growls. "I don't know how you haven't been fired already."

"Fired? For what?" I snarl. "For getting rudely interrupted while trying to do my job?"

"Collecting souls is not your job! Your job is to hand out chicken pox and cold sores!" Darkour comes closer to me, and we would be nose to nose if I were a few inches taller. "You're in over your head, Rakkason. You always have been."

"Enough!" A booming voice bounces off the walls, one that doesn't belong to Darkour or Sachar or me, yet one that was too familiar. I gulp.

Being summoned is like being sucked up in a vacuum; it's hard to describe. The room around the three of us disappears as we vanish and reappear in a different office, way off base and way different than Sachar's. This office is dark, so dark that if I wasn't a demon I wouldn't be able to see my hand in front of my face. Thankfully, though, I do have that demon vision every other paranormal entity envies, and so the pitch-black room just looks dimly lit.

Alistair, one of the highest-level demons, sits behind his desk, hands clasped in front of him. If we had souls, he'd be staring straight into them. He's the owner of Hellion, Inc., one of the scariest guys you'll ever meet, and one of Big Red's personal favorites. They play golf at the country club on Saturdays, I hear. I can't even get within a hundred feet of the country club.

"Mr. Alistair, sir!" Sachar scrambles, awkwardly trying to stand at attention. Darkour rolls his shoulders back, standing up straighter and taller. I just look at him, still a little woozy from getting summoned. "W-what's the problem, sir?"

"What's the *problem?*" Alistair replies mockingly, coldly, a sinister look crossing his sharp features. "Three buffoons arguing in the middle of my place of business, and you have the nerve to ask *me* what *my* problem is? Now, what's the problem with *you*, Sachar? Because it certainly seems to me that your problem is doing your job."

"I, uh," Sachar stutters. "I was, uh, just firing Rakkason. He ruined things, again. Not a shocker."

Alistair's glare sweeps over to Darkour. "I was helping Sachar," Darkour says matter of factly. "I was just about to escort Rakkason off the premises."

"This is ridiculous," I groan, unable to control my tongue even though I should keep my mouth shut with someone like Alistair in the room.

Alistair looks down at me. "And what exactly did you ruin, Rakkason?"

"*I* didn't ruin anything. I was told to collect a soul, but Sachar sent Darkour out to get the same girl, unbeknownst to me," I explain. "I simply had a normal reaction."

"You jumped me," Darkour deadpans. "I hardly think that's normal."

"I was upset."

"I was just handling the situation like I thought you would want," Sachar tells Alistair, yet again trying to regain control and, yet again, failing.

Alistair stares at the three of us for a long moment. "I'm not sure who to believe."

"Believe Sachar and me," Darkour says. "Rakkason cannot be trusted."

"Oh, I don't believe him, but I also don't believe you two.

I'm not sure that any of you can be trusted. Which leaves me with two options: fire the lot of you, or give you another shot. It all comes down to what kind of mood I am in."

He ends up giving us one more chance, which is a surprise. A very welcome surprise.

"You're walking a very thin line, Rakkason," Alistair had told me. "I'll be watching you like a hawk."

That's fine. Alistair can watch me like a hawk, stalk me like a vulture, surround me like a flock of pigeons, I don't care. I still have a chance to right what I did, all those years ago. And no one—not Sachar, not Darkour, and definitely not some fourteen-year-old girl—is going to get in my way. You know what they say, if at first you don't succeed and all that …. I think that phrase still applies after the first five hundred attempts. But I'm nothing if not hopeful! I'll win one of these days. I just know it.

Side note: I'm pretty sure I have a better chance with redemption than I do with Deteria.

Hellion, Inc.
Now accepting applications.
Send cover letter and resume to HellionHR@HellionInc.com

GABE MCCLURE is nineteen years old, was born in Indiana, bred for the most part in California, and graduated from Mira Costa High school in 2013 without honors. She has a ton (and she means a *ton*) of cats and a dog. She loves mysteries, paranormal things, and superheroes. Let her rephrase that: she loves super*villains*. Antiheroes are good too. And underdogs, of course. If she isn't writing (rare as that is), then she's acting or she's blogging about reality television. Follow her on Twitter @gabemcclure!

Afterword

As Henry the lemur might say;
Let creativity come first,
Never lose the joy of play.
Let your imagination burst,
And write a story today!

For more information about
National Novel Writing Month and its
Young Writers Program, please visit
nanowrimo.org and ywp.nanowrimo.org

Made in the USA
San Bernardino, CA
04 October 2014